REALLY CUTE PEOPLE

MARKUS HARWOOD-JONES

**carina
press®**

ISBN-13: 978-1-335-62195-5

Really Cute People

Carina Press
22 Adelaide St. West, 41st Floor
Toronto, Ontario M5H 4E3, Canada
www.CarinaPress.com

Printed in U.S.A.

For Andrew, Hannah and River.

Prologue

The view from up here sucks anyway. That's what I tell myself, while glaring at the brick wall that encapsulates my second-story-window view. Even on sky blue days, I rely on a sunrise lamp to get the minimum human requirement of vitamin D. *I should pack the lamp next,* I make a mental note. *The new place has good light but who knows how long that'll last.*

Crouched amidst piles of well-worn boots, vintage T-shirts, hand-me-down flannels, I've got a system going. And by system, I mean I've got four extra-large trash bags, their dark maws hanging open, ready to gobble up all that remains from the last four years of my life. I've only got a couple hours before Mako gets here with their mom's minivan. Then we'll load it up and drive away from the only place that's ever really felt like my home.

One bag is marked with a strip of white tape: *Charlie's Crap—TO KEEP.* It's the only one I plan to take to the new apartment. The rest, I'll donate. And by donate, I mean that they'll sit in the back of my car for the next few weeks. Every once in a while,

I'll open up the trunk and remember *I really should deal with all that* before slamming the lid and letting them vanish from existence again. One day, on a whim, I'll get fed up and drag the bags inside my new apartment, dump them on the floor, sort through them all again and post a few of the nicer pieces onto social media in hopes of orchestrating a clothing-swap. If that doesn't work, I'll try to pawn them off as gifts to my friends.

What friends? asks a voice in the back of my mind. I make a point to ignore it and turn up the volume on my portable speaker. Sure, the music cracks when the bassline kicks in, but it's better than listening to my own intrusive thoughts. Now, where was I? Right, sorting out my clothes and, by extension, the sad remnants of my old life.

I probably shouldn't have left this to the last minute. That seems to be a theme for me right now. Running on fumes, playing chicken with myself. It's easy to pretend that a dumpster fire will just run itself out. That is, until the sparks start flying. Then it's too late to do anything but stop, drop and roll away.

From beneath a wad of leggings and jeans, I find a pair of too-small pleather pants. Mei let me borrow them last fall, for a dance party at the local queer bar/café/plant store. I remember that night: there was a special on Slippery Nipples and I got so hammered in the first half hour, I had to come home and sleep on the bathroom floor. I guess after all that, I never got around to giving her pants back. I set them aside, next to the scratchy wool sweater that Mars stole for me, pilfered from the closet of a mutual ex. He knew I always coveted its giant pockets and extra-long sleeves. After a little more digging, I add a pair of lumpy slippers to the growing pile. Johanna knitted all of us matching sets during our first winter solstice together, when the power went out and our toes were close to freezing. Stopping to admire all these little pieces of nostalgia, I realize I've almost got a complete outfit on my hands. Gaudy and bizarre, yet functional. Sounds about right for Hillside House. A collective of Craigslist-roommates-turned-found-family, all our mismatched parts are what make us work so well.

Made. The voice reminds me. *What* made *us work.* Sure, we had a good thing going for a while, but that's all over now.

Scooping up the random assortment of bottoms and tops, I shove them all into the closest trash bag and tie it up tight. Down the street, there's a charity bin, nestled between the worst convenience store in the block and the best five-dollar pizza place in town. I'll get Mako to make a pit stop there, on our way out of the neighbourhood. It'll be easier that way, letting it all go at once. There's no point in lugging around bits and pieces of a broken dream.

The eviction notice had sat on our fridge for weeks. Like the garlic scapes going bad in our broken crisper, I think we were all waiting for someone else to take responsibility for the issue. Maybe we should have put on the chore wheel: *clean toilet, take out trash, deal with landlord bullshit.* On my end, I guess I had started to treat it like the mold between the bathroom tiles or that one bad step on the stairs. It was a problem, sure, but just one among many. We could learn to walk around it. Until we couldn't anymore.

Three weeks, four days, and—I check the time on my phone—*five hours.* That's how long it's been since our last house meeting. Our final house meeting, it turned out. I've still got the meeting minutes on my phone. Normally I'd give them a once-over and email the rest of the group, highlighting any extra chores or special events coming up. I'm not sure who I'm saving these ones for, though. Certainly not myself.

Mako was the one to bring it up. That's a talent they've got, saying what everyone else is thinking. After our standard go-around—name, pronoun, if-your-mood-was-weather-what-weather-would-it-be—conversation turned to house chores, projects, upcoming events. All fell silent when Mako placed the letter, face-up, on our tea-stained coffee table.

"Do you really think we can beat this?"

It was the kind of question that contains its own, unspoken answer. We could debate all we liked, weigh out the pros and cons, call the Landlord Tenant Board again, maybe even set up a sit-in in our living room. At the end of the month, though, all would remain the same. Our landlord claimed he was moving in, so we'd have to be moving out. A single guy with no kids, taking over a four-bedroom apartment? It was so blatant, we could almost laugh about it. Almost. It was obvious what he really was up to; by claiming an Owner Occupancy Eviction (thank you, Mars, for looking up the proper term), he could legally kick us to the curb. Then in a few months, he'd relist the unit for double (let's be real, triple) the old price. We'd all seen friends go through the same thing. Those that chose to stay and fight? Well, they'd had limited success.

I swear I used to have more books. Stacking paperbacks on top of hardcovers, my whole collection hardly fills a single cardboard box. We all merged our personal libraries onto one massive bookshelf in the common room. Mei had built it herself out of cast-off planks salvaged from behind the hardware store and bits of scrap metal found in the bike co-op's basement. It was just easier that way, sharing everything—plates and cutlery, crafting supplies, passwords for streaming TV services. Even the food in the fridge was bought using collective funds, cooked up into big house meals that we shared almost every night. Whether craving a sweet queer rom-com or double-decker pancakes, I was never hungry for long. Until now. In retrospect, I should have written my name inside the front cover of my favourite titles. I just never thought we'd have to untangle ourselves so quickly.

"Let's just focus on finding a new place instead."

That time, it was me who dared to state the obvious. I'm still not sure why the others couldn't see it like I could. How they couldn't understand, even if we beat him this time, the landlord would just find another way to turn up the pressure. Not to mention, Hillside itself had seen better days. No amount of homemade cleaning solution could clear the black mold from the kitchen ceiling. The bathroom sink had been dripping for the better part of a year. A pack of frat boys had just moved in across the street and within a few days of their arrival, we'd found our porch-side rainbow flag torn from its post. I didn't think it was so radical to suggest we pool our money, and our spoons, to focus on finding someplace a little less deadly.

"How can you even say that?"

"Is that why you haven't been sharing the GoFundMe to your socials?"

"I bet your dad and sister would give money if they knew."

"Why do you always have to see the worst in things?"

"It's not like he can call the cops on us, at least not right away."

They were on me like street cats on an open can of tuna. Mako was the only one to keep quiet. I nodded and mmm-hmmed my way through it, letting them all make their points, turning myself into a human pincushion.

It came down to a vote. We agreed, there had to be unanimous consensus. A fight like this needed total solidarity. Anything less and we'd all agree to drop it, give in, move on. After a couple false starts and a round of herbal tea, we stuffed bits of scrap paper into a mason jar. It was the yellow-stained one Mars had used during his bone-broth phase. As Mako spilled our crumpled votes onto their lap, I caught the faintest whiff of chicken stock.

There's a hum from under a nearby jacket. I dig out my phone and find a text from Mako. They've picked up the keys (a statement they've punctuated with several emojis including three hearts, a house, a cat that I guess is supposed to be Cashew, and a little slice of cake). I try to type a reply but my words are failing me. I give a thumbs-up react instead. As the screen goes dark, I experience a brief shift in reality. It's like one of those dreams where I've slipped out of my body and get stuck just watching things happening. I'm out of place, out of time, caught in a loop. The same few questions circle my mind like vultures, descending on half-dead prey. *How is this happening? Is it really all my fault? What am I supposed to do now?*

After the votes were tallied, Mei had left without a word. She shrugged on her tool belt and went out the back door to go fiddle with her bike. Johanna left next, muttering about getting the kettle on again. Mars followed, rinsing a handful of fresh veggies for a stir-fry. Even my cat, Cashew, poked his head out from the under the sofa and padded out of sight. Only Mako stayed, shuffling from their window perch to sit beside me. Fingers knit together, we held hands in silence. There was nothing more to be said. Hillside House—the queer collective home of my wildest baby-gay fantasies—had officially ended.

The following weeks have felt like a ride inside Cinderella's carriage. Smooth at first, even a little exciting, but ominously temporary. I've been watching the walls slowly tear down around me. All the things that made this place a home, *our* home, are transforming into pumpkin mush. The zine library has dwindled, now just rows of clothing pins and empty twine. The crafting cupboard has been reduced to a pair of broken scissors and couple of cheap glue sticks. When I went to make breakfast one morning, the household coffee maker and cast-iron skillet had both gone missing. The backyard garden has grown dense with weeds, the dirt deathly dry.

I'm just about done here. All the boxes and bags are piled up by the door, ready to be hauled downstairs. Among the dredges of my closet, I rediscovered my favourite denim vest. Stuffing my hands into the pockets, I find a small note: *tempeh, vegan mayo, snap peas (in season)*. An old grocery list, probably one I brought to the store and promptly forgot about. It's nothing remarkable. Even so, I neatly fold the paper in half and return it to my pocket.

The landlord will be here soon. With his many jangling keys

and menthol-cigarette smile, he'll wait politely for me to load out the last of my things. Then he'll change the locks. I have no doubt the whole place will soon be covered in off-white paint, coating everything from the light switches to the electrical outlets.

When I first moved in, the windowpane was sealed shut by several layers of globby paint. Even so, I picked the room for its view. Back before the neighbours built their double-decker laneway house, I used to look out at the top branches of an apricot tree. Full, green leaves that danced in summer sunlight, red and gold come autumn. In winter, its empty fingers rattled against the double-pane glass, sketching bits of abstract art among the frost. It was a benchmark, a reminder of each season and its inevitable passing. When working from home, I kept my desk pushed up against the windowsill. Occasionally I'd look up to find a red squirrel bouncing past or a cardinal warbling its springtime serenade.

After a full four seasons in my new-to-me bedroom, Mako helped me chip away the double layers of paint and pry the window open. A breeze ran through the whole house that day, fresh and sweeter than anything we'd ever managed to squeeze out from the failing AC unit. From then on, I always left my window open. Even in the coldest months. When that breeze would come, any tensions among the five of us would instantly lighten. Soon, we'd be cooking, talking, playing music like we always loved to do.

On the best of those nights, we'd all stay up late. Lying around the common room, we'd light candles and pull cards, making one-day plans; we could organize an annual, anti-capitalist pride picnic, or set up a network of community gardens laced through the downtown core. We'd daydream about future pets and babies, all the ways we could grow together. Those were the times when the house itself felt alive, breathing and sighing and laughing along with us.

Back in the present, I press my forehead against the window. It's cold on my skin but the rest of me is burning up. My stomach churns like an active volcano. I am absolutely fuming. This was supposed to be our home. These people were supposed to be my family. I knew our landlord could take possession of the former, but I never thought the latter would go with it.

There's a thump from the room next door. Heavy footfalls tell a story of strained movements down narrow stairs. Johanna and Mars are bickering about how to fit their bedframe down the hall. Mei left earlier today without so much as a goodbye and I guess those two are following suit. After a few minutes, there's one last round of bangs punctuated by a heavy slam. The whole house shudders on its foundations, and the quiet that follows is even worse. Regret slips down my throat, cooling molten rage into rock and steam. I've got no right to be so upset. I was the only no vote. If not for me, Hillside might still be standing. What a way to find out I was the weakest link in our chain.

Snow drifts down the narrow passage between my window and the opposing brick. I hold still and watch the tiny flakes, trying to remember what it was like to see the apricot leaves bloom. After a few moments, I turn away. I shove the last of my stuff into a couple tote bags and carry them downstairs. I'd crack open my window, but there's no need for a cool breeze in winter. Besides, I'm not sure the wind would blow like it used to anymore.

Chapter One

One Year Later

Wind at my collar, I shrug my jacket tight. This time of year, my daily walk to the office turns into an uphill battle against a winter wind tunnel. Heavy grey skies promise freezing rain before the day is through. City grit mixes with day-old snow to form a perfect, grey slush, nipping my toes as it seeps through the cracks in my secondhand leather shoes. On the plus side, the soft wool lining of my new overcoat has managed to keep the cold from soaking through to my major organs. My hands are warmed by a fresh coffee I picked up at the local weed-store-slash-overpriced-café. Sharpie marker on one side proclaims this cup is for *Charlese*. The barista always gets my name wrong. To be fair, I also never correct her. Today of all days, I was quite happy to just take the cup, and treat myself to a croissant while I'm at it.

Bay Street hums with Thursday morning traffic. Plumes of exhaust intertwining, sprawling into hazy mist; I walk through a particularly foggy patch, oddly comforted by its warmth. The sidewalk is traced with familiar stains and I navigate, with ease, a maze of littered cups and twisted plastic bags. A city bus rolls through a nearby puddle and I sidestep the resulting splash without so much as a flinch. A year of walking the same route every day has made such reactions second nature.

Busy people in tight suits stand clustered around the doors to skyscraper office towers. They suck on cigarettes and vape pens, scrolling on their shiny phones. A woman in a navy suit looks up and her steely gaze meets mine. Neither of us makes any acknowledgement. A moment later, she blinks away and I do the same. Exactly how I like it.

I shove my emptied cup into an overflowing garbage bin around the nearest corner. Squinting into a face-full of wind, I'm faced with a familiar concrete cube. Smack in the middle of downtown, its faded signage lists the offices of several chiropractors, a resident dentist-slash-psychic and something the directory simply calls *CMM*. Basement level, no elevator access. I take the stairs down to Call Me Maybe headquarters.

"Charlie!" Hassan leans back from his desk and flashes a pearly-white smile, just like every morning. "Looks like I beat you to the office, again."

"Yep." I stomp the slush off my shoes. "Looks like it."

Beneath the fluorescent lights of a drop ceiling, CMM's skeleton crew rubs their tired eyes. Shuffling around narrow cubicles, they sip on mugs of instant coffee brewed in the office kitchen-slash-break-room. Mornings around here used to be a bit more lively, back when we had free doughnuts and snacks set out a couple times a week. But that little morale booster got cut along with just about everything else last quarter. The budget was slim since before I got here, but lately it's gone absolutely skeletal. Not that I care. I never partook in the doughnut days—a single maple-glazed is simply not enough compensation to suffer through coworker small talk. If I want a treat, I'll stop at Tim Hortons on the way home and get a dozen crullers for myself, thanks very much.

I can hear Hassan's oxford heels clicking after me. Eyes forward, I take to my desk. My cubicle is nearly identical to all the others, save for a small plaque that reads *Assistant Manager*. Not that I'm really assisting anyone these days; another consequence of the new budget, the Actual Manager was laid off four months ago. And for around three months, three weeks and five days, I've quietly been waiting for a new brass plate to appear on my desk. Presumably, one with the title of *Interim Manager*. But I guess plating services are beyond our financial capacities right now, too.

"Got a minute?" Hassan appears at my side before I've even slipped off my coat. "We should touch base about the new user questionnaire—"

"I thought we finalized that last week." My laptop screen hums awake as I nudge it open.

"We sure did!" Leaning over my shoulder, Hassan prods at my computer's trackpad. "But last night, I realized some of the options we've got are pretty binary."

"Isn't that the point?" I cross my arms and lean back, my chair softly whining. "We're trying to generate stats here, not host a philosophy class."

"Sure, but shouldn't we have a write-in option?" he asks. "Or a comment section!"

"Hmm." I shouldn't be surprised that he's going the extra, extra mile. Hassan's desk has the same plaque as mine. Once upon a time, he and I almost shared a sense of camaraderie. That was back when there were plenty of us Assistant Managers around, monitoring multiple departments. Now that we're in CMM's no-doughnut era, our friendly rapport has simmered into a quiet yet potent sense of competition. After all, there's only ever been *one* Manager.

Fingers drumming on the back of my chair, Hassan impatiently clicks my trackpad again. The program isn't loading. His perfect smile twitches, ever so slightly. "Looks like the Wi-Fi's getting a late start, too."

"Yeah, maybe." Rolling backwards in my seat, I wave in the direction of our server room. "Say, Augustine, what do you think—things running smooth in there?"

From her desk inside the IT office—which, let's be real, is a glorified closet—our one-and-only tech gives a brief thumbs-up. Augustine and I got hired around the same time, yet I can count on one hand the number of idle chats we've exchanged in the last year. Honestly, I couldn't ask for a better coworker.

"Guess that's that." I stand and make a line for the break room. "How about you just Slack me the edits and I'll get them back to you after the weekend?"

"Um, sure, I could do that but—" Hassan outpaces me with a few long strides and stands right in my path. "Except, didn't Angie say she wanted the update ready by Monday?"

"Yeah, well, these things take time," I mutter, and move to pass him. But Hassan just steps in the way again.

"Mmm-hmm. Makes sense." He shoots a quick look over his shoulder, tilting on his heels. "And hey, if you want to extend the deadline, I'm sure the big boss will understand."

I pinch the bridge of my nose. He's got me there. If there's one thing our Executive Director can't stand, it's a missed deadline. "Fine," I tell him. "I'll get on it, after I get some more caffeine." Somehow in the year since I started here, I've gone from a green-tea drinker to someone who can't start their day until their second (sometimes, third) cup of coffee.

"On it!" Hassan pivots. "Two milk, no sugar, right?"

"Uh, right." Before I even finish my answer, he's skipped away towards the break room. I stare after him for a few seconds—Hassan's always been the chipper type but making coffee for me? Way too extra, even for him.

There's no way he could know what today is... I dismiss the thought before I can even finish it. No, that can't be it. I've been so care-ful. *He's probably just buttering me up for something,* I decide. I bet he wants more credit for the questionnaire update.

Settling back into my desk, I soon hear the telltale sputter of our coffee machine. I guess he really is making a fresh pot. The sound is soon drowned out by the second stage of Hassan's daily routine—belting renditions of Broadway show tunes, in all-too-perfect pitch (of course). My eyes flit to Augustine and we share a momentary, knowing look. She pulls out a pair of noise-cancelling headphones and sets them snugly in place. *I've gotta get myself a pair of those.*

In the bygone era of phone books and dial-up internet, the CMM hotline was listed as a *24/7 Mental-Health Support Service.* Shortly after I got hired, the actual phone lines were all unplugged as CMM doubled down on texting instead. Then even our texting line was shut off, replaced with an online chat that operates five days a week. Faced with government fund-ing cuts and the rising costs of renting office space, every bit of CMM has been chipped and shrunk and streamlined. Last fall, more than half the in-house staff got laid off—including all of our trained therapists and counsellors. They were replaced by a quippy AI chatbot. These days, when our clients get sick of talk therapy with a glorified version of Clippy, they're for-warded to a Referral Database. It's basically a list of resources that could do a better job than we can; community centres, psychologists, that sort of thing.

Enter, Charlie. The database started as my pet project, a bit of busywork that I took on as an intern. Now, it's become our main offering. Despite all the changes, the name CMM still holds a serious amount of sway in certain circles. Being on our list gives local services a mark of legitimacy, and an eager client base. On my end, it's how I've managed to keep my job. I'm the only one who truly understands how the program works.

It also helps that I'm pretty good at flying under the radar. I show up, do my work, keep my opinions to myself. Sure, I've thought about mentioning that our name is officially a misnomer. You can't call us, and even if you could, there is no real "me" to talk to. I guess the "Maybe Hotline" doesn't have the same ring to it, though. And it's that kind of self-restraint that'll get me promoted to full-on Manager. I just have to be patient.

"Hot bean juice, coming through!" Hassan sidesteps a couple passing coworkers, cradling a steaming mug with both hands. He sets it down on my desk with a triumphant smile. "You know, my fiancé got me into adding a splash of maple syrup to my morning cuppa. You ever tried that?"

"Can't say I have." I take a sip without looking up from my laptop. Damn if he didn't get the milk-to-coffee ratio just right. "Thanks."

"Ah, you got things up and running!" He grabs a nearby chair and wheels it over. "Hope my edits aren't too much for you."

"I'm sure it's fine," I say, scrolling along a few pages of back-end code. Hassan and I have been tasked with making a pop-up questionnaire, something to gather user data. This stuff isn't usually my department, but since the layoffs, everything has sort of become everyone's job. Not to mention, after seeing a bunch of coworkers replaced with a computer program, now seems like a good time to broaden my skill set.

This side project was all polished up and ready to hand in, until today. Now it's covered in Hassan's fingerprints on everything. Some awkward wording, a couple spelling errors. "No big deal." I click through the next page. "This is nothing that can't be—"

My words run out mid-sentence as I stifle a gasp. The questionnaire's second page is in total chaos. Overlapping text, broken links, strings of exposed code. Nothing is where it's supposed to be. "What even happened here?"

"Yes, right, that." Hassan clicks his tongue. "The thing is,

I was sort of halfway through the edits last night when I realized, my fiancé and I were totally supposed to have a date night!
Guess in my rush, I left things a little messy."

"You...guess?" My face is getting hot. When I look at Hassan, all I see is rows upon rows of broken code—and the hours
it'll take to fix.

"Let's focus on the positive, partner." He gives what I'm sure
is supposed to be a charming shrug. "Now you and me can
work together to make it even better!"

He starts reaching for my laptop again, but I snap it up and
spin aside. "No!" I shout, catching looks from nearby coworkers. Dropping my voice, I mutter, "It's fine. I can handle this
myself." Mentally, I'm already running through my options.
If I can find an old draft of this file, maybe I can salvage this.
Why didn't I set up an auto-backup?

"You sure?" Hassan's brows fold together, like hands forming
a tiny prayer. "If you've got other things to get done, I could
try to fix it myself."

"No, that's all right," I tell him. "I'll get it done." *It'll just take
all of today, probably most of tomorrow and maybe some weekend overtime.*

"Well, don't work yourself too hard!" Hassan snaps his fingers and steps backwards to his desk. Just before he turns, he
adds, "Oh, one more thing—think you can swing by the break
room in say, fifteen minutes? I need some help setting up the
L-A-L today, please-and-thanks!" Before I can answer, he raises
his voice so the whole office can hear, "Everybody catch that?
L-A-L kicking off in a hot twenty! I sprang for *two* veggie trays
this time!"

Curious heads peek up over various cubicle walls, glancing between Hassan and myself. I cup my face and I keep my
eyes down. Augustine passes my desk, frayed Ethernet cable in
hand. Without looking towards me, she asks, "Do you think

he knows spelling out that acronym takes the same number of syllables as simply saying 'Lunch-And-Learn'?"

I snicker under my breath. "It's also not even close to lunch yet. At best, it's brunch."

The hint of a smile traces Augustine's lips as she digs into a nearby storage cupboard. "I suppose B-A-L doesn't drip off the tongue quite the same way."

With some coaxing from Hassan, my coworkers begin to zombie-shuffle towards the office break room. Though I'm trying to focus on my actual work, I overhear Sophia from Finance ask, "You know who the guest is this week?"

"Not a clue," answers Aditya, the last bastion of our HR department. "But hey, have you signed that card yet?"

"Shh!" Sophia hisses back, not so subtly nodding in my direction. Aditya clamps her lips and hurries past without another word.

I look to Augustine but she's busy patching up a cable with a layer of gaff tape. As usual, she's got the right idea. No need to get sucked into office chitchat or workplace drama. I've got more important things going on.

When my buddy Mako hooked me up with this job, it was supposed to be a part-time thing. Running coffee orders, taking down meeting minutes, that sort of thing. The folks at Hillside House were always doing that for each other, sharing tips on fast money and easy work. Mei would sometimes have me in at the biker's co-op, working the front desk. Other days, Johanna might share her food-delivery routes and let me keep the tips. Whenever Mars was working a festival, he'd add my name to the list of volunteers willing to get paid in free pizza.

In a blink, I'm there again. In a sweaty T-shirt, the logo for some local music fest on the back. My arms are heavy, carrying a load of half-eaten pizza in boxes stacked taller than my head. One roommate holds the front door open while another helps Tetris this haul of leftovers into our communal fridge.

We eat like royalty for the rest of the week, so much food we hardly know what to do with it all. We try pan-fried-pizza, panini-pressed-pizza, pizza-for-breakfast-with-maple-syrup. All is warm and cheesy and good.

A sharp pang in my chest rocks me back to the present. Just as quickly as it came, the memory fades. In a blink, I'm back where I'm supposed to be. In the CMM basement, listening to the sputtering of the office fax machine and the buzz of the fluorescent lights. I clear my throat and sit up straight. I hadn't planned on getting emotional today.

A lot can change in a year. Hillside House seemed like it would last forever, until it didn't. My many roommates and I were scattered to the wind like dandelion fluff. Meanwhile, this supposed-to-be-temp gig has turned into something stable. My latest quarterly review was full of words like *impressive work ethic* and *clear attention to detail*. I stuck it up on the fridge in my bachelor apartment. That is, until Cashew knocked it down twice and bit off a corner of the glossy paper. Guess next time I'll try to put it somewhere more cat-proof.

This Lunch-And-Learn thing is new, too. Hassan's big idea, a series of lunchtime workshops intended to help with "team bonding" and "boosting morale." So clearly a ploy to get on our boss's good side, I'm not sure how anyone can stand it.

Hassan never fails to find the drabbest "guestperts" to teach us about things like "self-care" or "employment equity." It's not that I think the topics are totally unimportant. I'd just rather spend my precious break time hunched over my desk, eating microwave ramen, scrolling through my phone and avoiding any eye contact while I pretend that I work completely alone. You know, like a normal person.

"Charlie!" Hassan calls my name in a singsong voice and a shiver runs down my back. It's like something from a horror movie. Reluctantly, I push away from my desk and look towards the break room. Why does he have the lights off in there?

I eye over my shoulder, hoping to share another look with Augustine. Except, she's not there. The storage cupboard hangs ajar. A quick glance around the office reveals all the cubicles are empty too. This is starting to get freaky. I swear, I can hear the strings building.

"Charlie?" Hassan beckons me again. "We're just about ready. I saved you a *seat!*"

The lights above me flicker as I take uneasy steps. There are whispers in the kitchen. Childlike giggling. People must be in there, but why are they hanging around in the dark?

Unless. I freeze. Standing at the threshold of the break room, I peer into the shadows. It looks completely empty. *They couldn't have,* I tell myself. *They wouldn't have. Unless.*

"Surprise!" The lights clap on and my coworkers leap out from their hiding spots. Cheering and hollering, they toss fist-fuls of shredded paper like makeshift confetti. Magnetic letters on the office fridge have been arranged to spell out a message. My stomach sinks as the whole room speaks it aloud: "Happy birthday, Charlie!"

"Oh." The floor tilts. "Oh wow." I'm suddenly dizzy. Maybe, seasick? Can you get seasick standing still inside a basement? "You...shouldn't have."

"Don't be silly!" Hassan stands at the front. "As if our work-fam would forget your special day!" In his hands is a massive sheet cake, drizzled with blue icing and topped off with a shoddy printed photo. My own face stares blankly back at me.

"Is that..." My brain is making a sound like the fax machine when it's got a paper jam. I drag the edges of my mouth into what is hopefully a passable smile. "Where did you get that photo of me?"

"It's your LinkedIn profile!" Aditya helpfully chimes in.

"So smart, right?" Sophia nods. "It was Augustine's idea!"

Et tu, Augustine? I'm struck speechless once more. Augustine quietly shuffles at the kitchen counter, setting out paper plates and plastic forks. "I like photo cakes," she states plainly. "They have a good crunch."

"Aren't you going to blow out the candles?" Hassan shimmies his shoulders. "Oh, oh! Should we sing 'Happy Birthday'?"

My heart starts racing. *Please for the love of all that is*—

"Charlie?" There's a brief, yet firm double-tap on my shoulder. "Might I have a word?" Short brown bangs, chunky earrings and a many-layered scarf draped around her shoulders; Angie Bane, Executive Director of CMM, stands at my back. Lowering her cat's-eye glasses, she eyes the rest of the break room. "I hope I'm not interrupting."

"Angie, great timing!" Hassan hoists the cake like he's about to offer her the whole thing as a single piece. "Are you joining in the L-A-L today, too? Our guest speaker should be here any minute!"

"Wait, wait." I shake my head, slowly returning from my stunned stupor. "There's still really a workshop happening?"

"Well, yeah!" Hassan's eyes sparkle. "So, Ang, what do you say?"

"Wish that I could. Unfortunately, I'm far too deep in conference prep." Angie nudges her glasses back up her button nose. "This weekend is the third annual Paradigm Shift Symposium. I'm speaking on a panel about Metamorphic Breakthrough Leadership."

"Ah." Hassan's perfect smile doesn't move an inch. "Well, that sounds very important. Another time, then."

"Indeed." Angie gives a curt nod and turns on her heel. "Charlie, are you coming?"

I've never been so happy to be called in for a one-on-one with the big boss. With a shrug to Hassan and the rest of the crew, I hurry after Angie.

Or I'm about to, until I see *her*.

Shoulders squared, she walks with all the grace of a trained dancer. The collar of her layered blouse is slightly unbuttoned.

There's the hint at an elaborate tattoo across her collarbones, black ink on brown skin. A pair of bright yellow glasses accentuate the contours of her cheeks, the tender bend of her jawline. They match her earrings, too. When she turns, the springy tips of her hair tease along her shoulders. Her lips are the colour of an early sunrise; her eyes, sparkling like light breaking over the horizon.

I stand in the break room doorway, awestruck. The rest of my coworkers mill about, snacking on veggie trays and murmuring about when the workshop might get started. Have none of them noticed the goddess who just walked into our dingy office basement?

"'Scuse me, bud." Hassan ducks around me. He hurries over to take her coat.

My mouth is dry from hanging open. "Is that *the* Elizabeth Hawkshaw?"

"Yep." Augustine shuffles beside me and offers a slice of cake. It's the bit that's got my own eye on it. I shake my head, no thanks. "Apparently, Hassan knows her through a friend-of-a-friend. Neat, eh?"

"That's one word for it." I was thinking more *impossible*, or *fantastical*, or maybe just *amazing*. This has to be the most incredible happening to ever grace CMM's dismal doorstep. From the corner of my eye, I catch Augustine watching me watching her. I admit with a shaking laugh, "I'm a bit of a fan."

"No kidding." Augustine stabs her fork into the centre of my iris. "Yeah, her stuff is pretty good. I liked that TED Talk she did."

"Queer Body Art as Feminist Revolution?" My voice cracks, coming out louder than I meant it to. "Um, yeah. I know that one." I used to watch it at least once a week, and not just for the part where she strips down and coats herself in multicolour oil paints.

"So good to see you, Elizabeth!" Hassan leads her towards the break room. "Or, sorry, do you prefer Dr. Hawkshaw?" Even from across the office, I can tell he's got the jitters. Not that I blame him.

"It's actually Haw*thorne* now," she tells him, fidgeting with the collar of her blouse.

She changed her last name? How did I not know that?

"And the doctorate was only honorary," she adds. "You can just call me Buffy."

"Buffy," I whisper to myself.

"I didn't even know she was in Canada," says Augustine, polishing off the last of my icing-based eyeball. "She hardly posts online anymore."

"*Social media is a modern-day panopticon*," I murmur. "That's um, something she posted a few years back." Five years, four days, three months ago. Approximately speaking. "She's been pretty much offline since then, though I had heard she moved north in hopes of getting some extra privacy." *Though I never imagined I'd actually run into her like this.* I pat down my bangs and check the length of my undercut. I should have got a haircut last week, like I meant to. *Why didn't I get a haircut?!*

"Mm. Makes sense." Augustine elbows me, nodding to a stocky ginger guy clambering in after Buffy. He's got two tote bags, one on each shoulder, and his arms are full of art supplies. "Who do you suppose that is?"

"Assistant, maybe?" My eyes narrow for a second before I dart them back to Buffy. If I look away too long, she might vanish entirely.

"Must be," says Augustine. "Kinda cute, though."

"Yeah, kinda." I give the assistant a brief, second glance. Augustine has a point. In just a grey hoodie and jeans, he follows after her like a shadow. Tousled hair and scruffy beard, he looks like he just rolled out of bed, but in a good way. His cheeks are pink, still nipped from the cold outside. He says something to Buffy that's just out of earshot. She cracks a smile.

Hassan laughs along with them and suddenly, I'm burning with envy. How did he end up the one over there, making jokes with Elizabeth-*freaking*-Hawkshaw and her arm-candy assistant? Meanwhile I'm stuck, frozen in place.

"You know," Augustine whispers, "Hassan might introduce you, if you wanted."

"What? No. No way." I vehemently shake my head. "I'm sure they don't want to be interrupted by some random fan."

Even if I wanted to go over, Angie is staring at me from her glass-walled office. She taps her heel, expectantly. I can't keep her waiting much longer. Dragging my feet, I force myself to cross the office floor. It's never felt so impossibly far, until now.

"Right this way, please—we're so excited to have you!" Hassan waves for Sophia. "Would you show *Buffy* through the office? I'm going to prep the projector."

Sophia? Really? I clench my jaw, willing my snarky tone to stay as an inside thought. *I bet she's never even heard the name Hawkshaw before today.*

"Oh, uh. Sure." Sophia shovels down her last bite of cake and hops into action. "It's really nice to meet you." She ushers Buffy and her assistant towards the break room, pointing out a few notable features of the office. "I'm excited for your talk on collective arts and mental wellness."

"Is that the topic for today?" Buffy looks back over her shoulder. "Damn. I thought this was 'zine-making as a tool for wage-labour resistance.' I could go back to my car and get some different supplies?"

"No, we can do zines!" Hassan shouts from behind the projector. "I love zines!"

"Yeah." Sophia nods along. "Those are like, little cookies or something right?"

"Um, not quite." Buffy's assistant laughs under his breath. Both the bags he's toting are covered in colourful pins, iron-on patches and several iterations of the rainbow flag.

Hassan calls out again but I don't catch the specifics. All the chatter and background noise, even the sputtering photocopier and the hum of the vents—everything slips away. Because, just for a moment, Buffy looks at me.

We're moving past each other. An arm's reach apart, if that. We lock eyes for what could be a second, or a lifetime. It's impossible to say. My legs feel like jelly and cement all at once. Her lips twitch. I could swear she's smiling at me. *Really* smiling.

In a blink, the spell is broken. She turns back to Hassan to ask another question. Her assistant must have caught me staring; he smirks like we're sharing a secret. There's a warmth that radiates from him. It washes over me like ocean waves and I remember how to breathe again.

I stare after them, even as I grip the cool handle of Angie's office door. In the break room, Hassan is holding up a hand, motioning for everyone to take their seats. Buffy's back is to me. She digs through the bags her assistant carried over. I've never so desperately wished I could stay for a freaking Lunch-And-Learn.

Chapter Two

The walls of Angie's office read like an archive. Banners, buttons, flyers and posters cover nearly every inch of the walls, up to the ceiling. Framed photographs and newspaper clippings show a more-or-less consistent group; a half-dozen young women and a couple token gay guys, all sporting matching T-shirts. Their '80s-style geometric design spells out the words *Central Mental Monitor*. The largest image shows the team sitting at a circular table covered in chunky, corded phones. Everyone is busy, save for one face that looks to the camera. Thick-rimmed glasses can't hide the twinkle in her eyes. Decades later, Angie looks largely the same. Her round cheeks have grown creased and heavy, her wispy brown hair now flecked with grey. She still wears the same glasses. There's a spark to her that has not been doused with age.

There is a gap in the memorabilia. One side ends with a corkboard of mid-'90s flyers and button-pins. The story picks up again with a tacked-up T-shirt that pronounces the line's official reopening in the early 2010s. Hassan has told me before about this break in CMM's history. It's not exactly surprising. A bunch of twenty-somethings, without any training or proper funding, trying to run a free therapy hotline for the entire country? It would be much more shocking if there *wasn't* major drama, trauma and burnout.

Angie sits at the midpoint of these two eras, quite literally. The broad-backed arch of her executive chair is perfectly framed by either side. She was the last member of the old team to stick things out to the bitter end. So, when a new crop of prospective board members decided to relaunch the line, she was an easy pick for Executive Director. In the decades between CMM's two iterations, she had also picked up a few skills around finance and government granting. In her first year, Angie managed to get the hotline back together, fully funded, and secure our (somewhat dungeonesque) office space. She hired a proper team to run the program, including licensed therapists (all of which she then had to lay off this past year). I've heard a rumour she even picked the line's new name—Carly Rae Jepsen released "Call Me Maybe" the same year as CMM's big relaunch and, well, the rest is history.

Personally, I think it was a bit dicey going for a song-based title. Especially one that impacts our ability to have pretty much any branded merchandise. But what do I know? Angie's the expert here, and she knows it. She has clawed CMM back from the depths of dysfunction and disendowment more than once. Anyone who wants to keep their job will do right not to forget it. And as for our merch, turns out we can *technically* put the words "call," "me" and "maybe" on a shirt, so long as we space them out right.

The thick glass walls of her private office have an insulating effect. Tinted on the outside, she can watch all of us worker bees running around without herself ever being on display. It's quiet in here, too. Her chair gently sighs as she settles in behind her desk. Adjusting her glasses, she peers at two massive computer monitors. Her chapped fingers take to the grooves of her ergonomic keyboard and instantly set to work. For a woman in her late sixties, she types like a Zoomer.

"Charlie, Charlie, Charlie Dee." Angie repeats my name in a singsong voice. She always does that, makes a little tune of it. She told me once, it's a strategy she learned from an old advisor to help remember people's names. I'm also pretty sure she likes showing off how she's *not* misgendering me. "Tell me, how *are* you?"

"I'm okay." I balance precariously on a small, round stool that sits opposite her desk. "Actually, I'm pretty swamped with a couple projects right now and—"

"Great. That's great." Her chunky earrings clack together as she tilts her head towards me. There is no pause in her rapid typing. "You're welcome, by the way, for the rescue. Hassan's little lunchtime lessons are always so exhausting. I'm sure you were just itching for an out."

"Today's didn't seem *so* bad." The back of my head is burning, begging me to turn around. Maybe I can catch another glimpse of Buffy, or her cute assistant setting up the workshop.

Angie tuts her tongue. "Ever the optimist. That's what I like about you, Charlie. Still, I'd rather work through lunch, wouldn't you?"

"Oh. Yes. Definitely." I try to sit up straight, but the squeaky wheels of my makeshift seat get away from me. Wrestling the stool back under myself, I focus. The last thing I need is for Angie to reconsider my work ethic. The last time anyone was called into her office for a *quick chat*, they left with their stuff in a cardboard box that same afternoon.

If I am getting fired, though, Angie doesn't seem in a rush about it. She starts bringing up performance reviews, adjustments to the annual schedule—she even reads a few lines from her upcoming conference presentation. I hum and nod at the appropriate times. Yet a thread keeps tugging at the back of my mind. My attention sneaks out from under me, slides under the glass wedge of Angie's office door, around wayward cables and cubicle walls, slipping towards the break room. *What might Buffy be saying right now?*

"I know what you're thinking." Angie smacks her mouse a few times and spins with flourish, snagging a freshly inked page from her personal printer. My jaw clamps shut and I hold perfectly still and she starts reading over the document. Sipping from a massive travel mug, she exhales through her teeth. "I can't say I blame you. After everything, I'm sure everyone's still a bit jumpy when asked for a one-on-one."

"Yes, well." I take a deep breath. I've practiced this speech a hundred times. "Angie, you know that I respect your decisions during the last quarter. After the province pulled back our funding, you did what you had to do. However, given our remaining numbers, I don't believe it would be in CMM's best interest to lose the lead coordinator of the referral database. Not to mention that I've—"

Angie holds up a finger while she goes back in for another swig. From behind me, there's the hint of laughter and clapping. It's coming from the direction of the break room. I start to bounce my leg, growing restless.

"Given the gaps in our office team right now," I press onward, "I really think my role has become indispensable."

With a wag of her finger, Angie quiets me again. She drains the last of her mug and sets it down on the far end of her desk. "We are not here to discuss a termination, Charlie. To the contrary, I have an opportunity for you."

"I think you would find it more expensive to hire and train a new—" My knee freezes, mid-jump. "Sorry. Did you say, opportunity?"

"Indeed." Angie snags a pen from the plain white mug that sits beside her computer monitor and starts scribbling out a few notes. "This will be a chance for you to take on some greater responsibilities, really show yourself to be a team player." She sharply glances up at me. "You've got a car, don't you, Charlie?"

Speechless, I nod yes. If I ever had an idea of where she was going, it's lost to me now. Has this whole conversation been a long way of asking for a ride to the airport?

"Excellent, excellent." She makes a quick checkmark on the printout in front of her. "Be sure you fill up the tank tonight. Now tell me, have you ever heard of a place called Elmridge?" Before I can answer that I haven't, she's already swivelling in her chair and busy typing again. "Lovely little place. My brother's cottage is near there, right on the riverfront." She tilts one of her computer monitors to offer an aerial view of the town, courtesy of Google Maps. "It's had a real population jump in the last few years, what with all you millennial kids moving out of the big city."

I don't bother mentioning that most "millennial kids" are in their thirties now, if not older. "Looks nice," I say with a shrug. Truly, it looks like a small dot on an otherwise empty landscape; like most of small-town Ontario, it's probably just a cluster of strip malls and suburban housing, a half-dozen churches and a one-street downtown strip. "Quaint."

"Quaint is just the word for it." She spins the monitor back to herself. "Now, what might you say to an all-expense-paid trip to such a darling little town?"

This has to be a test. "I'd say, no room in the budget for something like that."

"Ha! That's a smart answer." Angie gives another few clicks to her mouse. "However, we may need to find funds for it anyway. We've been invited for a site visit."

I fold my legs, trying to get comfortable. This stool doesn't offer much in terms of support. "A site visit—to what, their local park?"

If Angie catches my sarcastic tone, she doesn't show it. "All those new young people have brought with them quite the progressive mindset," she explains. "The city has even invested in a new community centre, of sorts. It appears to be growing in popularity—enough that the centre now feels they should be added to our referral database." She pulls up a flashy website, its front page littered with acronyms and smiling stock photos.

"And you think so too?" I ask.

"It doesn't matter what I think." She flips the monitor back to herself. "I'd like you to go and run an assessment. See if they make the cut."

I roll my neck, working out a pinch between my shoulders. "Isn't that more of a job for the outreach department?" *Except, there is no more outreach department,* I remind myself. "Or, how about one of our volunteers?"

Angie pinches her lips. "Between you and me, we've been struggling a bit with volunteer retention. Some of our long-standing supporters appear to be quite flustered about the recent restructuring."

Who could have seen that coming? I fight the urge to roll my eyes. "Gotcha."

"I'm sure the issue will resolve itself." Angie waves her hand, as if our community relations crisis can be shooed like a fly. "Besides, I think it looks better to have a true representative of our organization go front and centre. I'd do it myself, if it wasn't for the convention." She sips her travel mug again. "Now, I've already set aside all the outreach materials you'll need. I trust you can manage the transport."

"Sure but…" My words trail off. That tugging sensation is back again. *If I can wrap this up soon, maybe I can still catch the end of Buffy's talk.* "Wouldn't it make sense to send more of a people person for this job? I bet Hassan would go for it." I can't believe those words are coming out of my mouth right now. We both know it's true, though. "I've already got a few projects on the go this weekend."

"I know that we're *all* feeling stretched at the moment." Angie's whole face squeezes into an expression of sympathy, like one might ring out water from a dishrag. "But that's all the more reason to pitch in the extra effort. Not to mention, the database is *your* project, Charlie. Who better to assess a new addition?"

"But—"

She holds up a finger and downs the last of her drink. I sit in silence, listening to the smacking of her lips. "I've been watching you, Charlie," says Angie. "You keep your head down, you do your work. You don't get caught up in petty office politics." She spins in her chair to face her wall of photos and memorabilia. "To be honest, you remind me of a younger version of myself."

I have to admit, that gets me. For a moment, I forget about Buffy and her assistant. Hassan and the questionnaire. Even the possibility of my promotion seems unimportant now. Everything takes a back seat as I wait for Angie's next words.

"You believe in CMM, don't you?" she asks, back still turned towards me.

"Sure." I nod. "Yes, I do."

"Well, *that* is why I've hand-picked you for this assignment," says Angie. "You'll have to trust me. This is a big-picture thing." She swivels once more, instantly returning her focus to the computer screens. "Not to mention, Hassan has already booked off his vacation time. Apparently, he's got some kind of wedding coming up this year?"

"I…see." It takes a moment for everything to fall into place. It's a budget thing. Because, of course it is. "We can't actually afford to send someone for a site visit so far out of the city, can we?" I say my question like it's a statement. Angie's silence is its own answer. "But if I just so happen to take a short trip to Elmridge this weekend—"

"Then the funds come from an entirely different source," Angie confirms with a subtle nod.

"That source being my vacation pay." I didn't mean to say that part out loud. Though, it's the truth, isn't it?

For about a minute, it seems like Angie's not going to reply at all. She finally releases a long sigh. "It is a big ask. I know that. But I also know you'll rise to the occasion." There's a glint in her eyes as they meet mine. "And while this trip won't be counted as *billable* hours, I would certainly take it into consideration when reviewing candidates for that open Manager position."

Visions of a new, shiny bronze plaque dance through my head. She certainly knows how to get what she wants. "All right. I'm in."

"Of course you are." She taps a key and her printer starts up again. "Truly, I'm almost jealous. It's been ages since *I've* gotten to take vay-cay!" She laughs and I force myself to laugh with her. "Now, how about you take the rest of the day off? Pack your things, plan your route."

Find a last-minute cat-sitter. "I'll do that," I say while clambering my way off the stool.

"Anytime!" Angie waves me off. "I'll send along the info for your accommodations in town."

"Perfect." I walk backwards and give a short wave. "See you Monday."

The rest of my officemates are chatting about in small circles or making the slow move back to their desks. Compared to the quiet of Angie's office, the sound in here is cacophonous. Most everyone is carrying small paper booklets, some with hand-drawn doodles or scribbled title pages. Leftovers from the work-shop, I suppose.

The break room has all but emptied out. I head there any-way. I couldn't tell you why—even if I managed to catch Buffy and her assistant, what would I even say? *Hello stranger, I've been planning to get your quote on "realizing possibility" tattooed across my forearm?* Or, *Did you really move to Canada—if so, why haven't you updated your Instagram bio? And who's this guy you're travelling with, your chauffer?*

"Psst!" Hassan cuts me off midway to the break room, eyeing Angie's glass-walled office. "What's going on, did you grab that manager spot?"

"Hmm?" I lean over his shoulder. "Maybe. I don't know." *Is that her packing up in the kitchen? No, I don't think so.*

"But you did talk about the job." Hassan strides beside me. "Any chance my name came up or, you know, any certain words?"

On my way over, I snag my laptop from my desk. "Oh, she definitely used words. Phrases, even."

"Were you let go?" Augustine pops up from under my desk holding an internet router box and a small Wi-Fi booster. "I've been watching the numbers and we *should* be through the major cuts. So if you were laid off, it was not due to budgetary needs."

I snag my coat off the back of my chair. "It'd just be a reflection of poor performance, then. Thanks, Augustine. Very comforting."

"No problem." She nods.

I start to button up my coat. "No, I'm not fired. No, she didn't hand me the promotion. I'm just supposed to go on a work trip."

"Damn, really?" Hassan snaps his fingers. "I'm jelly! Where are you going?"

"The middle of nowhere." I shrug towards the exit, eyeing the break room one more time. "Anyway, it doesn't matter. How was the lunch-and-whatever? Is, uh, that speaker of yours still here?"

"You mean Buffy?" Hassan bounces alongside me. "What a get, right? It was so cool to hear her talk about all her shows and stuff. And did you know, she's Canadian? I thought she was from California but turns out, she was born in Vancouver—while her folks were on vacation!"

"Yeah, I think I read that somewhere," I mutter, as if I hadn't *absolutely* remembered that fact from when she mentioned it in an interview with *Medium* magazine, nearly a decade ago. I've only read that piece maybe a dozen times. "Is she still here, though?"

"I just can't believe she even had the time for us!" Hassan is still beaming. "When my buddy connected us and said she'd started taking on gigs, I never really thought—"

"You just missed her," says Augustine. Her words sink like a knife to my chest but I keep my face completely placid.

"Bummer," I mutter.

"Yeah, but hey!" Hassan snaps his fingers, "How about we all go out for some bubble tea after work—we could recap the talk, maybe have a little b-day celebration?"

"That sounds *so* fun." I slip aside. "But actually, I'm heading home early. Lots to do before the trip, you know."

"But what about—"

"Another time!" I wave him off. "See you later."

Coaxing Hassan aside, Augustine gives a short thumbs-up. "See you. Glad you're not fired."

"Thanks." I nod. "Me too." Once their backs are turned, I duck into the break room one last time to just be triple-sure Buffy didn't sneak her way back in, or forget anything. All that's in there is a mess of loose papers, markers and pens, one-and-a-half untouched veggie trays and a cake that still has a good chunk of my face on it. Eyes darting around, I snag what remains of the cake and slip out the building's side exit.

The building's smokers prefer the front-side parking lot, since the end never catches the sun. A newly built condo has seen to that, casting most of the street in perpetual shadow. A small pile of snow sits shoved around the outer door, so dense I can barely get it open. Especially with my arms full of pilfered cake.

There's an unfamiliar minivan in the parking lot. A figure in a puffy coat smacks a handful of ice off the windshield. Whoever it is, they're awkward with the snow scraper. Someone comes out from the passenger side to give a hand. When she lowers her hood, my heart skips a beat. It's Buffy. She's wrapped in warm layers, including a thick, knit scarf. But there's no mistaking her. Even among the grey city slush, she shimmers like starlight.

That means the guy scraping off must be her assistant. Yes, I spot the ginger beard. When he smiles at her, they both radiate with warmth, like heat rising off a melting snowbank. They whisper a few soft words together and she reaches across to—

My breath is caught in my throat. She kissed him. She's *still* kissing him.

I turn around and quickly walk in the opposite direction. The moment I turn the next corner, a passing bike messenger runs through a massive puddle and splashes me with ice water. I'm instantly soaked, down to my socks. Heart heavy and toes slowly freezing, I begin the long march uphill towards my apartment building. Cake box tucked under my arm, a fresh bout of snowflakes start to fall.

Chapter Three

My keys skitter across the chipping plastic of my kitchen counter. I set down my sort-of-stolen birthday cake and begin to delayer. Kicking off my soggy shoes, I toss my jacket onto the barstool that serves as both my singular dining chair and coatrack. "Cashew, I'm home!"

I run the sink, hot water nipping my chilly fingers. While physically present, mentally I am still in the CMM parking lot. The steam of Buffy's breath as she leaned in towards him. The subtle way he slipped an arm around her waist, clearly practiced. It sits like a scratch on the record my brain is playing over again on loop. *Why am I even upset?* I scold myself. *Of course someone like her already has a partner. Did I even think I had chance, anyway?*

"Ah!" I cry out and pull my hands from the stream of hot water. My palms are pink and fingertips pruned. Carefully drying myself off with a hand towel, I call again, "Cashew, buddy!" I crack open a can of wet food. "Want a snack?"

There is no padding of tiny footsteps, no fluffy white ears or yellow eyes peeking out from under the bed. I take a quick look around the shoebox that is my apartment—in a place this size, how many places can a little cat really hide? *Maybe he got stuck in the bathroom again.*

No sooner does that thought occur to me do I hear a muffled meow. It's followed by a flush. I go rigid, waiting for any other sounds. I know he spends a fair amount of time alone in the apartment, but it seems unlikely that Cashew has taught himself to use the toilet. Am I in the middle of what is about to be a very awkward break-and-enter?

Better question, what kind of robber uses the bathroom?

I look around for something to defend myself and grab the silicone spatula sitting on the edge of my sink. I snag it, hoping the intruder will mistake it for a steak knife. *Why don't I keep my steak knives somewhere easier to grab?* Too late for second-guessing now. The bathroom door is swinging open. Cashew bounds in my direction. A moment later, a figure steps out. They're wrapped in a towel—one of *my* towels—and shaking out a wave of lime-green hair.

"Shit." I drop my not-so-deadly weapon. "Mako, what the hell?"

"Jesus!" Mako jumps back. "What're you doing here?!"

"What am I—what are *you* doing here?" I cover my eyes and turn aside as Mako drops the towel. When I look back, they've pulled on a pair of mermaid leggings and oversize sweatshirt. I recognize the top as one of mine too, though I haven't seen it since our (latest, for-real-this-time) breakup.

"I *was* in the middle of setting up." Mako shakes out their hair, water droplets cascading across the carpeted floor. "Way to crash your own surprise party."

"Oh no." I brace myself, half-expecting several more uninvited guests to leap out from behind my various houseplants and minimal furniture. Thankfully, the only sound comes from Cashew as he fervently rubs against my legs, mewing for attention. "Yes, I hear you." I crouch to scratch his chin. "Just a minute, buddy." Rising to my feet, I drop a spoonful of wet food into his bowl. "So, Mako, should I be expecting more company or is the surprise that my ex still has keys to my apartment?"

"It's just me." Mako brushes past me and prods open the cake box on my kitchen counter. "Mars and Johanna are busy, unfortch. And I still can't get a hold of Mei."

"Yeah, I'm sure." I pat Cashew on the small of his back as he digs into his meal.

Mako runs one finger along the cake's edge, swiping a fingerful of icing. "I wouldn't take it personal."

"No, *you* wouldn't." I toss the half-empty can of wet food into the fridge and let Cashew lick the spoon. "I get not making the drive. But no text? Not even some crappy birthday GIF of a cat blowing out candles—that's not personal either?"

"I don't know what you want me to say." Mako sits themself onto the kitchen counter, legs swinging in midair. "Maybe they just need more time, Chuck."

The hair on my neck bristles. That old pet name sounds much less sweet now that we've gone from roommates to lovers, to exes on both fronts. "Whatever. It's fine."

The apartment's forced air somehow feels colder. After a few moments, Mako breaks the silence. "So, how was work?"

"Brutal." I motion for them to scoot off the counter. They oblige and I fetch us a couple small plates from the cupboard. "Everyone remembered it was my birthday."

"Only you would find that *brutal*." Mako tugs open the closest kitchen drawer and grabs some forks. "Cake's pretty good, at least."

"Yeah?" I cut us each a slice, giving Mako the last remaining corner slice. I know the icing is their favourite part. "And oh man, I almost forgot, you'll never believe who came into the office today—Elizabeth Hawkshaw!"

"Am I supposed to know who that is?" Smacking their lips,

Mako graciously accepts their slice. "Wait, don't tell me. Is that your ex, the one from high school?"

"What? No!" I stab a fork into my serving of cake, which happens to have my left eyebrow on it. "She's that public artist I really like, the one with the TED Talk? Do you remember that woman who coated herself in tar, feathers and rainbow stickers on the steps of the White House—that's her!"

Mako carefully scrapes down all the icing off the side of the cake, nibbling on it, one scoop at a time. "Would you say she's more or less popular than Elliot Page? That's pretty much my only metric for queer celebrity."

"They're—she's not—" My words falter. "They're not comparable."

Cashew licks his bowl clean and mews loudly for more. "What about Janelle Monáe?" asks Mako. "Vivek Shraya?"

"You're the worst," I laugh, exasperated. "You know that, right?"

Mako cracks a smile and giggles along with me. Spearing a forkful of cake, I go in for my own first bite. And it *is* pretty good.

Cashew winds around the kitchen, vying for attention until eventually he settles in for a nap on Mako's discarded towel, which sits by the bathroom door. Pretty soon, Mako and I are sitting on the counter side by side, both eating cake straight out of the box. We swap gossip and stories, delving into moments of nostalgia. Even after everything, it is just so easy to be around each other—hours pass like minutes. Eventually though, the conversation circles back to where it always goes.

"It's not like it's *my* fault the Landlord and Tenant Board wouldn't return our calls." I dab my lips with a paper napkin, one saved from my many orders of takeout-for-one. "Going to the tribunal would have just delayed the inevitable, anyways."

"You're preaching to the choir, Chuck." Mako pulls apart two layers of cake and licks the icing off each one. "If we'd shelled out for a lawyer or got arrested for squatting, I'd have never been able to start up the Cut-In Studio."

I offer them a napkin for their sugar moustache. "How is the whole CIS thing going these days, anyway?"

"You know I hate it when you call it that." Mako shoos me away, preferring instead to use their shirtsleeve. "It's good, though. There's a real market for queer-friendly, gender-neutral salons—I'm even thinking of expanding to the East End!"

"That's great," I mutter. Hopping down from the counter, I start tidying up. Cashew gently purrs in his sleep.

"You know," says Mako, "I've been doing a lot of thinking lately."

I carry our dishes to the sink. "That's always trouble."

"Shut up." They shove my shoulder as I pass. "I'm being serious. All the crappy stuff that's happened in the last year—losing Hillside, getting fired from the Coalmines."

I shake my head. The "Coalmines" was Mako's not-so-affectionate nickname for the CMM office. "Angie would die if she heard you call it that."

"That's exactly why I do it." They grin. "But yeah, it was a lot of rough stuff. Not to mention our whole *situation*."

"Is that what we're calling it?" I start the tap and get to scrubbing our forks.

"For a long time, I was pissed." Mako's voice softens. "Wondering like, why me, you know? But maybe it's all happened like this for a reason. Because now, it's hard to even imagine where else I'd want to be."

"And isn't that *so* great for you." I laugh like I'm just teasing, but there's a bitterness beneath my words; we both can taste it. "For what it's worth, CMM still isn't the same without you." Secretly, I am thankful Mako got taken out with the layoffs. There's little quite so awkward as being your double-ex's de facto manager.

Without turning around, I hear Mako slide off the counter

and slip up behind me. "Speaking of," they ask, "have you taken my advice yet?"

"Shockingly, no. I have *not* tried to get myself fired," I say, clenching my jaw. I think all that sugar is hurting my teeth. "Something about needing money for rent, food, kitty litter?"

"But Chuck," Mako whines. "That place is sucking the life out of you!"

"I think you're projecting." I shove the clean cutlery into my overflowing dish rack and get started on scrubbing a saucepan that's been soaking in the sink since last night. "Besides, not all of us have a big inheritance to fall back on in case of a quarter-life crisis."

"Here we go," Mako grumbles. I glare down at the dish pit, refusing to engage.

I can still sense them behind me. Part of me wishes they'd soften, say something sweet, maybe put their hands around my waist. The way they used to, back when we first got this apartment together. When we thought maybe we were falling in love. I used to think that the end of Hillside wasn't so bad because, in a way, it brought us together. And at least in those early days, when we got tired of bickering, we'd switch to having sex.

I shake aside those memories and remind myself there's a reason Mako and I didn't work out. We hardly lasted a month sharing this bachelor pad. Turns out, you can't force love, even if it means cheaper rent. We've tried again a few times since, but the spark just isn't there.

"I don't think your thirties counts as quarter-life anymore," Mako announces as they step aside, moving over to give Cashew some attention. He rolls onto his back, exposing the white of his belly for pets. "It'd be more like a thirty-three-point-three-percent-repeating life crisis."

"If that, considering my luck." I laugh and go to dry my hands. My phone rattles on the kitchen counter. An incoming call.

Who the hell calls people anymore? That thought barely crosses my mind before Mako has leaped into action, snagging my cell before I can answer it myself. "I bet it's Johanna!" They grin. "She told me she'd try and get the day off. Or maybe Mei managed to find a ride!"

"I thought you said you couldn't reach her?" I ask. Mako ignores my questioning. For a brief second, I allow myself to hope they're right. Maybe it is Johanna, or even Mars on the other line. He was the only one who ever bothered to check in on me, after Mako and I broke up (the first time). It was just a text, but that was more than anything else I got from the people I used to call my "chosen family."

"Oh." Mako's smile drops. "Um, you should take it." They toss the phone towards me and I catch it against my chest. Despite everything, I squeeze my eyes shut and allow a flicker of a birthday wish. *What if it's all three of our old housemates calling to say they're outside my apartment? What if Mako has been bluffing this whole time and really did manage to pull off a surprise party?*

When I open my eyes, my father's face stares back at me. His profile photo, a frozen grimace. "Oh." I let it ring for a few minutes until it stops. The screen falls black.

"You're not gonna answer?" Mako leans across the countertop, fist tucked under their chin.

"I'll message him later," I decide, slipping the phone into my back pocket. With the dishes done, I dig out a duffel bag from my closet and start sorting through my clothes.

Mako pads after me and flops onto the bed. Cashew peeks one eye open and stretches, hopping onto the bed in hopes of more affection. "I thought you two were on good terms these days."

"I said I'll call him later." I hold up a couple of collared shirts and pick the least wrinkled among them. "I'm just not feeling super chatty. You never heard of setting a boundary?"

"Have *you* ever heard of opening up?" Mako grumbles as

Cashew nuzzles into their lap. I slap my closet shut and head to the bathroom, digging out a night's worth of toiletries. "You gonna tell me what you're packing for?"

"Work trip." I shove my toothbrush into the side pocket of my duffel bag, alongside some socks and underwear. "Leaving tomorrow."

Scratching under Cashew's chin, Mako stays quiet for a moment. "I guess I should get going, then."

I shrug. "Yeah, I guess."

Silently, Mako bids goodnight to Cashew before sliding off the bed. They head towards the front hall, taking out a pair of knee-high boots from the coat closet. "Hey, Chuck?" they ask while zipping up a pink, puffy coat, "Has it ever occurred to you that instead of worrying about all the people who aren't around, you might want to appreciate those of us that are?"

"Are you adding life coaching to the services at CIS?" I snort. "Or is that just your birthday gift to me?"

After a long, steady inhale, Mako lets out a sigh. "No. This is, though." They dig into their jacket pocket and pull out a small, brown box wrapped with twine. They place it on the kitchen counter without a word and turn to leave.

"Wait," I call out after them. Mako's hand lingers on the doorknob as they look back, over their shoulder. "Could you maybe watch Cashew this weekend?"

Mako's smile is a flat line. "Sure thing." They step into the hallway, silhouette framed by golden light. "HBD, Chuck."

The door clicks shut. I stare at the empty space left in their wake, for longer than I probably should. Eventually, I turn my attention to the countertop where a small box sits in waiting for me. I don't move to open it.

Cashew is doing the razzle-dazzle. I roll my eyes and coax him off the bed. "So, what do you think, maybe we watch something while I pack?" I flop down and reach for my laptop. Cashew briefly mews at me before getting back to business.

As I reach over to charge my phone before starting up a retro movie marathon, the screen starts to blink. A series of texts arrive in short succession.

Dad: Did you get my call?

Dad: You're probably out with friends.

Dad: I hope you're having fun. Happy birthday.

I glare down at the messages, Mako's words still ringing in my head. *It's not that I'm ignoring him,* I tell myself. *I'm just busy.* Tossing my phone onto my bedside table I tell myself, *I'll call him back later. Definitely. Probably.*

Chapter Four

Something in my car doesn't sound right. There's a steady thudding sound, getting faster as I pick up speed. Humming along Highway 401, its rhythm almost blends into the background. Almost. I flip on my windshield wipers, turn up the radio and try not to think about it.

The road is a stretch of grey, flagged by empty trees and snow-filled farmers' fields. Billowing clouds hang heavy in the sky. My gaze is fixed on the horizon. The radio crackles, slipping between pop songs to country music to local news broadcasts. "—heavy snowfall," a bland voice cuts into my latest jam. "Polar vortex from the west…hunker down, gonna be a big one." I fiddle with the dial. "—and now, an oldie and a goldie to keep you all cozy!" The music kicks in and I hum along, tapping the steering wheel.

"How is this an *oldie*?" I wonder aloud. I could've sworn this track just came out a couple years ago. I grimace as it occurs to me, this is what it means to be thirty. I shift lanes and take the next exit.

When given the chance, I always opt for the side roads, even if it means taking extra time. It's a bumpy ride but it usually means less stop-and-go. Other than a couple rusty pickup trucks and the occasional speedster, it's quiet. Not many people are going north in the middle of a cold snap, I guess.

Country houses and McMansions fade into dilapidated farms and small-town churches. While passing an overgrown graveyard, the wispy snowflakes on my windshield start to turn into fat, wet globs of ice and snow. I click my wipers up a notch, then another. I go a full hour without seeing another soul. *Maybe the main road would have been a wiser choice,* I think to myself. *Too late now, though.*

When I slow for a turn, the thumping returns with a vengeance. "I hear you." I pet the dashboard. "I'll get you to a shop as soon as we're back." Ideally one with the least number of straight cis dude mechanics. I guess I could go in boy-mode, try to blend in. "Or I'll luck out and find some hard femme mechanic who gives discounts for flirty butches."

I guess on some level, I'm still not used to doing all this kind of stuff by myself. Back at Hillside House, we all took care of each other. Mei was our handyman—or handy-gay, as she liked to be called. Bikes were her passion but she knew her way around cars, too. Johanna was a wicked gardener and Mars, her partner, a fantastic cook; they'd work together, merging our backyard harvest with the random produce salvaged from the supermarket dumpster. We ate like royalty and always had leftovers to share. Meanwhile, Mako—brash, brilliant Mako always had *something* going on. Our house was perpetually covered in half-dry canvases, loose-stitch quilts, unstapled zines. Mako breathed life into the world like a fire lets out heat, with ease and to the great awe of all those nearby.

In retrospect, I'm not sure what I contributed. My calendar reminders got our bills paid on time, and I usually volunteered to take meeting notes. Not especially special skills. Maybe that's why it was easy for them to cut me out.

Thump-thump-thump. It's getting even louder now. Knuckles tight on the steering wheel, I press down on the gas. It's better this way, I remind myself. Sure, all my houseplants are on the brink of death. And yeah, I order takeout for most of my meals. But at least I can afford to do so. If we'd stuck it out in that death trap, we'd all be worse off. In the end, I guess I did contribute something after all—I was the scapegoat. Everyone else could walk away believing they would have done something, if it wasn't for Hillside's resident coward.

Sleet sprays in all directions. I can hardly see the lines on the road. Without my GPS, I probably would drive right through Elmridge and end up somewhere north of Montreal. Even with its help, I miss the first turn and have to double back.

Elmridge is marked by a long bridge across a narrow river. Ice on the road makes me slow my approach. Far below, deep green firs cluster in on both sides of a half-frozen stream and large rocks line the riverbank. Someone's even fishing down there! I haven't a clue what they're trying to catch in this rotten weather, but it's kind of quaint. Cute, even, for nowhere-ville.

Rumbling through what passes for the Elmridge downtown, I see roadside shops display specialty items in both French and English. Locally made jam and honey, fresh-caught fish. A handful of pedestrians hustle along the sidewalk with hats and scarves pulled tight. I pass a chipped mural, the meaning of which is a mystery—probably some colonial fever dream about the town's history, its faces and figures warped by the erosion of time. A used car dealership promises *25%! Limited time only!* Twenty-five percent of what? I have no idea.

You'd think it would be hard to get lost in somewhere so small, yet somehow I manage. Windshield fighting a steady stream of hail, I peer out at the slanted street signs in search of my next turn. The GPS doesn't seem to know where I'm going, either. I wind through a labyrinth of wide houses, conservative yard signs, picket fences. The hair bristles on the back of my neck. *Where the hell has Angie sent me?* I try not to make eye contact with locals as they shovel snow off driveways. Slowly, the houses shrink down and stretch into duplexes, town houses and four-unit apartment blocks. Vacancy signs are taped into the windows of laundromats and corner stores. I even spot a couple pride flags. The tension in my shoulders relaxes, slightly.

By the time I figure my way through the town's winding sprawl, the sun has dipped to the west. A blood-orange glow is cast across the misty sky. My phone announces my destination is on the right. A two-story home, decorated in dark red brick. It stands out against the evening's snowfall, tucked at the edge of an isolated cul-de-sac.

I'd pull into the driveway but a large minivan sits parked in place, layered with snow. I double-check the listing info Angie forwarded. *Perfectly Private Oasis,* boasts the title. *Cozy House in Family-Friendly Area, "Home Away from Home." Use Lockbox for Entry.* I could have sworn there was on-site parking. Oh well, it's not like there's a fight for space on the street.

I find the lockbox tucked under a garden stone. Duffel bag slung over one shoulder, I twirl the keys around my finger. Excitement starts to rise in my stomach. Compared to my tiny apartment, this place is going to feel like a mansion. This really is starting to feel like a vacation. I'll get set up tonight, spread out my clothes for tomorrow and then just soak in the solitude. No noisy upstairs neighbours, no sirens on the street. For breakfast, I'll make myself avocado toast and pretend I'm a homeowner—a true millennial fantasy.

Shuffling through a layer of fresh snow, I climb the brick-laid steps. The handrail is chilly on my bare skin. I should have packed gloves but oh well, it's just one night. I give one final check of the house number and pull open the screen door, setting the key into its lock.

What happens next hits me all at once.

A small creature, a blur of grey and white, flies within a breath of my nose. The panicked bird—*is that a cockatiel?!*—makes a sharp bank, straight towards the waiting paws of a bright-eyed cat.

"No, Miss Kiki!" A child with puffball pigtails and snot running down her chin careens past, grabbing at the cat's tail and tripping over herself instead. "Miss Kiki, Mango's not your dinner!"

She knocks into the cat's scratching post and Miss Kiki is pushed off-balance. The bird dives in the opposite direction, skating death as it banks around an armchair. The cat takes a flying leap. She lands onto the mantel of a nearby fireplace, scattering a series of knickknacks and framed photos. The girl on the ground lets out a sob and smacks her fists.

"Ren—Rosie!" A man rushes through the nearest doorway, his broad chest plastered with a pink kitchen apron that instructs one to *Kiss the Cook*. Something about him tugs at my memory, but there's little time to think as the cat lunges again, claws extended. Mango the cockatiel scrapes the popcorn ceiling, spraying flecks of white like fresh snow.

"Are you all right?" The man scoops the girl into his arms, checking her for bumps and scratches. Her sobs are inconsolable.

"Daddy, no!" She smacks against his chest, wiggling to be free. "Miss Kiki's gonna eat Mango!"

"We're not going to let—" His brief attempt to quell her fears is cut short as the orange cat lets out a howl, readying for another attack. Mango titters with anxiety, bobbing back and forth in search of some escape.

"Hayden!" A woman's voice, from the top of the stairs. "The bird, watch the bird—the door is open!"

As if Mango just learned of that fact too, I'm suddenly facing down a sharp beak and flustered wings. The bird barrel rolls straight towards me.

My years on the high-school softball team snap me into action. I snag Mango like a fly ball, a second before its great escape. Fists tight, hands gentle, I pull the bird to my chest and feel it shivering. There are a few pecks and scratches, but I don't let go.

"It's okay," I whisper. "You're okay."

Mango settles. Or at least accepts this fate. When I look up, everyone is staring right at me. The man still holds his daughter in his lap, the two of them sharing matching looks of awe. Even the cat seems shocked at my presence as it stands, perfectly still, on the back of the couch. I clench my teeth and shrug, "Uh, hi. This your bird?"

"Uh-huh." The man and his daughter share a short look before they both stand and beckon me closer. I start to take a step but my foot catches on something warm and dense. I trip and start to blunder forward, arms jutting out in a reflex. There's a cacophony of shouts and hollers as everyone moves towards me at once. Mango slips free from my grasp.

I crash to the ground beside a large, sleeping dog who does not stir in the slightest. The whole, chaotic scene starts up again—a series of screeches and cries, tweets and meows.

One voice rises above the rest. "Mango, perch." A hand outstretched, an invitation and a command. Mango does not have to be told twice. "There you are. Good baby."

I must have fallen asleep at the wheel. There's no other explanation for it. Or maybe I never got out of bed in the first place and this is one of those weird dreams where you go through the motions of your day, only to wake up and find it hasn't started yet. Because how else could she be here, standing over me like this.

Elizabeth freaking Hawkshaw looks me up and down before

nodding towards the door. "Would you close that?" she asks. "No need to let the cat out."

Mango rests in her right hand and she coos to it gently, guiding it back to a birdcage that takes up a large corner of the room. Once all her pets are settled down, Buffy takes a minute to check in on her daughter and—now I know where I saw that guy before. It's her assistant! Or lover? She cups a hand under his bearded chin and I spy matching silver rings on their left hands.

"Is that—are you—?" My brain is taking its sweet time reconnecting. "How did you even get here?"

Buffy arches a brow in my direction. "I might ask you the same thing."

"Sorry." The words get stuck in my throat, raspy and dry. "I'm so sorry. I must have the wrong address or something. I'll—I'll go."

"Were you expecting anyone?" Buffy asks her partner, who shrugs in reply.

"We've got that Bnb-er coming tomorrow…" His words trail off as plumes of dark smoke start to trickle across the ceiling. A fire alarm kicks on in the next room over and he scrambles to his feet. "The oven!" he cries, racing towards the kitchen. "My eggplant bites!"

A king-size bed with fluffy white pillows. Bay windows. A walk-in closet and en suite bathroom. I hug my phone to my chest and scroll through photo after photo of the bedroom that was to be my *private oasis*. So much for all that. Instead, I sit cross-legged on a thin, grey mattress strung atop a wire metal frame. I'm surrounded by stacks of cardboard boxes, a dust-covered stationary bike and a handful of sealed plastic bins. There's a sack of birdseed on top of a pile of old newspapers. A small space heater chugs away in the corner, desperately fighting against the cold that drafts in around the window. I wasn't expecting I'd ever have to live in a closet again.

A scheduling mix-up. We agreed that's what happened. Maybe an issue with Angie's booking, maybe some kind of glitch with the site. Whatever the reason, my luxury vacation spot has become something closer to a hostel. Buffy didn't have much to say about it but her husband, Hayden, apologized profusely. He swears, they planned to clean up the place and clear out before I arrived *tomorrow.* Apparently they're new to hosting guests in what is otherwise their family home. And the last thing they need is a bad review. He even offered for them to take the "spare room" and let me sleep in the master suite. But this bed is hardly big enough for a single person, let alone two. I've had worse though, and I'm not about to drive back in this weather or go track down a motel. *It's just one night,* I tell myself. *Just one night.*

I'm so close to the kitchen in here, I can catch the lingering scent of burnt eggplant. This house was clearly never meant to have a guest room on the main floor. If I had to wager, I'd say I'm in an old pantry cupboard or maybe a neglected mudroom. The narrow door to my extremely humble abode sits slightly ajar, its hinges at odds with the slanted floorboards. Its singular window faces towards the road, offering a view of the closest streetlamp. Not that I'm complaining.

Hushed voices trail from the kitchen. Though I can't make out much of their conversation, I can guess what they're talking about. The interloper who arrived a day early (at least, according to their own schedule) and now expects to spend the night. They're probably kind of weirded out. Hell, this *is* weird! Consider me weirded, too!

Angie isn't answering my texts or calls. I dig into my duffel bag and try to remember into which compartment I shoved my toiletries. There's no point in unpacking anything else. First thing tomorrow, Hayden promised, they'll be off to stay with a family friend. Then the king bed, the bay-window reading nook—it'll all be mine.

The thin whine of a door nudged open. Someone is peeking in, spying through the crack. A sliver of a child's face carefully watches me.

I zip my bag shut. "Hey...kid." I offer a wave. "Can I help you?" A gasp and giggle, feet scampering back. She vanishes from view as quickly as she came.

"Rosie!" Hayden calls after her, "What did we say about going over there?" A moment later, he stands in my doorway in the exact same spot. "Sorry about her." He stands with one hand on his hip, still in his apron. "We're still working on boundaries. And respecting personal space."

"Aren't we all." I shrug and shuffle my feet. The floor is cold and it seeps into my socks. "It's no big deal. She seems like a sweet kid."

"She does seem that way, doesn't she?" There's a tilt to his smile, like he's biting back on half of it. He stands there a touch longer than he needs to, his eyes locked with mine. Something about the way he looks at me makes me dizzy. I blink away.

"Um, how old?" That's a thing people ask about kids, right?

"Five, next month." Hayden crosses his arms and leans against the doorframe with a wistful sigh. "If you can believe it."

"Nice," I mutter, intentionally *not* admiring the definition of his biceps and forearms. The guy must work out. "I used to work at a day camp for kids around that age. They're pretty busy, but plenty fun."

"That's a good way to put it." Hayden nods. "Still, I can't believe our little baby is growing up so fast."

"Maybe *you* can't." The door is pushed all the way open and Buffy stands there, clutching a tray of extra-crispy eggplant bites. She's wearing oven mitts that match the colour of Hayden's apron. Their edges are scorched black—both the mittens and the bites. In the background, the kitchen fan is working overtime to suck up the remaining smoke. "Five years feels exactly right to me, if a bit short. Are we sure she's not turning six next month?"

"Don't even joke about that!" Hayden pries an eggplant bite off the tray. He tries to take a bite and there's a sharp crack as the whole thing crumbles between his fingers. Making a face, he sets aside what's left of the burnt-up nugget and wipes his hands on his apron. "I swear, it's like we brought her home from the birth centre just last week."

"I can't imagine—" My empty platitude is cut off by a clatter from the living room and heavy thump. On instinct, I jump to my feet and Hayden gets ready to run over.

Buffy stops the both of us with a raised hand. "Give her a second," she whispers. "Let's just see if..."

We hold our breath in unity for a few seconds. The silence is pierced with a high-pitched cry. Hayden and Buffy look to one another, sharing a silent conversation of pursed lips and raised brows.

"All right. I'll handle this one." Buffy passes over the charred baking tray. "You go throw these out and order us a pizza."

"You think they'll deliver in this weather?" Hayden whines, in nearly an identical pitch with his daughter. "Besides, we can scrape off the burnt parts!" Buffy just stares at him. Silently, she tilts her chin and he lets out a sigh. "All right, all right. I'll call Pizza Town. But I'm making it for *pickup*." He pulls out his phone and starts muttering to himself, "One small gluten-free, a large meat lovers with extra-extra cheese... Hey, Charlie, what you want on yours?"

"Me?" I hold a hand to my stomach. It rumbles at the very suggestion. My food so far today was leftover cake, followed by about four stops for cheap roadside coffee.

"Who else?" Hayden taps on his phone. "It's the least we can do after the mix-up." He glances up and when our eyes meet, it's just like before. A spark in the air, stirring something up inside me. It's more than hunger.

"Uh, I'm good." I crouch over and fiddle with my duffel bag. "Thanks."

Hayden hangs back for a moment, as if waiting for more. After a minute, he shrugs. "Okey doke." Just like that, he heads the same way as Buffy. Two rooms over, I can hear her using the same soothing tone she had with Mango, but this time it's to calm Rosie.

There's a part of me that wants to follow. To go out there and ask for a small pineapple pizza, maybe some garlic bread. I'd see if Miss Kiki the cat would enjoy a pet. That dog looked sweet too, if inconveniently placed. More than anything, I want to go talk to Buffy—there's a single wall between myself and one of the greatest political artists of this era! Yet my legs won't stand. My hands move as if of their own accord. They pull out my laptop.

At least I have work. Probably better to stay busy, taking care of something that actually matters instead of getting sucked into awkward small talk. These people don't know me—why should they want to spend their otherwise pleasant evening entertaining this weirdo who's crashing at their house? And I'm sure Hayden is relieved not to have to cover the cost of an extra pizza. I'll just eat the granola bar that's been sitting at the bottom of my bag for who-knows-how-long. That's plenty.

Someone kicks on music in the kitchen. There's the shuffle of busy feet, dance breaks. I keep my eyes fixed on the screen, fiddling with this damn questionnaire that was supposed to be finished last week. I find myself running over the same lines again and again. Walls of text, punctuated with tiny boxes, brackets, semicolons. My orange nighttime screen filter makes everything start to blur together. My eyes are getting heavy. The bustling Hawthornes fade into a constant background noise. Hayden sets out for their pickup pizza and spends the rest of the evening talking about how hard the storm is coming down. Rosie helps Buffy clean up the kitchen and set the table. Something about their flow, the hum of a busy house— it feels soothing. Familiar.

Like a pebble dislodged from the bottom of a riverbank, a memory rushes to the surface of my mind. Mako, cross-legged in front of a worn wooden coffee table. They always said Hillside's floor was more comfortable than our frumpy old couch. Johanna is of the opposite persuasion, preferring to splay out across the entire sofa, preferably atop a mountain of blankets. Her loose blonde hair is traced with streaks of cotton-candy pink and Mars plays with it as he cuddles on her lap. He's nursing a fresh stick-and-poke tattoo and telling us about how he's flunked out of yet another apprenticeship. Mei is laughing at the story and strumming tunelessly on her ukulele. I lie in the middle of them all, eyes half-shut, Cashew beside me on an unfinished crochet blanket, purring. I am so warm.

My dream pops like an ill-fated bubble. I'm suddenly awake. Fully clothed, I'm halfway falling off the bed. My computer screen glows, a lantern in the dark. I blink as my eyes adjust. It takes a minute to remember where I am. The sun has gone down completely and my solitary window is a square of white. Snow is still falling like static on an old television set.

My phone buzzes again. I belatedly realize that's what woke me. It's my dad calling again. I send it to voice mail. Somewhere above me, Rosie is whining about brushing her teeth.

I try to will myself back to sleep but it doesn't come. This is always the problem with a late-day nap. I curse myself for drifting off so easily; it's a small slight but swiftly falls into place along many on my ever-growing internal list of *Poor Choices Made by Charlie*.

Rosie is crying again. Something about a lost stuffie? It's hard to make out the details couched between high-pitched squeals. Eventually, the upstairs bustle dies down and I am left alone, lying in darkness, listening to the creaks and moans of an unfamiliar house. The wind is howling outside. I never understood that expression quite so acutely as I do now.

There are murmurs through the vent. If I had to guess, I bet they're coming from the room directly above my own. Buffy and Hayden are probably getting ready for bed, engaging in a bit of pillow talk. One voice is a rumble, a train passing in the distance. The other soothing and consistent, ocean waves as they meet the shore. I think Buffy mentions something about the workshop yesterday. Hayden mumbles a reply. And I swear, it sounds like my name. The two of them snuggled up, talking about *me* of all people—the very thought sends shivers all the way to my toes. Of course, with the wailing outside and the groaning walls within, it would be easy to imagine something that isn't really there.

Chapter Five

The first thing I notice is the quiet. It's been so long since I couldn't hear the drone of a busy street or neighbours arguing in the unit next door. Even back at Hillside, with five house-mates and several pets, the house was never truly still. I wonder if the Hawthornes have taken their dog and cat with them, wherever they went off to. Do they expect me to feed their bird?

The silence is actually kind of eerie. The creak of the floor-boards, the tension of the hinges on my door—it's all so loud in comparison. I busy myself in the kitchen and find a small speaker plugged into the wall. It's got a Bluetooth connection. I kick on Robyn's first album and turn it up, max volume. Every glass and plate in every cupboard starts to rattle and bounce—okay, maybe not *max* volume. I tap it down a couple notches and start bobbing to the beat.

Nothing in this house matches up. For starts, the plates and bowls are all different colours and textures. I find the coffee beans are shoved behind a bag of rice, alongside a mason jar of rubber bands and chip clips. I have no idea where they might keep the sugar, but I manage to find a pack of reusable filters in a jar marked *Sweets*. It's shoved next to another jar marked *Savories* that's full of loose markers and pens.

The buttons on the coffee maker are worn to the point of being completely illegible. After a couple of false starts, I manage to get *something* brewing. The gurgle of water as it approaches a boiling point helps me to relax. I lean against the kitchen counter and study the Hawthornes' household calendar. It's one from the Trans Visibility Project. Yesterday's date is circled in red pen.

Even their fridge magnets are all out of sorts. Most placed at Rosie-height, they're a mishmash of rainbows, flags, peeling photos of snow-capped mountains. Most seem like souvenirs but from places I've never thought of as tourist destinations: Brandon, Manitoba; Lumby, B.C.; London and Paris (the Ontario ones). I find even more on top of the fridge, littered in bite marks. I wonder which house pet left those, or maybe Rosie used to be a bitey baby.

The coffeepot is full, but I can't find anything to pour it into. Turns out, every mug in the house is crammed onto the dishwasher's top rack. I pick out the least chipped of the lot and, in the fridge, I find a veritable smorgasbord of dairy alternatives—oat milk, rice milk, almond milk, soy. I grab the carton that's closest and mix it in till my cup is the colour of creamy hazelnut. At last, I take a long sip and let the warmth radiate through me. The beans are rich, well-roasted and freshly ground. A little taste of luxury. Someone in this house knows their stuff.

The household clocks are all out of sync but my phone tells me it's approaching 10 AM. No wonder I feel so well-rested. That razor-thin "guest bed" mattress wasn't even so bad after all, though I should get myself going. I'm supposed to be across town and setting up in an hour. Oddly, I don't feel that rushed. Maybe it's the fact that I'm not getting paid for all this overtime, but I'm quite content to do a wee bit of exploring first before rushing out to the car.

Every room in the house is painted with multiple colours. I guess the Hawthornes really love an accent wall—and accent walls *for* their accent wall. Some are traced with geometric shapes or hand-painted leaf motifs. Someone's been getting interior decorating tips from DIY-TikTok. Pictures, placards and drawings are strung up in every manner possible, from boxy wooden frames to handfuls of Scotch tape, scraps of yarn held up with pushpins. Alongside professional family photos and several child-crafted creations (all signed in the corner with an *R*), they've got a handful of high-quality posters. I recognize a couple from the Justseeds Artist Co-Op and one that looks like a Beehive Collective original.

Just like everything else, the Hawthornes' furniture is all kinds of eclectic. One might even call it queer. A heavy, well-worn armchair and matching footrest, both of which look older than the house itself, shoved alongside a cheap IKEA coffee table covered in clutter and crayon doodles. The sofa's velvet upholstery is sunken, holding tight to the memories of at least a hundred butts. I find a pair of mismatched socks tucked between the cushions. The in-built bookshelves look like real wood but they're overburdened; the slats bow beneath the weight of too many books that have been shoved in at odd angles. Tucked in the corner, I spot a beat-up acoustic guitar covered in colourful stickers. The fireplace looks completely decorative and is home to a dozen or so stuffies.

I find a cork-foam coaster carved in the shape of a fish. Setting down my coffee on the table, I flip through a loose stack of magazines. They've got back issues of *Broken Pencil*, *Labour Action* and a few glossy editions of a university newsletter. That last one is the magazine that does not sport dog-eared corners and underlined passages.

Is this Buffy's handwriting? I study a small note in the margins of a Canadian Tire catalogue. Did she find any special inspiration when circling ads in last week's paper? A copy of *Fierce Femmes and Notorious Liars* sits sideways on the bookshelf; is that *her* bookmark held within? I'm just brimming with curiosity. I've always admired her political performance art, but Buffy has never shared much about her personal life. At the same time, I can't help feeling like I'm poking through someone's closet, or their undies drawer. There's plenty more house to investigate, anyway.

On the stairs, the banister acts as a makeshift clothing rack. It's draped in several scarves, hats and sweaters. I sidestep a pile of colouring books and a couple pieces of Lego. What really attract my attention are the family photos on the wall. Affixed in dollar-store frames—one still has a price sticker on the edge— a few shots are carefully posed, clearly from some local portrait studio. The rest are all candids, blurred and grainy like they were taken with an old smartphone or maybe even a disposable camera. One picture shows Rosie riding her mother's shoulders in a crowd; in another, curled up on her dad's lap beside a campfire. She reduces in age with each step upwards until, at the top, Rosie the infant sits in a high chair, her face covered in strawberries and a prominent gap between her two front teeth.

There's something odd about these pictures. Once I see it, it's everywhere. The one with the campfire has a marking in the corner: *Riley and Papa at the Lake*. But when she's on Buffy's shoulders the caption reads *Ramona's First Pride*. In the bathroom, I find a pair of framed handprints credited to *Rowan, 5 weeks*. A handmade soap dish is signed by *Renee, Age 4½*. I have to wonder, *How many kids do these people have?*

On the floor below, the music fades out. The album has played through to its end. I look over my shoulder, edging open the door to the master bedroom.

The walls are the same colour as the pictures. I guess whoever's been doing the interior design hacks hasn't reached this room yet. There's the walk-in closet and the reading nook, bay window with a view of pure white; the snow is still falling. But one thing takes my attention above all others. The bed. The California king. It calls to me. Silky sheets, a fluffy duvet and *so many pillows*—I take a running leap, clamber to the headrest and roll onto my back. It wraps me up like a long-lost lover, sinking into an embrace. I spoon it back.

When I was a kid I was always scared of quicksand, for some reason. There was a stretch, around the same year my parents separated, where just the idea of it would send me into panic. So many nights, I woke up gasping for air, certain I'd been pulled under. Turns out grown-ups run into quicksand a lot less than I thought. If I really wanted to worry about something, I could have stressed over the rising cost of housing or impeding recession. After all, now I truly know what it means to be drawn in and enveloped to near suffocation among all that is soft and cozy. And it isn't a nightmare—it's the dream.

Swimming my way from either side of the bed, I take a peek at Hayden and Buffy's side tables. One side has a sunrise lamp, like the one I've got at home, a small jewelry box and a pair of reading glasses. The box is decorated in childlike drawings and says *Happy Mother's Day* on the back. Well, technically it says *Hapy Moth ers Day*, with a backwards "D." I get the idea though. The opposing bedside table has a tiny library underway, layered with science fiction novels, romance stories, several poetry collections and dense nonfiction texts. They're all stacked on top of each other like a game of literary Jenga. In the drawer, I find a handful of used tissues—yuck. Probably should have left that one closed.

The book-dense side has one other curious detail. A wallet-size photograph, held in a miniature frame. It shows two couples, neither of which appear to be Hayden or Buffy. The adults proudly stand before a gaggle of children, all dressed in Sunday best with matching dresses and suits. At the back, a slouching teenager refuses to smile for the camera. Their face is covered in acne—or are those freckles?—and I can barely make out the trace of long red hair that's pulled into a loose braid. All further details are obscured by layers of dust. Something tells me I should leave it be.

A gust of wind sweeps through the home, windows shuddering. The front door opens and slams. I clamp up, completely silent, listening carefully. There's the stomping of boots. Short, muffled words. There's someone downstairs. Multiple someones.

Could it be another schedule mix-up? Is there someone else who thinks they've rented out the house for the weekend? *Or,* my mind races to the worst possible option, *maybe it's an intruder.* Is it possible someone has been casing the joint, waiting for the Hawthornes' departure? What if I'm in some terrible, B-rate knock-off of a *Home Alone* movie? If so, I haven't even set up any traps yet. That hardly seems fair.

Was the front door locked? I ask myself. *Why didn't I check?* There's no time for self-flagellation. I grab at my pants pocket and find it empty. I didn't even think to bring my cell phone up here! *What the hell was I even thinking?*

The noises downstairs are getting louder. I recognize the hushed tones of a brewing argument.

"I've never seen it like this!" A woman's voice. *Is that Buffy?*

"I have," someone answers. "But not for a long time, that's for sure." He sounds a lot like Hayden.

"Is Monday gonna be a snow day?" Okay. That's definitely Rosie. "Is it? Is it?"

"At this rate?" Hayden laughs. "I wouldn't be surprised if it's a snow *week*."

"Not that it makes a difference for *you*." I peek around the corner. Buffy is stomping her boots. "No need to lose progress on your curriculum just because of a little snow."

"Aw, babe, can't we cut her a break?" I catch a glimpse of

Hayden. He's hanging up the family coats. "If public school kids are getting a day off…"

"Don't you start." Buffy kneels down to help pry off her daughter's boots but Rosie scoots away, insistent on doing it herself. "You're not the one who has to play catch-up when we miss a day."

"I'm not trying to start anything—" Hayden catches himself and straightens up. "Oh, Charlie, you're up! You seen outside?" He pulls out his phone and flashes his weather app. "Check this out, twenty-three centimeters! Just an hour ago, they said it was only seventeen!"

"*Only* seventeen," Buffy repeats with a click of her tongue. She's busy chasing after Rosie, who is now tracking puddles around the living room. "Back home—*oof*—four inches—*honey, please*—was enough to stop traffic for a day and a half!" Tackling her daughter onto the couch, Buffy manages to get both her boots off. But now Rosie has broken free and is running around in wet socks.

"Here, babe, I got her." Hayden hurries over to assist.

I step downstairs and pull aside curtains in the living room, only to be met with a wall of pure frost. I wipe a small circle with my sleeve and look out. It's a sea of white. Cresting waves and mountains, the landscape of this quiet street has been written overnight. Snow covers every inch of every lawn and sidewalk— I can't even see my car! Not a bit of it appears interested in melting. And there's more still coming down.

A solitary neighbour struggles to clear their driveway with a handheld snow shovel. Every scoop they hoist is replaced just as quickly. Otherwise, the world is empty. Quiet. A handful of boot prints trace around the Hawthornes' minivan; they tell the story of failure. There is no way they're getting in that vehicle, let alone driving it anywhere.

"You've got to be kidding me." My words appear as fog against the window glass. "We're stuck in here?"

"Seems that way." Hayden returns and joins me at the window holding two small, damp socks. He's close enough, I catch a whiff of him; light sweat, mixed with something more. An oaky sort of smell. It's nice. "I called around all morning," he tells me. "It's like this all over Elmridge. Apparently the plows can't even get started until the snow stops falling."

Buffy props herself up on the couch. "Have you received any word from your office?" she asks. "I hope they don't expect you to go anywhere today."

"No, I…" My voice slips away from me. "I haven't checked my messages yet."

"As well you shouldn't!" Hayden claps me on the back and heads towards the kitchen. "At least not until you've got some food in you. Rosie, wanna help me make breakfast?"

"I want Eggos!" Rosie claps her hands and hurries after him. "Chocolate Eggos, with chocolate chips! And chocolate milk!"

Hayden chuckles, "I'm not sure that's a balanced breakfast."

"Can't we *cut her a break*," says Buffy. "Let her *just be a kid*?"

"That's not—this isn't—" Hayden huffs. "You're such a butt, Buff!" He snags his apron off a hook by the fridge. "All right, kid. Let's get you loaded up with sugar. After that, we're going out to enjoy this *snow day*!"

Rosie squeals with delight. Soon, there's the scraping of chairs across linoleum, the clink of ceramic bowls. Miss Kiki hops from her cat tree to follow after them. The family dog snuffs his way out from under the couch. Somewhere, Mango is singing.

I just keep staring at the window. It feels like I'm falling backwards but I never seem to hit the ground. I'm just suspended here, watching the frost slowly creep.

"This yours?" Buffy draws my attention towards a coffee mug that sits beside their magazine rack. I stare at it for a few seconds before I remember how to nod. "It's gone cold," she tuts. "Let's go make a fresh cup, shall we?"

The warmth of her smile only makes everything worse. I mumble something like, "I'm good." Then, avoiding all eye contact with *any* of the Hawthornes, I rush through the kitchen and back into my makeshift bedroom. My door still doesn't shut right so I push a large bin against it. Grabbing my phone from its charger, I desperately check for any texts and calls. There are a ton of automated weather alerts.

Warning: Polar Vortex in Southern Ontario.
Heavy Snowfall Expected.
Stay Indoors.

The highways are all completely covered. Every route in and out of Elmridge is shut down. There's no word from Angie or any of my coworkers. I doubt that the centre I'm supposed to visit is operating in these conditions, anyway. Even if it was, how would I get there—strap Wellesley, the family dog, to a toboggan and have him pull me across town? No. There's no escaping it. I can't do my job, and I can't go home. Even so, all I want to do is run outside, start my car and head back to the grey, dismal city where no one ever would take the time to notice my coffee's gone cold.

Chapter Six

(10:05 AM) Charlie Dee: Good morning, Angie. Not sure if you're online as it is a Saturday. Please contact me as soon as you see this.

(10:15 AM) Charlie Dee: There is a weather situation here. It is not safe to drive to the centre.

(10:39 AM) Charlie Dee: Waiting on advisement from your end. Hope you are having a good morning.

"Do you think I should fill the bathtub with water?" I wonder aloud into the phone.

"What?" Mako's laughter crackles through the other end of the phone. "Why would you do that?"

Hunched against a wall of cardboard boxes and old VHS tapes, I stare intently at the window. How is it still snowing? "Just seems like a thing to do in a crisis." The narrow bedframe squeaks as I lie back and grab my computer. Still no word from the office. "Twitter says they might send in the army to clear the roads."

"Is that a good thing or a bad thing?" asks Mako. Their words are muffled as Cashew mews with impatience.

"He's past due for breakfast," I remind them. "Do you need me to tell you where his canned food lives?"

"I *know* where the cat food is." Cashew's yowls are getting more insistent. "But I suppose it might be helpful to know where you keep the can opener nowadays."

I will myself not to laugh. "Bottom drawer, next to the stove." There's rustling, the banging of pots and pans. "No, not that drawer." My laptop screen lights up, a notification coming in from Slack. "It's Angie. Gotta go."

"Tell her to shell out some overtime for this!" Mako hollers as I hang up. "Also, if you die in an avalanche this weekend— I'm keeping the apartment!"

"Sounds good. Talk soon." I click off and quickly scroll to Angie's message.

(11:10 AM) Angie Bane: can u walk there?-A

I clamp down on the inside of my cheek. Has she really not seen the news? There's a province-wide blizzard going on! I didn't really read past the headline of those news alerts but the words *polar vortex* sure seem intimidating.

Channelling my best customer-service tone, I type a reply.

(11:13 AM) Charlie Dee: Local officials are advising all residents to stay indoors.

Three little dots hover next to Angie's name. After what feels like millennia, she responds.

(11:15 AM) Angie Bane: R u sure? Cant be that bad-A

How does one best tell their boss to *google it*? Thankfully, I don't have to find out.

(11:15 AM) Angie Bane: K yes they are closed...stay put. Go tmrw.-A

There's a piercing whine from the next room over. Someone is running the blender. My jaw is starting to hurt from gritting my teeth.

(11:16 AM) Charlie Dee: I am not so certain that will be feasible. Can we arrange to touch base tomorrow morning?

(11:20 AM) Charlie Dee: Angie? Are you still there?

(11:25 AM) Angie Bane: just keep me posted. Save receipts for gas and food.-A

Angie's icon goes dim. She's logged off. My phone buzzes, an incoming picture message. It's a snap of Cashew's butthole, his face buried in his food dish. I roll my eyes and reply to Mako with a single laugh emoji. At least I know my cat is well cared for, if nothing else.

"Knock, knock!" Hayden taps at my door and starts to push it open, only to be stopped by a strategically placed box. "Sorry to bother you." He shoulders his way through the gap. "But it's brunch-o-clock—eggs and toast, all gluten-free!"

"I'm all right," I mutter, though the scent of fresh bread and butter is hard to resist.

Hayden grins. I think he heard my stomach grumble. "If you'd rather some gluten-full options, we might have a loaf buried in the deep freeze. We're making smoothies too, if you're so inclined."

I take one last look at my Slack messages. Angie is still offline. With a long exhale, I shut the laptop. "I guess I could use a pick-me-up."

"That's the spirit!" Hayden doubles back out of sight. I shove the barricade-box away from my door and follow after him.

Hayden's pink apron is flecked with eggs, flour and a handprint that looks about Rosie-size. Blender under one arm, he spoons in large globs of peanut butter, jam, several frozen bananas and a handful of—is that *spinach*? I make a face, trusting he won't see it. "So, what's your go-to milk? Almond, oat, cow?" Locking on the blender lid, he smacks a button on the side and shouts over the ensuing whirr, "You're not allergic to nuts, are you?"

I raise both hands in surrender. "I'm good!"

The blender dies down but now there's shrieking coming from the foyer. I grab a piece of toast—pretty good, for gluten-free—and I peek into the living room, curious as to all this commotion.

"Mom! My zipper's stuck!" Rosie squirms and whines, pulling at her snowsuit. "It's pinching! Mom, help!"

"Just a second." Buffy is crouched by the shoe rack, trying to coax a set of booties onto the family dog. "I just need to get Wellesley ready for outside." Every time she grabs at one of his heavy paws, he instantly pulls back from her grasp. "If you could just—please, Rosie."

"Stop! Stop!" Rosie wiggles and stamps her one snow boot. Her other foot doesn't even have a sock. "Stop calling me that!"

"Sorry, yes, I'm sorry." After several tries, Buffy manages to grab hold of Wellesley's back paw and shoves it into a small red boot. "There's one." Before she can velcro it shut, Rosie's cries rise another octave. "Okay, just hold still." Buffy bends in half, one hand still on the dog and the other fiddling with Rosie's snowsuit. "Mommy can't help you if you—"

She yanks the zipper and pinches even harder. Rosie starts fully screaming, stumbles backwards and smacks into the shoe rack. A series of heavy snowshoes scatter to the ground. Miss

Kiki leaps downs the stairs and scurries away. Mango squawks in his cage, getting in on all the noisemaking. In all the commotion, Wellesley has managed to slip out of his bootie again.

"Hayden, babe?" Buffy cries out, exasperated. "We could really use a hand!"

"Coming!" Hayden downs his peanut-butter-and-chaos smoothie in three gulps, wipes his face with the back of his hand and rushes into the fray. "Wells, let's do this." Hayden tackles the dog shoes while Buffy tries to console a sobbing Rosie. Piercing through the turmoil, the telltale ring of an iPhone left on loud. "Oh, crap." Hayden yanks his cell from his pocket. "Buff, I gotta take this. I think it's the committee."

"On a Saturday?" Buffy groans. Hayden shrugs apologetically. "Fine. Go." She waves him off. "I'll figure things out."

"Hello?" Phone tucked against his shoulder, Hayden hurries his way upstairs. "Yes, this is Dr. Hawthorne speaking…" Buffy is left to grapple with Wellesley, who has somehow managed to now slip from his collar, while Rosie whimpers herself into a puddle.

I grab the open jar of peanut butter off the counter. "May I?" Buffy stares at me, then the peanut butter. "I picked up a trick, from when I used to be a dog walker." Kneeling beside Wellesley, I let him sniff the back of my hand before approaching farther. "There we go. Let's see if we can make this a little easier for everyone."

I take a fingerful of peanut butter and wipe it on his nose. Wellesley's shaggy brows perk up and his nostrils flare. His big pink tongue starts licking with enthusiasm, giving me just enough time to grab at his booties and slide each one into place. I secure the Velcro and top it off with a scratch behind his ears. His fluffy tail thumps with appreciation.

When I look up, Buffy is smiling at me. "That was brilliant," she murmurs.

"Thanks." I can feel myself going flush, cheeks warm.

Buffy's not the only one watching. Rosie clutches at her mother's back, watching me intently. I give Wellesley another pet and explain, "Even puppies need help sometimes putting on their outside clothes." I take a peek at the design on her multicolour snowsuit. "Do you like unicorns, Rosie?"

"NO!" She scowls. "I *love* them. And my name's *not* Rosie."

"Oh. I'm sorry." I don't think I heard it wrong yesterday, but what do I know? I glance towards Buffy but she's busy resecuring Wellesley's collar. "Would you mind telling me your name, then?"

"I'm *Rainbow*, now. Obviously." She sticks out her little tongue at me. I try not to laugh.

"Now, *Rainbow*," Buffy echoes as she finally gets to buttoning her own coat. "We've been over this. Just because *you've* decided to change your name doesn't mean everyone *else* knows about it." She gathers up the wayward shoes, sets them back onto the rack and grabs a rainbow dog leash. "So, what do we say?"

"Hmph." The-child-formerly-known-as-Rosie crosses her arms. After a tense couple of seconds, she juts out a small handshake. "Hi-my-name-is-Rainbow-she-her."

"Nice to meet you, Rainbow." I kneel to take her hand. "I'm Charlie."

Rainbow stuffs her fists back into her snowsuit pockets. "Charlie what?"

"Charlie… Dee?" I sneak a look at Buffy.

"She's asking for your pronouns." Buffy clips Wellesley onto his leash. "If you don't mind sharing, that is."

"Oh!" A genuine smile flutters over my face. It's been a while since anyone thought to ask. "They and them, please."

"Okay-nice-to-meet-you." Rainbow wiggles past her mom to grab at the door. "*Now* can we go play outside?"

Buffy nods and grips the door handle. "Coming?"

"Me?" I stumble backwards. "Uh. That's very nice to offer but—"

"I really could use the help." Buffy grips the leash in one hand and holds back her daughter with the other. "If you don't mind."

Snow piles around my ankles. My sleek city boots were not built for marching in the snow. The drifts formed by last night's storm rise up to my knees. Buffy had the foresight to loan me a pair of snow pants but I doubt even a triple-thermal ski suit could keep my socks dry.

The sidewalks are completely impassable. Instead, the four of us wade down the middle of the road in single file. Buffy forges ahead at the front, Wellesley plodding along at her heel. Rainbow jumps in her mother's footsteps and I hold up the rear. Our path is buried almost as quickly as we made it, vanishing beneath still-falling snow.

"Mom, my face hurts!" Rainbow slumps into a snowbank. "My feet hurt!"

"What about your butt?" Buffy laughs over her shoulder. "Does that hurt, too?"

"No, no, no!" Kicking her feet, Rainbow sprays snow in all directions—including right into my face. "My butt doesn't hurt!"

"Are you sure?" Buffy presses onward, undeterred. "It kinda sounds like it does."

Wiping aside the ice that's collected on my eyebrows, I offer an arm and help Rainbow to her feet. An icy gust of wind whips past and we all brace tight, waiting for it to pass. All those objections Rainbow has been spouting, they're starting to feel pretty reasonable.

A wave of white washes over us and I can't see farther than my own nose. "It's getting pretty windy out here!" I shout at the purple blur up ahead that I'm pretty sure is Buffy. "Maybe we ought to head back?"

"Just step where I step!" she hollers back. Sure enough, the wind dies down soon enough and Rainbow scurries up ahead, dragging on Buffy's waist.

I close my eyes and picture home. I bet Cashew is curled up right now, sleeping on the bed in that one spot he likes. Mako is probably sipping on hot chocolate. I bet they're using my favourite, extra-large mug. To them, the storm is nothing but a backdrop. An easy excuse to work from home. I try to take a deep breath but it freezes in my nostrils.

Buffy is nothing if not determined. She leads us out of the cul-de-sac, down a path marked by broad trees. Their branches are empty hands against the sky's unforgiving grey. We pass old brick homes, frosted windows, eaves troughs overflowing with icicles. I watch as an old woman in a heavy parka shovels a path to her mailbox. She makes a fair bit of progress in the time it takes our little group to march past. Just as she's finished collecting a handful of flyers, a neighbour appears with a snow blower; the machine's haphazard spray undoes all her hard work in a matter of seconds. Buffy offers to stay and help but the woman waves us on.

Wellesley is having the time of his life. He had a slow start, stopping occasionally to gnaw at those dastardly little booties, but he's in a groove now. He and Buffy work as one, clearing out a path for the rest of us. He shoves his face into the ground, coming up with a snootful of snow that gets Rainbow giggling every time. Who, herself, is still hanging off her mother's waist.

"Mom," she half-whines, half-sings. "When we go back can we have hot chocolate?"

A child after my own heart. I grin.

"Mmm-hmm." Buffy fumbles with her thick wool mittens, resetting the Velcro strip on one of Wellesley's shoes. "Sure."

"With marshmallows!" Arching backwards, Rainbow lolls her head so far that the puffball of her hat is touching the snow. "Mom? Mom, can we have it with marshmallows though?"

"I'm not sure we actually have any marshmallows at home," says Buffy and Rainbow shrieks in horror at the thought. In a fit, she loses her grip on Buffy's side and tumbles into the snow—vanishing from sight. Off-kilter from acting as a coun-terweight, Buffy stumbles in the opposite direction. Wellesley takes his chance and kicks off both his front-paw boots, skirts out of his collar and makes a break for it.

"Wells!" Buffy flails after him but it's too late. He's already legs ahead, galloping into a nearby park. "Rainbow, are you okay?" Buffy swims over and joins me in fetching Rainbow whimpering from the embankment. "You're okay." She breathes a sigh of relief.

"No, I'm not!" Rainbow sobs. Her hat's been knocked off and her mittens are astray. "I'm cold and I'm wet and I wanna go home NOW!"

"Sure thing," says Buffy. "We've just got to—"

"Now!" Rainbow cries again. She's shivering, snow melt-ing into her coat.

"Hey, Rainbow?" I jump in. "You were moving pretty fast in the snow, before. Bet I'm quicker though." Lifting my knees as high as they can go, I start jogging after Wellesley. "Wanna race me and find out? Last one to the park's a rotten egg!"

"No way!" Rainbow instantly stops quivering and takes off after me.

"Coming, Buffy?" I shout, and she smiles back at me. Not a single inch of me is cold anymore.

It's quickly clear, there's little contest. Rainbow gallops past me like a reindeer—or a unicorn. She might as well be frol-icking in an open meadow. I push and shove my way after her and, along the way, spot a fleck of red among the white—one of Wellesley's lost boots. I hold it up for Buffy to see and she does the same. There's one problem solved, at least.

I'm well out of breath by the time I reach the park. Wellesley has circled back, fascinated with a patch of off-colour snow. I lean against a fir tree while Rainbow's already moved on, kick-ing up snow while practicing her cartwheels. "Mom! Mom, are you watching me?"

"Keep your gloves on!" Buffy shouts after her. "If you lose one, we're not coming back for it!" Nestling alongside me, under the fir tree, she whispers, "Thanks."

"No biggie." I shove my hands into my pockets. My thin gloves are soaked through. "You all right?"

"About as much as usual." She rubs her arms for warmth. "Nice one, Rainbow!" she hollers. "Can you do a back hand-spring next?" Rainbow's face lights up at the challenge and she starts jumping into summersaults, desperately trying to vault herself through the snow. Buffy shakes her head. "I've never seen a kid with so much energy."

"No kidding." The pine tree's branches rustle with the wind. Clouds parting, the sun peeks through for an afternoon flirtation. Only when the snowflakes start to settle do I realize Buffy is holding my arm. *Surely, just for extra balance,* I tell myself. "So, um—" *Why are you living in Canada? When are you going to do another performance? Would you ever start posting on social media again?* "Does Hayden work a lot?"

"More than he used to." Buffy wipes the fog from her glasses. "I never thought we'd be one of *those* families. Where the dad is always working and I'm left to do… Well, everything else." Her gaze drifts aside, lost among the snowflakes.

"I'm sorry?" I say, not because I didn't hear her but because there's not much else to say.

"It's—oh, no." Buffy drops my arm and books it, leaving behind the tree's shelter. "Not that one, honey! That's too tall!" I duck out after her and spy Rainbow, clambering up the branches of a nearby pine.

"I can do it!" Rainbow insists, already a few feet up and climbing higher. I grab Wellesley's leash, which Buffy dropped in her pursuit, and clip his collar back on.

"I don't think that tree likes you climbing it, honey!" Buffy scampers over an icy patch. Across the road, a few neighbours have stepped onto their porches and are watching the commotion. "You're gonna get stuck up there!"

"I can do it, Mom!" Rainbow hugs the tree's trunk. "Are you watching?"

Buffy clutches at her coat. "Yes, I'm watching! Just be careful up there—trust your body!"

"I'm trusting!" Rainbow hops to the next branch up, raining needles down onto her mother.

I tug at Wellesley's collar and nudge him forward but it's like trying to drag a boulder on a leash. "Hey, uh, Buffy?" I call out. "Any tips for getting this guy going?"

"Hmm?" Buffy glances back. "Oh yeah. Come on, Wells! Wanna treat?" She slaps the pocket of her coat and something rustles inside.

"Mom, do you see me?" Rainbow waves down from her perch, now halfway up the pine. "Do you see me?"

"Sure do!" Buffy's voice catches on the wind. "Got a plan for how you're gonna get down?"

"Didn't you hear her, Wellesley?" I tug at the leash again. "Your mom's got treats for you." He snorts and digs his face in deeper to the snow. Kneeling down, I venture a light scratch along the base of his neck. "I bet that smells great and all, but your family needs you, bud." His ears perk up as I find just the right spot in his thick, snow-soaked fur. "That's it. Come on now, let's get moving." His big, brown eyes study mine for a moment and he stands, trotting off to join Buffy and Rainbow. I scurry to my feet to keep up.

"I can't do it!" Up ahead, Rainbow teeters on a long branch. Needles are stuck into every bit of her snowsuit. One of her mittens rests on the snow below. "Mom, I can't do it!"

"I'm right here!" Buffy stands with her arms wide open. "Just take one step at a time!"

Rainbow meekly nods. She tries to put one foot down on a lower branch but there's a loud snap. It cracks beneath her weight and she shrieks as she falls. Buffy dives to catch her and they both land in the snow. Wellesley and I race towards them.

"Are you all right?" I ask, out of breath.

Rainbow sits up, her eyes wide with shock. Her face is full of white, fluffy snow. Some is already starting to melt down her cheeks and Wellesley licks it off her. She breaks out into a fit of giggles and Buffy groans, rubbing her own shoulders and back. "We're okay." She nods. "Let's just get home."

Chapter Seven

"Toronto's had its share of snow days but I've never seen anything like this." I stand with a shawl wrapped around my shoulders, looking out the screened-in windows of the Hawthornes' back porch. Mountains and slopes of shimmering white stretch across the backyard, layered like the strokes of a paintbrush. Long, glimmering icicles decorate the windows and rooftops of neighbouring houses. It's like standing inside a snow globe. "It really is quite pretty."

"Isn't it just?" Buffy passes me a warm mug of tea. Her cheeks are a ruddy crimson, still pinched with cold. She huddles in beside me, so close I can feel her body heat. "I've always had a thing for snowy days. Hayden thinks I'm goofy for it, but I love the way it makes everything so clean and quiet." Outside, Rainbow frolics across the yard. She moaned the whole way home but has now decided she wants to stay outside all day. Wellesley chases after her with a friendly bark.

Like every other room in their house, this one is packed to the brim; a set of moth-bitten love seats and an old rocking chair—pieces that look like they were already vintage when Hayden's mom lived here; layers upon layers of homemade quilts, puffy blankets and a needlepoint pillow that reads *Don't Let the Cops In or the Cat Out*; a small writing desk with a thin layer of dust sits littered with pocket-size notebooks, dried-out pens and stacks of books like *Queerly Ever After: A Parenting Playbook for the Modern Family* and *Fifty Easy Meals for Your Toddler's Picky Palate*. The only piece of paper that appears recently touched is a short list of names. I recognize a couple of them, artists and authors that Buffy has worked with in the past. Several are crossed out.

"I'll admit." Buffy pauses to sip her tea. "Some days I miss the years I spent living in California."

Was that for the four-year-long art installation you did in San Francisco? I wonder. *The one where you climbed a flagpole each day and read out the Pledge of Allegiance, backwards?*

"How long has it been since you moved up here?" I ask.

"Well, let's see." Buffy stirs the spoon in her cup. "Rainbow is turning five? So, subtract about seven months from that." She takes a thoughtful sip and exhales, slowly. The heating in this room is slim. I can see her breath. "It was Hayden's idea. Once certain we were expecting, he didn't want to bring our baby into a country without free health care." She stares out at the yard, watching Rainbow fall to her back and make a snow angel. "His mom had just passed away and left him the house. It all just made sense back then."

"And now?" I ask. Buffy stays quiet. When I look to see if I've accidently offended her with all my questions, I find she's scowling at her phone.

"Crap," she curses to herself. "Goddamn it."

"Is everything okay?" I ask.

"Yeah." She scrolls her screen a few times, frown sinking. "Well, no. I missed a grant deadline."

"Ah, been there." I shake my head. "What was it for?"

"It doesn't matter now." Buffy tosses her phone onto a nearby recliner. It kicks up dust on impact; I get the feeling they don't use this room all that much. "It's just—I was thinking of maybe writing a book. This funding would have been perfect for it."

"A book?" I'm so taken with the idea I forget to play down my enthusiasm. "What about? What's the genre?"

Buffy shrugs. "I wanted to do an anthology. See, I used to do these big talks and performances—I figured I could write down the old scripts, put them all together into a book. But then I was like, who am I to do something like that?"

"Mmm-hmm?" I nod along like my insides are not screaming *I would absolutely read that book. You're Elizabeth. Freaking. Hawkshaw.*

"So I reached out to a bunch of my old artist friends." She cracks open the screen door and waves for Rainbow to wrap it up, come inside. "I was thinking I'd get some funds, turn it into a collection of different performers. Maybe hire an editor."

"I love that!" I clap with excitement. "That's so *you* too—making a book that's also a piece of community art! Amazing. Just amazing."

"I just don't know how I messed this up." Buffy's grabbed her phone off the chair and is scrolling again. "I thought there was another month still to go."

"Hey, it happens." I gently step around to face her. "But if you really want this thing to work, you could do a fundraiser for it. I'd sure donate." She peeks up at me over her phone screen. "Um. I guess now's a good a time to tell you, I'm kind of a fan."

"Oh." Her eyes flit down and she starts typing something. "That's nice."

Whatever heat was left in this room gets sucked out the windows. I stand in silence for a few seconds, then ask, "I'm sorry. Is that weird? I don't mean to put you on the spot or anything."

"No, it's nothing like that." Shoulders slumped, she sets herself down in the armchair. "I truly do appreciate the compliment. It's just that lately, *I'm* not a fan of my own work."

How can she even say that?

"How can you even say that?" *Oops. That was supposed to stay an inside thought.* Now that I've broken the seal, the truth is pouring out. "Your stuff is brilliant! Groundbreaking! Avant-garde!" With every compliment I launch, she shrinks deeper into the chair. I snap my mouth shut, guilt pooling in my guts. I'm making her uncomfortable. I should just shut up, say thanks for the walk and go back to my room. *She's probably tired of entertaining me anyway.*

Yet my legs don't listen to my head's advice. Instead, I crouch onto a nearby footrest and fold my hands in my lap. Buffy watches me, curiously. Slowly, she sits up a little more and mumbles, "Thanks."

"I mean it." My heart is pounding. This is going way too far. And now my hands are the ones rebelling, delicately reaching towards her. I offer them, palms up, like a prayer. She hesitates for just a second before taking them in her own. "Do you remember the year you did the Chicago Art Show?" I ask. "When you coated yourself in wax?"

"The one where I invited the audience to come forward and carve their initials as it dried?" She chuckles, eyes twinkling. "How could I forget?"

"I was on the livestream." I blush to admit it. "The commentary you made, about how we carve our impacts in one another?"

"'Be in the lasting touch of momentary encounters,'" she quotes herself. "'Or the flash-pan of love-at-first-sight.'" My heart pounds just remembering it. Hearing her speak those words, right next to me, it's unreal.

How I had wished to be in that room, to have been bold enough to scratch the initials *C.D.* in the wax dripping down her back. "It spoke to me. I was going through a really hard time."

"You have no idea how long it took to clean off after that," Buffy laughs and sits up a little taller. "I swear I was soaking in hot water for a week. I ended up shaving half my hair off just to get it out." She squeezes my hand and, for the first time, I notice the thin creases around her eyes. "I don't know. Something's just changed in the last few years. I just don't have the stamina I used to."

"Mom, do you see?" Rainbow shouts from outside, pointing at what I thought was a snow angel but now looks more like a giant human-moth hybrid. "Mom? Mom!"

"Can't imagine what could be keeping you busy." I nod towards Rainbow.

"Tell me about it." Buffy taps my hand once more and stands herself up. "I thought school age would be easier but—" Mid-conversation, she opens the screen door and calls for Rainbow to come inside, *for real this time*. "Now it's all parent-teacher committees and extracurriculars."

Scampering in, Rainbow squeals as Buffy catches her mid-step. She gets set on her butt and instructed to remove her boots.

"Not to mention, playdates on the weekend. And oh my god, so many holidays—arms up!" Buffy peels off Rainbow's coat, coaching her along the way, "Up! There you go—And do you have any idea how long I spent making Valentine's Day cards for all her classmates? I don't even believe in Valentine's!"

I silently marvel at Buffy's ability to have two separate conversations at once. "No kidding."

"Charlie? Hey, Charlie!" Once free of her snowsuit, Rainbow races towards the living room, then doubles back to ask, "Are you a boy or a girl?"

Buffy winces at her daughter's question and starts stammering an apology but I hold up my hand, motioning for her not to worry.

"Hmm." I scratch my chin, tilting my head and turning in

a circle. "Let me think, let me think. A boy or a girl? That's a tricky one! What do you think?"

Rainbow giggles. "I think you're funny!"

"Well, that answers that." I nod and she's off again, cartwheeling down the hall. I glance to Buffy. "Smart kid you got."

"Too smart, sometimes." Buffy hangs back for a second and drops her voice. "Thanks for being sweet with her."

"It's easy." I run a hand through my hair and shrug. "She's a great kid."

"We like to think so," says Buffy. "Her teacher does too, though the name-change stuff has been tricky."

Mentally, I roll through the many R-names I clocked across the household art and family photos. "Seems like she's working on finding one that fits, eh?"

"You have no idea." Buffy's cheeks dimple when she's fighting back a smile. "Once she found out people can choose their own, she's gone by Riley, Ringo, Rocket—Racecar was the hardest to explain. At least she's been consistent with the pronouns."

"For now," I point out.

"For now." She pulls on the screen door, whistling for Wellesley to come inside. "You know, you're very easy to talk to."

"I like to listen." I watch as Rainbow climbs her way along the staircase, using the outside of the banister. She turns to make sure I'm watching. I give a thumbs-up.

"You like to study people too, don't you?" Buffy asks it like a question, but one to which she already knows the answer. "I saw you the other day, watching me." I blink back at her in stunned silence. "What? I like to study people too." She winks. "Especially really cute people."

Wellesley trots his way inside and shakes himself off. Buffy manages to avoid it but instantly, I'm soaked. Looking up, she's got one hand over her mouth. She can't hold it in for long and soon, I'm laughing along with her. Wellesley snorts his way over for a lay down on the living room couch. There's a puddle forming around my feet.

Between giggles, I say, "These were the last of my dry clothes!"

"Go get yourself changed." Buffy nudges me towards the stairs. "You can borrow something of mine." Before I can argue, she's busy leading Rainbow aside. "Come on, kid. We should get started on lunch—or, whatever mealtime this is. Afternoon snack?"

"Brinner!" Rainbow decides with confidence and barrel-rolls into the kitchen. While she and Buffy get to work, I kneel beside Wellesley to give him a good scratch behind the ears. He huffs and nuzzles into my hand.

From the kitchen, Rainbow starts belting out a rendition of "Baby Shark"—but, she's made it about unicorns instead? Buffy seems to know all the words as she joins into the sing-along. The whole thing reminds me a bit of Hassan's morning routine at the office, how he always starts the day with show tunes. Sure, it can be a bit disruptive. But if I'm honest with myself, I miss it on the days he's not there. There's something truly special about letting yourself go like that, just being all of who you are. I wish I knew how to do that.

Wellesley sighs and rolls onto his back. In a matter of seconds, he's already starting to snore. I give him one last pat before heading upstairs to change out of these wet clothes. Only once I'm on the upper landing do I notice, I'm humming that song. *Hmm,* I chuckle softly to myself. *Maybe getting stuck here will do something good for me after all.*

Chapter Eight

The closet's sliding door has jumped its track. No matter what way I push or pull, it's stuck half-open. My wet clothes are piled beside the bed, waiting to be hung up to dry. Buffy told me to borrow whatever I might need but now that I'm standing in her bedroom, wearing only a pair of boxer briefs and a T-shirt, I'm starting to think I should have picked an outfit before getting undressed. I can still faintly hear her and Rainbow, singing in the kitchen downstairs. All I want to do is hurry up and get dressed so I can go join them. And if that means clambering into a broken closet, I guess that's what I'll do.

Nudging my way inside, I peer at a selection of unfolded sweatpants and wrinkled flannel shirts strewn across the floor. A few warm knits, sweaters and a couple dresses all hang up neatly. The only pieces that look like they'd fit me are all out of reach. Given few other options, I suck in my gut and pull my arms tight, squeezing into the closet.

Everything is muffled in here. In the dark, the soft arms of empty cardigans pull at my shoulders. I push through a tangle of stray hangers and spot a pair of purple leggings that seem like they'd fit my waist. Before I can grab them, there's a creak. The bedroom door is pushed open.

"But I thought it was just a formality." Hayden's voice is hushed and firm. His footfalls cross the room. *Didn't Buffy tell him I was in here? Or was I supposed to say something?* I press against the back of the closet. A windbreaker beside me rustles slightly and I clench my teeth. Thankfully, if Hayden heard anything, he's too preoccupied to care.

"I know, I know, publish or perish." His voice rises like a teakettle starting to boil. "It's not as if I haven't been trying, but mid-century, neo-Marxist, trans-feminism is a niche research topic!" The closet door still sits ajar. His shadow passes, briefly. "What about my student feedback—doesn't that mean anything?"

On the pads of my feet, I sneak to look outside. Hayden stands with his back towards me, sitting at the edge of the bed. There's an unfamiliar stiffness to his posture. "Yes, I understand." He mutters. "Please convey my respects to the committee."

Should I say something? I hold my breath. *No, it's too late now. I'll just wait until he leaves.* But Hayden doesn't seem like he's going anywhere. He clicks off the phone and tosses it aside with a groan, stands and cracks his back. Unbuttoning his shirt with one hand, he slips it from his shoulders and reveals the trace of freckles down his neck, onto his back. My stomach flutters. I shove myself back into the closet, giving him some semblance of privacy.

Hayden is muttering under his breath. I can't make out the details but I can certainly recognize the tone. He's carrying out one-half of an argument, a scolding that will almost certainly never truly come to pass. *Been there.* I'm reminded of my breakups with Mako, all the arguments I had with my showerhead.

There's a thump on the closet door, then a hand. "Damn thing," Hayden grumbles. "Always gets sticky when it's cold out." I sink deeper into the sweaters and collared shirts but there's just nowhere else to go. With a firm shove, he sets the sliding mechanism back onto its track and the door rolls open. "There we go."

We lock eyes and time holds still. Hayden's lips are parted in shock. I stand with a pair of purple leggings pulled to my chest. He's still topless, a soft belly hanging over the waist of his faded jeans. I can't help but notice his chest hair; how soft it seems, and the way it blends along two faded, pink scars that define his pecs. I recognize those scars. Mars had a pair like that, too. *Noted*.

Everything speeds up again, now in double time. We both scramble to apologize and dress ourselves. "I—What're you—?"

"Buffy sent me to find some dry clothes." I stammer my way out of the closet and manage to trip twice on stray hangers. "I wasn't trying to—"

"No! Yes! Clothes!" He jumps sideways. "Clothes, good."

"Good to wear things," I agree while stuffing myself into the purple leggings and a stray green hoodie. "I'm so sorry. I should have said something."

"It's fine! You're so fine." Hayden trips over his own feet and smacks against the bedroom door. "Go. Or stay! Whatever you want."

"I—I'm good now. I'll go," I say, standing perfectly still. Hayden stays quiet for a moment too and we just stare at one another. Something in the air makes it feel like being outside in summertime, just before a storm. "Um."

"Oh! Sorry, again. I'm in your way." Hayden steps aside and swings the door open for me. As I pass, our hands brush against one another. Even once I'm in the hallway, he just stands there in the doorway staring at me. Even when I turn my back, I can feel his eyes on me. Weirder still, part of me doesn't want to go.

"I just can't believe they strung you along like that." Buffy is on her knees, rummaging through a drawer of loose containers and lids of varying sizes. "The way things were going, it was like it was all already decided."

"It was," says Hayden. "Just not in the way we'd hoped." He tucks away a stack of clean plates and mason-jar mugs, fresh from the dishwasher. "But let's focus on the positive. I got the inside scoop that there's another tenure-track position up for grabs, soon. If I just take a little more initiative, the commit-tee thinks I'd be a good candidate."

"That's exactly what they said *last* time," Buffy snaps. I can sense the ice in her words, even from the opposite end of the kitchen. I press against the window; its frosted glass is warm in comparison. I try to will myself invisible. The last thing I need is to get sucked into a back-and-forth with my hosts-slash-temporary-housemates.

Completely oblivious to the drop in room temperature, Rainbow skips her way into the kitchen. She's wrapped what looks like an adult, knee-high sock around her head and knot-ted it into something like a bow. "Mom, can I have some or-ange?" She swings open the fridge and grabs at a carton of juice that sits in the door. "Mom? Mom?"

"Yes, honey. Just a minute." Buffy lets out a long sigh and starts fiddling with the Tupperware again. "Well, anyway. This other job that's coming *soon*—is that using the normal defini-tion for the word, or are we talking university time?"

Rainbow stands on her toes and manages to grab the han-dle of the juice carton. Dragging it to her chest, she stumbles briefly beneath its weight. "Mom," she says again. "Mom, can you help me pour?"

"Mmm-hmm." Buffy pulls out a green container and even finds a lid of the same colour, but they don't snap together quite right. "Damn," she quietly curses and starts looking through the drawer again.

"So, I talked to the department head about it." Hayden tack-les the lunch-load of dishes piled in the sink. He rinses each one before loading it into the dishwasher. "She says the position could be posted as early as May."

"That's not so bad." Buffy tries to pair a red container with the green lid. No dice.

"… Of next year," Hayden says with a grimace. Buffy shoots him a *you've-got-to-be-kidding* kind of look. His shrugs as if to say, *I wish I was.*

"Mom, can I try to pour?" Rainbow shakes the jug in her arms, prying at the lid. Tiny orange droplets speckle the kitchen floor. "Mom! Mooooo—!"

"Yes!" Buffy snaps the green lid onto a yellow container and for a split second, it looks like it might fit. But the seal is warped and every time she pushes down one side, the other end pops open. "Gah!" She tosses both halves into the sink, splashing Hayden with dishwater. "Why is it so impossible to find *anything* in this house?"

Rainbow stands in silence. Hayden towels himself off and passes her a plastic cup from the dish rack. Buffy closes her eyes, takes a deep inhale through her nose and slowly breathes out. "Rainbow, thank you for asking. Mommy is just looking for something and then I can help."

"May I?" I offer a hand to Rainbow. She scowls at me, considering the offer, then gives a short nod. Balancing a cup in one hand and the juice carton in the other, she clambers to the kitchen table. I smile as I fill the cup. "Cool headband, by the way."

"It's *not* a headband." Rainbow grabs the drink and downs it in a few gulps. She ends up with a pulpy moustache and juice dribbling down her chin. "It's my *unicorn horn*, obviously." She shoves the cup back into my hands for a second serving.

"Oh, so obviously." I tut to myself. "How didn't I see that?" Rainbow shrugs and moseys over to the living room, slowly sipping her juice. While I stow the carton back in the fridge,

I venture a question to Hayden. "So, what kind of *initiative* do they want you to take?"

"The committee said they like my work." Hayden wrings out the towel in his hands. "But apparently, I don't have enough articles under my belt."

"Why should it matter how much you publish?" asks Buffy. She scoops the leftovers of our mac-and-cheese meal into an old pickle jar. "What about all the extra hours you've spent on committees? You basically planned the entirety of their Pride programming last year! Not to mention, your students love you. Isn't that worth something?"

Hayden's shoulders slump. "It's one of those weird academia things. The university wants to look like it's on the cutting edge of everything—especially big, fancy journals and funded research." He passes over the pickle jar's matching lid and Buffy screws it on tight. "Failing that, they suggested I could take on extra lectures. Really *demonstrate my commitment*."

A harsh laugh escapes me before I can help it. "So, extra hours, no boost in pay. Sounds pretty damn familiar." Inching around the kitchen table, I glance briefly towards my bedroom. I could excuse myself now, go *demonstrate* some *commitment* of my own. I'm still not done fixing up that questionnaire. Yet, I feel no rush. I should be freaked from my nearly naked run-in with Hayden. Not to mention, I still haven't fully processed that way-too-emotional outburst I had with Buffy earlier. But instead of nerves racing through me, there's something else. A warm, easy kind of feeling. They're both just so easy to be around, any awkward tension just doesn't seem to stick.

I motion for Hayden to pass me a spare cloth. He obliges and asks, "I take it they don't pay you well at that hotline gig?"

"Not enough to keep up with big-city rent." I start wiping down the table in figure eights. "Not that I'm complaining. Really, I'm lucky to have a job at all."

Buffy finally stows our leftovers and gets busy tidying the stovetop. "What makes you say that?"

I stare down at the faint lines left by my washcloth. They shimmer in the midday light, then fade. "Did you hear about those austerity cuts the government pushed through last year? We got hit hard. Ended up running a serious deficit. More than half the staff got laid off. I was just lucky that my job wasn't so easy to replace."

"Damn," Buffy mutters under her breath.

Hayden leans against the sink counter with his hip. "That's brutal, Charlie."

"I guess so. I've been so focused on just getting through, I haven't let myself feel any sort of way about it." The both of them staring at me like this, it makes my skin prickle. I force myself to laugh it off. "It is what it is, you know?"

"Yeah, I get that." Hayden scratches his beard. "Working as a sessional prof can be that way too—keeping your head down, doing what has to be done." He rubs his eyes and sighs towards the ceiling. "It can be exhausting after a while, but I don't see another option. We need the money."

"Babe, I've told you, you can't stretch yourself forever." Buffy gently rests a hand on his forearm. "I could always try booking some more gigs. Those small-time workshops pay pretty decently."

"True. But…" Hayden finishes his thought with a flat-line scowl. Buffy lowers her glasses and arches her brows. They're having another one of those silent conversations. I'm not sure they've even realized that they slipped into it. Maybe I've gotten too comfortable here, thinking I had anything to add to a dialogue it seems they've had many times before. I should have just retreated to my bedroom after all. "I just worry." Hayden speaks aloud again, at last. He puts a hand over hers and squeezes back. "We both know what happens when you push yourself too hard."

Before I can look away and offer them privacy, Buffy's eyes dart to mine. I'm struck with an impulse to apologize but she cuts me off before I can start. "Well." She claps and gives the kitchen one last look-around. "We've got the kid fed, cleanup done. I've set up everything for her language lessons this afternoon, and we'll make some time for music practice tomorrow." Hands folded, she nods at Hayden. "I'm sure you've got more work to get done today—why don't you go get to it?"

"I *do* have some essays to mark." Hayden scratches his beard. "And I had an idea for a research project. There's a part of my old thesis that I never got around to publishing." He catches Buffy stifling a yawn. "But hey, that stuff can wait. What if I did a swap-in, give you a quick break?"

"It's fine." Buffy snaps her jaw shut. "I'm fine."

She moves to stow the leftovers into the fridge, but her foot connects with a trail of orange juice. In one smooth motion, she slips one leg out, approaching an accidental split. Buffy manages to regain her balance but the jar falls from her hands and lands with a crash, splattering glass and macaroni across the tiled floor. The silence that follows is absolutely crushing. Buffy stares at the floor, nostrils flared and lips quivering.

"Hey, it's okay!" Hayden jumps over with a broom in hand. "I got this."

"Are you all right?" I ask, offering a hand to help her step over the mess.

Buffy looks herself over, inspecting for any damage. "I'm good," she mutters. "I guess I could take a breather, though."

"That's what I thought." Hayden scoops up the shambles of lunchtime leftovers and dumps them into a bin under the sink. "Go on, then."

Buffy's knees are still a bit jittery as she steps aside. "I'll be in the shower if you need me for anything." She stops, one hand on the kitchen's archway. "Oh and don't forget—"

"French, then Spanish." Hayden fetches a spray mop to clean

any remaining residue. "Then a snack before four if we want to make it to dinner without a meltdown. I'm on it, babe."

Buffy hangs back for a few more seconds before finally marching her way upstairs. Dropping his voice to a whisper, Hayden tells me, "This stay-at-home thing was supposed to be a chance for her to slow down. But some days, I think she just found herself a job that runs around the clock, three hundred and sixty-five days a year."

I rinse off my cloth and squeeze it out in the sink. "It's hard to take it easy. Especially when no one has ever shown you how."

"Spoken like someone with experience." Hayden stows the mop into a kitchen cupboard, standing shoulder to shoulder with me. Up close, I find his eyes are hazel. No, more than that. They're rich, deep green like an oak tree, flecked with strips of gold. Only when Hayden blinks away do I realize I've been staring.

"Now." He snaps the cupboard shut. "Let's go find that kid of mine."

The living room appears empty, save for the pets. Miss Kiki is perched on the fireplace mantel, where she licks her paws. Mango is prodding at a puzzle game that spits out seeds every few seconds. Wellesley has resumed one of his favourite sleeping spots—the front door welcome mat.

"Hmm." Hayden walks in a circle around the room. "Now, where did that Rainbow get off to?"

There's a giggle from under the couch cushions. One of them is distinctly wiggly. "Gee, I wonder," I wonder aloud. "Do you think she could be upstairs?"

"Or maybe she's gone outside!" Hayden grins and winks at me. The giggling gets louder. "Well, I guess we've lost her. I think I'll just take a little sit down right…here."

He slowly lowers onto the squirmiest sofa I've ever seen. Rainbow sticks her head out from behind the cushions. "Daddy, it's me!"

"Who said that?" Hayden looks around in shock, turning to me. "Did you hear something?"

"Nope." I shrug, desperately trying not to smile.

"No! Dad!" With peals of laughter, Rainbow starts to push and kick as Hayden settles right on top of her. Hands behind his head, he leans back even farther, giving a deep sigh of satisfaction. "Dad, I'm right here!"

After a few more seconds, he lets her push him off the seat. "Rainbow!" Hayden turns and smacks his cheeks. "What are you doing in *my* seat?"

"It wasn't *your* seat!" She clambers out of her hiding spot and rolls onto the ground. "And I was being the Invisible Unicorn!"

"The invisible...unicorn?" I smirk.

"Yeah!" Rainbow gives a cheesy smile, showing off the gap between her front teeth. "It's only the best game *ever*!"

"Rainbow invented it." Hayden nods sagely. "She's very clever like that." He reaches an arm out and I help pull him to his feet. In a whisper, he explains, "It's basically hide-and-seek. But, add unicorns."

"Okay, let's go again!" Rainbow claps her little hands and points at each of us in turn. "Daddy, you and me are gonna be the Invisible Unicorns. Charlie, you can be the Unicorn Tracker—they're a unicorn too, but they're also the one who looks for everybody else."

"Got it." Just as I nod, there's a buzz in my pocket. Holding up a finger, I quickly peek at my messages. It looks like Hassan wants an update on how the questionnaire is coming along. "Hmm. Actually, can I take a rain cheque on the Tracker job? I've got a...work thing."

"Yeah, and kiddo..." Hayden kneels to rest a hand on Rainbow's narrow shoulder. "Your mom has set aside some time in the schedule for you to work on your languages. We should at least *try* and get that done."

She crosses her arms and pouts the saddest pout I've ever seen on such a small face.

"Well, okay. Here's an idea." I tuck away my phone. "What if we did just a *couple* rounds of Invisible Unicorns, but *en français*?"

"Hey, now there's an idea!" Hayden snaps his fingers. "What do you say, kiddo?"

Rainbow's sorry expression blossoms into a beaming grin. "Yeah! Yeah, yeah!"

"I think you mean, *oui-oui!*" He pats her on the back and she scurries off for a place to hide. Before he gets going, too, he stops to ask, "You sure about this?"

"Dad, come on!" Rainbow pokes her head back in the living room, "And Charlie, *tu ne pas*—um. Don't peek!"

"Wouldn't dream of it!" I wave for Hayden to get going and turn around, covering my eyes. I start counting backwards from ten, trying to remember my elementary French. "*Dix, neuf,* uh, *le* eight…" Somewhere not too far away, Hayden and Rainbow both start tittering.

Chapter Nine

The unicorn's brilliant purple hue dims as dark vines encroach around all sides. She scampers one way, then another, but can't outpace the attack. Crying out, she is ensnared and lifted off the ground while a brown squirrel laughs wickedly at having caught her in his plot.

"But why doesn't she use her powers?" I shake my head and look to Rainbow, who sits within just a few inches of the television. Eyes wide, she clutches a unicorn stuffy in her lap.

"They got stolen by Acornius Maximus," Hayden explains while holding up a T-shirt from a large stack of laundry. After a quick once-over, he sorts it into one of three smaller piles that lay around the living room. "Back in the Hovel of Nightmares."

"Haven't you been paying attention?" Buffy smirks, standing on her toes to water a hanging spider plant.

Hayden pulls out a bright yellow sock and starts searching for its mate. "If you wanna know a really wild twist, in season nine, it turns out he isn't even a squirrel—he's a robot, built by the *real* big bad of the series."

"I thought he was more like a cyborg?" Buffy pauses to check in on Mango. She mists him with the water a few times and he preens in appreciation. "Also, babe. Spoilers."

"Shh!" Rainbow hushes all of us. "This is the best part!" She scootches even closer, nose nearly against the screen.

The music builds and just as Sparkles-the-Resplendent is swallowed up, three more unicorns appear, all different colours of the rainbow. They charge on Acornius and a battle ensues, sparks and pastel rays flying all over. By the time they've completed their rescue, I find myself clutching my chest with relief. *Who knew they made kids shows so good these days?*

It's been only a few days since I arrived at the Hawthornes' house but we've settled into something like a routine. Buffy and I tend to wake up first. We take out Wellesley for his walk while Hayden helps Rainbow get herself going. By the time we're back, breakfast is underway. Scrambled eggs, turkey bacon, fluffy pancakes and local maple syrup—I feel like I'm staying at a high-class hotel, even if Hayden does manage to burn at least one course per meal. The Hawthornes nearly always eat their meals together, talking and laughing and swapping stories. Even though I keep meaning to excuse myself, it's hard not to get sucked into the fun. The close quarters have sometimes made for dry nerves, once in a while. But this house has a way of diffusing tension before it can bubble over into something bigger.

Rainbow got her snow day, and then some. She's been doing virtual kindergarten during the day, under Buffy's daily supervision. Hayden shuts himself in the master bedroom for a chunk of the day to mark papers and make calls. I'm left to my own devices most afternoons, hours I should spend catching up on projects from the office. Yet I find myself listless, distracted. So far away from the gleam of condo windows and constant hum of downtown traffic, I find it hard to concentrate. My inbox is clogging up with emails, updates, last-minute-reminder memos. The weight of all those unread messages is growing in the back of my mind.

Sunday night, I tried to dig out my car but only managed to clear off my trunk before my fingers and nose felt like they might fall off in the cold. I grabbed a couple CMM-branded T-shirts from the pile of otherwise-untouched outreach materials. At least now, Tuesday afternoon, I could have something of my own to wear other than the two business-causal looks I brought up.

I've been scanning the weather radar for updates. The storm shows no signs of letting up and, while the major highways are slowly getting cleared, Elmridge seems in no rush to plow the local roads. At least Angie doesn't seem too concerned about my extended stay. She's hardly texted anything, even when I missed the deadline for that questionnaire by a full day.

Time moves differently in Elmridge. The questionnaire was a mess but hardly unsalvageable; back at home, I could have knocked it out in a weekend, with time leftover to order take-out and snuggle my cat. Who, as it happens, seems to not miss me—Mako sends daily updates, pictures and videos of him batting around his toys and sleeping on their lap. *Why doesn't he ever snuggle on* my *lap like that?*

The credits for *Brightbriar and the Uni-friends* start to scroll. A timer appears on screen. It counts down the seconds till the start of the next episode. Before Rainbow can grab the remote and get us started on Season Three, a doorbell chimes. A real-world doorbell. Hayden, Buffy and I all look at each other, sharing the same thought. *Who the hell could that be?*

"I'll get it!" Rainbow hops up and skips her way to the front door.

Buffy touches Rainbow's shoulder to intervene. "Maybe Mommy should help you."

Before either of them can make a move, Hayden's at the

peephole. "You're never gonna believe this." He grins and turns the lock. "It's—"

The door swings open in a wide burst, fat flecks of snow cascading in from the storm. A man, nearly as tall as the entrance itself, stomps his sway inside wearing a pair of massive snowshoes. He unwraps the scarf around his face and shakes loose an array of icicles from his big, bushy beard. Strapped to his broad shoulders are two bulging backpacks and he's got more under each arm.

"Uncle Franny!" Rainbow squirms and leaps into his arms.

The mountain of a man swiftly drops all his bags at once to whip her up in a hug. "There's my favourite little nugget!" He spins her twice and Rainbow shrieks, still spinning in circles when he sets her back down.

"Frances." Buffy beams and extends her arms. "What a delightful surprise!"

"Get on over here, Buff." The man grabs her by both hands and pulls her tight. "You too, Hay-day!" In one fell swoop, he's lifted them both off the ground into a deep squeeze. "How the heck are ya?"

"How are we? How are *you*?" says Hayden, stumbling briefly as he's returned to two feet. "How are you even here?"

The man kicks up one leg to display his mode of transport. "Sure glad I kept these around from when I lived up north. Given the whole snow situation, I figured you could use a refresh of supplies." He hoists several bags and loads them into Hayden's arms. "What with the stores all closed up for the storm."

"Look at you, being so thoughtful." Buffy scoots around him to close the door.

"This is amazing!" Hayden hollers from the kitchen. The unzipped backpacks overflow with fresh greens, kale and spinach, bright yellow bananas and deep green avocados. There are several bags of milk, even a fresh block of cheese. "This is *way* more than we need, though. I don't think we could even fit it all in the fridge."

"Just pick out what you like." The man kneels to unbuckle his shoes. "The rest is coming with me to Saint B's!" Buffy starts helping Hayden unload in the kitchen, Rainbow flitting after her. I start to follow but hesitate, briefly considering the stranger who just touched down in the Hawthornes' living room. At that exact moment, he looks up and catches me staring. "And who do we have here?"

When rising to his feet, it's clear he's a head taller than me—at least. I will myself not to take a step back. "Charlie." I wipe the sweat off my hands before offering a shake. "Charlie Dee."

"Good to meet ya, Charlie-Charlie Dee. The name's Frances." He's got a grip like a bear trap, yet it doesn't crush me. Rather, his skin is soft and oddly silky. "Fran, if you're friendly. Franny, if you really wanna have fun." I clock his painted nails and when I pull my hand away, it lingers with the scent of lavender.

"Charlie was supposed to stay here on the weekend," Buffy explains as she comes back for the last of the bags. "They got stuck here when the snow-pocalypse hit."

"Right!" Frances arches his back, stretching out his shoulders. "The Bnb-er! What the heck brought you out our way in this weather?"

"For uh, kind of a work thing." I point to my shirt. "I was supposed to go hand these out, over at the new community centre."

"New community centre?" He scowls, picking out bits of frost from his brows. "I know you're not talking about ECIC."

"That sounds right." I'd only glanced at the name in Angie's email when it first came in. That feels like a lifetime ago. "The Elmridge Centre for something-something."

"That's the one the city just dumped all that money into last year, yeah?" Buffy returns from the kitchen with a thermos of hot tea. "I thought they called it Innovation Plaza or some other such nonsense."

Rainbow flits around her mother like a fast-moving shadow. "I wanna give it, I wanna give it!" Buffy seals the thermos's cap and hands it to her. Rainbow has to stand on her tip-tippy toes to pass it up to Frances.

"Thanks, nugget." Frances uncorks the lid, downing several hefty gulps. He sighs and wipes his chin with his sleeve. "I guess you could say they serve a *community* of sorts. Little different than the kind of folks we work with, though."

"You run a centre too?" I ask.

"You could put it like that." He taps his nose like we're sharing a secret.

"Frances works at Saint Brigid's, a few streets down," Buffy helpfully explains. "He's the pastor there."

Frances must read the surprise on my face because he lets out a bouncing belly laugh. "I know, right? I can't believe they ever let me into theology school, either."

"Brig's has some good local programming," Hayden chimes in from halfway in the fridge. "Not just religious type of stuff." Jumping back to the grocery bags, he pulls out a full carton of eggs. "Fran, this is perfect—I just burnt the last ones we had in the house!"

"Some things never change." Frances tilts his head to one side until there's a loud crack. Shaking it out, he pops it again in the opposite direction. "I'll never forget the first year we lived together in dorms. You must have set off that smoke detector a dozen times."

"Maybe *half* a dozen," Hayden chuckles. "At most." He picks through the eggs and takes only a handful to store in the fridge, returning the rest to their carton.

There's a hand on my shoulder. It's Buffy's. With soft eyes, she assures me, "I was skeptical too. As a sworn pagan, I thought

I'd never touch foot on holy ground again, lest I turn to dust. No offence, Fran."

"None taken." Frances crosses his heart.

She says something else but I don't hear it. The whole of my awareness has curled up in the palm of Buffy's hand as she rests it, still, on the curve of my shoulder. The small of her thumb teases the collar of my shirt, tenderly rising to the base of my neck. My baby hairs prickle with attention. *There's no way she's really*—Before I can even finish my thought, she squeezes. It's so brief, I almost think I dreamed it. But there it is again. Two small pulses, like the beating of a heart. My breath freezes in my chest and I don't dare to look directly at her. Maybe she's just distracted—she probably plays with Hayden like this and it's just become a habit. *Or, maybe,* I dare to wonder. *Could she really be flirting with me?*

"Oh hell yeah!" Hayden shouts, "A lemon! Two lemons!"

The moment he speaks, Buffy's hand drops. "This guy and his citrus," she laughs. "Am I right, Frances?" He chuckles with her as they both move in to help unload. I shiver, already missing the warmth of her. That moment between us could not have lasted more than a couple seconds but I'm going to be thinking about it for much, much longer.

"I can do it!" Rainbow jumps, grabbing at her father's arms. "Dad, let me!" Hayden passes over both lemons and she runs them to the fruit basket.

I hang back for a few seconds, standing in the kitchen's arched doorway. Buffy doesn't look my way. Maybe I imagined the whole thing. *Can being stuck inside so long cause hallucinations?* I shove aside the layers of panic that arrive with that thought, and instead clear my throat. "So, uh. You said the rest of this was going to the church. You all doing a potluck or something?"

"Or something." Fran draws up another bag and zips it open, revealing packs of socks, mittens, hand warmers, all tightly packed together with elastic bands. "We're running a drive for supplies." He turns to Buffy and Hayden. "If there's anything you can spare—foodstuff, sure, but also baby formula, warm clothes, menstrual supplies. It's a give what you can, take what you need kinda deal."

"On it." Buffy steps towards the spare room. "Charlie, do you mind if I go in and see what we've got on hand?"

"Oh. Uh, sure." I shrug. "It's your house."

Her hand rests on the door. "But it's *your* room, for the time being."

I smile in thanks and nod permission. Buffy ducks inside. Taking a seat at the table, I start helping with the sort. "So, Frances, how long are you going to be running the drive?"

"As long as it takes!" Frances snags an apple from the Hawthornes' recently replenished fruit basket. He wipes the wax off on his sleeve before crunching down.

Hayden inspects a slightly squished head of purple cabbage. Looks like that one was maybe at the bottom of the bag. "Do y'all need any volunteers?"

"Probably, yeah." Frances takes another bite of apple, grinning with every inch of himself. It's almost hard to look at, like trying to stare into the sun. "I've been trying to spread the word online but you know how these things go."

"No kidding." Buffy returns with a crate of supplies. Mostly old baby stuff. "I can't count the number of times I've tried to promote an action and get like, a hundred *maybes*."

"And then five people who actually turn out," Hayden agrees. "Well, you can at least consider *us* on board, right, Buff? We'll layer up and meet you down there."

"Yeah!" Rainbow pops up from under the table and scurries over a kitchen chair.

Buffy softly laughs, "She has no idea what she's just agreed to."

"Sounds like fun." I sneak a peek at my phone. Five more

unread emails—how did I ever manage to keep up with all this back home? "I should probably hang back, though. I've got some work I'm supposed to be doing."

"That's all good," Hayden chimes in. "You can enjoy having the house to yourself for a couple hours! To be honest, I'm a little jelly."

"Yeah, thanks," I mumble. He's right, of course—I've been itching for some personal space. We all have, over the last few days. So then, why do I feel like *I'm* the one who's going to be missing out? I look to Buffy, almost hoping she might push me, *ask* me to go along. But she just shrugs.

"For sure, no worries!" Frances polishes off the last of his apple, core and all. "Now, let's get a move on! I've got a couple more stops before heading back."

With the whole family's help, plus mine, we restock Frances's supplies, and then some. Hayden has to fish out a couple extra-large IKEA bags to make room for all the added donations. On the plus side, after this haul, my supply-room-slash-bedroom is now substantially roomier. Sitting on the stairs, I rest my chin on both hands and watch Frances prepare himself for a return into the storm.

"We may have gone a little overboard here," says Buffy, looking around at the many varied piles. "Are you sure you can carry all this—we could try to bring some over later on?"

"Made it here, didn't I?" Frances squats into a dead lift. Multiple backpacks over each shoulder and bags slung under each arm, he strains upright. A couple large veins pop up along his neck. At full height, he turns to open the door but the momentum of all those supplies knocks him off-balance—he wobbles, one of the packs slipping down his shoulder. When he tries to catch it, one of the IKEA bags starts splitting at its seam. Fully off-kilter, Frances braces himself and smacks against the front-hall closet; packs of pasta, a box of dried baby formula and a large ziplock of kibble scatter to the floor. "All right!" He bursts into laughter and lets down the remainder of his load. "All right. If you're swinging by later anyway, maybe I *could* ask you to bring a bit with you."

"Except not all of us have snowshoes on hand," Buffy points out, eyeing Hayden. "I'm sorry, I do want to help—but it's hard enough just taking Wells in this weather. There's no way we could carry this all down there."

Rainbow scurries to help clean up the mess, passing back each item to her mother. Hayden pouts. "But what if we—?"

"Ah-ah." Frances holds a finger to his lips. Brings it to Hayden's cheek with a gentle tap. "Don't stress. If I've got to do it, I'll just run two trips. Or three, maybe."

"You never knew how to take it easy." Hayden sighs, cupping the hand against his cheek. He rests a hand against Frances's upper arm, lightly squeezing.

My eyes dart to Buffy but she's busy on Rainbow maintenance, picking something out from one of Rainbow's pigtails. "When were you even eating peanut butter?" She grimaces. Rainbow answers with a shrug.

"Okey doke." Frances gets himself situated, taking on only around a third of the weight he did before. "Good to see ya, Hawthornes." He nods at me with a sparkle in his eye. "Charlie."

"Hold up." I grab the banister and rise to my feet. "I just got an idea." The whole room turns to me, expectantly. My lips twitch with a rising smile. "Any chance you folks have a toboggan?"

"Wait!" Rainbow scampers back up the slick steps leading to the Hawthornes' residence. "One second!"

"Watch your feet!" Buffy reaches both arms after her, bracing to catch an impending fall. "Remember to—" Her words are drowned out by the smack of the screen door against the house's brickwork. "Go slow."

It took ages just to get Rainbow into her snowsuit. Frances went on ahead, promising to meet us at Saint B's—whenever we manage to get there. The screen smacks open again and Rainbow grips a fresh pair of mittens. "I had to get my purple gloves," she explains. "They go better with my hat!"

"Great." Buffy huffs and adjusts her own toque, brushing a stray curl from her face. "Now come on, let's get going. And close the door behind you."

Before her boot can even meet the top step, Rainbow turns again and rushes back in, tracking snow up the stairs. "Oh, oh—I have something I wanna bring for Uncle Fran!"

"Of course you do." Hayden just laughs. He leans over and drapes an arm over my shoulder, giving a playful shove. "Anytime we go anyplace, she always needs an extra ten minutes."

"Or twenty." Buffy grabs one of Rainbow's purple mitts that's already been dropped into the snow. "There's always *one more thing*."

"Charlie, are these fitting okay?" Hayden kicks at the heavy borrowed snow boots on my feet. "We might have another pair somewhere."

"Oh, no, they're great." I stuff my hands into my jacket pockets. "Thanks a ton for loaning me all this stuff. I really should have packed better."

"Families are meant for sharing." Buffy shimmies over and snaps a missed button on my coat. "And so long as you're staying with us, you're part of the fam."

Family. It's been a long time since anyone used that word for me. Buffy's hand rests on my chest, a few moments longer than she needs to. Her deep brown eyes flit up, meeting mine, and for a moment I let myself believe that she really means it.

"I got it! I got it!" Rainbow bounds downstairs with a crumpled bit of paper in her hands. "Let's go!" In an instant, she's grabbed the toboggan's red rope and is desperately attempting to drag it on ahead.

"Well, we're off." Hayden locks up and joins his daughter in pulling the sled, which itself is piled high with two back-packs, several tote bags and a couple smaller cardboard boxes. I step to follow but a mittened hand rests on the bend of my arm. Buffy holds me back.

"You sure you want to come?" she asks, in a whisper. "We don't blame you if you'd rather have some time alone."

Without a word, I offer her my elbow. We link arms and step into the sunlight, together. This is already so much better than sitting around by myself, answering emails.

In the hush of midday, we wind our way around and out of the Hawthornes' sleepy cul-de-sac. The clouds have parted to reveal pockets of brilliant, endless blue, though the wind still kicks up such massive squalls of snow it's hard to tell if the storm has truly broken. Through frost-kissed windows on either side of the road, I catch glimpses of people going about their day. They watch television while running on treadmills, smack the ice off their frozen mailboxes or simply stand there to watch our silent procession with looks of utter awe.

As we venture closer to Elmridge proper, the streets stretch on either side, yawning wide. We march past town houses and squat apartment blocks, laundromats and corner stores. There's a singular café with its windows lit up by a row of string lights, but there is no sign of anyone inside. Occasionally, we pass other souls out to brave the storm: a young couple walking their two corgi puppies (Rainbow stops in her tracks to pet both dogs, who enthusiastically lick her face in return); a man touting a large, potted ficus on top of his head; a pair of dedi-cated joggers, decked out in spandex and matching leg warm-ers. Hayden and Buffy stop once in a while to say *hello, so nice to see you* or *can you believe the weather we're having?* They always take the time to introduce me to *so-and-so who runs the antique shop* and *such-and-such from the EarlyON program.*

The sloping trail of an overloaded sled carves its way through the snow, marking our collective path. My scarf is wrapped tight, tucked into my coat. Even so, gusts of freezing wind still sneak under my hood and down my neck. My fingertips are nipped with cold, borrowed mittens wet from a brief yet raucous snowball fight. The showdown was initiated by Rainbow but dominated by Hayden. He now marches in front, stomping out a trail for the rest of us. Over his shoulder, he shouts, "Everyone still doing all right back there?"

"All good!" Buffy hollers back. Rope slung over one shoulder, it's her turn to pull the cargo.

Rainbow bounds between the three of us grown-ups, clambering a small snowbank and sliding down on her butt. She lands in a heap and groans, "Are we there yet?"

"Just another couple blocks, now!" Hayden's smile glitters in the sunlight. "We got this!" He turns to lead the way again but stops short with a gasp. "Oh my god—do you see that?"

"What?" Rainbow scampers up and races to his side, "What is it?!"

"This!" Uncovering a half-buried branch, Hayden breaks off one end with his boot and wipes aside the snow. "It looks exactly like an arm, don't you think?" Rainbow frowns at him, but nods in agreement. "Well, if we can find a matching one, we could make a perfect snow-friend!"

"Oh!" A smile breaks out across her rosy cheeks and Rainbow scurries ahead. "What about that one?" She's already grabbing at the low-hanging branches of a nearby maple.

"No—honey!" Buffy drops the rope and reaches after her. "We don't break the arms of living trees!"

"I got her, babe." Hayden holds up a gloved hand. "Don't worry." He wades through the snow after Rainbow.

Buffy lets out a long sigh and takes off her glasses to rub her eyes. "That kid," she mutters and glances towards me. "What about you—holding up okay, Charlie?"

"Oh, I'm fine." I dig out a handful of snow from around my ankles. "I've only lost feeling in four out of five toes. No biggie, right?"

"Nothing a bit of hot cocoa can't fix." From the folds of her jacket, Buffy pulls out a small thermos. "Here."

I nod in thanks and twist off the cap. Steam wafts into the air and the smell alone starts to heat me up. "You were so smart to bring this."

"I know." She winks. "Now, see if you can guess the secret ingredient."

Gently, I take a sip. The flavour is rich, almost like velvet. But there's something more. A subtle heat, in the back of my throat. "Is it… Cayenne?" I ask.

Buffy raises her brows. "I'm impressed. Most people don't get it on the first try."

"My old roommate used to do the same." I pass the thermos back to her and she sips too. "Back at Hillside—the furnace never worked very well. So, on really cold days, Mars would whip up a batch of this stuff in the biggest pot we owned. We'd let it simmer all day, adding extra milk or cocoa powder whenever it needed top up." My stomach tingles, radiating warmth. I can almost feel the blankets wrapped around my shoulders, hear the laughter of my housemates. "For days after, the whole house would smell like chocolate."

"Sounds like you made some good memories together." Buffy's glasses are all foggy from the heat of her drink. She passes it to me again while nearby, Hayden is rolling snowballs and Rainbow is still desperately in search of the perfect, matching arm-stick.

"Yeah. We did." For some reason, my second sip just doesn't taste the same.

"You okay?" Buffy wipes her lenses with her scarf. "Is it too hot?"

"No, it's not that." I twist the thermos cap back into place. "It's just, I don't really talk about those days anymore. We had kind of a falling-out." Even without looking, I can feel her eyes on me. "Okay," I admit. "More than just *kind of*. And it was basically all my fault."

Buffy tuts her tongue. "I've got a hard time believing that's true. In my experience, relationship breakdowns are rarely one-sided."

"Well, this one was." The wind picks up again. I tug my toque, keeping it snug over my ears. "Basically, we'd been sitting on a rent-controlled unit for ages and our landlord wanted to up the price. So, he claimed he was going to reno and we had to get out."

"Renoviction." Buffy tucks away her thermos and zips her coat tight. "Classic."

"Yep." I poke at a patch of ice on the sidewalk with the toe of my boot. "Some folks wanted to fight it, some weren't sure what to do. But me, I argued that we should spend our time and money looking for a new place instead." The frozen puddle starts to crack. Dark water bubbles under its surface. "When we came down to it, I was the deciding vote. We didn't fight. But we didn't find a new place either. Everyone ended up scattered." The ice breaks and I pull my foot back, splashing droplets in the snow. "Anyway, they all basically ghosted me. Except Mako, but they'll be friends with whoever."

Buffy shuffles over to stand beside me. We watch Hayden judge each of Rainbow's sticks. One of them has used rocks to give the snow-friend eyes, complete with pine needle lashes. "From the sounds of it, you were *all* going through a hard time," she whispers. "You're not single-handily responsible for the housing crisis. If anyone's at fault, it's that landlord."

"Yeah, maybe." I shrug.

Her gloved hand slips around my elbow and draws me closer. "You made the best choices you could, with the knowledge you had. I can tell you really loved that place and I'm so sorry it was taken from you."

"Isn't that just life?" I sniffle. My nose is getting runny from the cold.

"Sometimes, yeah." She squeezes my arm. "Doesn't make it right, though." Rainbow starts running towards us and Buffy drops her grip, but not before adding, "And those housemates, if they really cared about you—they should have at least tried to talk it through."

"Mom, mom!" The pom-pom on Rainbow's hat jumps with her in excitement as she points towards their finished product. "What do you think—is it perfect?"

Buffy taps her chin and moves to inspect the snow-friend. After a good think, she announces, "Perfection is overrated. This is better—this is *art*."

"But Mom," Rainbow whines. "I didn't *want* to make art!"

"Too bad, kiddo," says Hayden, tousling her hat. "Looks like we did it anyway. Now come on, I'll race you up the next hill!" The two of them take off up the next slope, leaving behind their (slightly lopsided) snow-friend.

"Thanks," I say to Buffy. "For you know, listening."

"Thanks for sharing." She nods, heading back to retake the reins of our sled.

"Oh, oh!" Jumping with two feet at a time, Rainbow hurries back down the embankment. "Mom, this one is perf—it's great! Can we ride it? Can we?"

Buffy looks on ahead to Hayden, who gives a thumbs-up. "Sure thing. You know the drill." With my help, we drag the toboggan to the top of the hill and take our positions. We've done this a few times now, though not quite so steep a slope.

Buffy settles in front, perched atop a bag of rice. It settles under her with a soft crunch. I take up the middle seat, balanced on a box of canned beans. Hayden brings up the rear. When his arms wrap around my waist, that tingly feeling returns in my stomach. Except, a little more persistent than before.

Once we're all carefully arranged, Rainbow climbs to her mother's lap. "You got the reins?" Hayden digs his boots into the snow, holding us steady.

"Yeah!" she shouts back, grabbing the rope with both mittens.

Buffy grips her daughter's shoulders. "And you're to actually steer this time, right?"

"Uh-huh!" Rainbow wiggles with anticipation, "Let's go! Let's go!"

We start to slowly push forward. Hayden's voice is in my ear. "You ready for this?"

"Not even a little." I grin and hold on tight.

"Heave!" Buffy coaches us to lean forward. "Ho!" We all lean back. "Heave, ho! Heave, ho!" We all join in on the chant, rocking back and forth. Slowly, we begin to pick up speed. Reaching the crest of the hill, the nose of the sled sticks out and for a few sweet seconds we are perfectly balanced on the precipice. I close my eyes and let myself imagine that we're about to start flying. It feels about as likely as everything else in this moment. All pressed together like this, it's as if I really do belong here with all of them. Part of the family.

Momentum builds so much faster than I anticipated. The wind picks up and starts howling past my ears, snow splashing against my face. The hood of my jacket is knocked back and my hat quickly goes with it. Hayden holds me to his chest and I bury my face into Buffy's neck. We all howl and holler,

Rainbow easily the loudest among us. Even still, we pick up speed, going faster and faster.

We smack into a bump and the sled lifts off the ground, sailing through the air. Our shouts turn to screams as collectively, we begin to teeter. Hayden is yelling something but his words are lost to the wind. Buffy lurches forward, trying and failing to grab at the rope that Rainbow has dropped entirely. She's got both arms raised high like she's on a roller coaster.

"Bail!" someone cries out. I think it might be me. "We gotta bail!"

The ground is rushing up to meet us. There's no time to do anything but leap. Hayden's arms vanish from my waist and I let myself follow suit. Tumbling into a face-full of snow, I sit up just in time to watch our whole toboggan-load of groceries soar into the sky—not a single one of us still riding with it. Bags tip sideways and zippers rip open; all at once, our cargo is scattered across the snowbank.

My heart pounds in my ears and my lungs are burning. Incredibly, there's no blood or broken bones. Buffy sits up, glasses askew and snapped on one side. She manages to set them back into place, a short-term fix. Hayden climbs to his feet with Rainbow on his back. Her eyes are absolutely wide, like she can't decide if she should scream or cry or laugh out loud. To be honest, neither can I. The four of us hang in panting silence.

"So, that went a bit sideways," says Hayden, offering me a hand up.

"Just a tad." I laugh and spot my wayward hat, halfway back up the hill.

"I'm so glad you're all right!" Buffy takes Rainbow into her arms and squeezes her fiercely.

"Can we go again?" Rainbow squirms and wriggles against her mother's embrace. "Can we, can we?"

"Maybe on the way back," says Buffy, still panting for breath. She points ahead and that's when I see it—beyond the crest of the next hill, a tall grey steeple sits against the blue-grey sky. Its shimmering, stained glass windows glow with orange light.

Hayden leads the effort to re-gather our supplies and leads to the entrance. As we grow close, I spot the name, carved into the stone-wrought walls. *Saint Brigid's Cathedral.* Underneath, someone has posted a laminated pride flag. "Come on." He nods. "Let's get this stuff inside."

Chapter Ten

Saint Brigid's heavy oak doors groan their way open. A rush of wind shoves at my back and I stumble inside, alongside a cascade of snowflakes. Buffy helps Rainbow to unzip her snowsuit while Hayden gets started on the unload. The church ceilings are lofty and curved, vaguely reminiscent of an upturned ark. The air is dense with the smell of dusty old books and rugs in dire need of a steam-clean. Stained glass windows line the hall; impressive at first glance, many of their delicate patterns traced with narrow cracks. Rows upon rows of wooden pews sit empty, save for one figure with short, frost-white hair. She sits hunched over, carefully folding a stack of pamphlets.

"Hey, Maggie!" Hayden sets aside the last of our baggage and tromps his way over. Rainbow whines her way out of her snowsuit and darts away, crawling over and under the pews. "Good to see ya!"

"Hayden Hawthorne!" Maggie stands to greet us, thin arms braced against the pew back for support. "And I see you've brought your lovely wife—Elizabeth, isn't it?" Buffy gives a polite wave. "And your daughter... Apologies, dear one, but I've forgotten your name."

"Rainbow!" she shouts before diving out of sight again.

"My, how have you gotten so big already!" Maggie claps her hands.

I spy a rack overflowing with winter coats and scarves. Grabbing our own, I move to hang them up but my chilly hands lose their grip. The whole coatrack tumbles with a heavy thud against the woodgrain floor. I wince as it echoes across the church hall.

"This is our friend Charlie," Buffy makes my introduction for me while I try to tidy up the mess. "They're staying with us for a few days."

When she smiles, the creases that layer Maggie's cheeks are thin as wet rice paper. "Is all that for the drive?" She motions towards our haul. "You really didn't have to bring all that."

"Sure we did!" Hayden passes around the bags, totes and bins, heading towards a set of stairs leading down. "How's the party going down there?"

"Quite well!" Maggie nods and sees us off. "Frances always manages to draw a crowd, no matter the weather."

The narrow passage downward is as dark as it is cool. My stomach sinks with every step. My mom was a churchgoer, off to Mass every Sunday. She never forced the rest of us to go, said she'd rather we make our own choice once we were old enough. I wonder if my sister every got into the practice. I can say for certain, my dad never did. One time, in my mid-twenties, I developed a mild curiosity in the whole Jesus-fan-club thing. Tagging along with Mako for a visit to their parents' congregation, I don't remember much about the service. The looks we got, though, those stand out clear to me still. The way people whispered, the cold politeness of their smiles. I shiver as we follow the bend of the stairwell, stepping through another heavy wooden door and into a wave of white light.

"You made it!" A worn Doc Marten boot kicks around the

corner, propping open the basement door. A sturdy woman greets the lot of us; she's maybe in her mid-forties, hair the colour of fresh cotton candy and a denim vest covered in colourful pins. Careful stitching on each breast pocket announces her pronouns, *She* and *Her*. She touts a stack of papers under one arm and around her neck sits a white clerical collar. "A little birdy told me you were heading our way!"

"Did that little birdy happen to be, say, around six-foot-four with a big bushy beard?" Hayden greets her with a hug. "Toby, Charlie. Charlie, Toby."

"Love that you brought a friend." Toby offers her hand but I can only shrug. "Oh, and let me grab those for you!" She takes several bags from my arms and turns on her heel, announcing to the room, "Fresh load coming in! Make way!"

It looks like Frances managed to get a decent turnout, after all. Saint Brigid's basement is a flurry of activity, a couple dozen volunteers milling around plastic tables and folding chairs. They sort through cases of oddly shaped fruits and veggies, dry goods and stacked cans. A parallel array inspects boxes of crochet hats, mismatched gloves, ugly Christmas sweaters and unopened packages of socks and underwear. The two assembly lines meet in the middle, putting together care packages in any box or bag they can spare. The finished products are set aside an emergency exit that sits propped open, snowflakes drifting in. Every few minutes, someone pokes their head in to grab the latest batch of deliveries—they're carried out with snowshoes and on sleds; one person even shows up riding a personal plow.

The motley crew carrying out this collective task are a far cry from any congregation I've ever met. There are leather jackets, cuffed jeans, multicolour hair. An androgynous trio compares their crystal necklaces while picking through winter outerwear. I spot a handsome couple of fitness-gays making eyes at one another while packing up a haul of potatoes and onions. A slender woman in a deep green hijab fills her rainbow-coloured water bottle at the church kitchen sink, making small talk with a young man with a blue turban and a trans-pride pin on his lapel. Toby parts the crowd for us as we go, stopping briefly to touch base with an early-twenty-something in a pastel turtleneck.

I've seen fewer visible queers at drag shows in the Village. There are a few buttoned-down boomers thrown into the mix but their very presence is such a rarity, they stand out just as much as anyone else. The most eye-catching of the bunch has to be the drag queen posted in the far corner of the basement, dressed in full face with a purple glitter-beard. On a makeshift stage, she holds a microphone and serenades us all in a beautiful baritone. Several wide-eyed children are gathered around, staring up in awe. I can hardly blame them. If Toby wasn't keeping us on such a quick pace, I'd stop and watch the show.

We sidestep open crates and tables of busy volunteers. Toby sets down our supplies at their designated stations before tasking Hayden with a check on their sound system—apparently they've already blown a couple speakers and the last one is on its last legs. Rainbow darts into the crowd, greeting several children with friendly hugs. Buffy stays close to my side.

"Here we go!" Toby grabs the papers from under her arm and drops them on a table, alongside similar stacks in likewise disarray. "I know the work's a bit mindless but our expert-folder—did you get a chance to meet Maggie, upstairs?—she's taking care of the church bulletin so I was hoping you two could try and catch us up on these?"

I pick one up and read it aloud, "*Tuesdays, Dinner & Drop-In. Wednesdays, Peer Support. Friday and Saturdays, Glitterbug Child Care.* What is all this?"

"It's our newsletter!" Toby takes the page from my hand and flips it over, revealing the title: *Saint Brigid's Affirming Services.* It's arced like a greyscale rainbow, placed above a delicate line drawing of the church exterior. The ink is smeared, the trace of an errant thumb. Someone likely tried to grab the page too soon after printing. At the bottom, a bold line of text proclaims the programs are *Multi-Faith, Nondenominational. All Are Welcome.* "We're putting one in every basket," Toby explains. "Just to remind folks what we've got on offer."

"Seems doable." I pull out a chair for Buffy and sit myself beside her. "I've folded my fair share of zines."

Toby gives us a double thumbs-up. "No questions, then?"

"Just one." *Actually, I have about one hundred. But we've got to start somewhere.* "I thought Frances was the priest here. Or uh, Reverend. Minister...dude. Person. Whatever you folks all call it."

"Oh, he is." Toby touches her collar and gently adjusts it. "I'm an apprentice—kind of a minister-dude-guy in training." She points with her chin towards the corner stage. "But if you need anything, just holler for me. Fran's a wee bit occupied, at the moment."

I follow Toby's eyes and land on the drag performer as she's wrapping up the set. It takes a full half-minute before I clock the face that's under the glitter-beard and heavy makeup. "That's *Frances*?"

As confirmation, Rainbow scurries through the crowd, over a stack of chairs, and lands at the drag queen's feet. She offers up a crumpled bit of paper. Frances kneels to accept the gift, unwrapping it with her and smiling. They share a hug.

Toby whistles. "Cleans up nice, doesn't he?"

No kidding. "I'm not sure I've ever seen a priest in drag."

"As Frances likes to say, all priests wear drag, his just has more glitter!" Toby snaps her fingers and I break into laughter.

"That's actually pretty clever!" I admit.

"It is, isn't it?" She grins. "When he came in, Saint B's became the first affirming ministry in the whole county—our folks started flocking to it. He's the reason I asked to do my apprenticeship out here, that's for sure!"

"It hasn't been easy." Buffy speaks softly, not looking up from her work. Her busy hands carry out the rhythmic process of press-fold-staple-repeat. "There's been a fair bit of pushback. But if nothing else, Frances is not the type to back down."

"You can say that again," says Toby. A twinkie volunteer in a lime green turtleneck swings by our station, prodding her with a clipboard. "'Scuse me, friends, I'll have to circle back with you in a minute." Toby gives one last wave before she seamlessly slips into the crowd.

"Guess she doesn't want to see my CV, double-check my references?" I elbow Buffy but she's focused on her work. By the time I'm on my first fold, she's already set aside a tall stack of completed pamphlets. "So, um." I try a shift of gears. "I wasn't expecting for this place to be so…"

"Bursting with more homos than anyone knows what to do with?" Buffy peeks up with a smirk. She smacks a stapler into her latest fold and holds the pamphlet up to the light. She scowls, finding it askew.

"I was going to just say queer." I run my thumb down the centrefold crease. "But yeah, that works too."

"I was pretty surprised myself, the first time I came around." Buffy pries out the wayward staple with her fingernails and tries again. "Should have figured, though. I've known Frances for ages now—he's actually the one who introduced me and Hayden." She pauses for just a moment to glance across the hall, where Frances is currently setting up a drag queen story-time for the kiddos. "He leaves a trail of fairy dust on everything he touches."

Lime-green-turtleneck reappears at our table to collect a handful of our busywork. Just as they're reaching for the hand-off, they gasp and point to my T-shirt. "*Central Mental Monitor?* Oh my god, so vintage!"

"They actually changed the name—" I start to explain but decide against it. "But yeah, thanks. I work there."

"Do you really?" They let out a tiny round of applause with just the tips of their fingers. "I seriously used to call in, like, twice a week back when I was first coming out." Hand over their heart, they look at me with the biggest puppy-dog eyes I've ever seen. "Thank you, for real. For all the work you do."

"I don't actually do the..." My words trail away from me. "It's not actually much of a hotline anymore." Turtleneck pouts and tilts their head, confused. "The actual therapy team got laid off. Funding cuts."

"Oh." They stand at the edge of our table, quiet for a moment. "So, what do you *do* now?"

I shrug. "We have a chatbot?" Heat is starting to rise up my neck. I'm keenly aware of Buffy's eyes on me. "And my job is pretty much resource management."

"Oh." The volunteer takes our folded pamphlets and shuffles through them, running a quick count. Popping back up to attention, they nod goodbye. "Still. Cool T-shirt."

"Thanks," I mutter. Looking down, I notice I've just folded the last two booklets backwards. I sigh and start to pull them apart again.

Without a word, Buffy takes a few of my poorly pleated pages and helps uncrease my mistakes. Just as she's lining them up for stapling, Frances gets on the mic for another number. There's a sudden pulse of feedback, a shrill whine that makes everyone in the room groan at once. Buffy slams down on the stapler and it jams.

Around us, people are hustling, shouting around their tables. Someone calls for a speaker check and I spot Hayden running across the room. Gritting her teeth, Buffy smacks the stapler again, and again. The top few pages start to tear under the pressure. Delicately, I rest my hand on her wrist and whisper, "Are you okay?"

She stops and blinks at me. "Why wouldn't I be?"

"You're trying to murder a church bulletin?" I point out.

Buffy looks down at the mess in her hands and takes a slow breath through her nose, out through her mouth. She drops the failed pamphlet into a nearby recycling bin. I take the stapler off her hands and set about getting it unclogged. "You don't have to apologize for being in a bad mood."

"I'm *not* in a mood." She huffs and sets her shoulders away from me.

"Got it." I dig my nail into the stapler's jammed-up head, wincing as the underside of my finger is briefly stuck between two bent bits of metal. Turtleneck swings back, this time with a handful of fresh papers still warm from the printer. Under my breath, I ask, "Did you want to maybe talk about it—the *not-mood*?"

"Maybe," she mumbles. I stuff the remaining staples back into the magazine and pass it back to her. As she takes it, I catch sight of a slight tremor in her hands. I open my mouth to ask another question but my phone starts to hum. Hassan's profile photo smiles back at me.

"Sorry," I mutter, standing up. "Work thing. One second."

Saint Brigid's basement might be a lot of things but good on reception, it is not. Not about to shove my way through the crowd, I take the back exit instead. My skin prickles in the cold and I wrap my arms around my chest. "Hassan?" I press the phone against my shoulder, "What's up?"

"So you *are* alive!" Hassan's voice crackles from the other end. "I owe Augustine a fiver."

The snow is picking up again, twisting into flurries. I have to cup one ear just to hear him clearly over the wind. "What?"

"What do you mean, *what?*" His words break up, cut off by the sound of the office photocopier. I'd know that mechanic whine anywhere. "You've been triple-O since Friday afternoon! And you stole your own birthday cake!"

"It was *my* cake, wasn't it?" I press my back against the church's cold exterior. The door beside me sits cracked open, leaking warmth and idle chatter. "I told you, work trip. Then, storm. I'm still getting my job done, remotely."

"Then what about the team meeting this morning?" Hassan points out. "I sent you a Zoom invite so you could conference in."

"Damn, that was today?" I shudder. Snow is leaking in around the corners of my borrowed boots. "I was supposed to chair that, wasn't I?"

"Don't worry," he says. "I took over. And I took notes. But Charlie, I had a question—"

The wind screams across Saint Brigid's parking lot and I duck for cover. "What?" I shout into the phone.

"I said," Hassan raises his voice, "is Angie with you?"

"Why would you think that?" I shake my head.

"She disappeared around the same time you did," he explains. "Though at least she's still answering her Slack messages."

My eyes are starting to sting, like they're frosting over between each blink. "She had some kind of conference, right?" I shrug. "Maybe it's still going."

"Yeah, maybe." Hassan's voice is fading. I'm losing signal. "Anyway. I've been covering for you best I can, but we need you back here. Or at least, get yourself online."

"Got it." From the corner of my eye, I spot Buffy. She stands with a shoulder braced against the back door, holding up a large puffy coat. Beckoning me closer, she wraps it over my shoulder and under my chin. Instantly, my chest grows warm and slowly defrosts the rest of me. In my ear, Hassan is going on about some other project we're supposed to finish by the end of this quarter.

"Gotta go," I mutter. "Bad connection."

"Wait, can't you—" His words are cut short as I tap off the call.

I bury my face into the coat's downy layers. "This is pretty cozy."

"Snagged it off one of the donation lines," says Buffy, rubbing her arms. She speaks through chattering teeth. "I didn't want you to freeze out here while on your call."

"Didn't think to get one for yourself?" I ask, and she just shrugs. Unbuttoning the jacket, I lift up one arm for her to come join me inside. It's a tight fit but we manage it. Pressed together, she snuggles against my chest.

Huddled on Saint Brigid's back stoop, we hold quiet and watch the snow. The small parking lot is blanketed white, dotted with the snowshoe steps and sled marks. There are other tracks too—signs of a bunny that darted for cover under a nearby bush; the indents of a fox or some other nimble pursuer. Among the ice-laden branches of a nearby fir, the rustling of a busy squirrel.

If anyone has noticed us missing, they are in no rush to find us. The busy efforts of all those volunteers play out in shadows across the snow. I make a subtle move to head back but Buffy stays planted. Face bathed in a slice of orange light, she furrows her brows at the commotion inside.

"Need a break from the crowd?" I venture a guess. "Do you have a hard time in crowds?"

Her touch slips from my chest, down my arm. She clasps my hand. "Let's just stay here for another minute."

I squeeze her back. "Okay."

What kind of a question was that? I wish I could swallow it back. *Of course Elizabeth Hawkshaw doesn't mind a crowd—she lives for them!*

Except, this isn't Elizabeth Hawkshaw. At least, not the version of her I've been carrying around this whole time. She's so much more than that. There's a stillness about her, like the surface of a pond. Every now and then, I get just a glimpse of all that lies beneath the surface. She's curious about things, about me, even though I should be no one to her. She's witty and sharp and—she's looking right at me.

Buffy draws herself against my waist. The fog of our breath intermingles, swirling into mist. My cheeks burn, heart pounding in my ears. My eyes flit to her lips. *Does she want me to?*

Laughter echoes from beyond the open door. Easy, smooth and familiar. I spy Hayden, surrounded by a group of fellow volunteers. His hands are animated and when he hits the punch line, his laugh carries all the way across the church hall. It's picked up by the wind, dancing skyward, tickling the trees. Frances slings an arm over his shoulder, still in full drag. He plants a kiss on Hayden's cheek.

"What's the story with those two?" I wonder aloud. "Did they used to date or something?"

Glancing at the scene inside, Buffy smirks. "It'd be easier to list the people here Hayden *hasn't* hooked up with." Her grasp on me softens as she adjusts our shared coat. Slyly, she points to a tall femme hanging at the edge of Hayden's inner circle. "Hayden met them while busking in Vancouver. Hooked up on and off for a few summers." Buffy nudges her chin to a couple holding hands together, near the gender-neutral bathrooms. "Those two, he actually went to high school with. Apparently they did a triad thing for a while, until Hayden moved away for school in Montreal."

"Sounds messy." I look around, silently gauging who else might be one of Hayden's old flames. "Lots of history."

"You could say that." Buffy nods. "Don't get me wrong, they're all lovely people. And everyone's worked hard to help me feel at home. We're always getting invites to brunches and dinner parties, backyard barbecues and book clubs…"

"Sounds exhausting!" I blurt out. Luckily, Buffy laughs with me.

"It *is*!" She shakes the snowflakes from her hair, releasing a sigh the size of a small cloud. "You know, five years into Elmridge and some days they all still feel like *his* friends first. I'm forever just his *plus-one*."

My breath is tight, throat raw from breathing in the cold. "There is at least one person here who you met first," I point out. "By at least a few seconds. Whole minutes, maybe."

Buffy's heart-shaped lips part with dawning understanding. "Well, not to lean into the hierarchy of it or anything." Her cheeks begin to dimple. "But yes, I suppose we did."

"So, that makes me *your* friend, first," I tell her. "Technically speaking."

"Just technically, of course," she murmurs. "Thanks." With a shiver, she tugs towards the warmth inside. "Jesus, it's freezing out here. Let's head back."

Chapter Eleven

Rough hands grasp along the dip of my waist, drawing me closer. A moan escapes my lips. A hot, wet mouth presses into the space between my thighs. I buck and shiver as a second set of hands appears, teasing at my nipples. Gentle nibbles along the bend of my shoulder, along my neck, up to my ear. I ball my fists, clawing at bedsheets, lost in a medley of soft flesh and panting kisses. There's no holding back. A cry escapes me as I'm about to—

Crash. Thump. I wake to a bang on the ceiling. It's shortly followed by the patter of hurried feet. "Rainbow, what did we say about going in there?" Hayden's voice echoes through the vents. "Mommy is resting. She can play with you later." Instant sobbing, crying, stomping.

Well. I groan and prop my elbow against the mattress. *That's one way to zap the steam out of a perfectly good, late-afternoon sex dream.* The bedsprings creak under my shifting weight.

Wellesley starts barking and Mango kicks up too, chirping and squawking up a storm. Miss Kiki pokes her face through the crack in my door and nudges her way inside, ears back and tail twitching.

"I hear you, pal." I motion for her to come say hello. "It sure does get noisy here sometimes, doesn't it?" She eyes my out-stretched hand, darts around it and slips under the bed. Can't say I blame her.

"How about we go put on some *Brightbriar* while Daddy wraps up his work for the afternoon?" says Hayden. From the sounds of it, he's trying—and failing—to coax Rainbow down the stairs. I, on the other hand, would love to watch some more of that cartoon right around now. Last night's episode ended on a cliffhanger! Literally, the *Uni-friends* were hanging by the edge of a cliff as the squirrel army closed in, led by (either a cyborg or clone version of) the dictator Acornius.

Pawing the sleep from my eyes, I reach for my laptop. It's slumped over on its side, screen flickering with endless rows of green and grey. The last twenty-four hours drip back into focus like water from a leaky tap. I pulled a late one last night, trying to catch up on my work. Hassan had sent a dozen more *last-minute tweaks* to various projects, even ones I didn't think he was collaborating on. A check of my email shows an update from Augustine, warning of system-wide updates to start late Wednesday. A glance at the corner of my screen reveals that is, impossibly, today.

The Hawthorne house has been quieter than usual since all of us came home from Saint Brigid's last night. The walk home felt so much longer, despite the fact that we were carry-ing only an empty toboggan. We were all exhausted, but none more than Buffy. While Hayden, Rainbow and I geared up for a night of frozen pizza and cartoon streaming, she dragged herself straight to bed and hasn't come out since. By midmorn-ing today, Wellesley was pacing at my door. I took the initia-tive to walk him myself but marching through the snow is far less fun by myself.

My eyes keep having trouble focusing. I keep mistyping my password for my work email and end up locked out. I've got more missed calls, rescheduled Zoom meetings, pushed deadlines. Cracking my knuckles, I set into my work. Just a few minutes later, I find myself staring into space. Through the porthole-view of my window, snowflakes curl and collide. It radiates with cold. I pull a blanket over my legs.

Miss Kiki mews and pokes her face out from under the bed. "I'm sorry, were you using that?" I ask. She flexes her whiskers. "Come on up, then," I say, patting the mattress. After a moment's consideration, she accepts my offer and hops directly onto my laptop keyboard. She promptly curls up and falls asleep. *I guess I could take a break,* I decide, giving her a scritch on the neck. Her ears twitch and she stretches with appreciation.

The news is calling it *the storm of the century*. A sure sign of climate change, except to all the conservative talking heads on Twitter who keep saying things like *if the earth is getting warmer, then why is it cold outside? Checkmate, libs.* I hate-slash-doomscroll for a while before coming away with the singular conclusion that we need a new word for *unprecedented*. That one is over. Put it in the back of the dictionary, alongside all the other defunct words. I know that's not how dictionaries work. But maybe it should be.

I recognize a familiar theme song, blasting from the living room TV. Seems like Hayden has managed to corral Rainbow after all. I wonder if he's in there, gearing up to watch with her, or if he's maybe at the kitchen table working on his new research paper. He told me the idea for it as I brewed my coffee this morning. Something about the literary themes in some Danish lady's 1930s autobiography. Or was she German? Anyway, he seems amped up about the idea. I spent my half of our conversation smiling and nodding, pouring oat milk into my coffee. The taste is starting to grow on me.

Another *crash*, followed by a *bang* and a *thump*—Rainbow
screams, surely clambering on every piece of furniture in the
Hawthornes' living room. Hayden's laughter echoes after her.
Miss Kiki purrs, gently nudging my hand for more pets. I desperately want to shut down my laptop, silence my phone and
go join in the fun next door. But Hassan's phone call from yesterday still hangs over me. I don't have the luxury of playing
make-believe in this family that's not even my own.

Gently nudging Miss Kiki to the side, I prod my computer
back to life. With a few clicks—and only *two* attempts to get
my password right—I'm back into it. Scanning through the latest updates, it looks like our feedback form is set to go live as
soon as Angie gives the go-ahead. Whenever that might be. I
haven't managed to get a straight answer on whether she's back
at the office by now or what. I'm tempted to message her myself.

"What's going on in here?" Buffy's singsong voice joins the
medley from next door. It sounds like Hayden and Rainbow
have roughhoused their way into the kitchen.

"Sorry, babe!" Hayden quickly answers. "Did we wake you?
We can keep it down."

"It's all right," she laughs. "I've had enough me-time, anyway. I'll get myself dressed and then let's see if we can't squeeze
in some music lessons before starting on dinner."

"Mom, Mom!" Rainbow's voice trails after Buffy, calling
her to join in their game.

My phone buzzes, facedown on the mattress. I'll bet that's
Mako with an update on Cashew. Or maybe Sophia from finance managed to send over the updated resource budget I asked
for. I flip the screen and immediately a weight lands in my gut.

Dad: You free?

Dad: We need to talk.

I scowl at the message for a solid minute before typing a reply.

Charlie: Working. I'll call you later.

A rap at my door draws my attention. Hayden asks from the other side, "Now an okay time?"

Here we go—just when I was getting going on my work too. I guess I'll just *have* to take a break. I wonder what it'll be this time. *Does Mango need a new enrichment activity?* Or, maybe Rainbow and Wells need to burn off some energy in the backyard—that could be fun! I sit up straight and toss my phone aside. "Mmm-hmm?"

"Sorry, I know you're working in here." Hayden nudges open the door, just wide enough to poke his head in. At the same time, Miss Kiki stretches herself and hops off the bed, darting out of sight. I hear Rainbow squeal in the kitchen, chasing after her.

"It's all good." I adjust my laptop screen and pretend to review missed meeting minutes. No need to seem *too* eager. "What's up, you need something?"

"Oh, no!" Hayden flips his phone screen towards me. It's open to the weather app. "Just wanted to make sure you saw the good news—the storm's on its way out! Any luck, and you could be back on the road by tomorrow morning! Isn't that awesome?"

"Oh." My neck goes stiff, eyes fixed on the tiny screen in his hands. Sure enough, the next few days are full of "sun" emojis and temperatures well above zero. "Um, that's great." I drag my mouth into something that I hope passes for a smile. "Really. Awesome."

Hayden snaps his fingers. "I *had* to see your face when you found out!"

"Here it is. My face." My own phone starts to light up. Incoming call. I shove it aside. "Thanks for telling me."

"I'll leave you to it, then." He starts to back off. "I'm gonna get an early start on dinner."

"Wait." I snap my laptop shut and hurry up off the bed. "Um, can I give a hand?"

"Cutting with grain means milder flavour." I draw the tip of my knife down the length of the onion. "Tip to tip."

"Then going against the grain sounds like the way to do it." Hayden stands over my shoulder, carefully studying my technique. "More flavour the better, no?"

"Not necessarily," I say, picking off a stray bit of peel. "Depends on what you're looking for." With a firm shove, I slice the onion into two clean halves and get to work.

Twisting the tap, Hayden sets about rinsing a batch of russet potatoes. "You cook a lot at home?" he asks.

"I used to." I tuck my bangs aside but they just fall back into place. The sharp tang of the onion pinches my nose and makes me squint. "Don't seem to find much time anymore."

"But know your way around a kitchen?" Hayden pops open a jar marked *Flour* and pulls out a potato peeler.

"My old roommate worked in catering." Sniffling profusely, I wipe my eyes with my sleeve. "He passed on a few good tips." As I make my next slice, there's a sudden jolt of pain. I wince and drop the knife, clutching my hand to my chest. "Damn!"

"Hold still." Hayden drops what he's doing and is beside me in an instant, gently leading me to the sink. "Okay, let's get you cleaned off." He delicately runs my fingers under a splash of warm water. "Looks like you just nipped your fingernail. Did you want a bandage?" He dabs my hand with a hand towel and starts digging through the kitchen drawers. "I think we've only got ones with unicorns on them. And one box of plain horses that Rainbow absolutely will not ever use, no matter what."

"I think I'm all right," I say, giving my finger a close inspection. He's right, there's a nip taken out of the nail on my pointer but no sign of actual blood. "Thanks."

I resume my station at the cutting board but Hayden comes up behind me. "Here," he murmurs, drawing his arms along mine. "Hold your knuckles like this."

Heat rises to my cheeks. He's so close to me, I can smell the sweetness of his breath. There's something just so comforting about the way his chest presses against my back, and the way he guides my hands. "That's it," he whispers as I carry out his instructions. "You got it."

"Thanks," I murmur. When he backs away, the warmth of him lingers on my skin. I almost want to mess up, so he'll show me again.

"All good," he smirks. For a second, I could swear there's a touch of pink across his face. Was he blushing too? "When you're a shoddy chef, safety's extra important."

"I wouldn't call you shoddy." I shrug, trying to hold back my sniffles this time around. "A little distracted, maybe."

"Comes from a lifetime of managing too many dishes at once." Hayden drops his potato peelings into a compost bin. "I'm the oldest of a whole wack of kids and my folks just couldn't keep up with us all. So, I picked up the slack." He drops the compost bin back into the fridge and smacks it shut with his hip. "By twelve, I was managing house laundry, helping with homework and whipping up meals *at least* three times a week—did I do it well? No. But I did it."

"How many is a *whole wack* of kids?" I ask.

Wiping hands on his apron, Hayden quickly does a finger-count. "… Six? No, Seven!" He snaps his fingers. "Shit, London's gonna kill me. She's the baby and *always* resented getting counted last."

With the first onion sliced, I get started on a second. "London?"

"We were all named after capital cities." Hayden scoops a cup of water into the rice-cooker.

"Except you," I point out.

"Well, I'll say this." The machine gently beeps as he sets it to cook. "Rainbow didn't start the trend of name-jumping in our house." Tossing the remaining dishes in the sink, he moves to start up the stovetop. "Okay, potatoes chopped. Rice, cooking. Let's heat things up." He drops a hefty bit of oil into the cast-iron and starts up the gas range. "What about you—any siblings?"

"Just a sister. Emma." I shrug. "I really don't know her all that well though."

"No?" Hayden leans beside the stove, poking through an overburdened spice rack.

"She's a few years older," I explain. "The summer after our parents broke up, she got a scholarship for university and went to go live with my mom out west." My knife rises and falls in a careful rhythm. *Up, down. Up, down.* "Dad worked a lot so I basically was on my own most of the time. At eighteen, I moved out to Toronto. Haven't been home since."

"Hmm," Hayden murmurs. The gas stove *click-click-clicks* as the flame licks the bottom of the pan, oil sizzling.

"I guess I'm still sort of mad about it." My chops grow faster, slices thinning. "Like, she was my big sister. Why she'd ditch me, you know? Even now, she doesn't keep in touch. I know she's got work and her dude-bro fiancé but—"

"Charlie?" asks Hayden.

"And don't even get me started on my mom!" The groove of my knife cuts start chipping at the wooden cutting board. "She and I hardly talk at all these days. Meanwhile, my dad won't leave me alone. It's like, oh, *now* you want to get to know me?"

"Charlie?" A touch at my elbow. Hayden's presence slows my hand. I look down and find a mash of onion pulp dribbling down the board. My eyes sting, tears streaming down my cheeks.

"Sorry," I mumble, and clean myself off in the sink. "I swear, I'm not actually that upset about it. It's just the—"

"Onions. I get it." Hayden lifts the cutting board aside, scraping its contents into a small bowl. "No need to apologize. But I do think these are officially diced."

"Yeah, no kidding." I pad my face with a towel. "It's weird. I don't really think about that part of my life anymore. I didn't expect to get so worked up about it."

"It's no big deal," says Hayden, pouring me a glass of water. "Cooking always helps me process, too. Keeps my hands busy. Lets me just sit and think."

"Yeah, maybe." I accept his offering with a sniffle. Starting with a sip, I quickly gulp down the whole thing and pour myself a second cup—my throat was so dry, how didn't I notice that? I hold the glass to my chest and I catch my breath, watching Hayden poke at the spice rack. "Or maybe, it's you."

"Me?" The corners of his eyes crinkle as he smiles. "What did I do?"

Wind rattles the kitchen windows. Something under the kitchen faucet starts to gurgle. I stare down at the glass in my hands, gathering my thoughts. "You asked," I tell him. "You, Buffy—you take the time to get to know people. To listen. You make it easy, like I can say whatever's on my mind and it's not going to be *too much* for anybody."

"I'm glad you feel that way." Hayden elbows me while cracking some fresh pepper. "But Charlie, you could never be too much."

"Says you." I lightly push him back. "Anyway, what about you and your siblings—are you still tight like when you were kids?"

"Sort of." He adds a handful of paprika. The onion-mush turns faintly red. "It's hard when you're their de facto parent. Those boundaries never really come down. My mom and I were close, though." He checks the stovetop temperature. The oil is just starting to sizzle.

I look around the kitchen at all its funny odds and ends, wondering what pieces might have been left behind by Hayden's mother. The shelves near the ceiling packed with little knick-knacks, the ceramic cookie jar full of wooden spoons, the stack of recipe books (some with scorch marks on their sides). I rest my hand against the wall's woodgrain paneling, feeling the layered pulse of all the stories here. "This is her house, isn't it?" I ask. "Must be hard sometimes."

Hayden stays quiet for a few seconds. When he speaks again, it's softer than before. "It can be. But I'd rather have a piece of who she was than nothing at all." He looks up, eyes darting over my shoulder and towards the door. "Hey, babe."

"Hey, yourself." Curls pulled into a loose bun, Buffy leans in the archway wearing a holey sweatshirt and cozy flannel leggings. I've never seen anyone who can pull off a look like that, the way she can. She looks like she's modeling a new brand of distressed leisure-loungewear.

"Glad to see you're feeling better."

"Heard you took Wells out today." She momentarily rests her hand on my shoulder in thanks. "I just couldn't keep my eyes open this morning. Or this afternoon." Arching her back, she twists and stretches out her hips. "I caught up on a little reading, though. I'm working my way through this parenting book." She bends to touch her toes and slowly rises back up. "Just finished the chapter on schedule maintenance, and it said—" Freezing midway through her stretch, her eyes dart around the room. "Where's Rainbow?"

Peeling a couple cloves of garlic, Hayden shakes his head. "I thought she was with you."

"You mean you don't know?" Buffy ducks into the living room, scouring the couch cushions. "I ask you to watch her for *one* day." She ducks to check under the table, behind the chair. Mango chirps with interest, following her every movement.

"I did!" Hayden starts after her. "But I thought—" The stove starts smoking, oil splashing from the pan. "Shit. One sec." He races to flip on the oven fan.

"You don't think she went outside, do you?" Buffy is already grabbing for her coat. "Oh my god."

In all the commotion, a small rattle catches my attention. The cupboard under the sink is twitching and that gurgling noise now seems a lot more like a giggle. I wave to Buffy. "I think I might have an idea where to start the search."

Hayden reaches for the cupboard and it bursts open, Rainbow leaping out with hands like claws. "Raar!"

Buffy drops to her knees, dragging her daughter into a hug. "My baby," she laughs, still catching her breath. "You really got me that time."

"Do unicorns roar?" I ask Hayden in a whisper. He gives a noncommittal shrug, fanning the last of the smoke.

"I'm not a unicorn!" Rainbow shouts and bounds into the living room. "I'm a velociraptor!"

"Are we circling back to your dino phase?" Buffy follows at her heels. "Good thing I saved the old playsets."

"Whew." Hayden tightens his apron. "Crisis averted, meal prepped—let's get this party started!"

Just as he's about to drop the onions and get to sizzling, there's a bright flash. Every light in the house grows hot for a split second and then falls dim.

The oven fan quiets and the floor vents stop their hum. A scream pierces the darkness.

Chapter Twelve

"Looks like the whole block's out." Hayden stands as a silhouette at the window, one hand holding back the curtains and the other clutching a flashlight. "Even the streetlamps."

"I've still got service." Buffy's face is lit blue by her phone screen. She swipes, scanning for updates. "They're saying the storm knocked out a transponder."

"What's a transponder?" Rainbow shivers up against her mother, wrapped in several blankets. I suspect she's more frightened than cold. Her initial shriek at the blackout is still ringing in my ears.

"I don't actually know," says Buffy, holding down the power button on her phone until it turns dark.

"It means we're going to be without electricity for a little bit." Hayden shines his flashlight across the room. I wince as he catches it in my eyes. "Sorry."

"It's fine." I rub away the spots from my vision. "I thought things were supposed to ease off tonight, though?"

"Guess the storm had other plans." Hayden shrugs. "At least the gas range should still work. I can finish cooking dinner."

Buffy wraps her arms around Rainbow, coaching her through a series of deep breaths. "We should have some matches in the first-aid kit, to help you get it started. Hayden, babe, do you know where that got off to?"

"I already checked in the spot it's supposed to live. All I found was this." The flashlight flickers and dies out. Hayden smacks the side of it, then pops out the battery pack and gives it a shake. When he slides it back in, the beam holds steady once again. "I think I know where to find some more candles, though. And I'll grab us extra blankets."

Hayden darts to the back porch and returns with all he promised, and more. Together we get the stove running again and for a while we huddle around it for the warmth alone. A hot meal in our guts only does so much to keep us warm. The house is growing colder with every passing hour. We layer on sweaters and long johns. I'm starting to think I should have filled the tub with water after all.

Without speaking, we collectively drift back into the living room. Rainbow is superglued to Buffy's hip, following her around the living room. I busy myself by checking on the family's various pets. Mango's cage is safely blanketed but I can hear him twittering inside. Meanwhile, Miss Kiki has hidden herself at the top of the cat tree and refuses to come down, even for her favourite treats. Wellesley paces the living room rug, scratching for a place to rest but never actually lying down. I guess we're all feeling a tad anxious.

Hayden sits crouched on the floor, cranking the lever of a hand-pump generator; each turn comes with an awful grating crunch, one I'm pretty sure it's not supposed to make. "I knew we should have charged this thing. I just knew it." He huffs and turns the handle even faster. Not so much as a glimmer appears on the generator's battery light.

"If you knew so, why didn't you do so?" A tall candle in one hand, Buffy tries to strike a match. It flames brightly for a few seconds before snuffing out into a trail of smoke. "Shit," she curses under her breath. "Hayden, will you drop that damn thing and just come help me out here?"

"But this is—" He grunts his way through another rotation. "Why did we even buy it if not for—" There's a sickening crack and the lever snaps off into his hand. Hayden stares down at the broken bit of plastic for half a minute before letting it drop. "Fine. How can I help?"

"Just block the wind." Buffy beckons him closer. Hayden follows her instructions and cups his hands. "There's a wicked draft in here."

"It's the damn windows," Hayden grumbles, hunkering his whole body around the candle's wick.

"I knew we should have got them resealed." Buffy strikes another match but the flame won't catch.

"*If you knew so, why didn't you do so?*" Hayden mimics. Buffy's eyes glint in the darkness but they soften as she smiles.

"I guess I had that one coming," she admits.

"I've got a lighter in my jacket." I speak the thought as soon as it occurs to me. Buffy arches her brows towards me and I answer with a shrug. "My ex used to smoke."

A smirk tugs at Hayden's lips. "You still carry a lighter around for your...ex-smoker ex?"

"We're still friends." *And knowing Mako, they'll pick up the habit again.* "Besides..." I fumble through the darkness towards the front hall closet. I dig through layers of fabric until I am met with the familiar touch of my overcoat. I quickly find the old lighter in a zippered pocket. Giving it a good shake, I flick the flint wheel and a spark emits. I hold up the steady flame. "It comes in handy sometimes."

"Case in point," says Buffy. "Now, you hold on to that for one second. Rainbow, I'll need your help grabbing some cans from the recycling." Hand on the small of her back, Buffy guides her daughter towards the kitchen. "Oh, and Hayden? Find me something sharp."

With Hayden's penknife in hand, Buffy pokes a series of sharp holes in the top of several coffee tins. She sets up a small contraption where each out is balanced over several candles, which she lights using my Mako lighter. The heat coming off each one is more impressive than I expected. From there on, lighting the rest of the living room is a much simpler endeavour. Beeswax pillars, soybean tea lights, candles in cups and mason jars; she gets Rainbow's help to reach a set of small decorative wax sculptures from a shelf high above the television. The figures were likely never meant to be burned but they do so gloriously, all the same. Soon, we're surrounded by an array of twinkling firelight, dancing around us like fireflies. All together, the room is even warmer than before the furnace ran out.

Mango chirps in his birdcage, pleased to be free of the blanket. He preens on a small branch. Miss Kiki remains stuffed into the uppermost cabin of her cat tree, but she's purring softly. Wellesley is practicing his act of being a dog-size rug in the middle of the hardwood floor. Buffy lights the last candle and plants herself onto the couch next to Hayden.

"Even if it didn't work, thanks anyway for trying to get the generator working." She nudges his leg. "It was a good thought."

Hayden places a peck on her cheek. "That's the last time I'm buying anything off a Facebook ad."

"Thanks to all of you, for getting all this set up." Leaning against my knees, I inspect Buffy's candlelit heaters. "These are seriously impressive."

"Just something I picked up." Buffy taps her lap and Rainbow wriggles her way up. "One truly awful spring, I was in Chicago for a five-day protest-piece. Myself and a couple other artists were camped in Millennium Park, when an awful blizzard hit. Rather than abandon our project, a friend of mine taught us how to make these radiators. They got us through *that* storm so I figure, why not this one?"

"Five days, wow," I murmur, tucking back against my seat. "I bet there's a story there."

"Yeah. Maybe." Buffy gently fiddles with her daughter's hair. "Anyway, what shall we do now—maybe we call it a night, try and get some rest?"

"Go to bed?" Hayden drags his hands down his face. He flops onto Buffy's lap with an exaggerated groan. "It's hardly past eight!"

"Yeah, I'm not tired!" Rainbow grabs her cheeks, just like her dad. I start to chuckle and they both turn in unison, which only makes me laugh harder.

"I'm sorry." I shake my head. "But sometimes you two make the *exact* same face. Really, it's very sweet." A wide grin breaks out across Hayden's face and he turns to Buffy, who responds with a prod against his shoulder. Glancing between them, I get the feeling there's a joke here that I'm missing out on. "Sorry, did I say something I shouldn't have?"

"Hardly," says Buffy. "Everyone's *always* saying how much they're alike. It's just kind of funny."

"Apparently, it's a thing." Hayden nuzzles Rainbow with his beard. She giggles and squirms out of reach. "Kids always end up more like the non-genetic parent."

"You're not—right." *I just had to stick my foot in my mouth, didn't I?* "Sorry. I shouldn't have assumed."

"It's all good." Hayden props himself back up on the couch. "Just a reminder, I should flag myself a little harder."

"We could dye your hair the colours of the trans flag?" Buffy suggests with a scratch of his chin. "Maybe just your beard?"

"Don't even joke about that!" He gasps and covers his facial hair with both hands.

"I think there's some pride pins in that outreach merch I

brought?" I look over my shoulder. "I could try to dig them out for you, when the weather lets up."

"Ooh, got any bi-pride ones too?" asks Buffy. Her sly grin shimmers in the candlelight. "We need every defence we can get against people reading us as a couple of hetero-hashtag-allies."

"We could always have another kid?" Hayden digs under the couch and pulls out a couple of unicorn stuffies. Rainbow quickly grabs them from his hands. "When I was doing the seahorse dad thing, that threw off a lot of people's radar."

"So you actually carried the pregnancy?" I gawk at him. "That's incredible."

"It sure was *something*." Hayden taps Rainbow on the shoulder. "Kiddo, do you remember the story—how you were made?"

"Mmm-hmm." She's busy galloping her stuffies across the living room table, making small roaring noises.

"Would you *tell* us the story?" asks Buffy. "Charlie hasn't heard it before."

"Oh! Okay." Still holding tight to her small herd of stuffies, Rainbow scrunches up her face in deep concentration. "Um. Well, back in the olden days, before I was born, Mommy and Daddy loved each other *so* much that they wanted to have a baby."

"It was mostly Dad's idea," whispers Hayden from the corner of his mouth.

"Not true!" Buffy tries to pinch him but Hayden deftly dodges it.

"Shh!" Rainbow presses a finger to her lips, giving her parents a stern look. "So, um. Then Mommy went to a special place, where they make all the eggs that babies come from."

"The fertility clinic doesn't make the eggs, honey," says Buffy, hand idly resting against her lower abdomen. "Mommy makes them, and they help take them out."

"And then the eggy went in there." Rainbow points to her father's stomach.

"Right." Buffy nods. "In Daddy's... Do you remember the word? It starts with a *u*. Rhymes with *shmooterus*?"

"Wait, we missed a step already," Hayden jumps in. "Before the egg could go anywhere it had to get some help to grow into a baby."

"Do you remember who helped us?" Buffy sneaks a look towards me. "You've actually already met him, Charlie. Big guy, likes hugs and sparkly wigs?"

"Hold on." The pieces slowly start to slot into place. "Your donor was—"

"Uncle Frances!" Rainbow leaps up and Hayden gives her a high five.

Noted. I'm tempted to look for signs of him in Rainbow's face, her mannerisms. But more than anything, she still just looks like *Rainbow.*

"And then nine months later—" She starts up again.

"Forty-one weeks," Hayden quickly corrects her. "And three days. Just saying."

"They had a baby!" With a quick spin, Rainbow spreads her arms wide. "And the baby was me!"

"You?" I gasp, "But you're such a big kid!"

"I wasn't *born* a big kid." She breaks out into giggles. "I was a little baby first!"

Crossing my arms, I shake my head in disbelief. "No way."

"Yeah way!" Scrambling to her feet, Rainbow takes off towards the stairs. "I'll go get the pictures!"

"Oh, no, honey." Buffy stumbles over herself, hurrying after her. "The photo albums are too high for you to reach!"

"I got it, babe." Hayden holds up a hand, motioning for Buffy to stay put. "I'll go help her." Rainbow's already halfway to the upper landing.

"Quite the storyteller," I remark over the sound of footfalls over our heads.

"She is, isn't she?" There's a loud *thump* from upstairs and

Buffy braces the arm of the couch, ready to rush upstairs. A moment later, the echoes of laughter. She visibly rests back into the couch cushions. "Though she doesn't include *my* favourite part, when we tried to explain to our families what the heck we were doing." Buffy laughs under her breath. "Hayden got the bright idea to throw a party for it. I can tell you, it is hard to fit the words *Reciprocal IVF* onto a cake."

"And after all that, your dad *still* thinks I'm a trans *woman*." Hayden comes traipsing back downstairs, Rainbow in tow.

"Bless him." Buffy plays with the flicker of a nearby candle. "He's very supportive. He just keeps asking when you're going to shave the beard and start hormone therapy."

"I got my ukulele!" Rainbow gallops into the living room, instrument held aloft over her head.

"I thought you were getting the photo albums?" I point out.

"Got 'em." Hayden lays out a small stack of binders across the coffee table.

"Aww, honey, look," Buffy coos. "It's your baby book!" She starts flipping through the pages, stopping every few moments to show me pictures of Hayden at the birth centre, a sonogram, newborn photos. Buffy runs her hands over the pages. "Back when we started trying, I was going through a bit of a rough patch. My art just wasn't speaking to me anymore. I knew I needed a change, to do something completely different." Resting on an image of Rainbow's first birthday, she looks up at her daughter as she sits perched on the couch's armrest, plucking notes on her ukulele. "Something that felt like it mattered."

Hayden rubs Buffy's shoulder, flipping to the next page. "This is my favourite part." He turns the book around to show me a family tree. Down one side, Hayden's branches are mostly under the name *Thornton*. Buffy's half is, predictably, peppered with many a *Hawkshaw*. At the base, they meet on either side of Rainbow's birth name. All three are listed as *Hawthorne*. Someone has also drawn in a small, third branch, marking Frances as *Uncle (Donor)*.

"You merged your last names?" I wonder aloud.

Buffy nods. "When she got here, everything just changed overnight. It felt right to try something new."

"Not to mention *Hawkshaw-Thornton* sounds like a law firm." Hayden sticks his tongue out, making a face. "One that specializes in defending evil billionaires."

Running my fingers along the swooping letters that spell out Buffy's name, I ask, "Do you ever miss it? Your art, I mean. Performing."

Wrapping a stray curl around one finger, Buffy lets it spring back in place. "Sometimes. Now that we've hit her school-age years, I've been getting restless." Hayden pats her back and she rests against him. "I'm trying not to rush it. Small gigs, to start."

"Like the workshop at my office," I point out. "I did kind of wonder why someone like *you* would bother coming in to something like that."

Buffy tuts. "Never doubt the impact of doing small, grounded work. My politics are what got me into performance, not the other way around."

Scanning over the page again, another question surfaces to my mind. "Wait—where did the *e* come from, at the end of *Hawthorne*?"

"Now *that* was Hayden's idea." Buffy taps his knee. "He said it added *flair*."

"*Everything* in life is better with flair!" He snaps a set of finger-guns at Rainbow. "You know what I'm talking about, don't you, kiddo?"

"Yeah!" She laughs and smacks all the strings at once, head-banging.

"Wow!" I wince. "You sure are playing that."

"You can see why I've been pushing for more practice!" Buffy shouts over the noise.

"I love it!" Hayden slips away from Buffy's side, standing up. "Raw—very punk. But hey, how about we try something a little different?" Reaching to the corner, he grabs an acoustic guitar off its rack. There are stickers on every inch of it, some that appear to be just as structurally necessary as they are aesthetic. "Now, I might be a little rusty," he says while setting the strings in tune. "My fingers don't have calluses like they used to."

"He's just being modest." Buffy hops up and joins me on the living room's love seat. "Hayden's sing-alongs are the stuff of legends," she whispers. "Especially around a campfire."

"Or at a sit-in." Running through the notes with his thumb, he gives a satisfied smile. "I still remember a couple protest songs, if you're feeling nostalgic."

"Just play whatever you feel like," says Buffy. Beneath our shared blanket, her hand reaches for mine. The warmth of her legs curl up with mine. I keep my head pointed directly forward, even as the hair rises on my neck.

Shouldering the strap of his guitar, Hayden runs through a few basic instructions with Rainbow. "People always need a little music," he says. "Gets the blood flowing, keeps the spirits up. Now, you ready, kiddo?" She fiercely nods. In unison, they strike the first chord.

Rainbow only knows around three notes, but Hayden proves that's more than enough. He lets her set the pace, gently helping her hold her fingers steady. They make their own song together, Hayden making up lyrics on the spot based on suggestions from Rainbow, then Buffy, then even me. When her little hands start to cramp up, Hayden does some solo work. Pretty soon, she's curled up with all her stuffies on a pile of blankets, fast asleep.

Hayden shifts to a serenade, a slow ballad. He seems unperturbed, even as Buffy nestles herself in the crook of my neck.

Before long, I'm lying on her lap while she strokes my hair. Wellesley shuffles over and I let one arm fall, giving a lazy pet. My eyelids are heavy and I allow myself the luxury of simply lying still, breathing steady.

Chapter Thirteen

I'm not sure I've opened my eyes. All I see is pitch-black. One by one, my senses return. There's a cushion under my chin, a fuzzy blanket is stretched across my shoulders. Something cold and wet pressed against my toes—I squirm away from Wellesley's snoot and draw my knees to my chest.

The air is touched with cold. My eyes slowly adjust. Hayden's guitar sits on its side, alone on the opposing couch. Rainbow's tower of stuffies has been toppled over. The living room window is laced with frost and all the candles have all been doused. Face-up on the coffee table, a screen flickers. My phone. It's ringing.

The battery is down to its last ten percent. A familiar face stares back at me, frozen in time. My thumb hovers over the red button. I'm tempted to ignore his call. *And why shouldn't I?* Except, part of me is tired of all this dancing around. The voice mails and texts left on read. It's been like that between us for so long. A voice in the back of my head tells me, it's time to cut against the grain; it sounds a bit like Hayden.

"Hello?" His voice is tinged with the static of a weak connection. "Charlie?"

"How are you calling me right now?" I ask. "I have, like, one bar."

"Am I supposed to be able to answer that?"

Fair enough. I rub the sleep from my eyes. "Do you even know what time it is?"

"You should turn your phone off and leave it in a separate room when you go to bed." Behind his words, there's the sound of a chattering crowd, automated announcements. "That's just good sleep hygiene."

"Where are you?"

"Just finished meeting with a client—" He cuts out for a few brief, treasured seconds. "Waiting for a connecting flight."

I sit up, wrapping the blanket around me like a shawl. "Do you need something?"

In the background, I can hear the rattling of change. The whine of an espresso machine. Someone wishes him good morning. "So," he asks, "how is work?"

"Fine." Wellesley snorts and kicks his legs in his sleep. I pat his belly. "I'm actually on a work trip, too."

"What kind of trips do professional dog walkers take?" He laughs. "A bus to the next neighbourhood over?"

"I haven't walked dogs in ages," I remind him. "I'm with that nonprofit now, remember? The one that—"

"I remember. I was just teasing."

"Sure you were."

The grating pitch of feedback on a speaker system. A mumbled announcement, listing upcoming flights and their related gates. "I want to talk to you. It's about Emma."

Of course it is. "I know I haven't RSVP'd to her wedding yet. I'm just not sure I can get the time off."

"What? I didn't—" We're breaking up again. And there it is. Like so many wealthy men in the world, my dad is a massive cheapskate. When we're out to eat, he never tips more than ten percent. Our shower at home was always stocked with hotel shampoo, which he swore was "just as good" as any supermarket product. And, when he travels, he always picks the cheapest option for accommodation. This is far from the first time he's asked to crash at my place. My last bar of service is holding on for dear life. "Let's try this in person. I'll be flying into Toronto in—" Someone on the other end asks for his ticket and passport. There's a brief shuffle on the line, the faint sound of pleasantries; *have a good flight, sir.* "What do you say we grab a bite while I'm in town?"

"I'd say, sounds like you're short on entertainment."

"What was that?" he shouts over the sound of rolling bags and boarding calls.

"I said," I push my phone against my cheek, "I'm not sure if I'll have time."

"Well, let me know when you know." The background noise drops to a hum. He must be heading onto the aircraft. "I'll send you the—"

A series of short beeps. Call dropped. Out of service. Low battery. The screen goes dark. "Bye," I mutter to no one. My eyes sting again, like I've been chopping onions. After a few minutes of sitting in silence, I wrap the blanket around my shoulders and shuffle to the kitchen. If I'm not going to fall back asleep, I might as well grab a snack.

The kettle mutters to itself, licked by blue flames from the gas range. I pass my lighter between my hands, thumb picking at the flint wheel. My head is swimming, memories passing by like scenes on a moving train. They all start to blend. The echo of my father's footsteps, coming home late. They merge with the slamming of Hillside's front door, which itself soon merges with the hum of midday traffic as Mako and I debate who will keep the microwave post-breakup. I am in every season of my life at once and each one ends with me here, standing alone in a strange kitchen, listening to a kettle as it struggles to boil.

"Can't sleep?" Wearing a pair of puppy-dog slippers and a fluffy pink robe, Hayden stands in the archway.

"Not really," I mutter. "You?"

"Rainbow's in our bed tonight. And she's a side-sleeper." He shuffles to the stove, adjusting the heat. Digging through the cabinets, he sets a French press on the counter along with a bag of ground coffee beans. "As in, she sleeps sideways. She kicks, too."

"I can picture that." I chuckle to myself. Hayden fetches us a couple mugs, picking out one for himself that has Rainbow's toddler-face printed on it. "She's such a lucky kid, to have you two as her parents."

"We're the lucky ones. For sure." As the coffee steeps, he gives himself a splash of oat milk and a spoonful of brown sugar for sweetener. I let him do the same for me.

Staring into the gas range, I let myself get lost in the flicker of its firelight. "Can I ask you something?" Hayden nods. "Have you ever felt like life is just moving past you?" The kettle starts to rattle, gurgling. The spout begins to sputter. "Like, you're just a rock in a riverbed—and maybe, you stuck in one place for a little while. Or a long while. But eventually, the current wins. It takes you and it sweeps away everything you've ever known. And you're just sent tumbling. Over, and over."

The water boils to a shrill cry, cut short as Hayden takes it off the element. "Damn, Charlie." He pours it into the press. Tiny bubbles rise as the coffee starts to steep. "You're wasting your talents in the nonprofit world. You should be a poet!"

"Sorry." In a blink, I return to my senses. I pull the blanket tight around my shoulders. "I don't mean to dump on you. It's just been a bit of a weird week."

"No kidding." He pushes down the filter and pours fresh coffee for us both. "I don't blame you for feeling out of sorts. You must really miss home."

"Weirdly, I don't." I move beside him, leaning against the counter. "I miss my cat, sure. And maybe sleeping in my own bed. But I think what's got me weirded out is how easy it's been to leave the rest behind."

"What about your job?" Hayden gently blows on my coffee to cool it, before passing me the mug. "Or your friends?"

"Work is work." I take the cup with both hands, heat radiating through my palms. The rising steam warms my cheeks. "If anything, I like being able to set my own schedule. And working remote means there's no coworkers bugging me for small talk." I inhale deeply, soaking in the rich scent of fresh beans. There's a faint hint of hazelnut. "I'm behind on some projects, sure. But I'm starting to think there's more to life than meeting deadlines." *As for friends,* I think to myself, *I've only got the one. And we've got a messy history.*

"That's the truth." Hayden pauses to savour his first sip. "I'm bummed about losing out on tenure track this year but there's a blessing in it too."

The moment the coffee hits my tongue, my whole body starts to warm. A tingling sensation rises behind my eyes, waking me up. "Yeah?"

"Yeah." He grabs a spoon from the kitchen sink and uses it to stir his drink. "I can stick around here more often, be present with Rainbow. Make sure Buffy's not doing things *totally* alone."

"She works hard, eh?" I ask, though it's not really a question.

"Mmm-hmm." He nods. "This has been her trying to keep things *casual.* Loosey-goosey." He takes another long sip and deeply exhales. "I worry about her. The last thing she needs is another burnout."

There's a small chip in the handle of my mug. I pick at it with my thumb, absentmindedly. "She mentioned going through a rough patch before."

"More like a pull-the-brakes, screeching-halt, stop-drop-

and-roll patch." I start to laugh but Hayden doesn't. He just stares down at his cup, watching the milk and coffee swirl. "It was towards the end of my PhD. Buff was just so dedicated to her work. Constantly on the road, booking shows, planning her next works." Brows knit tight, the bags below his eyes seem to deepen in real time. "She kept trying to push herself harder, make a bigger statement, do something *meaningful*. She was always talking about that. The both of us, we came up through the organizing world—marching with unions, working at co-ops. Her art started as means of protest but then it took on a life of its own: *Elizabeth Hawkshaw* became the main draw, not the message, not the movement. I know that ate at her."

The frosted window shimmers blue with waning moonlight. Dawn is on the horizon and the freckles splashed on Hayden's cheeks almost seem to glow like early starlight. "Around the time my mom got sick, Buffy started really hurting." His voice has dropped to a whisper. I move closer, carefully listening. "She was spread too thin. And when she still tried to push it, her body started giving out. People think burnout is just a mental thing. But it's so much more than that."

"Right," I whisper.

"She wasn't sleeping," he explains. "Then, she couldn't get out of bed. One morning, her jaw was all busted up—just from clenching so hard, in her sleep." As he lifts his gaze to meet with mine, his easy grin settles back into place. "That was right around when we found out the IVF had worked. I was pregnant."

"Wow," I murmur. It hardly feels like a big enough word, but all others seem to be failing me. "All this time, I've been watching her online, reading interviews. I had no idea what was going on behind the scenes."

"She's a great performer." He polishes off the last of his coffee and rinses out the mug in the sink. "Anyway, it's really her story to tell. But it was a hard time, we had to make some big changes." He motions for my cup. I gulp down what's left before passing it over. "Buff's in a much better place these days. She still works too hard but she's getting better at balancing it out."

I watch the silhouette of his side profile. The way his shoulders rise and fall. "And what about you?" I ask.

"What about me?" He stops the tap and grabs a hand towel.

Venturing a hand against his forearm, I point out, "It just seems like you've been through a lot too. Your mom's passing, Buffy's health stuff. The whole having-a-baby thing."

Hayden crinkles his eyes at me. "Honestly, I'm not sure I've had a minute in the last five years to think about it!" He pats my hand once and then busies himself, wiping down the countertop. "I've been taking care of people my whole life. It's what I know how to do."

"Well, maybe once in a while, you deserve to be taken care of, too." I turn to find a cloth, intending to lend a hand. But I'm caught off guard by a blurry face, standing far too close for comfort. Stepping back, I realize it's my own warped reflection on the polished surface of the fridge. "Man." I lean in and study myself, fidgeting with my bangs. "I need a haircut."

"Really?" Hayden wipes his way up beside me. He shakes off his hands before running them through my hair. "I kinda like the bedhead look. It suits you." Fingertips tracing down my temples, behind my ears, he cups my face. The heat of his touch draws me in. I lick my lips, trying to control my breathing.

"Hayden, can I ask you one more thing?" He nods yes. "Are you and Buffy…" *Monogamous?* "Happy?"

"I'd like to think so," says Buffy. A lit candle in one hand, she yawns and shimmies her way to Hayden. I step aside, heart still racing.

"Morning, Buff." He greets her with a kiss. "We were just talking about you."

"All good things, I hope. Have you two seen outside?" Following her suggestion, I use my sleeve to rub a circle in the frost. Sun peeking over the horizon, the sky is painted rose and amber. Not a cloud in sight. Along the streets, heavy tire tracks; the roads have been cleared of snow.

"Guess the plows came through after all," says Buffy. "Looks like you're heading home."

Chapter Fourteen

"It can't *all* be in my head, right?"

I brush my teeth with an urgent fervor while cradling the phone against my shoulder. The little bathroom under the stairs is more of a cupboard that just so happens to have a toilet and sink. A slope of layered, yellow paint coats the walls. The awkward angles and carpeted flooring make this the best spot for a clandestine phone call.

"You should have seen the way he was looking at me." I stare at my reflection in the toothpaste-flecked mirror. "He was *definitely* going in for it."

"Google says the vortex is moving south." Mako's words are broken up by the scraping of a can opener. In the background, Cashew mews for breakfast. "Problem now is, as soon as the highways get sorted everyone will be rushing back in. Traffic's gonna be brutal."

The power came back on sometime in the midmorning, right around when I'd gone back to bed in hopes of sneaking a teaspoon of sleep. All at once, the lights clicked on, clocks started beeping and music began to play full blast from the speaker in the kitchen. The commotion woke Rainbow, who soon came barreling down the stairs. Wellesley started barking at the ruckus, Mango joining in, while Miss Kiki slipped into my room for a place to hide. So, there went my chance at being well-rested. But at least the furnace is back on, and my phone's had a chance to charge.

"It's just wild to me that he'd even think about cheating on Buffy. There's no way he really meant it like that." I spit a gob of toothpaste into the sink. "Then again, she's totally been making moves, too. Which is just like, bizarre." Just as I say her name, there's a shuffle over my head. Someone is stepping down the stairs. "She's basically a queer *icon*. Not to mention an easy ten—an eleven! I'm what, a six? On a good day?"

There's the clatter of cutlery, the tap of a spoon against a cat dish. "I don't think you want me to answer that." Mako laughs.

"Shut up." I turn to lean against the sink. "Seriously, what would you do if you were me?"

"I'd think about going to the labour board," says Mako. Cashew is purring in the background, smacking his lips. "It's criminal that Angie had you out there during all this. A little weekend trip—and now it's literally Thursday! What, are you supposed to just relocate indefinitely to, what was it, Enbridge?"

"*Elm*ridge. And you know that's not what I meant."

"When you're back, I'll help fix up your résumé. See if we can't get you a better gig." There's a series of *tap-tap-taps*. Mako must be fiddling with their phone screen. "Do you know the Jobs for Queers page on Insta? They've usually got some good stuff." My phone vibrates with an incoming text. "How about getting into dog-sitting again? Check out this gig."

I pull up the posting. "*Seeking a full-time, live-in pet-nanny* for a *prize-winning Labradoodle*—I don't know, Mako."

"But look at the pay!" They pipe in, "For $1,800 a month, that's not too bad right?"

"In *rent*." I scroll down to the details. "It says, *great opportunity for anyone seeking affordable housing.* I think they're looking for a tenant who will also pick up their dog's crap."

"That wouldn't be so bad," says Mako. "You like animals and stuff, right?"

There's a quick knock on the bathroom door. The knob starts to rattle, tiny push-lock straining in place. "Buff, you in there?" asks Hayden, "Have you seen the charger for my laptop?"

"Sorry, I—" I stand up and smack my head against the slanted ceiling. "One second!"

"You calling for me?" Buffy's voice drifts in from some-where above my head. "Also, why is your laptop charger sitting on the stairs?"

"Oops!" Hayden backs off. "Apologies, Charlie! I thought for sure you'd be back in bed."

I peek the door open just in time to spy Hayden and Buffy share a tender kiss. When they part, Buffy's eyes flit towards me. A sly smile rests on her heart-shaped lips. "He filled me in on your whole early-morning rendezvous."

"He did?" Slinking from my hiding place, I brace against the banister. "Okay but Buffy, you know I wouldn't—"

"Say, is that my shirt?" Hayden tucks his way towards me. "It looks good on you."

"Agreed." Buffy fiddles with my collar. "Very cute."

Muttering thanks, I rush back to my bedroom. "Did you catch all that?" I whisper into my phone. "*So* flirting, right?!"

"All I heard was your pocket," Mako grumbles. "Chuck, is this really the most important thing to be worrying about right now? You're all stressed about Muffy and Brayden—"

"You know that's not their names." I kick through the clothes tossed across my floor.

"My *point* is," Mako continues, "you're totally missing the big *question* here."

"Big question?" I dare to ask.

"Yeah!" There's the clatter of dishes in the sink on their end of the line. "Namely, what time do you think you're going to be home? I was thinking of bringing a date over but I don't want to make it awkward."

"A—what?" I grab the pieces that look to be mine, tossing them in handfuls back into my duffel bag. "I don't know. I was thinking of staying one more night, if Buffy and Hayden are okay with it."

"You sly fox!" Mako giggles. "All that fussing over these signals that they're sending. But you *like* it, don't you?"

"I don't know what you're talking about." I hold up the least wrinkled of my formal shirts. It'll have to do. "It's like you said, traffic's going to be brutal going into the city. And I've still got stuff to finish up in town before I start the drive back. What's one more day out of the office?"

"You tell yourself that." There's a crack. The sizzling of egg in a hot pan. At least I don't have to wonder if my food's going bad in the fridge.

"And Mako?" I ask. "Please don't bring rando dates into my house while I'm gone."

"I was just kidding." They laugh.

I zip up my bag. "Sure you were."

"And for what it's worth, it sounds like you're having a very nice vacation," says Mako. I catch the scraping of a spatula in the background—I just hope they remembered not to use a metal spatula on my Teflon pans. "But there's also a life back here for you. You may want to return to it at some point."

I click off the call and find Hayden in the kitchen, working at the stove. "Can I tempt you with a spot of breakfast?" He adds in a singsong voice, "It's fried tempeh."

"Wait, first." Buffy waves to me from the front hall. "Charlie, can you come work your magic again? I'm already late taking him out and Wells won't put his boots on. I tried the peanut butter trick but he keeps eating it too fast."

"Just a second." I shuffle my bag from one shoulder to the other. "I just want to go check on my car, see how deep it's snowed in."

"I already dug it out for you." Hayden flips the tempeh with a flick of extra flair. "Shoveled the whole driveway and the sidewalk this morning, while you sleepyheads went back to bed."

"Aw, babe!" Buffy presses her face to the window. "You didn't have to do that."

"I know." He winks. "I made a couple big piles of snow for Rainbow to jump in, whenever she drags herself out of bed."

"Oh, wow. Thank you." Sure enough, there's my car—he even scraped the ice off its windshield. "Um, if that's the case, though, I should probably go to this work thing. The place I was supposed to visit—ECIC or whatever—my boss set up a meeting for me with someone there to drop off all those outreach supplies." It's pretty much the only task Angie's asked me for directly since she sent me out here. I feel a certain obligation to it.

"Gotcha." Hayden's smile falters but only for a moment. "You thinking of hitting the road after that?"

"Oh, not really." I tap my duffel bag with one hand. "Just figure I should bring a change of clothes. I'm not sure how professional this place is supposed to be."

I go join Buffy, distracting Wellesley with a long chin-scratch. "If it's anything like I've heard," she tells me, "they'd probably like you better if you showed up in some Lululemon yoga pants. If you happen to have any in there."

"Unfortunately not." I smirk and slip into my coat. "I'll be back, though, don't worry."

"Sounds like a plan." Hayden waves goodbye. "I'll be sure to cook up enough supper for all of us."

I slip outside with Buffy and Wellesley. He whines when I don't follow for our usual walk, but she eventually coaxes him along. I watch them trot down the paved road together, waving at neighbours and stopping to watch the squirrels.

My breath rattles in my chest and comes out in quick puffs of fog. On the third crank of my car key, the engine finally starts. My windshield wipers kick on, smearing a mix of ice and slush across my view. The radio starts blasting a song that hasn't been popular in at least two decades. I crank up the heat, little as it is, and pull onto the freshly plowed street.

I squint at the grey strip of road ahead in search for any sign of a yellow line. I'd even take a clear definition of the sidewalk curb. The streets may have technically been cleared but there are long stretches of raw slush and mountains of snow on either side. At least there are only a few other drivers out. If I run off the road, I'll probably only hurt myself.

Residents of Elmridge begin to peek out of their porches. A few brave optimists are shoveling their driveways. Heading towards the downtown, I see a few of the businesses have cleared their walkways and welcome customers again. The hardware store has a display of hand-held snowblowers, on sale for half-off. A small café has its neon sign lit, windows foggy. From the looks of it, everyone and their dog is lining up for the simple joy of buying a coffee. The gas station is up and running too, its steadfast clerk standing outside and smoking the stubby end of a cigarette.

I pass over the town's central bridge. As soon as I start to pick up speed, that percussive rattle is back again. It's coming from my engine, louder than before. I'm almost tempted to pull over but when I round the corner, it fades again. My attention is drawn instead to that sparkling, glass-walled structure that towers over the Elmridge skyline. On my approach this time, I notice a small plaque out front. *The Elmridge Centre for Innovative Connection.*

The parking lot is crowded with Teslas, a couple BMWs and—is that a Lexus? The sliding doors open smoothly but my eyes need a minute to adjust. Sunlight cascades across the polished wood floors, tall ceilings and a chandelier of dangling light bulbs. People dressed in everything from three-piece suits to high-brand athleisure sit in small groups around a series of round tables, working on laptops and iPads. Several thin women step out of a yoga studio, gathering at a water station to re-fill matching Hydro Flasks. Opposite them, a pair of men in beanies and short beards climb a winding staircase composed of exposed slats. They pass a wall of living vines and step into a clear-walled office on the second floor.

So this is ECIC. I take a deep breath, bow my head and move in.

"Are you a member?" A woman in her early twenties sits behind ECIC's central, circular desk. She wears a perfectly flat smile. "Excuse me—are you here to sign up?"

"Sign up?" I nudge the box of outreach supplies under my arm. It's weighed down with buttons, pins, flyers—pretty much any cheap thing we could slap our logo onto. "I'm just supposed to drop some stuff off."

"Well, we'll need you to sign in, if you're here as a guest." The woman directs me towards a touch-screen kiosk around the bend of her desk. "Do you know the plan member who invited you?"

"My boss told me to ask for..." Quickly, I double-check the contact name Angie sent over. "Sam?"

"Oh, that's me!" She claps and eyes the box under my arm. The *CMM* logo is plastered on one side. "Ah yes, we had you down for a weekend tour! Such a shame about the weather, getting in the way of everything." She whips around, snap-ping her ponytail. "Come along, then. I'll show you around."

With nowhere else to go, I hurry after her. Sam guides me through ECIC's many co-working departments, exercise stu-dios and in-house gym. They've got a minibar, a juice bar and a salad bar. There's even a health-food store with a pharmacist on staff, though I note the shelves are mostly stacked with sup-plements and essential oils. With every step, Sam's hair flicks out behind her like an arrow pointing the way. Her shiny beige nails never stop tapping on her phone.

"We operate on the cutting edge, the intersection of social enterprise and wellness," she explains to me their mission statement. "We provide opportunities for upcoming innovators to actualize their full-body potential! Grass shot?" We've stopped in front of something called *The Free-Thought Café*. Several people wait to place their order but a man in a *One Love* T-shirt scans some kind of card at the register and skips to the front.

"I'm not thirsty." I move the outreach box to rest under my other arm. Sam has already taken off again in a full-on power walk. "I've got to say, I'm surprised how busy this place is. I didn't think Elmridge even had this many people in it."

"Oh, most of our members aren't from the local community." She taps the button for the elevator. "We picked this location for its accessible price point, not to mention proximity to several important social centres."

"So the building was cheap," I translate. "But people from big cities could still drive here."

For the first time since we left her desk, Sam stops to look me in the eye. "You're funny," she decides. "I like that." She rings for the elevator again, heel clicking with impatience. "How about we take the stairs?" In a blink, she's on her way again.

"Sure," I mumble. These supplies are starting to get heavy.

Sam takes the stairs two at a time. "We provide unique spatial environments in which our members can actualize their holistic potential."

"So, you rent out space," I huff, trying to keep up the pace. "Kind of like a mall?"

"If you want to be reductive." She stops, only briefly, to adjust the base of her ponytail. "All our services are absolutely free, for anyone with a membership."

"That's actually pretty cool," I admit.

"Isn't it?" We stop to look down from the second-floor balcony. The first-floor Pilates studio is emptying out. Based on the sweaty faces of those carrying rolled-up mats under their arms, I guess it was a particularly active class. "We're big believers in accessibility. Which is why we have flexible payment plans, and the option to manage fees through volunteer hours!"

I watch the Pilates crew all go line up at the café. That one guy who cut in line still looks like he's thinking on his order. "I thought you just said it was free?"

"For *members*." Sam swipes her phone screen to pull up the ECIC website. Sure enough, there's a list of titles and associated costs. "To join up, we only require a one-time commitment to an annual investment. And anyone who volunteers for a minimum of fifteen hours per week gets fifty percent off their dues!"

Mr. Cut-in-Line finally places his order and the barista gets busy blending up a bright green smoothie. "Volunteers. All these people, they're working here for free?"

"Oh, no!" Sam turns on her heel, nearly smacking her hair into my face that time. "They're *donating* hours. Think of it like a library. You put resources in, check other ones out." She starts us off on another flight of stairs, this one nearly at a ninety-degree angle. "There's also the option to pay down fees by bringing in new members—for every successful recruit, you can either pay your dues down or upgrade your plan privileges. Some people even end up *earning* cash!"

This whole building is starting to look a lot more pyramid shaped. "And how often does that happen?"

"All the time!" Around a curving hallway, Sam dips in and out of sight. I follow the *click-click-click* of her heels. "Just ask anyone. We're just all one big happy family around here." Turning a corner, I almost smack right into her. Stopped at a foggy glass door, Sam scans the card on her lanyard and enters a quick pin. "There's also plenty of room for upward mobility. I've only been here three months and I'm already an Executive of Creative Cultivation!"

"And that means what, exactly?" I ask.

"That's such a great question." A light goes green and Sam grips the door handle. "Now get ready, this is my favourite part."

Steam spills into the hallway as Sam leads me inside a rich greenhouse. Raised beds of dark soil, verdant greens; crops of spinach and kale, flowering zucchinis, all are misted by sprinklers lining the atrium's arched ceiling. I'm reminded of the bountiful garden Johanna managed to cultivate in the Hillside's crumbling backyard soil. I can only imagine what she would have done with a place like this. We pass swaths of blooming flowers—geraniums, petunias, chrysanthemums, even a few monstera.

"This fully functioning greenhouse is designed to run through all seasons," Sam explains as she inspects a few of the smaller buds. "I like to come up here and sit with my own thoughts."

"I can see why." This is beyond anything I would have imagined from looking at ECIC's cold, glassy exterior. Maybe there's something to be said for this membership model they've got going, if it allows for a place like this. "It must take a huge staff to keep this place running smoothly," I wonder aloud.

"That's the beauty of it all." Sam perks up. "Most day-to-day operations are managed by our members alone!"

I stop in my tracks. "So, wait. This *whole place* is staffed with the unpaid interns?"

"*Members.* Gaining valuable work experience, and discounts on their dues." Sam digs out a few of the smaller sprigs before wiping the dirt off her hands. "Of course, our board of directors do receive small dividends for their efforts. But that's all plenty covered by what we earn in dues, public funding and on-site enterprises." She turns and beckons me towards a supply room. "How about we wrap up our chat in my office?"

At long last, I drop the crate of outreach supplies onto Sam's desk. What she calls her office appears to me more like a garden shed. The small, windowless room is musty scented, crammed with bags of soil. I'm pressed against a shelf of anti-pest sprays. "Sorry for the tight squeeze." Sam sweeps aside several file folders dusted with dirt. "Still a bit of a work in progress going on in here."

I would have thought her office would be a bit more, well, executive. "Not to be rude, but aren't you *CEO of creativity* or something?"

"I'm part of the Executive *tier.*" Sam spins her chair, moving from typing on her phone to swiping on a tablet. "I donate around twenty hours a week. Hardly enough to get my own suite." She flicks on a table lamp, granting a bit of light to our dim surroundings. "But I have basically claimed this little spot as my own. Most people don't even know we have a workspace in here!"

"I can't imagine why," I mutter.

"I must say…" Sam reaches under her desk and roots through various drawers. "It's been such a pleasure to have you here. I always love giving tours, even on my days off! It's like seeing the ECIC through fresh eyes every time."

"Today was your day off?" I grimace. "You didn't have to do that."

"Sure, I did!" She pops up with a fistful of pamphlets. "We're *so* thrilled you're going to be adding us to that database of yours—we can't *wait* to connect with all your users!"

"Right." I stifle a cough. The thick smell of manure is working into my throat. "Well um, I can't promise anything… I'll have to write up a report, share it with my team."

"Mmm-hmm, mmm-hmm. I totally get that." Sam's ponytail bounces as she nods along. "In the meantime, how about you just forward me all the contact info for your client base? That way, we can reach out to them directly!" She pushes several pamphlets into my hands, "Oh and your higher-up— Angela, was it? She mentioned you would want to learn more about our social enterprise model?"

"She did?"

"Oh yes. She *specifically* asked about it, multiple times." Sam spreads out her many flyers, all of which detail different types of programs—workshops on intermittent fasting, tips on getting into cryptocurrency, workouts with private trainers. "Lucky for you all, we've actually just started up a new workshop series all about expanding the ECIC model! Can I sign you up? I'd love to add you to my downstream team!" She hovers over her tablet, ready and waiting.

"That's very generous." I smile, politely. "But I really should talk to Angie first."

"I get what's happening here." Sam waggles her finger. "You're bargaining for a discount! Well, you're in luck, because the Executives Tier gets five percent off all on-site workshops."

"Maybe another time." I start backing towards the exit.

"What's the rush?" Sam stands up after me. "How about we hop back downstairs to the café—are you more for still or sparkling water?"

"Neither—thanks, though!" I grab the door handle and get ready to sprint my way back down all those stairs. "I really do have to go. I'm, um, supposed to call my cat sitter."

I can hardly make it back down those stairs fast enough. Through the sliding doors, I don't even button my coat before hopping in my car. All I want to do is get back home; I can't wait to see Buffy's and Hayden's faces when I tell them about all this.

Chapter Fifteen

A hazy amber sun hangs low, casting long shadows along the Elmridge bridge. Sitting in my parked car, I peer out at the riverbank. Shallow waters shimmer, fresh ice starting to crack. I'm still processing my walkthrough at ECIC. All the jargon and hierarchy of a sketchy corporate office, repackaged to look like a community centre. How many other Sams are there— going in on their days off, trading all their time and money for hazy promises of *wellness* and *productivity*?

What the hell was Angie thinking, sending me there? Sure, CMM has changed a lot in the last few years but I didn't think we'd sunk *this* far. The referral database is the last bastion of our old mission, something made to really help people when they need it. When we give that stamp of approval, it means something—to our clients, and the programs too. I, for one, am not ready to just hand it out, and certainly not to a glorified multilevel-marketing campaign.

Maybe I'm missing something here, some kind of bigger picture. I'll admit, my work-brain has been running at reduced capacity. After my stay with the Hawthornes, visiting ECIC was like getting dropped from a hot-air balloon into a submarine. I dove down to the bottom of the ocean and now I'm on the surface again, struggling to catch my breath.

After. The word circles back to me. I didn't even notice it the first time. *After my stay.* That's true, I guess. The work-side of my work-trip is officially over. I did what I came here to do. When I'm back at the office, I'll write up a report (one that does *not* recommend we add ECIC to the database). Then I can go back to my usual projects, my usual life. Days spent under the fluorescent lights of a basement office, followed by evenings alone at my bachelor pad. I wonder if Cashew misses me. He's probably curled up on Mako's lap right now, getting all the cuddles.

My duffel bag sits in the back seat. The GPS says, if I left now, I could be home before midnight. Highway traffic would be stop-and-go. Now that the storm has lightened up, everyone and their dog will be trying to get wherever they were going before the roads were shut down. But the side roads, they could work. It would take a little longer but I don't mind taking my time. No more squeaky storage-room cot—tonight, I could fall asleep in my own bed. Wake up tomorrow, put on my own fresh clothes and walk my usual route to work. I'm sure that's what Angie would prefer. There's nothing technically keeping me in Elmridge anymore, except the fact that I want to stay.

The fog on my windows is starting to frost. I start the engine and watch the ice melt again. Water droplets grow and streak down my windshield like fresh rain; they weave together, a litany of silent dancers acting out stories of upheaval and breakdown, marriage and separation. Sometimes, several cling to the glass and slowly coalesce, forming a sort of midair puddle. I count down the seconds until they grow too heavy to hold their shape. It's always just a matter of time until they fall apart. I click on my wipers and in a matter of moments, the whole grand performance is blotted away.

The rattling is back. I make a point to ignore it as I back up, pull a three-point turn and cross the bridge. Square apartment blocks, fast-food restaurants, a secondhand clothing store; their varied heights stand out against the skyline like crooked teeth. The laundromat has its neon sign lit. A singular patron leans beside a whirring washing machine, fiddling with their phone. I round the corner of a residential street. An old man sits on his front stoop, the orange light of his cigarette as bright as any streetlamp. He stares at me as I slowly drive past.

Another few blocks and a familiar grey tower crests into view. There's a light on at Saint Brigid's. I wonder if Maggie is still up, folding pamphlets. Maybe Toby is there, keeping her company, or Frances could be rehearsing one of his drag routines. A part of me almost wants to pull over and knock on those oak wood doors. But I keep moving, in the direction of a now-familiar cul-de-sac. I could drive home tonight, yes. But the shape of that word has started to change for me.

A house of mismatched everything. Nothing ever in its place. Raucous mornings, corralling all the pets and people. The lingering scent of something burning on the stove. Mundane tasks like laundry or dishes, made into adventures all their own. Laughter, singing, overlapping conversations. Everything the Hawthornes do, they do together. Even when they're apart, they think about one another and the ways they can make each other's lives easier. Hayden and Buffy take care of each other—and Rainbow! I've never seen a kid with so much freedom to be all of who she is, without any judgement at all. The love that radiates through that house stands like a beacon, drawing everyone in. Including me.

Piles of freshly plowed snow stand high on either side of the street. I pull into the imprint my own car left hours earlier and let the engine idle. It's a marvel, how much the sight of the

Hawthornes' glowing porchlight fills me with warmth. There's a light on in the living room. Shadows dance across its drawn curtains. *I wonder if Hayden's got dinner going yet.*

Pulling out my phone, I shoot off a quick text. Does he need me to pick anything up? It's not too late to turn around and grab a few supplies from the gas-station-slash-corner-store. A few seconds later, Hayden appears in the kitchen window. He's wearing his pink apron. *Adorable.* I watch him poke at his phone, swipe at something and then tuck it away. But looking down at my own phone, there's no reply. "He's probably just focused on the food," I decide.

From day one, the Hawthornes managed to make me feel welcome. That's something I don't come by often. Even more than that, they genuinely seemed happy to have me around. *They're just being nice to me.* That's what I'd normally tell myself. *Surely, they'll be relieved when I leave and everything goes back to normal.* My head might believe that but the rest of me isn't so sure. I know the way Hayden looked at me last night, how close we were together. That was more than being *nice*, wasn't it? What about Buffy, in the church parking lot—what would have happened, I wonder, if I'd been bold enough to just make a move?

I scroll to Buffy's contact in my phone and shoot her a text instead. She should have a moment to read it; Rainbow's probably watching her nightly episode of *Brightbriar* around now. Sure enough, two checkmarks appear beside my outgoing text. Anticipation pulses through me like static electricity. I stare at her name, waiting for the three dots of an incoming message. A minute passes, then another. Nothing. I've been left on read.

Maybe Rainbow was too restless for TV tonight. She's probably climbing the banister right now, or kicked off a round of Invisible Unicorns. The driveway is plowed, the door only a few paces away. I could go in and find out. *Unless.*

Unless Hayden said something to Buffy. What if I really was picking up all the wrong signals—worse, what if I wasn't? He was all but ready to cheat on his wife, and I was going to let him! How could either of us do that to her? Of course he'd tell her. *I* should have told her. And if he did fess up, she would too. All our secret hand-holdings, stolen glances, moments when time stood still. The heat of her breath, mixing with mine. She has sacrificed so much over the past five years, building up this family—this community! We came so close to ruining it all. I was going to let her throw her life away, on *me* of all people! An out-of-towner, home-wrecker, here to devastate all of Elmridge before running back to the Big City.

Hayden and Buffy have been nothing but generous to me. And this is how I repay them. I wouldn't text me back either. My stomach sinks as I smack hard into the truth. Some people might not care about me, and that's fine. A few folks might actually like having me around, but only for a while. Eventually, everyone sees me for who I really am. Selfish, and cowardly. I should have known better than to hope for something different this time.

My phone screen lights up. For a split second, I take it all back. Buffy must have just had her hands full. Or Hayden's calling me, phone pressed against his shoulder as he minds the night's sauté. I have about a hundred fantasies which all pop at once, when I see the name.

Incoming Video Call: Mako

With one last glance towards the Hawthornes' house, I swipe right and take the call. The screen is dark. Not black, like their camera is off. It's more brown with flecks of light. There's a rustling sound, some kind of music. The static of overlapping voices. One or two seem almost familiar but it's impossible to pick them out. *That tracks,* I think to myself. *For once, Mako calls me when I really need to talk. And it's a butt dial.*

I'm about to hang up when suddenly, there's motion. The

smudgy movements of fingers blocking out the camera lens. Mako's face appears as a blur at first but slowly it's in focus. "Oh my god, hi!"

Flashing lights in the background, a glimpse of something like a stage. Someone walks by carrying a flight of beer. "Are you at a bar?" I ask. "It's Thursday night!"

"What?" Mako shouts over pulsing beats. "What's going on, dude—why you calling?"

"You called me!" I shout back.

"What?!" They stand and sip a bright pink cocktail. "One sec, let me find a quiet spot!" As they turn, I catch sight of who they're with. It's just a flash, but I'd recognize that bright green mullet anywhere.

"Is that—" My question is answered before I can ask it.

"Where you going, Mako?" Mars hollers after them. Beside him, someone's head is turned. But I only know one person who French braids her hair like that.

"Yeah!" Johanna's voice is so clear, it's like I'm in the room with them. Except of course, I would never be invited. "You're up next for karaoke!" Sure enough, the camera tilts and I spot who's up on stage. It's Mei, finishing up her set before Mako takes the mic.

"One sec!" The screen goes dark again. There's shuffling. Mako reappears flanked by scarves and winter jackets. "Okay yeah, hi. What's up?"

"Where are you?" I ask.

"Coat check." Mako peeks up. "It's cool. I know the guy who runs it and he won't mind me hiding out in here for a minute. He's a client at CIS."

"You know that's not what I meant," I mutter, fiddling with my car's temperature controllers. *When did it get so hot in here?* "So what, you all having a Hillside House reunion tonight?"

"Oh." Mako fidgets with their septum piercing. "You clocked that, eh?"

I roll my eyes and prop the phone up on my dashboard. "I thought you couldn't even get a hold of Mei."

"Yeah, she just got back in town!" Mako cracks a smile, "Get this—turns out she met this woman living out in Colorado, they've been living on a weed farm together! But apparently it didn't work out. She's moving home now and actually looking for a roommate."

"I'll be sure to ask around for her." I briefly swipe away from the call to double-check my messages. Still no word from Hayden or Buffy. "Seriously dude, nobody even thought to tell me you were all getting together?"

Mako digs in the pocket of a nearby coat and pulls out a pack of gum. "It's not like you're in town anyway!" They nab in a couple pieces for themself and start to chew. "And, well. You know."

"Yeah, you don't have to say it." I grimace. "I know I'm not wanted there."

"It's not… Okay, maybe it is that," Mako admits. "But trust me, you're not missing out. I don't even really like hanging with these folks anymore, I'm just showing face to get the latest goss."

"You sure about that? Because it looked like you were having a good time." I cross my arms and lean back in my seat. "And what about Cashew?"

"What about him?" Mako pops their pilfered gum.

"Have you even checked on him lately?" I ask. "Or did you ditch him to go party?"

"Chuck, chill." Mako's eyes dart away for a moment. There's muttering, someone asking for a ticket. "Cashew is fine. I stopped in this morning, cleaned the litter box, gave him breakfast and an extra scoop for dinner."

"What?" I snap. "You can't just do that! He's got very specific mealtimes—I was counting on you for this!"

"Yeah, I know," Mako hisses. They retreat farther into the coats. "You also asked me at the last possible minute. *And* you've extended that ask like, five times already!" Their voice is a whisper now. "I don't mind doing you a solid, but I still have a life. I'll go and hang with him again, after I'm done here."

"Don't bother." I adjust my mirrors and click on my headlights. "I'll go take care of him myself."

"What're you talking about?"

Arm against the passenger headrest, I slowly back myself out. "I finished my work stuff out here. I'm heading home now."

"Are you sure?" Their voice is starting to break up. The connection is getting weaker. "You'll be back pretty late."

"It's like you said, you've got a life." I weave my way around piles of plowed snow, heading back towards the main road. "It's time I get back to mine."

"Chuck, wait—" Their end of the call cuts out completely.

"Tell everyone I say hi." I tap the red, end-call button and step on the gas. The Hawthornes' porchlight glow shrinks in my rearview mirror.

Chapter Sixteen

The highway stretches before me like an arrow; a single grey line cut long through a valley of farmlands, fields still blanketed with snow on either side. Thin strips of pink and gold line the sun as it sets at my back. Every few minutes, the right side of my engine lets out a series of short thumps. I'm growing accustomed to the sound, almost looking forward to it. Each time, it's a reminder of how much distance I've put behind me, how much closer I am to home.

I glance at my dash. My fuel tank is running low. Scanning the horizon, I search for any sign of a gas station—I thought Buffy said there was a cheap one out this way. The last few wisps of warm sunlight dip from my rearview. The few highway lights lining this side road flicker to life. Their glow spills across my lap in rapid sequence. I push on the gas and pick up speed. Why does driving back in always feel longer?

The growing darkness makes me wonder if I should have taken the 401 after all. I figured it would be jammed up—commuters rushing back to wherever they were going before the storm. Though now that I'm driving through this seemingly endless, desolate patch, I'm starting to long for the busy lights of traffic. Maybe getting stuck in the stop-and-go wouldn't have been so bad.

I let out a long sigh and loosen my grip on the steering wheel. *How many times am I going to let myself be disappointed by other people?* One day, I'm going to have actually learned my lesson. Part of me is still upset with Mako, but can I really blame them? If the roles were reversed and the old Hillside crew had asked me out to drinks, I probably would have gone too.

As for Hayden and Buffy, they really are great people. Their family and whole community—it's just so easy to get sucked in and feel like I really belong. But they're still just people, living their lives, taking care of one another. And I came crashing in, expecting them to just bend over and accommodate me for however long. It's not their fault that I kept reading more and more into all our little moments together. They were just that. Moments. And now, they're over.

Homo Sweet Homo. Mako's birthday gift to me, a custom key chain. It rattles as my car hits a rough patch of pavement. More than ever, the words are bittersweet. That was our house motto, back in the day. Mars, Johanna, Mei, Mako and me—after struggling to find our place among our bio-families, we had all decided we could make our own instead. We were supposed to last forever, to *be* each other's home. We were bonded by our queerness, all the parts of ourselves that never fit anywhere else. Then it all ended. And life went on. Just as it will now.

But what if I'm wrong? The thought bubbles its way to the surface. I've been fighting it since I left the limits of Elmridge. *What if I really did have a chance this time, to find my people?* Hayden and Buffy could be waiting around right now, wondering where I am. What if they really do care—what then? I'm not sure what would be worse, believing that I'd made up all the tenderness between us, or knowing it was real but that I'm too chicken to turn back. *Maybe I should—*

Before I can finish that thought, everything goes dark. My car lights, the headlights, everything. There's an eerie quiet and it a takes a second for me to realize that clunking noise has stopped. A second later, the engine safety lights all click on; I'm awash in red and blue, flashing warning signs. My headlights flicker, just in time to reveal a patch of dark ice up ahead.

I swerve but it's a second too late. The moment my tires kiss the slickness of its edge, the whole car starts skidding sideways. I hold fast to the steering wheel, pump the brakes. It's doing nothing.

Isn't this what they told us to do in driver's ed? I think to myself, *Oh god, is that going to be my last—*

A rush of white streams upward and envelops my entire view. I close my eyes and brace for impact.

A trail of wispy clouds blots a path through the stars. If van Gogh got bored partway through making *The Starry Night*, it might have looked something like the sky tonight. The moon hangs low, drifting over fields of empty snow. A handful of tall highway lamps stare down at my stalled vehicle. Otherwise, there is no trace of electric light in any direction. What I wouldn't give to glimpse a set of distant high beams or a farmhouse porchlight.

I can't pick up even a single bar of service. Not even when I push my phone right against the roof. The battery is running rapidly into the red. I try starting the ignition, again. The first few attempts drag a raspy whine from the unknown depths of the engine. After that, deadly silence, too cold for crickets chirping in the fields or birds twittering on phone wires. The subtle noises of my own body start to overwhelm me. My heartbeat, a drum; my stomach, a gurgling pit. I hold my breath to keep the cacophony at bay.

I've thought about stepping outside, of course. I could pop the hood, stare down and pretend I know what I'm looking at. Or I could start walking. Try to track down a cell phone signal or search for some (gay-friendly or, failing that, gaydar-impaired) country folks willing to lend me a call on a landline. All these plans, however, would mean opening the car door. Once that lid is popped, there's no going back. The way the wind is running outside, there's no doubt I'd lose what little heat I've managed to keep. There's also no guarantee I'd even find anything, or anyone, out there. Not quite ready to make that jump, I focus on what I can do: surviving.

I find an empty pop can buried under the passenger seat—Mako probably stuffed it there the last time they borrowed my car. For once, I'm thankful to clean up their mess. Grabbing my *Homo Sweet Homo* key chain, I stab my house key into one end of the aluminum. I pry off the opposing end and I upturn my creation over a small, beeswax candle. The tea light is borrowed from the makeshift emergency kit that Mei made for me, years back.

When I first got my car, Mei was pissed. She called it a *betrayal to the biker movement*. She was a mechanic by trade but only worked on cars out of absolute necessity. All her spare time after work was spent at the feminist bike co-op. On weekends, she'd go wheat-pasting, putting up posters about the need for barriered bike lanes.

It took a full six weeks before she'd even accept a ride in my passenger seat. Only after she busted her ankle, trying to cart home a garbage bag of dumpster-dived vegan doughnuts, did she compromise her values in exchange for a lift to the laundromat. The name for Hillside House came from the fact that we lived at the very top of a very steep incline. Biking down to do our laundry wasn't so bad. Going back uphill? Not exactly an easy feat, especially with a compression wrap around your foot. Mei accepted a few more rides during her recovery period and a few weeks later, solidly on two feet, she knocked on my bedroom door. Without a word, she passed me a zippered handbag in which she'd packed a wind-up flashlight, miniature hammer and an orange tea light. A hand-stitched label on the cover called it *The Bike-Betrayer Disaster Kit*. We both had a good laugh about that.

The first candle is already burning low and stubby. It took a while to get the can balanced on top. The good news is, it's working. My car windows are already fogging from the ambient heat. Right now, this extra-small version of Buffy's homemade heater is all that stands between me and freezing to death on an empty country road.

The windows are sweating in a matter of minutes—or hours? My phone is off to conserve its battery life and without it, I've got no sense of time. I make a mental note to learn how to read constellations, for the next time I'm in this exact situation. I watch the drops of condensation slide into one another, lying with my seat back. I huddle in a pile of sweaters, scarves, socks, the entirety of my duffel bag splayed about into a makeshift nest.

When faced with such enclosing darkness, it's hard not to get existential. It feels a bit like I'm the only person left in the whole world right now. Maybe all those obnoxious evangelical preachers were right. The rapture came while I was stressing about my big queer feelings. Now I'm stuck here, waiting for whatever happens after everything ends.

I flick the lighter in my palm. Its flint wheel catches and I watch the flame dance for a few seconds, then die out. Fuel is getting low.

"Seems about right," I mutter to myself. "This is what I get for trying to do something. I should have just stayed at home."

And home is where exactly? I ask myself. My head and my heart have two different answers. I know the one I'd rather believe. Why was I in such a rush to leave? My reasoning is all fuzzy in retrospect, the way the stars look through the foggy lens of my windshield. I'd been hit with such an overwhelming urge to run, to race back to the safety of my shoebox apartment. Which itself started as a compromise, a second-best option after Hillside crumbled apart. And that house, too, was forged through loss—my childhood home, which had never held much childhood for me. A sister who hadn't been a sister. A father who hadn't been a dad.

Those early memories too painful to revisit, I sit instead inside dreamy recollections of Hillside House. I roll through a mental Rolodex of summer solstice parties, backyard potlucks, karaoke nights. They play out like scenes inside a snow globe, with me on the outside looking in. *Except.* Those years have all been tinted rose by nostalgia and heartbreak. But out here, with no distractions or niceties, the bitter truth is harder to keep at bay. I've always told myself the loss of that house was my fault. That's what everyone else believes too, no doubt. But long before that fateful vote, there were other signs. Cracks running through the home's already-shaky foundation.

Mei never managed to do her overnight dishes. No matter how many meetings we had, how many chore-charts and calendar reminders, she'd always slip back out of the habit. When we ended up with a wicked fruit-fly infestation, I took matters into my own hands. Every night, once all the others had gone to bed, I'd slip into the kitchen. Elbows-deep in dishwater, I'd scrub until my fingers pruned over. Then I'd scrub some more. I wasn't done until the bottom of the basin was fully visible. In the morning, everyone would wake up happy. That was a reward enough, for me.

Then Johanna got the idea to do a January Juice Cleanse. One of her favourite influencers was on a kick about it. The next thing we knew, she was dumping our communal groceries into the compost and proposing we all go in together on the trend as a New Year's resolution. Mako argued that cleanses were diet culture bull crap, toxic and fatphobic. Mei was more worried about the impacts on something called our *gut flora*, which I'd never even heard of. Mars was a fence-sitter, as to be expected—it's not easy to call out your own partner on her bullshit, though even he was pissed about the wasted food. I managed to talk Johanna out of the idea by simply pointing out we had no counter space for an automatic juicer. If she was serious about this plan, she'd have to make all the juice by hand. Just like that, she was suddenly back on board with solid foods and instead touting the importance of *intuitive eating*.

There was also plenty of that drama over Mako and me hooking up. I remember one particularly sweaty afternoon, Mars was prepping a dish to share with his D&D group. It was mid-summer and the preheated oven was turning our kitchen into a sauna. Mixing his vegan ricotta by hand, Mars turned to me and said, "Charlie, you two are like pickles and peanut butter."

"What's that supposed to mean?" I had asked, stirring the tomato sauce.

"You're both great on your own." In my mind's eye, his work apron sits loose around his neck; otherwise shirtless, top-surgery scars peek into view whenever he reaches for the spice rack. "Sometimes you can even be fun together, if you're feeling funky. But don't go tossing them in the oven and expect cookies to come out."

"But you and Johanna have been a couple for, like, forever." I flicked on the stovetop fan though I knew the dust vents were far too clogged to cut the heat. "How is that any different?"

Mars shook in a few fresh spices, then took the spoon from my hands to give a taste. "For one thing, me and Jo started dating before we all moved in together," he said, smacking his lips. "And we're for real committed to each other."

"What if Mako and I are serious too?" I pointed out. "You don't know."

"Except I do, because this is Mako we're talking about." By

then, he'd fetched some garlic from the garden and was dicing it. "I'm sure you'll have a fun honeymoon phase. But then you're in for a messy-ass breakup, the rest of us all mixed up in the middle. The whole house will end up going down in flames."

"You don't know that." Except he did. Maybe not in the way he saw it coming, but the house was doomed to fail. And I was going to be at the epicentre of its crash. He was right, too, about Mako. We were never meant to be a long-term thing. I don't know why I tried for so long to make them someone that they're just not.

Towards the end, every house meeting felt a long walk across a hot beach. We spent hours talking in circles, making broad statements. *Let's all check in more often this month,* and *Everyone try to give an extra 10 percent to their chores.* Sometimes we'd brainstorm ways to break out of our funk: *The group chat has been feeling so toxic, maybe we should make a new one?* or *What if we organize a neighbourhood picnic-giveaway-karaoke night?* Then we'd slide off to our separate rooms and vent on social media, vague-posting about how problematic *other people* can be.

After a few brief gurgles, the tea light falls dark. I'm alone in my car again, a sob rising in my throat. Hillside, as I remembered it, is rapidly unspooling. I pull at one thread, then another, trying desperately to knit this mess into something worth keeping. But it's not working. And it's like I'm losing my home, all over again.

I take a slow breath in. On the exhale, I sit up and stare at the sky. The clouds have pulled aside and let the stars reveal themselves. The moon rests, a sly smile on the horizon. Over the last few days, I've felt more alive than I have in years. Even at Hillside, I never felt so safe, so held. Buffy, Hayden—and Rainbow! Sweet Rainbow with all her big, brilliant feelings. They all hardly knew me, yet they shared their family meals, their long walks, their TV nights—hell, I even let them take me to church!

I find myself daydreaming about that cot in the closet they call a guest room. How the sun peeked in during the morning. I'm craving the sweet—sometimes crispy—taste of Hayden's home cooking. Laughing at Buffy's attempts to rally Rainbow and Wellesley for a walk. Miss Kiki, strolling along her cat highways; Mango tittering in his cage. That's what a life worth living feels like.

I dig out my phone and hold the power button. The screen flashes, five percent battery left. There can be no more idling. I've got to track down some reception—now or never. Squeezing into every layer of clothing I can find, it's not much but at least I won't immediately freeze. I pry open the driver's side door. A freezing wind rushes in, stealing the little heat I had left. Jaw set, I push out into the night. I keep my back against the wind as I march into the darkness.

My dimming lock screen teases the idea that I could call for help. If I even get a signal, I never got around to paying for CAA. At the time, it seemed a luxury. I could try Mako but, if they'd even answer, I'm not sure how I'd give directions. *I'm at the intersection of two empty cornfields, left of the moon. Can't miss it.* What if I tried Buffy? Or, maybe Hayden, if he's up late. *Who's to say they'd answer?* speaks a bitter voice in my heart. I shove it aside and tap the call button.

Before the first ring, my sneaker connects with a patch of hidden ice. Maybe the very same that drove my car off the road. Before the irony can hit me, the asphalt does—I whip around and land, hard. The air knocked from my chest. My lungs are burning. *My phone!* I grasp, desperately. *Where's my phone?* It's skittered a few feet away. The screen is dark.

I lie on the road, I don't know how long. The wind howls over me like a screaming train, running me flat. I want to cry but my tears are frozen. *What's the point of struggling anymore?* If anything, a good handful of folks would be relieved to see me go. To know we'll never awkwardly run into one another at the farmers market or a Pride social.

Just as I'm about to call it quits, something strange starts happening to my shadow. Its outline is growing long. A bright, white light is at my back. It's cascading on all sides. I didn't think dying would be this cliché. But that's not death coming for me. It's headlights.

Someone has pulled over a few paces back. Shadows step out of the vehicle and inspect the car that's pulled over to the side of the road. My car. I want to call out to them, the shadows. But my lips are cracked, mouth dry. I force myself to sit up.

"Here." My cry is quickly stolen by the wind. I try again. "I'm here!"

The figures look my way. A second later, they're rushing towards me. Warm arms pull me close. I know that smell, the softness of that skin. But I must be dreaming. How is it Buffy's face is smiling down at me? Tears are gushing down her cheeks. Hayden's voice is in my ear, telling me how glad they are to have found me. "Everything's going to be okay."

I believe him, as much as I believe anything right about now. If I died then at least I made it to my own personal heaven. The rapture's not looking so bad after all.

Chapter Seventeen

"Mako really contacted *every* Airbnb in Elmridge?" I pull my arms into the sleeves of the oversize T-shirt, on loan from Hayden. My own clothes are still half-soaked and hung up to dry in the bathroom. My back still aches from the fall earlier but Buffy brought me a warm compress, which has it feeling somewhat back to normal.

"To be fair, there are only about four in the whole town." Hayden reappears from the en suite bathroom with a brimming glass of water. I take it with a thanks. A deep, freezing cold lingers right down to my bones. "We were already on high alert, halfway out the door when we got the call."

"Not that you gave us much to go on." Buffy walks in, her arms full of extra pillows and fluffy blankets. She tosses the load of fresh linens onto the floor and starts sorting them into haphazard piles.

"The last message we got was that you were almost home," says Hayden, sitting cross-legged in the reading nook. Lines of worry are etched across his face. "But then you just never showed up. We didn't know what to think."

"Lucky Hayden remembered you don't like highway driving." Stripping the bed, Buffy whips off the duvet. "That got me thinking, when we were complaining about gas prices—I told you about that pit stop with the cheapest prices this side of the four hundred." She tosses aside a stray sock and it lands at my feet. I kick it into the closet. "But it was just an educated guess. We could have just as easily gone down any other road."

Hayden moves to help get the duvet into a new cover. "You had us really freaked."

Shoulders up, I slouch against the sliding closet door. "Couldn't have been that stressed out," I grumble. "Since you never texted me back."

"We did!" Buffy smacks a pillow to fluff it. "Didn't we?"

"I thought you—" Hayden gets caught up wresting with the corners of their duvet cover. "Okay," he huffs. "Clearly we've got some communication breakdowns going on."

"Agreed." Dropping my arms, I join Hayden in his efforts to locate all four corners of the duvet. Next up, we slide a fresh fitted sheet onto their king-size mattress; it's surprisingly easy, when there's three people all working together.

"Looking good." Buffy claps her hands in satisfaction. "Now. I think it's time we talked."

I take a step back from the edge of the bed. "I'm not really sure how to say this because I don't want to imply anything. Or risk messing with your marriage." Staring downward, I wiggle my toes in their mismatched socks. "And there's a good chance I've been completely misreading all these signals going on but, um." I hold my breath, like I'm about to jump off a high dive. And maybe I am. "Do you two realize you've *both* been hitting on me?"

"About that—" Buffy starts to explain.

Hayden jumps in, saying, "So, here's the thing."

They both pause and look to one another, having another one of those silent conversations. I clear my throat. "Either one of you want to finish that thought?"

Hayden tilts his chin. Buffy nods. "All right," she tells me. "After all the, shall we say, *miscommunications* going on tonight, Hayden and I had some time to talk."

"And I swear," says Hayden, "I thought Buffy had told you on one of your walks."

"But *I* figured you two must have gotten into it while cooking or something." Buffy sits herself at the edge of the bed, pressing down a crease in the sheets. "Then I didn't want to bring it up *again* and risk making you feel uncomfortable."

"Me, uncomfortable?" A weak laugh escapes me. "Never."

"We've been very aware you've been kind of stuck with us." Hayden scratches at the freckles on the back of his arm. "Which is why neither of us wanted to make the first move."

"First move?" I repeat, voice starting to crack. When did my mouth get so dry again? *Where did I put that water?*

Buffy flicks on the lamps on each bedside table. "Given all the power dynamics going on between us—you being our guest and all. There was a risk you'd have felt pressured into something you didn't really want." She turns out the overhead lights, the room cast into an orange glow.

"Then it dawned on us, you truly may not have known," Hayden explains. "But Charlie, we're polyamorous. You know that, right?"

The moment he says it, this room, the whole house, tilts slightly to the left. It all twirls and dips and then slots itself back into place in exactly the same spot. Except, of course, everything is now completely different.

"That…makes sense." My voice seems to come from somewhere far away. Still catching up from the world-jump, I guess. "I was starting to wonder if, maybe—but, I didn't want to assume." Pinching the bridge of my nose, I wait for the dizziness to subside. "I'm just not used to people being into me like that. Especially really cute people."

"Did you hear that?" Buffy shimmies up beside Hayden. "Charlie thinks we're *cute*."

"Well, yeah." He slides an arm around her hip. "Have you seen us?" When he turns to face me, there's a glint to his smile. "We're sorry for all the runaround. It doesn't help we're both a bit out of practice."

"I'll say." Buffy teases her fingers over Hayden's chest, playing with the chest hair that pokes at the neckline of his shirt. "It's been years since either of us had the time, or energy, to seek out a new playmate."

"A *playmate*?" The word slips out of me before I can even stop to think about it.

"Mmm-hmm." Buffy asks, "Any chance you would be interested?"

Oh my god yes. A million times yes. More than anything in the world, yes. "Uh, yeah." I bite back a growing smile. "I think I could get into that."

I can practically hear Mako in my head, warning me about falling into something casual again. When we were together, I was always wanting something more. Something that felt *real*. But with Hayden and Buffy, it's different. They've already got each other and weirdly, that doesn't bother me. If anything, it makes this easier. No expectations, no big questions about who we could become to one another. All we have is this time together and I don't want to waste it.

Before I rush into all that, though, there's something I should probably tell them. "I really meant to come back tonight," I say, shuffling my socks on the carpet. "I was actually parked out front and—this is gonna sound creepy. But I was kind of watching you, in the windows."

"Ha!" Buffy covers her mouth with a gasp. "Charlie Dee, you little voyeur!"

Hayden chuckles, "I didn't know you were kinky like that."

"I'm not!" A jolt of excitement through my stomach. "Well, maybe a little." I start to flush, heat climbing up my neck. "I texted about coming in, but then I saw you both read the message and not even try to reply. And I was thinking like, maybe you weren't so keen to have me back after all."

"Oh, bud." Hayden steps towards me. "Clearly we haven't inspired enough faith in you."

"No, it's my fault." I step backwards. "I overreacted. My buddy Mako called right around the same time. We kind of had a fight and—anyway, it doesn't matter."

"You sure about that?" Buffy asks with a tilt of her chin. "Seems like it maybe matters quite a bit."

"For what it's worth, I remember you messaging." Hayden offers his hand. "It was right around when we were getting Rainbow ready for her sleepover at Uncle Franny's."

Buffy tiptoes after him. "She was doing that one-more-thing routine. Times ten. It was a whole thing."

"Oh." Delicately, I let Hayden's fingers slip around my wrist and draw me close. "That uh… That makes sense." Buffy slides around my back and starts nibbling on my neck. A shiver runs through me. My breath shudders between words. "So, she's out of the house tonight, then?"

"You know it." Hayden whispers into my cheek.

"So…" Buffy's voice is in my ear. "Why don't you come to bed already?"

I allow myself to be lowered onto an expanse of fluffy pillows and soft blankets. Buffy's fingertips play along my jawline, drawing a path to my lips. "May I?" she asks.

"Uh-huh," is all I can manage to say.

Her lips meet with mine and for a few glorious seconds, time slows. I soak in every piece of this moment. The scent of her, the heat of her mouth. Our noses press together and she giggles into my lips.

I can hardly believe this is happening. My mind races, reading layers into her every tiny movement. Does she want me closer? Are my hands in the right place? Part of me wants to stop and ask a thousand questions, what she likes and doesn't like, what we're going to be to each other after all of this. But then, we come apart. Buffy backs away and I start to follow. Then, there's Hayden. Strong arms, yet his touch is so delicate. Running my hand through the roughness of his beard, I nudge him towards me. When we kiss, his moustache tickles my upper lip. Our tongues spill against each other. I come away panting. So does he.

Hayden still holds my wrist. "How is this feeling so far?"

"Really good," I answer, catching my breath.

"Did you want to take a break?" asks Buffy. "We don't have to take things any further than you want to."

I grip Hayden by his shoulder and nod to Buffy. "Let's keep going."

Without another word between us, we fall back into one another. Hot mouths, the nibbling of kisses along earlobes and chins. I arch my back as Hayden bites into my neck. At the same time, Buffy is teasing at the hemline of my T-shirt. "May I?" she whispers. I nod, enthusiastically.

Her fingers slip below the fabric, teasing at the softness of my stomach, climbing higher. Every touch between us feels like a lightning bolt. My pulse runs wild and I squeeze my knees, building anticipation. When she finally reaches my chest, my nipples are already hard. She toys with them, pinching and twisting. I buck and whine and beg for more. Lifting my arms, I let her tug my shirt over my head. Cold air meets my naked skin. All the more pleasant, the warmth of her mouth as it meets mine again.

"I think they like that, Buff." Hayden laughs.

"You think so?" She smiles up at him. "But love, you know how Charlie also likes to watch."

Straddling overtop me, they share their own passionate make-out session. Propping up on my elbows, I admire the ease with which they play with each other. Buffy runs her hands through Hayden's hair, grabbing a fistful of it. She guides him to her neck and without missing a beat, he nips along the curve of her throat. Arm around her back, he draws up her shirt to unclip her bra. Her shirt drawn halfway up, I spy the underside of her ample breasts. Eyes fluttering, she spies me ogling them. A smile edges across her open mouth. She whispers something to Hayden. In a moment, they're both back on me again.

Hayden buries his face into the crook of my shoulder, kissing down my chest, along my waist. Strong arms grasp me by the hips and slide me towards the edge of the bed. Fingers tug at my waistband, sending shivers down to my toes. "Can these go?" he asks.

"Yes," I whimper. Buffy's tongue is playing around my areolas. "You can—" The rest of my words are caught in my throat. Hayden draws my pants over my ankles and lets them drop onto the floor, leaving me in just my boxer briefs.

Softly, he pulls his mouth along my inner thigh, humming into the hardness between my legs. "Mm." He holds there, looking up at me. "You're stunning. Do you know that?"

I blush. Raising my hips, I let him peel off the very last layer that stands between us.

Hayden's stubbly beard is rough on the soft skin below my stomach. His lips move along the curve of my pelvis, seemingly in no rush. He slowly edges closer. I shiver beneath the flicks of his tongue, fighting the urge to buck my hips, grab his head and press him exactly where I want him to go. Instead, I reach back and grab at Buffy, bracing her for support.

I've managed to slide down the bed, close to Buffy's legs. I look up and find she has stripped down to the nude. From the curve of her stomach up to her collarbone, she's decorated with a garden of tattoos. Thorny vines of a rosebush, interwoven with a burst of orange daylilies, layered into the thin lines of daffodils. The work is so stunning, I almost want to stop and ask what each one means. Almost.

Straddling my face, Buffy takes a beat to meet my eyes. I answer her unspoken question by parting my lips for her. She inhales quickly, edging her hips. Her nectar is sweet, and just a little tangy. I don't want to miss a single drop. At the same time, Hayden finally takes the whole of me into his mouth. I let out a groan and Buffy pushes down harder.

The three of us push and pull against one another. I catch a glimpse of Hayden, pants around his ankles. Mouth still busy, his fingers pump a short, thick cock. Behind that, juice from his front hole is dripping down his legs. My tongue slides along Buffy's clit, deeper into her folds. She writhes on top of me. I drown in the ecstasy of her pleasure.

"I'm—I'm getting close!" Buffy squeaks, writhing on me.

"Me too." My words are muffled against her.

"Oh, I've already gone," Hayden laughs from between my thighs. "But I could—"

Buffy cries out, arching her back. I am soaked, her essence dribbling down my cheeks. I follow shortly after, legs clamped around Hayden. He groans and I'm pushed over by the rumbling vibration of him on me. The three of us rock and groan and quiver. Falling into the bed, we fall asleep as a sweaty, sticky heap. Before long, Hayden is snoring. Buffy leans over to grab a cup of water off her nightstand.

"You good?" She offers me a sip.

I take it and gulp down half the glass. "*So* good." And I mean it, more than I think I ever have before. The butterflies in my stomach are all exhausted but they keep fluttering away. The only thing that really scares me is that I could go to sleep and find out this was all a dream after all. That's why, long after

Buffy has put on her face mask and curled up with a pillow between her knees, I stay sitting in bed. In the dark, the popcorn
ceiling looks like starry sky. I count each one and offer thanks
for granting a wish I never dared to ask.

Chapter Eighteen

Buffy's hand rests on my chest. Hayden is still snoring, spooning my waist. My heart races. I hardly got any sleep last night yet I feel completely energized. The last twenty-four hours have blurred together but at least I know it wasn't a dream.

Slipping my way out from in between them, I let Hayden and Buffy curl up with each other. I find my underwear beneath the bed. On tiptoe, I make my way downstairs and get the coffee brewing. I've soon got the skillet warming. I'm sure Hayden won't mind me borrowing his apron. After everything that happened last night, I'm hardly in the mood to spoil my good mood with a grease burn. The toaster pops—I've already got a couple slices of gluten-free set aside for Hayden, and a wedge of rye with marmalade for Buffy. Saving myself for last, I spread both pieces with equal parts jam and peanut butter.

Hands slide around my waist. Buffy pulls me to her chest. "There you are."

"Don't worry." I let her kiss my cheek. "I didn't run away again."

"I wasn't worried." Her nose presses into the crook of my neck. "Mm." She deeply inhales. "What are you cooking?"

I crack a pair of eggs into the pan and listen to them sizzle. "Just a bit of breakfast. You two looked like you could use a sleep-in."

"Thank you." Buffy gives one last nip down my shoulder.

She's wearing only one of Hayden's T-shirts and a pair of ankle socks. It's hard not to stare at her perfect ass as she bends over to poke through the fridge. From the way she wiggles her hips, I get the sense that she likes to make me look.

Pulling out a jug of orange juice, Buffy pours herself a glass. "Last night was incredible."

"Okay, right?" I gesture with the spatula. "I was like, is it just me or are we *super* hot together?"

Buffy sips her drink with a smirk on her lips. "Definitely not just you."

"When you had your legs—"

"And you did that thing with your tongue?" She moans just like she did last night. "Oh my *god*. I thought I was gonna die!"

I nudge the edges of the pan, debating whether to make this a scramble. "You and Hayden are majorly sexy together. Like, you could do porn."

"Only if you would be our audience." Buffy rests against the kitchen table, head back. "You have no idea how badly I needed that." She sighs. "Just one carefree night."

That's all it was, then. I can be okay with that, I decide while sprinkling a handful of green onions onto the eggs. *I am okay with that.* "Seems like it's been a long time since either of you got to relax."

"I promise, we've been trying. But with a kid, and Hayden trying to find work in academia, and us trying to make a life out here..." She lists out each of their responsibilities on her fingers before throwing up her hands to declare, "It's just not practical!"

I add some shredded cheese that I found in the veggie crisper. Because of course that's where they keep their dairy products. "Not to mention trying to recover from your burnout." I sneak a look towards her. "Hayden told me."

"I know." She nods. "He told me you two talked about it."

I prod at the eggs, testing their yolks. "You know, I actually remember when you posted that you'd be leaving social media. Then how you cancelled all your upcoming shows." I twist the salt shaker and some ground pepper for good measure. "I thought you were just gearing up for something even bigger. Like, you'd come back with a bang, revealing that you just spent the last few years—I don't know, living in a tree house to protest old-growth deforestation. Or a submarine, to make a statement about oil spills."

"You're not the only one who had ideas like that." Buffy traces her socks across the kitchen tiles. "Sometimes people get a hold of my email. They ask when the *big reveal* is coming, poke for hints. I don't get back to them." She stops with one toe pointed, framed by the rising sunlight. "It's been five years of this, now. And I'm *just* getting myself back to something that feels like normal. I'm trying to ease myself in, taking small gigs—"

"Like the one back at the office," I point out.

"Exactly. But I still end up so wiped, and jittery. And oh my god, *irritable*." She laughs to herself. The curls of her hair dance along her shoulders. "I get Hayden to come help, mostly because I don't trust myself to drive back."

I click on the stovetop fan. "That's got to be really hard."

"It can be," says Buffy. "But it feels good to be making a difference again. Even if it's just a small one." She turns to me, cast in a golden halo. "Thanks for listening. It's good to talk about this stuff with someone."

I set the element on low. "You don't talk about it with Hayden?"

She shakes her head. "He's worried about me enough as it is."

"I get that." Stepping closer, I rest my hand over hers. "But also, he might be able to handle more than you think."

"You two talking about my love handles?" Hayden steps downstairs in his boxers. The soft plump of his stomach hangs just over their waistband.

"Maybe." Buffy smirks and greets him with a kiss. I head back to the stove, checking on our progress. Whites firm, yellows soft—just about ready.

"Charlie, I'm gearing up for a butt slap!" Hayden comes up behind me. "You down?"

"Slap away!" I bend and stick out my backside. The soft smack of his open palm against my tighty-whities leaves my skin all tingly. "Oh!"

"You like that, eh?" Hayden rubs his hands. "You know, we could have some real good times together."

"I think we already did." I turn and draw him closer with my finger. "But I'm down for more, if you are."

He takes my invitation, bracing me against the kitchen counter. His knee slips between my legs. "I'd like to kiss you now."

"I'd like to kiss you back." I cup my arms around his back and meet his lips with mine.

Soon, Buffy joins us. Both are nipping on my neck. "Does this feel nice?" she asks with a flick of her tongue against my ear. Her fingers are working their way down my chest. I groan and she works her hand lower. "How about, here?"

"Oh don't—yes." I shudder.

"Do you want to stop?" asks Hayden, easing off.

"No." I let out a whimper. "Keep going." Hayden lifts me by the hips and shoves me onto the counter while Buffy spreads my legs. Before either of them can take things further, the doorbell rings.

"No!" Buffy cries. "*Please* don't tell me that's Frances with our kid."

Hayden puts a finger to his lips and goes to check it out. "It sure doesn't look like him." He looks back at Buffy. "I don't know *who* that is."

Reluctantly, I slide off the counter and peek outside. "I do." Swinging open the door, I ask, "Mako, what in the world are you doing here?"

"Shit!" Mako looks me over, in my wrinkled apron and bare legs. They shove my chest and stamp inside, "Charlie, you absolute *asshole!*"

There's a tap at my shoulder. "Did you want to introduce us to your friend?" asks Buffy.

"What the hell are you doing here?" Mako shouts. A cold wind slams the door shut behind them.

"Where else would I—oh." I clench my teeth. "I never called, did I?"

"No!" Mako throws off their coat and starts pacing. "*Nobody* called or texted or told me anything!"

"I thought you followed up with Mako, after we found the car?" Hayden mutters to Buffy.

She shrugs. "You said you were on it."

"I meant—" He sighs and scratches at his beard. "We really *do* have to work on our communication."

"So you drove all the way here, just to make sure I was okay?" I step around Mako to peer back out the window. "Whose car is that?"

I bet its Johanna's. She was working on her licence when we spoke last. *Or maybe Mei finally caved and became a bike-betrayer too.*

"My coat-check buddy leant it to me." Mako shrugs.

I whistle through my teeth. "Must be a pretty good buddy."

"You could say that." They kick the snow off their boots and give me a sorry look. "Dude, about last night—I should have given you a heads-up, or just not gone at all."

I shake my head. "It's all good. I know you're all on good terms, it just sucks that I'm not."

"It does suck!" Mako prods their finger into my shoulder, "And for what it's worth, you are *way* more fun to hang with." Their eyes dart towards Hayden and Buffy, a smirk rising on their lips. "Guess I didn't need to rush out here after all, though. You seem pretty well taken care of."

"I'm going to go put some pants on," Buffy excuses herself.

"Right. Um." I smooth out my apron, as if that would make a difference now. "Mako, this is Hayden." I nod back towards the stairs. "And that's Buffy."

Hayden wipes his hands on his shorts and waves hello. "Care to join us for breakfast?"

Smoke trails the kitchen ceiling, spouting from the pan on the stove. Looks like I'm the one who got distracted, this time. "Maybe we should go out to eat," I suggest.

Elmridge may not have a bustling downtown, but they do have a decent coffee shop. The Red Tangerine is quiet from the outside, sidewalk still slushy from the dump of snow this week. Inside its foggy windows, a bustling scene is underway. The aroma of fresh espresso and baked goods wafts through the air. Lush, green plants hang in every corner, breathing life into the place. A bright display shelf shows off the many sandwiches and sweets they've got on offer, almost all of which are citrus-themed. Background chatter floats all around as the round tables—all designed to look like orange slices—are absolutely packed with customers. We're lucky to have found an open table when we came in, though we had to borrow a couple chairs when Rainbow and her uncle Frances showed up.

"I just don't get it." Hayden scowls at the foldout menu. He flips it over for the third time. "How many times have I written into the suggestion box—they need more gluten-free options!" He leans over to peer at the diner's front counter, reading through their chalkboard of daily specials. "At least have a good soup-and-salad combo going."

"Got it!" A tiny fist appears from underneath the table, a yellow crayon in its grasp. Rainbow clambers back onto her seat.

"Nice one." I pass her colouring book back to her. "For a minute there, I was worried your unicorn wouldn't get a mane."

"It's not a *unicorn*." Rainbow points to the lizard-like wings she's added to the back of her creation. "It's a uni-dactyl."

"Are you sure it's not a pteracorn?" Hayden leans over for a better look. "You might want to double-check." Meanwhile, Buffy deftly snatches the red among Rainbow's crayons before it, too, can take a diving leap off our table.

"You're kidding!" Mako smacks the table, rattling our drinks. "*You* know Avery Starling?"

"I played junior softball with her, three summers in a row," says Frances, delicately stabilizing his tangerine mojito— today's special. "Though that wasn't the name she went by back then." He thoughtfully sips his drink. "We were both *major* closet-cases."

Mako rests their chin in one hand. "Wow. What a small gay world."

"You don't know the half of it." Frances twists the tip of his fuzzy moustache.

"The fruit salad is gluten-free, Hayden." Buffy scribbles a note on a paper napkin. "You had that last time and you liked it." Making a quick round to double-check she's got everything just right, she passes the list to Rainbow. "Honey, this is our order. Think you can run it to that nice waitress over there?"

"Yeah!" Rainbow scrambles from her seat and dashes to the front counter. Buffy watches her carefully, fidgeting with one of the crayons. She shifts her knee under the table to gently press against mine.

"Gosh, you make me miss the city." Frances wistfully sighs, stirring the straw of his drink. "I should get out there more often, catch up with some old friends."

"You really should." Mako's brows are raised as their gaze

travels from Frances's chiselled jawline to the bursting outline of his pecs as they strain the buttons of his shirt. "And hey, if you wanted to get together, grab a couple drinks…"

"Can you *not*?" I groan and cover my face. To my left, Hayden's hand sneaks onto my lap and gives a tiny squeeze.

"What?" they whine. "If you get to have a flirty time in small-town-nowhere, why can't I?"

"Shh!" I glance to Rainbow, who, blissfully, is fully distracted by the dessert display. Her nose is pressed up against the glass. There's a distinctive trail of mouth-breathing condensation.

"Oh, who cares?" Mako waves off my concern. "You're having fun for once—just own it!"

"I like this one," says Frances in a stage whisper. "Can we keep them?"

"Hey, if you've got a spare room in that rectory, I'd consider it!" Prodding Frances in his shoulder, Mako laughs in the way they do when they're *so* not joking. "After a week at your place, Charlie, I'm *not* looking forward to heading back to mine." They stick out their tongue and fake a gag. "The pack of heter-bros I live with can hardly even pick their laundry up off the bathroom floor, let alone stick to a chore wheel."

"And *that's* the reason I left." Frances snaps his manicured fingers. "You never get any privacy when you're all sandwiched together like that. All that constant noise and smog and condos going up all over." He shudders.

"Not to mention the rent." I nurse my second coffee of the morning. A splash of oat milk and a spoonful of brown sugar, just like Hayden makes at home. It's growing on me. "Seriously, I'm starting to think you're all on to something, hiding out in a small town like this."

"Unfortunately, the cost of living is going up out here too." Buffy refills her mug with a small orange teapot the waitress left on our table. "That's part of why we ended up doing the whole Airbnb thing, to keep up with the cost of living."

"Has it been helping?" I ask.

Buffy tilts her head while Hayden waves his hand in midair. "Elmridge is more of an *up-and-coming* tourist destination," he explains. "So far we've only had...one person come to stay." He points his coffee spoon at me.

"I was your *first*?" I grip his forearm, bursting with giddy laughter. "That's so cute!"

"Get a room!" Mako crinkles their nose at us.

My cheeks start to burn. "I didn't mean it like that."

"I think they're cute," says Frances with a wink. He gulps down the last of his drink and waves towards the nearest wait-staff for a refill. "And while it would have been fun to have you all sleep over at the rectory, like we'd talked about, I think this little rom-com you've all stumbled into has been much more fun."

"Anyway." Hayden rolls his eyes and pokes at his phone. "My buddy with a tow truck found your car. She wants to know if she should drive it out to our place, or to her shop in Toronto."

"An excellent question." Frances leans on the table, tilting it slightly. "What's the story Charlie, you live here now or what?"

"I, what—?" I stammer. "Of course not."

"I'll take the lease to your apartment, if it's up for grabs," mumbles Mako.

"You know you're welcome to stay with us as long as you want to." Buffy rubs my shoulder. "But we also understand if you're ready to get back to life as usual."

Hayden pats my leg. "Even I hate to say it, but ghosting your day job seems maybe not the best call. You've still got rent to pay."

When Frances's mojito arrives, Mako orders one of their own as well. "And a cat to feed," they chime in. "Who misses you, by the way."

"I know but—" *But what?* They've all got good points. This was only ever supposed to be a short-term trip. I've already overstayed, now by a full week. "I'm just not sure I'm ready to jump back into everything."

Crossing his arms, Frances leans back in his chair. As he lets go, the table pops back up, plates and cutlery clattering. "Chuck—can I call you Chuck?"

"I always do," says Mako.

"Let me tell you a story." Frances folds his hands and for a minute, I think he's about to try and lead us in a prayer. "Both my folks were ministry people. My granddad, he was a preacher. I spent every Sunday morning sitting in a church pew and I couldn't stand a second of it." He sucks his teeth, picking at a speck of orange pulp. "I swore to myself, soon as I was eighteen, I was outta here. And that's exactly what I did." He grins. "You remember, Hay-day."

"It was all you talked about." Hayden chuckles. "If I remember correctly, you swore the only way you'd end up in a church again was if you died before your folks. Because they'd drag you back there before putting you six feet under."

"So morbid," whispers Mako. "I love it." They bite down on the straw of their drink.

"Sounds about right," says Frances, stroking his beard. There are still a few flecks of glitter in there. "For a long while, I just kept running. Gig to gig, city to city. But I learned, no matter where you go, there's always bullshit waiting for you. And the more I tried to fight it, the more I knew where I was supposed to really be."

Dimples rise on Buffy's cheeks. "Thanks for the sermon, Franny."

"Almost finished." He taps his nose and flashes his smile at her. "My point is, if someplace is where you're really supposed to go, you'll end up back there." He leans across the table to straighten the collar of my button-up. "Until then, there's no harm in taking a break to make sure it's what works for you."

"Order up!" The woman at the front counter waves our table number.

"I'll get it!" Rainbow hops from the display case and starts reaching for the dishes as they're set out for pickup. "I'll get it!"

"Let Mommy help you, honey!" Buffy scrambles from her seat. Hayden hurries after and they come back with arms loaded with fresh-baked goods, hot soups and loaded sandwiches. We're all more than ready to dig in.

"It's been awesome having you around, Charlie. Seriously." Hayden unwraps a muffin labelled *GF, DF, V.* He shares a piece with Rainbow but it crumbles before she can even take a bite. "But also we're not going anywhere."

"Agreed," says Buffy. "Besides, you know where we live."

My own reflection stares back at me from the depths of my coffee cup. Even with all their promises, I know there's no guarantee something like last night will ever happen again. But maybe that was enough. I guess it'll have to be. "Okay. Mako, mind if I catch a ride home with you after this?"

They down their mojito in one gulp and smack their lips with satisfaction. "I thought you'd never ask."

Chapter Nineteen

One time, when I was around twelve, I snuck out with my sister's skates. She always had the better pair between us—our parents said it was because she actually made use of them. Meanwhile, mine always spent the whole winter at the back of the shoe rack, gathering dust.

It was a crisp morning, snow still fresh. The dinky ice rink down our street had yet to be resurfaced by the community centre that haphazardly managed its maintenance. There were lines and cuts layered over one another from the dozen or so other skaters that had taken advantage of last night's free skate.

Silver blades gleaming in the early sun, I laced on my sister's skates as tight as they would go. I'd layered on two pairs of socks but it still was not enough. My feet were swimming in them. But there was no turning back.

Waddling across the rubber mats, through the push door, I gripped the sides of the rink. I did a couple laps that way before bracing myself against the wall for one last firm shove. If anyone had been around to see me, it might have looked like

I was trying to take flight, arms flailing at my sides. I stayed upright, forcing myself to carve the skates against the ice. Even if I wobbled and tripped and nearly twisted both my ankles. I was determined to circle the rink, at least once.

When I fell—because, of course, I fell—I didn't cry. I just lay still on the ice for a long, long while. I listened to the whistle of the wind while the cold sank into my bones. Staring up at an unforgiving sky, I knew no one was coming for me. Eventually, I crawled myself back off the ice and hobbled my way home. If my sister noticed the melting snow on her skates, she never said a thing.

That's how it feels to be back. Like trying to cross thin ice, wearing skates two sizes too big.

Everything is so much louder than I remember. Wetter, too. The so-called *storm of the century* coated the city for a couple of days. Then it melted, froze and melted again. The sidewalks remain slick with uneven ice while melting piles of brown slush line the roads.

Fat drops of freezing rain fall hard against the pavement. A man in a tight suit pushes past me through the Monday morning rush. His fancy shoes skid on an unseen patch of ice and his shoulder smacks into another pedestrian, a young woman in a long black coat. She shoves him off and keeps shuffling down the street. Neither looks up from their phone. To be fair, nor do I. I'm busy, scrolling down through my latest messages.

Buffy: Miss you already, beautiful.

Buffy: Can I call you beautiful?

Hayden: How about Dapper. Darling? Dazzling!

Buffy: Are you just looking through the 'D' section in the dictionary?

Hayden: No...

Hayden: I am using my Thesaurus app.

I scroll through the earlier messages in our newly formed group chat. Hayden has already sent a series of pictures: the morning sun as viewed from their kitchen window; a self-portrait of Rainbow as a magical witch-cat (or possibly a cat-witch); a close-up of Wellesley's sleeping snoot. A moment later, Buffy chastises him for spamming the chat when he should be working on his course prep for the upcoming semester. But she also likes every picture, reacting with little purple hearts. So far, it looks like they're making good on their promise. Maybe what we had won't be forgotten so quickly, after all.

"Hassan, how the heck are you?" I stomp my way into the CMM basement with a huge grin on my face. "Feels like it's been ages."

"Hey, looks who's back!" Hopping up from his desk, Hassan claps me on the shoulder. "I was starting to wonder if we'd see you again."

I shake off my coat and toss it over the side wall of my cubicle. "You know I could never leave you all high and dry like that," I laugh. "I'd at least give you a chance to throw me a surprise *goodbye* party."

While the city might feel unfamiliar to me now, the CMM office hasn't changed a bit. The bright lights still hurt my eyes and the photocopier is still jammed from last week. But there is something comforting about seeing the same old carpet stains, squeaky chairs, water damage on the ceiling panels. Maybe it's just the fact that now, this is more than just my office. It's the place where Buffy, Hayden and I first met. With easy strides, I head towards the office kitchen. I think I'll start my day with a fresh cup from the communal coffeepot. "Good morning, Aditya!"

"Morning," Aditya mumbles back. Hunched over at the break room table, she's busy typing on her phone.

Hassan eyes me over as I splash a heaping helping of cream and sugar into my cup. "You feeling okay?"

"Never better." I draw a long sip from my mug. The beans here have never tasted so good. "How's things at home, with the fiancé?"

Hassan's eyes sparkle with excitement. "We're so great!" He claps. "We just spent the whole weekend shopping for our wedding wear. I'm thinking of getting a custom piece—do you think a flower crown would be too much?"

"Not for you." I raise my mug to cheers him. "I say go for it. It's your day!" Leaning back on my heels, I sneak a peek towards Angie's office. Its mirrored walls are layered with dust and the door has been left ajar. "What's going on there?" I ask. "Still no sign of her?"

"No." Augustine appears, standing at the sink. She rinses out the emptied coffeepot. "She has not turned off her out-of-office auto-reply, either. All my emails keep bouncing back."

"I've had luck on Slack." Hassan shrugs. "She's still handing out work. Just not here to oversee it."

I get busy replacing the coffee filter. "Where do you think she's at?"

Aditya sits up, slipping her phone onto her lap. "I heard she's at an exclusive spa out in Banff, rubbing elbows with richie-riches. Maybe trying to rake in new donors?"

"What if she's been skimming money off the top of CMM?" Hassan suggests. "She could have run off to some tropical island—she could've programmed a chatbot to give us all busy-work until we figure it out!"

"That seems unlikely," says Augustine, dryly. "I've been watching the numbers. There's hardly enough funds in to justify a scheme like that."

My phone buzzes in the breast pocket of my shirt. I peek at

the screen, on the off chance it's Angie somehow weighing in on her own disappearance. I wouldn't put it past her to have set up this whole mystery just to see how we'd react when not under constant supervision. But rather than Angie's bespectacled profile photo, my dad's face scowls back at me instead. It's the third time he's called this morning. I silence it. The question of Emma's wedding still hangs over my head and I'm hardly in the mood to be interrogated about it. Besides, there are bigger things going on right now.

"Since when do you *watch the numbers*?" I ask Augustine as she pours in the water for a fresh pot.

"When the finance department was reduced, I took it on myself to double-check our balance sheets." She looks up and finds us all staring. "I've got a degree in labour economics."

Then why are you working here, of all places? I wonder. *And in IT?* Maybe I really should join Hassan and all of them for post-work bubble tea. It could maybe even be fun to learn a little more about these people I'm around all day. "Well, all I can confirm is, she's not in Elmridge." I finish off my drink and rinse out the mug. "The town's just not big enough—I would have run into her."

Aditya narrows her eyes at me. "But isn't that *exactly* what someone would say if they *were* covering for her?" she points out. "Now I'm thinking that's where she is for sure."

I start to stammer. "But—I really didn't—"

"We're just messing with you, Charlie." Hassan shoves my shoulder. "It's good to have you around, again." He beams with that sunshine smile to me, and I find myself returning it. "Well, Angie or no, I'm going to get my day started."

"Same here," says Augustine. The rest of us mutter in agreement as we shuffle back to the bustle of the office floor.

Aditya stops short at the entrance to the break room. "And just who is that supposed to be?" She points towards a narrow man in a dark navy suit. Hands behind his back, he appears to be inspecting the artwork and awards posted on our walls.

"Perhaps we're getting audited," suggests Augustine. I'm inclined to think the same, until he turns.

"Dad?"

"You can't just show up at my work like that." I slump my way into the booth. Its faux-leather seating crinkles and groans.

"I wanted to try your apartment." Dad lowers his glasses to the bottom of his nose, scanning the tiny printout menu. "But Mako said I'd have better luck at the office."

"Since when do you talk to Mako?" I shift in my seat, trying to get comfortable.

He flips the page over. There's a QR code on the back. "We're Facebook friends," he mutters.

Of course you are. My seatback whines as I push against the table. It's going to be a long night.

At least Dad let me pick the restaurant. I agreed to meet up after work, if only to get him out of the office. That was, of course, before Hassan jumped in and insisted on giving a quick tour. Even Augustine seemed mildly interested in our unexpected visitor, chatting with him about some of our IT systems. I doubt my father had any clue what she was talking about but he seemed at least nice about it. Apparently, folks in the coal mines are desperate for anything to break up the day. Maybe that's a side effect of Angie's long absence. I did try to contact her, too, throughout the day but only got more of the same— one-word replies, if that. No news as to where she's been or when she's coming back.

Under the soft glow of the exposed Edison lights that decorate Fisticuffs Eatery, he looks thinner than I remember. The little hair that remains on his head runs thin and wispy. His bony arms hardly fill the sleeves of his sharp navy suit. Even his tie is skinny. In person, he's much less intimidating than the man who hangs at the corners of my childhood memories. But maybe he just wasn't around enough for me to form a good mental picture.

"Is this all they have for drinks?" He scowls at the palm-size page.

I point to the white square on the back. "You've got to scan that thing with your phone. It'll pull up their full listing."

"Your generation and technology." He tsks and tosses the menu aside, waving down one of the servers. "Always making everything more complicated."

"It's not more—here, I'll just do it for you." I pull out my phone. There are already more messages in my group chat with Hayden and Buffy. All I want to do is get out of here and read through all of them. But instead, I scan the code and pull up the restaurant's app. *I don't know why I even bother,* I think to myself. *We both know what he's going to order.*

Arms crossed, he watches me scroll for a few seconds. "Do they have a whiskey sour?"

"Already on it." I tap the button to order and add an Old Fashioned for myself.

Our drinks come quickly, handed to us by a server dressed in all black. They've got bright green hair and piercings poking out from every visible part of their body. I thank them with a polite smile. My dad stares openly, all the way until they've walked back into the kitchen.

We cycle through the standard small talk. Recent weather, how his flight went (he rode business class yet he still complains about the legroom), how long he's in town. Outside, rain drapes down the restaurant's long windows. People hurry past in broad umbrellas, getting splashed by passing cars. Seems like the snowstorm has traded itself in for an early spring.

Our drinks arrive, along with a couple appetizers. I dig into a tray of dumplings that arrived with a dark, tangy sauce. Dad nibbles on a bowl of shrimp-chips. "Your workplace seems…"

He smacks his lips, searching for the word on his tongue. "Pro-ductive. And very centrally located."

"That's all true." *And all perfectly vague.* I spin the ice in my drink. I'm two-thirds through it and we haven't even got the main course yet.

"It sounds like you're doing good work." Dad pokes at the chips, ignoring the peanut sauce they came with. "That gentle-man who showed me around, he told me about how you help people. Some kind of phone line, yes?"

"Used to be." I crunch down on another dumpling. At least the food is good.

"Why didn't you tell me you got the assistant manager posi-tion?" he asks. "That's quite impressive, at your age."

"Dad, I'm thirty," I remind him.

He mutters into his drink, "I know that."

Soft blues plays through the restaurant speakers. Every few minutes, Uber Eats and DoorDash drivers arrive soaked from the rain. They grab large paper bags off the counter and then hurry back to their e-bikes and idling cars. I watch them come and go. After what feels like an endless minute of awkward si-lence, I admit the truth. "I guess I just didn't think you'd be all that interested."

"Well, I am," he insists. "You should celebrate your accom-plishments."

"Thanks." I knock back what's left of my drink. "What about you? What's with all the travelling for work lately—I thought you were supposed to be retired."

"I'm just wrapping things up with a few of my clients." He adjusts one of his cuff links, its polished silver glimmering even in the low light. "Once that's done, I'll step back from the practice."

"That's what you said the last time I saw you," I point out. "What was that, two years ago now?"

He blinks up, seeming genuinely surprised. "Has it really been that long?"

Silence hangs between us once again, punctuated by the shuffling of plates and drinks on nearby tables. A family in the corner is trying desperately to get their toddler to sit in a high chair. I smirk as I watch one of the dads make silly faces, cracking up his kid long enough to get the straps clicked on.

"I've been wanting to talk to you." Dad folds his napkin over once, then twice. "It's about your sister."

"I know, I know. The wedding with Bentley." *I still can't believe she's marrying that guy.* His name makes him sound like some kind of schnauzer. I hear he's actually a well-off pharmacist. I'm sure Mom and Dad love that for her—their doctor daughter marrying one of her own. "I'll get to the RSVP this week, I swear."

"You may want to hold off on that." He adjusts his glasses. They make his eyes so big, it's like he's peering out from inside a fishbowl. "From what I've heard, they are postponing. Apparently, Emma is thinking of leaving Edmonton."

"What about her practice?" I ask. "And Bentley?"

He shakes his head. "I was wondering if you might know what's going on with her."

"Why would I?" I stifle a laugh. "Ask her yourself!"

"I would." He clears his throat and takes another sip. "But she answers my calls even less frequently than you do."

"Oh." The rest of our food arrives. An array of skewers, grilled chicken and savory mushrooms, designed for sharing. Dad doesn't lift a finger. Once the server is out of earshot, I mumble, "I'm sorry. I could probably pick up more often than I do."

"It seems to be a Dee family trait," he sighs. "My father, in his twilight years, he was always coaxing me into quality time. He wanted to rent a cottage, go fishing—like we did when I was a kid." He rolls up one sleeve to check his watch. "I always told myself, I'd get to it after I got established in the firm. Then, after I made partner. But that title only came with more responsibilities, more travel and late nights." He smacks his lips again, carefully thinking over his next words. "Charlie, I owe you an apology."

The words knock me back so hard, a bite of chicken gets briefly lodged in my throat. I smack my chest and sputter into a cough. "What're you talking about?"

Dad just stares past me, looking out at the restaurant's long, tinted windows. "When you and your sister were young, I thought the best thing I could do was keep you taken care of— materially, speaking. Your mother tried to intervene. I didn't listen." His gaze falls to his own hands, still folded in his lap. "I should have let the both of you go, when she went out west."

"The both of us?" I echo.

He gives a solemn nod. "After Emma got her scholarship, your mother offered for you to go and live with her, too. She said it wasn't right to separate you kids." His shoulders slump beneath the weight of his suit jacket. "But I was selfish. I couldn't stand the idea of coming home to an empty house."

A highlight reel plays out inside my head, all the times I came home after school to microwave my own meal. All the nights I tucked myself into bed. "So you left me to do so, instead."

In an instant, I see my words cut across his face. His frown follows the hard lines on his cheeks. He's had plenty of practice, making that face. "I did. And I'm sorry."

I don't know what to do with that. Am I totally sure he even said those words? Maybe it was a fluke, or he really said *I'm sore, eh?* He's always had a bad back. But no. The longer I sit here, watching him stare down at his hands, the louder his words seem to echo. They overwhelm the music, the chatter around us, until there's no denying it anymore. He really did say that. And I have no idea how to respond.

"It's whatever." I slump into my seat. "Don't beat yourself up about it. It was good practice for when I moved out."

A meek smile rises on his face. It pushes against the hard lines of his face, like he's out of practice. "I'm proud of you, Charlie." He tells me, "You're stronger than I was, much better at being on your own."

Am I? "I have been starting to question that lately," I admit. "I, um, recently connected with some…" How do I even describe who Hayden and Buffy are to me? "Very nice people. And it's all still very new, but it's made me wonder if I need to reevaluate a few priorities. Maybe give myself a chance to connect, again."

Dad picks at one of the mushroom skewers and takes a bite. "Well, if you're willing to take the advice of an old man, success can be a fickle thing," he says between chews. "I've found, if there's no one to celebrate the milestones of life with you— whatever they may be—any victories you gain will end up hollow." He swallows and meets my gaze. Reaching across the table, he awkwardly pats the back of my hand. "If you think you've found your people, hold on tight. From there, everything else will sort itself out."

"Thanks, Dad." I nod towards his whiskey sour. "Want another one?"

"I've got an early flight." He pushes his drink aside. "But I'll take a soda water. And maybe after this, we can go for a walk in the rain?"

"Sure thing." I nod and pull up the app to place his order.

Chapter Twenty

Buffy: its so quiet here without you

I smile down at my screen, setting a bubbling pot of pasta on the back burner. It'll need time to cool before I add the sauce. I'm trying out a new recipe, one Hayden sent over.

Our group chat fills with messages each day, conversations spilling into one another. The winding threads of *Really Cute People*—Buffy's idea for a chat name, which Hayden and I quickly seconded—chronicles a long series of selfies, pet pictures, work stories (usually from me), global news articles, ASMR YouTube videos (Buffy's favourites), forwards from foodie influencers (always Hayden) and an endless number of times that we've asked each other *have-you-seen-this-TikTok?* My head buzzes as I swipe through our latest texts. It's almost like I'm drunk. Except instead of booze, it's on warm-and-fuzzies.

Hayden's name pops up alongside three dots. He's typing.

Hayden: very quiet

Hayden: except for Wellesley barking at the garbage truck outside. and Mango singing for his supper. and R chasing Miss K around the living room.

Buffy: yes, other than that

I laugh-react to both their messages. From beyond my apartment windows, sirens wail. My next-door neighbour is blasting EDM again and, based on the sounds coming from the folks upstairs, I'm pretty sure they've installed a bowling alley right above my head. What I wouldn't give for some of that Elmridge peace and quiet. It's been almost a month now since my first sleep at the Hawthornes' house. Our texts, calls, FaceTimes and VoiceNotes—they've been keeping me afloat. Even so, that cot in their spare room has never seemed so appealing as it does right now. I wish I had my car back from the mechanic already so I could drive out for a day trip. If they'd have me.

Buffy: I said to H, I've been thinking about you all day

Charlie: yeah? what have u been thinking 👀

Hayden: wouldn't you like to know

I fill a glass of water and stop to scratch Cashew under his chin. He's curled up on my kitchen stool, cuddling a dishrag. He chirps in appreciation of the attention, stretches one leg, then gets back to the busy work of sleeping.

Charlie: I miss u too ♥

The late-day sun has warmed my bed. I splay out, phone held over my head.

Buffy: I miss your lips

Buffy: I should have kissed you more when I had the chance.

Hayden: i miss the way you smell

Buffy: I wish you were here right now

I wiggle my hips as I type out my reply.

Charlie: what would you do if I was there?

I'd be lying if I said I hadn't been worried about the distance. How it might dampen our connection. It's not that I don't trust Hayden and Buffy. But myself? That's more of a question mark. Back in my old shoes, it would be easy to imagine that week as just a dream. A bubble, too delicate to touch. In a decade or two from now, I could see myself living in a (hopefully, slightly nicer) version of my bachelor pad, dragging myself into the office each day and marching home again to eat microwaved meals and fantasize about that one time I felt truly happy. I've never been so happy to be proven wrong.

Hayden: i would start by kissing your neck

Charlie: that sounds nice

Hayden: then massage your shoulders, down your back

Buffy: I'll take a massage too, if you're handing them out

I roll onto my front, propping myself up on a pillow. Shivers of excitement play across my skin. Buffy's typing again.

Buffy: I'd kiss you next. Press my lips to yours and just hold you.

Buffy: arms around your waist, I'd push you onto the bed

Charlie: that's so hot

Charlie: wait, are we sexting right now?

Hayden: do you want to?

Heat simmers in my stomach, spreading lower. I squirm and squeeze my legs together. I've never seen the appeal of dirty talk like this, until now. Whenever I tried it with Mako, I always got the feeling they were scrolling Instagram or TikTok at the same time. But with these two, it's like I'm there in the room with them.

Hayden: okay if you're on top Charlie, th'n I'll join you on the bed

Charlie: I like the sound of that

Hayden: while you're kissing her, i lift up your shirt and start teasing your nipples

Buffy: mm nice. I think I'll take a minute to just watch

Almost on their own, my own hands travel to grasp my chest. My nipples are growing firm, rubbing against the thin cotton of my shirt. My breath is quickening.

Charlie: I run my hand through your hair, H.

Charlie: your mouth feels so good but I want more

Hayden: i twist and pinch you with my hands while my face moves lower

A moan escapes me. My blood is rushing, heart pounding in my ears. I roll onto my side, hands shaking as I type.

Charlie: yes. please.

Hayden: I kiss down your stomach and start to unbutton your pants

Charlie: asdf;lkl

Shit. I grab for my phone from where it fell. It's managed to skitter all the way under the bed. Every second it takes for me to collect it feels like an eternity. Leaping back onto the bed, I quickly catch up on what I've missed.

Buffy: ?????

Hayden: don't leave me hanging here

Charlie: sorry. sweaty hands.

They both laugh-react, thank goodness. Mako told me once, the best lovers are the ones with a sense of humour. In retrospect, I wonder if that was supposed to be a compliment or dig at me. But that's a question for another time.

Buffy: Are we turning you on?

Charlie: absolutely.

Hayden: oh im already hard over eher

Hayden: *here

I pause for a moment to let the mood seep its way back in. Buffy gets us going again.

Buffy: I stand over you, C.

Buffy: I take off my shirt. No bra underneath.

The chat lights up. A picture message. Sure enough, Buffy stands in front of her bedroom mirror, without a top on. My pelvis twitches with excitement.

Hayden: goddamn babe you're so sexy

Buffy: I know 😊

Charlie: you really are.

Charlie: I reach for you to come closer

Buffy: I think I'll make you beg for it

I curl my toes and start to squirm. It's so hard not to start touching myself. But I'm not sure I can manage typing with only one hand.

Charlie: please

Hayden: pants unbuttoned, i slowly slide them down your legs

Hayden: i kiss my way back up, bury my face into the softness of your thighs

Charlie: I want you so bad

Buffy: how bad

Blood rushes through me. I moan, grinding against the air. They're really going to make me work for it.

Charlie: I'll do anything

Hayden: will you bend over

Charlie: yes. yes.

Hayden: show me

I'm not sure I've ever gotten undressed so fast. I strip off all my clothes and throw them across the apartment floor. Setting up my camera just right, I put a timer on and crouch onto the bed, butt raised in the air. After a couple tries, I get a good angle and send it off in an instant. Seconds later, heart-reacts, sweaty-face emojis. Blushing with heat, I grin. They like it.

Buffy: very good

Hayden: I give that gorgeous ass a smack

Charlie: yes. harder.

Hayden: i whip out my best paddle and give you a proper spanking

Buffy: oo this is giving me ideas for later

Hayden: same

A quiver of jealously races through me, for an instant. But it's met with an equal amount of pleasure at the thought of them together. I only wish I could be there in person, to have the option to join in.

Hayden: how are you feeling Charlie

Charlie: so good

Charlie: i want you in me

Hayden: can Do. how does this treat you?

His latest message is followed with a picture. Hayden stands with a fat dildo in his hands. It's sparkly pink, because of course it is. I laugh and text back.

Charlie: I think I can take it.

Hayden: i grab u by your hips bend you over, rubbing it against you

Buffy: babe, even still in a fantasy, we cant forget the lube

Hayden: haha true

Hayden: how about you drizzle it on?

Charlie: I love that idea

I can hardly take it anymore. Phone in one hand, I reach down and run a finger over myself. I'm starting to drip with excitement. All I want is more.

Hayden: now that youre good and ready for me, i slowly push myself inside you

Charlie: it's so big

Charlie: i love it.

Buffy: while he's got you from behind, I come around and spread my legs for you

Buffy: you want to taste me?

Charlie: so bad. please.

My fervent hands can barely keep up on either end. Moans rise from deep in my gut as I buck my hips. I can almost feel Hayden taking me from behind, the sweetness of Buffy on my lips. I'm getting close.

Charlie: I lick your slit and tease your clit with my tongue

Buffy: I pull you by the hair and ride your face

Hayden: hell yeah

Hayden: Im pumping you from behind. getting close now

Charlie: me too

Buffy: me three

My climax rushes up on me with such force, I collapse to my knees. I've never been such a screamer before. These two really know how to get me going.

Collapsing on the bed, I make sure they're both well finished too. We send pages of heart-emojis and smiley-faces. I curl up against a pillow and put a second at my back, imagining myself as the middle spoon. The last of the day's sunlight gleams off nearby office towers and sky-high condos.

My heart rate slows as the skyline turns to its nightly orange. The buzz of a truly good orgasm lingers in my brain. But even after that fades, too, something else lingers. It's hard to put it into words. It's more a feeling. One that just keeps on growing.

Hayden and Buffy told me about my predecessors. Their other *playmates*. It's been a few years but they all follow basically the same pattern. A chance meeting, a flurry of fun times and a slow fade into friendship. I've been trying, really trying, to make my peace with that story. But if we've got a short time together, I'm going to get the most out of it.

Charlie: I wanna come back and see you, soon

Hayden: yes please

Buffy: we would love that

Chapter Twenty-One

Buffy: so your boss has been MIA for how long? and ppl are just fine with that?

Nose to my phone screen, I sidestep cavernous potholes and street-wide puddles. It's been weeks of wet, dreary weather and the whole city feels soaked completely through. On the plus side, the plants seem to love it. Sprigs of green grass and dandelions poke up through the holes in the sidewalk.

Charlie: not missing exactly.

Charlie: she's just working remotely. but hasn't told anyone why.

Hayden: wish i could just stay home whenever i felt like it

I turn the corner with a skip in my step. On a whim, I took the long way to work this morning. There's no rush to get in now that Angie is indefinitely out-of-office. Though Hassan has taken it upon himself to start organizing incentives for the folks who come to work in person. Doughnuts have returned to the office kitchen, twice a week. Probably purchased with his own paycheque.

Rumours continue to fly about where Angie might be. I've found myself spending my lunch hours hanging around the break room, brainstorming all kinds of conspiracy theories. *She bought an RV and is working on the road, travelling across the country*—Sophia came up with that one. Yesterday, I overheard someone speculate that Angie was never actually our real boss but instead a paid actor. Paid by whom? I wish I knew. Seems like easy money.

I pass the usual pack of Bay Street vapers, huddled outside their shiny revolving doors. Glancing up, I catch the eye of a woman I've seen a few times before. Without thinking, I smile at her. She takes a beat, then smiles back. *How about that—maybe I'm not the only one in need of a little human connection, from time to time?* A skip in my step, I close the last few blocks between myself and CMM.

The *Assistant Manager* plaque on my desk hasn't been bothering me like it used to. In fact, I took a picture of it the other day and sent it to my dad. Just because. I'm starting to think that it might just be the perfect role for me—still a decent salary without all the pressure of being the one everyone's supposed to go to for everything. Truly, I've been wishing that Hassan would get that promotion already so he can get paid for the work he's doing already. It'd be one less thing for me to worry about, plus he's clearly suited for it. He's stepped into Angie's shoes more times than I can count since her not-so-formal exit. He even worked with Augustine to play music through the office sound system; now every morning, we start the day with some pump-up jams. That keeps my morale up, that's for sure.

More than any of the office politics or daily bits of drama, I find myself most often fixated on what's in my pocket throughout the day. Namely, my phone, as it is where the RCP chat lives. And wow, is it living. There are days where we send a hundred messages back and forth before I've even hit my lunch hour. Hayden and Buffy have started using it to log little, daily-life things—what food they need at the grocery store, who is picking up Rainbow from kindergarten. Those are always my favourite. I love sharing in a slice of their life like that.

Today, more than any other day, our texts are a flurry. Because after work today, I'm finally getting my car back from the mechanic. The issue itself turned out to be pretty fixable—something about wheel alignment, I think—but the cost set me back a ways. Now all that is sorted and, as an added benefit, it just so happens to be a Thursday. Which has now become my Friday, since no one is going to complain if I take a *work-from-home* day once in a while. If Angie ever does find out, it's not like she'll be in any position to argue.

If I jump into that driver's seat and hit the road before nightfall, I can get a good forty-eight hours with Hayden and Buffy, plus Rainbow and the pets. Sunday, I'll head home in the afternoon and be able to stroll into the office (likely, a bit late) Monday morning.

The scent of roasted coffee beans breaks through my weekend fantasy. There's a small shop around this way. It's a hole-in-the-wall, really, one I used to swing by more often. Back when I lived at Hillside, it was right on my route to work. Maybe I have time for just a quick detour, for old time's sake.

A bell rings as I slip my way inside. The place hasn't changed in the slightest. If I remember correctly, a sweet pair of old butches set this place up as a post-retirement project. They passed on ownership to their granddaughter a few years back. But the brickwork walls remain covered in local art and posters advertising community events—looks like they're hosting a poetry reading in a few weeks. Maybe I'll ask Buffy and Hayden if they'd like to go. We could make it a city-date.

At the counter, I peruse through their baked goods, debating whether I'd rather have an apple-butter croissant or double-chocolate muffin. I opt for a drink instead and place my order with the smiley woman working at the front cash. Her tip jar reads: *This doubles as a wishing well.* I smirk and drop a loonie inside. Because, why not?

Elbows against the counter, I listen to the sweet sound of steaming milk and drip espresso. I study the other café patrons, telling myself stories about each one. That guy with the jogging stroller is having a hell of a morning. I can tell by the way he downs his green tea. The guy chatting loudly on his phone? The way he's standing at the window, I bet he's a hopeless romantic, waiting on a blind date. And that woman hunched in the corner on her laptop, the one with the thick glasses and giant travel mug? *Actually she kind of looks like—*

"Angie?"

I half-expect her to sing my name, the way she does at work. *Charlie, Charlie, Charlie Dee.* Instead, Angie startles as she looks up from her computer and spies me at the counter. She quickly snaps it shut and starts shuffling through a massive purse that hangs off the seat beside her.

Looking around, I take a tentative step in her direction. "What are you doing here?" I ask.

"I just needed a change of scenery," she mumbles from the depths of her purse. "Just catching up on a few projects." She sits back up and adjusts her glasses. "How about yourself?"

I nod in the direction of the office. "I stop here sometimes, on my way in."

"Large oat latte?" The barista sets my drink onto the counter. "Two pumps of syrup!"

"That's me." I stand with my hands in my pockets.

"Don't let me keep you, then." Angie waves me off.

I shuffle backwards and grab my order off the counter, heading for the door. But something makes me turn back. "Angie," I ask, "what are you doing here?"

She blinks up at me. "Did we not just have this conversation?"

"No. Well, yes, but—" I motion to the café walls. "I meant, why are you *here*. If you need a change of scenery why not, say, go find it in your office? It's like a block away."

Angie steeples her fingers. "I am aware of that."

Looking over my shoulder, I half-expect Mako to be standing there filming me. This has to be a prank or something. I drop my voice to a whisper. "Everyone's been wondering what's up with you."

Touching fingertips to nose, she inhales deeply. "I imagine they have been." She sighs and takes the purse off the chair beside her. "Would you care to take a seat?"

I awkwardly look around, like someone's going to catch us together. Doing what? Who knows. Eventually, I accept her offer. "Thanks," I mutter.

For what feels like forever, the two of us sit in silence. The café bell chimes with customers' arrivals and departures. The steamer seems to run nonstop, whipping up hot drinks for this drizzly day. The whole time, Angie is staring down at her hands. She seems almost meditative.

"Charlie, tell me about your life outside of work." The question—or demand, as it feels like—catches me off guard. "Do you have friends, a family?" she asks. "What do you do for fun?"

"Um." I sip my latte to buy myself some time. I'm not really in the mood to explain my current three-way-situationship to my boss. "Mako and I are pretty close," I decide. "I don't know if you remember, they used to work in the fundraising department?"

She pinches her lips. "Colourful hair, funky clothes?" I nod. "Yes. I remember. I remember all the people who have come and gone through the doors at CMM." She tuts. "I'm sorry. I didn't know you were close."

It's not like they're dead. She's so somber, I almost have to laugh. "It's fine," I assure her. "They actually went on to start their own business. It's going pretty well."

"That's great." Angie smiles, but only with her eyes. "Really great." She lifts open her laptop and speaks to me from behind it. "I have two sons, all grown up now. One is in school. The other's going through a bit of a renaissance period."

Is that code for being unemployed? "Sounds nice."

"The older one just had a daughter." She pokes her head out from behind the screen. "My first grandchild. Care to see?" Before I can answer, she tilts the computer towards me. Sure enough, she's pulled up a series of family photos. She slowly clicks through each one. "He and his partner, they're down in California now. I have been meaning to go out and visit, but with work the way it's been…" She turns the laptop back to herself and stares at it for another few seconds before closing it again. "I'm not sure he'd be thrilled to see me, anyway. We don't talk all that much."

I want to tell her *I'm sorry.* But also, I don't really know Angie all that well. I certainly can't imagine her as a doting grand-mother. Maybe there's a reason they're out of touch, but that seems far too cruel to say out loud. So instead, I just say, "That must be difficult."

"I don't normally allow myself much time to think on it," she explains. "The hotline—" She catches herself. "Though, I suppose we can't call it that anymore, can we? It's not exactly accurate."

"It's up to you." I shrug.

"Yes. It is." Angie takes a long drink from her travel mug. I sit quietly, waiting for her to finish. "CMM has been strug-gling these last few years. More than I think most of the staff are aware."

"The layoffs gave all of us a pretty clear idea," I point out.

"Mm." She rhythmically taps her nails on the table. "I want you to know, it was not my call to close the therapy department. I never believed a robot or any other such nonsense could replace true human contact." Jaw clenched, her tapping grows more fervent. "That was a decision made by the board of directors. My job was just to see it through, as best I could. I tried to minimize the damage."

"You did what you had to, Angie," I say. "We all understood that."

Her fingers come to an abrupt halt. "Thank you," she speaks, voice dropped. "That is very kind of you to say."

Angie still hasn't explained where she has been all this time. But I'm hardly going to push her. After another long silence, I decide to just shift the subject. "So, um. How was the conference?" She just stares at me, gaze unwavering. "The annual paradigm something-something? You were heading there last time I saw you."

"Ah, yes." She wags her finger at me. "I remember. I can't say I know how it went, as I wasn't able to make it." She starts digging through her purse, pulling out a small notebook and pen. "I sent a prerecorded version of my lecture and instead spent the weekend at a retreat. It was one my therapist recommended to me."

"Oh." I watch her scribble a few notes. Am I being evaluated on my reaction to finding out my boss has a therapist? "Um, how was that, then?"

"Insightful." She smacks the pen against the page like an exclamation point. "It was completely silent. Meditation three times a day. No phones, no internet. Exactly what I needed."

"That's great for you." I eye the door. Is it too late to bail on this conversation? I'm not sure how long I can hear about Angie having more time and money for mental health care than any of the CMM employees.

"Indeed," says Angie. "And when I left, I knew what had to be done." She flips a page of her notepad and pauses to adjust her glasses again. "I've decided to hand in my resignation at the end of the next quarter. And as my final act, I plan to nominate you for Executive Director."

Midway through a sip, I choke on my drink. The awful sting of milk and coffee hits the back of my nose. "Me?" I grab a napkin off the table and try to clean myself up. "Angie, I'm not sure if—"

"I can think of no person better suited for it." She tucks away her notepad again. "The title of the role may change, though. If we cannot find a way out of our current deficit, the board's next plan of action involves changing our status from that of a nonprofit. They're also currently looking into new options for revenue streams." This time, she pulls out a bottle of hand cream from her giant bag. She carefully applies it. "I'm afraid I'm not sure I understand the mechanics of it but I understand the new chat program could allow for something called *data mining*," she explains. "There has also been some chatter as to whether other staff positions could be replaced by some of these AI programs. Other people on the board are more interested in that social enterprise model that Elmridge centre is running— that's why I wanted you to go check them out for yourself."

"I see." My stomach sinks, slips down past my feet and onto the floor. None of that bodes well. "Well, I'll tell you right now, we do *not* want to turn into a copy-paste of that ECIC place. And all this, it sounds like more reasons for you to stick around, not less," I tell her. "We need someone like you, who knows what CMM is really supposed to be like."

Angie rubs the lotion into the creases of her skin. "My perspective is too clouded on such things," she says. "If it's a matter of sink or swim, perhaps CMM really does need to make that kind of change." She pops the lid back on the cream and studies the label. "However, I do know that I, personally, cannot bring myself to go through another round of layoffs. And I certainly cannot stick around to watch this organization, into which I've poured the best years of my life, become something so unrecognizable. The stress of it has already taken a toll on me."

"Why me, though?" I can hardly believe I'm asking this, but the words come through me anyway. "Why not someone like, say, Hassan? I'm sure he'd jump at the position."

"He's a family man." Angie tsks her tongue. "Him and that fiancé of his, I know they want children. In my experience, this job leaves very little capacity for personal matters." She points a (well-moisturized) finger to me, then to herself. "You and I, we know how to set such things aside."

Do we? I'm not so sure I love being in that club together. If I was in charge, I wouldn't want to be the type of boss that passes over someone for a promotion just because he wants to start a family.

"The future of CMM will need someone who can think outside the box," says Angie. "And who is willing to see the forest for the trees. I believe you are that person, but I leave the choice to you." She stows her lotion and clips the bag shut. "As a personal favour, I'd appreciate if you kept all this information private, until I officially announce my retirement."

My mouth is dry from hanging open for so long. "Uh, yeah. I understand."

Angie stands with her purse slung over one shoulder. "Good. Now, I believe you have somewhere to be." She tucks her laptop under her arm. "I think I'll finish these emails at home today."

Just like that, she's gone. After a few moments of stunned silence, I head out too. On the way into work, I start furiously typing to the RCP chat.

Charlie: you are never going to believe who I just ran into.

Chapter Twenty-Two

"Are you sure you know what you're doing?"

"This is literally my job." Mako fiddles with the trimmers. After some struggle, they manage to snap on the size guard. Looking at me in the mirror, they laugh. "Don't you trust me?"

"I'm not sure you want the answer to that." I smile back. The clippers hum against the back of my head. Locks of hair fall and scatter on the bathroom floor. Cashew paws at the bathroom door, quite offended that we'd exclude him. I wish I'd set this up before my last visit out to Elmridge but at least, when I go again in a week, I'll arrive looking fresh. And for what it's worth, Hayden seemed charmed with my shaggy look last time. Buffy did too—she likes having something to grab on to. I hope Mako leaves at least a little extra length on top.

While Mako works on the tricky spot at the back of my neck, the topic of conversation shifts to the precarious state of CMM. Angie asked me not to tell my coworkers about her upcoming career change, but she never said anything about *past* employees.

Mako positions my head just-so to get at my baby hairs. "So, she snaps her fingers and what, the ED spot is yours?"

"I don't really know," I say to their reflection in the mirror. "I didn't think to ask."

"Seems like something you should find out, if you want the job." Mako glances up at me, trimmers still running. "You *do* want the job, right?"

I take a moment to adjust the towel around my shoulders. "Hey, you never filled me in—how was your date the other night?"

"Blah. So boring." Mako scrunches up their nose. "She was an aerospace engineer and a dominatrix on the side. Which on paper, so hot, right?" They draw the clippers up to my hairline. "But all she wanted to do was talk about how sexy prime numbers are."

"Mako!" I pop my tongue. "I'm shocked at you, kinkshaming like that."

"Shut up." When they giggle, the clippers come dangerously close to my ear. I duck out of the way and they grab my chin, righting me again. "What about you and your trip out to see *Bayden*—did you have time for more hot-hot threesomes?"

"I'm not sure Buffy would love that nickname," I say, biting back a smirk.

"We can call them *Huffy*, then." Mako waves aside my concern. "Or *Chuffy*, if you wanna add your name into it." They lean down to whisper, "Also, don't think I didn't notice you avoiding my question."

"Yeah, well." I pick at my nail beds, avoiding Mako's penetrating gaze. They've always had a way of seeing right through me. "We had fun, yeah. But we're just trying to keep it light and breezy right now. Casual."

Mako chuckles. "You don't know how to do *anything* casually."

"What're you talking about?" I grin back at them. They push me back into place again. "I am super chill, all of the time."

"No, you aren't." They laugh while buzzing around my ears. "And that's fine. You do you."

"Ouch!" I wince as the clippers pinch my earlobe. "Careful!"

They pop off the guard for a second and inspect the blade. "Somebody's gotta clean these trimmers," they mutter.

"Didn't you bring those from work?" I ask. "If anyone's going to—"

"Anyway." Mako clicks the trimmer back on. "That's why it never worked out between you and me." They get back to work. "I'm just never gonna care as much as you care. I don't have the fucks to give."

They're right, of course. But I'm not about to just give that to them. "And I do?"

"Mmm-hmm. You're basically made of them." They crouch to do my neckline. "You always give a hundred and ten percent to everything and everyone. *Especially* if you like them." Their head pops up in the mirror again. "Do you remember the love letters you used to leave me in the morning?"

I stare into the sink basin. "No."

"Don't lie to your barber." Mako flicks my shoulder. "But yeah, they were always super sappy, full of deeply poetic de-scriptions." They take a moment to coif their hair, which is currently dyed the colour of ocean algae. "How beautiful I looked dappled in the sunlight. Yadda-yadda-yadda." They catch me blushing. "Now don't be embarrassed. It was all very charming."

I'm growing certain that this is the longest haircut in all of human history. "What's your point?"

Mako runs their hands through my bangs. "I'm just *saying*, you didn't feel even an itsy-bit resentful that I never wrote you one back?"

I shrug. "But that wasn't why I gave them to you."

"That's not what I asked." They swap their clippers for a pair of scissors. I wince at every cut.

"Okay. Maybe just a little," I admit. "But like you said, you're just not the type to do that kind of thing." I grit my teeth as they snip a particularly large chunk from the back of my head. "Besides, that's in the past—it doesn't even matter anymore."

"And what about at Hillside?" asks Mako. "Weren't you ever a bit angry when you got home after work to a big load of dishes?" *Snip, snip, snip.* Bits of hair start to fill the sink. "Everybody knew you were doing them, yet nobody offered to lend a hand. Or even say thank you! That didn't piss you off?"

"I think that's short enough." I start to reach for the scissors.

Mako smacks my hand away. "And what about all this stuff with your dad, and your sister?"

"What about it?" I blink at them. I'm watching myself balding in real time.

"Now hold still." They splash their hands with water and wet the tips of my hair. "You still haven't called her, have you?"

"That's totally irrelevant," I insist. "Besides, it's on my to-do list. There just happens to be some other stuff going on in my life right now. Not sure if you noticed."

"*Or* are you avoiding her because you're scared you'll spill your guts. And have to have a real-ass, grown-up conversation about your feelings." Mako starts pinching random sections of my hair between their fingers and cutting them at the ends. I'm certain they're just making things up now.

There's not much left to do at this point but accept my fate. Why didn't I just shell out the money for a real barber? I grumble under my breath, "I can talk about my feelings."

"As your ex-roommate, ex-lover and current best friend, I beg to differ," Mako snaps.

Cashew starts scratching louder, mewing for our attention. I try to telepathically communicate with him instructions on how to turn the bathroom doorknob. *Come on, bud, you can do it. Free us both.*

"All I'm trying to say, Chuck, is you gotta start telling people how you really feel," says Mako. "Even if it's scary, even if they get upset. You're not the kind of person who can just let it go, and I've seen how it eats you from the inside out." At long last, they put down the scissors and turn me around. My back to the mirror, they tease at what's left of my hair. "It also turns you into kind of an asshole."

I grimace at them. "No it doesn't."

"Case in point." Mako fetches a jar of styling gel from their barbering kit. Which is less a formal kit than it is a tote bag filled with a bunch of random hairdressing supplies they've picked up over the last few years. I hang silent while they put together the finishing touches. I'm in no rush to turn and face my reflection. I guess they found a couple stray hairs because they end up snipping more off, despite my protests.

"You should know something." They speak a touch softer than before, eyes focused above my eyebrows. "Before we had the vote to disband Hillside, Mars had already found a three-bedroom apartment."

"What?" There's no way I heard that right.

"It was out of our price range, but he was gonna try for it anyway." Mako pulls out a small comb from their pocket and adjusts my part. "Johanna asked Mei if she'd go with them. And Mei asked me." They take a moment to step back to double-check their work. "It wasn't personal. More like a kind of cruel practicality. A luck-of-the-draw type of thing."

It's like someone just grabbed my guts and gave a twist. The bathroom mirror wavers, my reflection spinning out of focus. Mako must be messing with me. Or maybe this is some sick way of making me feel better. I open my mouth to try and give a witty comeback, shrug this all off like one big joke. But I can't play this off. Somewhere deep down, it rings too true. Instead, all I can ask is, "Why are you telling me this?"

"Because you deserve to know," they say, in all seriousness. "You weren't the death of Hillside. That creep of a landlord was. And you weren't alone in wanting to jump ship, you just didn't get an invite to the lifeboat."

The bathroom fan sputters. I listen to it struggle, my jaw clamped shut. "I don't know what to say."

"Anyway, I only ever gave them a *maybe*. And the rental Mars found turned out to be full of black mold. So we would have all ended up scattered, anyway." Mako takes the towel off me and shakes it out into the bathtub. I'm going to have a hell of a time cleaning that up. "Sucks, I know. I didn't mention it until now because I knew you wanted to try and stay friends with some of those folks again. But when I met up with them the other night, it was like nothing had changed. They're all just selfish people, caught up in their own worlds and petty drama."

"I don't know if I'd go that far," I mutter. Snuggles on the couch. Pancake breakfasts. Our annual backyard Pride party. The little warmth that remains among my memories of Hillside starts to fizzle. I'm not sure I can throw away all the good, with all the bad.

"Yeah, you wouldn't." Using a small brush, Mako dusts the hair from my shoulders. "Because even after everything, you still care. Like I said." They grab the arms of my chair. Crouched face-to-face, our noses are almost touching. "You're the type of person who's always gonna pour their heart into whatever you're doing—or whoever. So, do me a favour? Just make sure they're worth it." They spin me back around and I meet my new reflection.

"Wow." Crisp lines, a perfect part; they even managed a decent fade up the sides.

"Looks good, right?" They lean over me and start fussing

with it again. "Now, next up, I'm thinking we do frosted tips with lime green sideburns."

"You're the worst." I shove them off with a smile. "I love you, bud."

Mako poses for themself in the mirror. "Oh, I know."

Chapter Twenty-Three

New leaves, unfurling in the warm breeze, dance with light and shadow. They whisper to one another along the riverbed, melting with the chatter of birds and forest creatures. The water ripples along, sparkling in the midday sun. My shoes squish into the mud with each step as I navigate rows of interwoven roots. Even with the occasional tricky section to the trail, I'm surprised we haven't passed many other people walking out here on a Friday afternoon. My last few visits to Elmridge, it's been too muddy for a proper hike but today is just perfect. "It would mean more hours." I clamber over a boulder that juts out into the trail. "I'd have to work most weekends. There are lots of meetings with the board, and with donors. Galas and stuff. I'd sort of become the face of CMM."

"Sounds like there could be benefits, though." Buffy is a few paces ahead of me. She clears the path of a few fallen branches. "I assume there'd be a pay bump."

"And better benefits?" asks Hayden, holding up the rear with a walking stick in hand. He found it under the Elmridge Bridge when we passed underneath it earlier.

"Pretty good ones, yeah." I grab at a nearby tree for some extra support. The bark is rough and sticky with fresh sap. "My dad would probably be ecstatic. I might outpace my sister for the favourite child spot." Buffy looks over her shoulder at me. "I'm just kidding. Mostly."

"Sure you are." She offers her arm for my support instead. I thankfully take it and right myself on the path. "How *is* Emma doing, anyway?"

"She's all right." I roll up my sleeves, quite aware of how much I'm sweating through my shirt. "We got some time to talk last week. That Bentley guy sounds like a real prick—I'm glad she figured out that she doesn't have to put up with his crap."

Hayden pauses to dab his forehead. "Is she still thinking of moving?"

I nod. "Toronto's on her list of *maybe* cities, so I actually invited her to come stay with me for a bit."

"Wow, that's huge!" Hayden gives a loud clap. "Is it huge—are we celebrating this?"

"Same question," says Buffy. "How are you feeling about that idea?"

"Pretty stoked, if I'm being honest." I thought reconnecting with Emma would be hard but we hit it off pretty quickly. It's funny how many old stories I'd forgotten about the old days, when we lived together. "I'm still figuring out how to open up, tell her how I really feel about her moving away. But maybe some quality time is just what we need—we're talking about her coming around the end of summer."

"Let us know the dates, when you know them." Hayden gets us marching again. "Because we had kind of an idea."

"Oh?" Following Buffy's lead, we arrive at an outcropping with a good view of the river. Together, we rest against a fallen tree.

Hayden passes me a bag of trail mix. "What do you think about taking a little vacation together?"

How soon can we go? Do I have time to pack a bag? My heart instantly picks up a beat, which is saying something after all this exercise. "I'd really, really like that." I crunch on a handful of almonds, unable to fight back my smile. "This time though, let's do it while the weather's good. I'm not in a rush for another snowstorm vacation."

"Agreed," says Buffy. She takes a bit of our mix and tosses it over to a chunky chipmunk. It freezes for a second before hungrily stuffing its cheeks. "I'm also putting a veto on any Airbnb rentals. Let's just do something low-key, like rent a cottage for the weekend."

"I could get on board with that," I agree.

The river laughs, small waves pattering across the shoreline. They pick up twigs and stones. We watch them come and wash away. After some time, I say the words that have been resting on my heart. "I've really been enjoying our time together. Like, *really* really."

"Us too," says Hayden with a glint in his eyes. "You're something special, Charlie." Buffy darts her eyes towards him with one of her unspoken messages. He just looks away. "This whole job though, you still seem pretty indecisive about it. Is there something else holding you back?"

Buffy rests her hand alongside mine. She gently rubs her thumb along my wrist. "It's also okay if you don't want to get into it."

Angie's words of warning still ring in my ears. I've seen firsthand the kind of schedule she's had to keep. And I know at least a little bit about how it's impacted her personal life. "Well, it might make it hard to host long-lost sisters," I point out. "Or take spontaneous cottage trips."

I search Buffy's face for a reaction to that second point but she doesn't meet my eyes. Meanwhile, Hayden is searching for another smooth rock to toss. I know I could ask them outright—

are we really just playing around together? Or do they feel the same way I do, like something more is brewing here? But if I dare ask, tell them what I really want, what if it ends all that we have? *I'm not ready for that.*

I peer out towards the tree line. The very top of a crystalline structure rears its head just above the fresh layers of green canopy. Even out here, ECIC finds a way to cast its shadow. At least it serves as a good change of topic. "I keep thinking about that weird-ass trip that brought me out here." I kick at a nearby stone and watch it tumble into the river. "Remember how I told you about their whole membership model thing?"

"The one where they basically convinced people to pay for the *privilege* of working there?" Hayden picks at his teeth.

"We haven't forgotten," says Buffy. "I actually warned one of the moms at Rainbow's school about it. She was thinking of signing up."

"It definitely seemed pretty damn exploitative." I shrug. "But at the same time, I don't know. Sam seemed happy?" I frown at the tree canopy above us, searching it for answers. "I keep thinking about the board, all that stuff about other sources of income. Like, damn. If CMM could figure out how to make money like ECIC does, we'd be done with our financial problems."

"And waist-deep into a bunch of ethical issues." Hayden gently rubs the small of my back. "Charlie, that kind of plan really doesn't sound like you."

"I know." His touch draws me back down to earth. "I'm just trying to think of anything that could work. I don't want to see a bunch of my friends lose their jobs again."

"Friends, eh?" Buffy pokes my arm, teasing me. "I don't know if I've heard you call your coworkers that before."

"I guess that's new, yeah," I admit. "Something feels like it's changed. Maybe it's just me but Hassan, Augustine—everyone there feels more like a team now."

"How about that." Hayden stands and stretches his back. He

starts skipping stones across the water. "No big boss to supervise you, and you work together even better."

"Yeah. Funny that." I run a hand through my freshly cut bangs. Mako made them a little shorter than I'd normally go for, but I'm liking the change of pace. "Which makes it even weirder keeping Angie's retirement a secret from everybody. I'm pretty sure Augustine has figured out that something is up."

"Seems like you've got a tough call, then." Buffy pats my back and stands up to stretch herself. "Whoever the ED is they'll be faced with difficult decisions and the staff may suffer for them either way."

"Sounds like maybe the workers need a seat on the board." Hayden throws another stone and it gets a good four bounces before splashing out of sight. "And some bargaining power. Given that you all know what it's actually like to *run* the place."

"On that note, I actually had an idea." Buffy shelters her eyes to check the time. "It might rock the boat a bit but I think it could work." She motions for us to get going again. "Before I get too much into it, we should be heading back. We're running out of time."

"What?" Hayden takes a quick look at his phone. "Rainbow's not out of school for another couple hours."

"Oh, I know." Buffy's smile dimples as she leads the way back home.

My bare skin prickles along the path of Buffy's hands. She cups my face, drinking me in. Guiding me down, she presses me into her chest. I lap at her, running my tongue around the darkness of her areolas. I love watching her grow hard for me. Bodies entwined, our hips rock against one another. She brushes against me and a moan escapes me.

Strong hands dig into my love handles and rock me steady. Hayden's pink dildo slips inside me and I gasp. He fills me up so well. Deft fingers find my most tender places and flick, pinch, stroke. My breath is rising, screaming through me. When Buffy laughs, it reverberates through her. She loves the sounds I make.

Once we've all reached the peak of our pleasure (some of us, more than once), we splay across the bed, a mess of arms and legs. I nestle in the middle, my go-to spot. The heat of us all mingles together. We catch our collective breath. Hayden cups my backside and gives a gentle pat. Buffy nuzzles my chin. I look up, watching the ceiling fan run its endless circle.

My bliss does not last as long as I wish it would. Unwanted thoughts crawl at the edge of my subconscious, flashing into view like lightning. I twitch as one of them hits too close to home.

"Hey." Buffy softly draws my face towards hers. "What are you thinking?"

"It's just the work stuff again," I tell her. "I can't seem to stop thinking about it."

Hayden props himself up over my shoulder. "Did you want to talk through it again?"

"I feel like I've been talking way too much about it." I bury my head into a pillow. "With you, with Mako—I even called my dad for advice! It's like I'm just spinning out, stuck running through the same things again and again."

"I get that, yeah." Hayden slips small kisses along my neck.

"It's just like, why wouldn't I take it?" I sit myself up and hug the blankets. "It'd be a good job. Busy, sure, but maybe it'd be worth it." My heart patters. "Maybe I'd even be able to steer CMM back into being something that makes a difference in the world."

Buffy draws herself up behind me. "I'm sensing a *but* is coming?"

"I already made that butt come." Hayden sneers and she smacks him with a pillow, so hard that he nearly tumbles off the bed. I laugh and help Hayden right himself.

"But I just can't seem to picture myself saying yes." Rubbing my eyes, I can't believe I just said that out loud. *That's got to be one of the worst reasons* ever *to turn down a legitimate job offer.*

They're doing that thing again. Hayden raises his brows. Buffy replies with a quick shake of her head. One of their silent conversations. I'm getting a little better at knowing how to read them. "What're *you* thinking?" I ask.

"You caught that, did you?" asks Hayden, still watching Buffy. She scowls and fidgets with her blankets. "Buff, we might as well just talk about it."

The tattoos along her back rise and fall with her shoulders. "It's just I—*we* don't want to pressure you."

"Pressure me?" I ask.

"I think that ship might have sailed, though." Hayden strokes my leg. "Charlie, I'll just ask. Do you think your feelings for us could be holding you back?"

"Because we would *never* want to be the reason you walked away from something like this," Buffy finishes his thought.

"What if I wanted you to be my reason?" *I can't just ask them that.* But, too late. I think I just did. "I know this is supposed to just be something casual. No labels and whatever. Which is so totally fine with me."

Buffy's eyes dart over her shoulder. Hayden nods. Tucking a strand of her curls behind one ear, she turns back to face us. "Charlie," she says, "the last few weeks have been so special."

"Better than we ever thought they could be." Hayden squeezes my knee.

I glance between them. "This is starting to feel like you're gearing for a breakup."

"More like the opposite." Buffy shimmies her feet to play with mine under the blankets. "When you're driving up to see us, it's all I can think about. There's this incredible buzzing that gets in my head all day." She draws fingers around the sheets. "I haven't felt a rush like that in a long, long time."

Hayden nods. "I keep getting distracted when I'm teaching,

because I want to just check my phone. When I'm home, Buffy and I sit and read over your messages!"

"Giggling like we're little kids with a crush, I might add." Buffy wrinkles her nose as she smiles. "A really, really big, oh-my-god how-is-this-happening kind of crush. And it doesn't hurt that you and Rainbow get along so well—even Wellesley gets excited now, when he hears your name!"

Hayden rights himself and faces me head-on. His eyes search mine for a moment before he tells me, "Charlie, we are *totally* falling for you."

"But we didn't want to say anything," Buffy adds in. "Just in case you didn't feel the same way, or like you *had* to do anything other than what you wanted to."

The window at the reading nook is filled with endless blue. I watch a plane soar in the distance, leaving a thin white trail. A part of me feels like I'm that far away, too. High above this whole scene and watching it play out. There's no way this is actually happening. Not to me.

Hayden is explaining something. I should probably try to get back into my body so I can listen. "Dating two people, especially an established couple—it comes with a certain dynamic."

"We have all this history and commitment," Buffy chimes in. "It can take a lot of work to negotiate things like equitable time and attention. For all of us."

"Well, um." My words find their way back into my mouth. "I think I've shown I'm up for it." I offer both my hands. "Or at least willing to figure it out as we go."

Hayden takes my left palm in his. "So are we."

"No question." Buffy intertwines fingers with my right.

The three of us sit in the circle we've created. "So, what are we saying here?" I ask. "You want to, what—go steady with me?" My breath catches as I say the words. They seem so silly, so small in comparison to all these big feelings going on inside me. Maybe I need to get back into writing poetry.

Buffy tilts her chin at the suggestion. "Yes, I think that could be a word for it."

"How about we call it offering a promotion?" Hayden suggests. "From playmate to date-mate."

Date-mate. The phrase washes over me like cool water. I had no idea how much I needed to hear that, until he said it. "I assume, good benefits?"

"The best." He winks and I shiver.

"Okay. Yes. Please." Any relief I had from sharing how I felt is quickly replaced by a growing panic. This is real. They do feel the same. I manage to choke out a question, "So, what comes next?"

"Well, this still might not look like your typical relationship," Buffy explains. "There's not going to be a simple step-by-step, going from dating to moving-in to marriage and baby-making."

"Hey, no need to keep pitching!" I laugh. "I'm not interested in finding something typical—I'm interested in *you*."

I offer an arm to Buffy and she takes it. "The feeling is mutual." Pulling Hayden with her, we land in a three-way hug.

"You have no clue how great it is just to *talk* about all this." Hayden tickles me with the scruff of his beard. "I've been *dying* to tell you everything!"

I giggle and nuzzle him back. "I think I have some idea. Since you know, it's mutual."

"I was scared to even hope that you really felt the same," Buffy murmurs against my neck. "That you would want to choose us—choose *this*."

"This is all I've ever wanted." I press my lips against her cheek. "All that matters right now is that we know the truth, how we all feel about each other."

"Agreed." Hayden's hands start to wander down my waist. "But hey, why stop now? Let's get a little deeper into all those feelings."

"Sounds like fun to me." I grin back. All that is left of the distance between us quickly falls away. I let go of any lingering *what-ifs* and *what-do-we-do-whens*. Something tells me, everything will sort itself out, in its own time. Right here, right now, I'm snuggled between the most incredible people I've ever met. And they think I'm just as amazing. How goddamn lucky is that?

Chapter Twenty-Four

Hayden always smells so good after his morning shower. It's his beard oil, sandalwood. He rubs it in afterwards and it makes all of him feel just so soft and sweet and kissable. After a weekend of sharing my bed, the sheets are starting to smell like him too. I love it.

We had to wait a couple weeks before getting together after our last date. I was hoping for another walk by the river but Rainbow had a school project, and Buffy got a couple speaking gigs. Our group chat has stayed active as ever, though. And when they arrived at my door, Rainbow and the pets left behind in the care of good Uncle Franny, it was like we'd never been apart. It's funny how time bends around us like that, making our time together feel so brief and so long at the exact same time. "Morning!" He greets me with a kiss. I wrap my arms around him, burying my face into his scruff. I could live there forever.

"*Mffph,*" comes a sound beneath the covers. Buffy peeks out from under the duvet, cheeks puffy. "What time is it?" she wonders aloud.

"Breakfast time." Hayden grins and drops his towel. My heart picks up so quick, I have to sit down as I watch him get dressed. *Damn. How did I get so lucky?* Soon enough, he's off to the kitchen and fixing us a bite to eat. I help tie the strings of his pink apron, which, adorably, he brought from home.

While the air sizzles with the scent of melting butter and a fresh-cracked egg, I curl back up under the blankets. I wrap my arms around Buffy's waist and spoon against her. She groans and turns over to nuzzle against my neck. I soften under her warm touch, lazing back into bed. Eyes closed, our lips find one another and fireworks go off behind my eyes. I don't even care that she's still got morning breath.

Cashew bats at my toes and starts chasing our feet below the blankets. Buffy giggles and tucks her legs up. Hayden pops open a can of wet food and taps on Cashew's food dish. There's something beautiful about the way he just does it, like something he's always done. It's amazing how easily he and Buffy just fit into my life. As if there was always a space open for them, and I just never noticed until now. "Order up!" says Hayden. "Breakfast is served for both kitties and grown-ups."

Buffy buries her face back under the blankets. "Can we just eat in bed?"

"I don't see why not?" I laugh.

Cuddled together in a pile of blankets and pillows, the three of us eat our scrambled eggs and bacon. We use a bowl, a plate and an extra-large mug, respectively. I make a mental note to source a wider variety of dishware before their next visit.

Buffy yawns and reaches for her glasses on my nightstand. "What's the plan for today, then?"

"I'll head out to grab supplies," I say, carrying our dishes to the sink. "We'll need some snacks and maybe, uh, some paper plates."

"Not a bad plan." Hayden scratches at his chin. "We're doing sort of a late-lunch, early-dinner thing."

"Linner," Buffy agrees. "We'll have to make sure we don't run too late. Frances is expecting us back in time to pick up Rainbow before bedtime."

"Don't remind me." Hayden groans. "Why did we promise an *evening* pickup? He could have dropped her off at school tomorrow!"

"Frances would say we should count our blessings." Buffy ruffles his hair. "So, let's just be thankful he agreed at all to a multiday babysit!"

"That's one solid uncle she's got there." I stoop to pick up Cashew's food bowl. When I stand, I sniff the air and wonder, "What *is* that?"

"Crap!" Hayden leaps off the bed and races towards the kitchen. Smoke plumes from the frying pan. "Sorry, sorry!" He clicks off the element and starts the overhead fan. "I must have left the stove on!"

I hop onto the kitchen barstool and click off the smoke detector from the ceiling before it can alert the whole building to our mild midmorning disaster. "Crisis averted." His cheeks run red and I rub his shoulders, telling him it's all right.

Buffy sputters and then starts to giggle. "I'm glad you're okay, but can we take a minute?" Her dimples peek into view. "You managed to burn a pan of *nothing*."

A smile cracks across his face. "Yeah." He starts to chuckle. "I think that's a first for me." Before long, we're all laughing with her, rolling back into the (now, slightly crumby) bed.

Our good mood turns even better as we start to get frisky with each other. I inch up the flap of Hayden's apron, playing with the hair along his upper thigh. I bite into the curve of his neck and sink my hands into his crotch, stroking him. "Mm," he sighs. "That's nice."

Buffy teases herself as she watches the two of us together. "Damn." She licks her lips. "I want you both so bad, right now."

"Same here." Hayden rapidly unties the apron behind his

back. "Also, I was looking up good positions last night—y'all ever heard of doing a daisy chain?"

"You'll have to show me later." I slip out of both their grasping hands and quickly get myself dressed. "I'm supposed to meet up with Mako—they're giving me a hand with everything."

"No!" Buffy cries and paws after me. I blow a kiss as an apology.

Hayden pouts. "You got me all worked up for that?"

"You two can take care of each other, I'm certain." I slip on my shoes and snag my *Homo Sweet Homo* key chain from the kitchen countertop. "For real now, I've gotta go! Love you, bye!"

Time holds still. One foot out the door, I don't even breathe for what feels like a full minute. The skillet on the stove still slightly smokes. The oven fan grumbles. Cashew pops his head up and watches me with curiosity.

"I didn't—" The flow of the universe hits into its boomerang effect. It all speeds up again. "That wasn't—that was a reflex!"

"Are you sure?" Buffy hides her mouth with her hands but she can't hide the rise of a giggle in her throat.

"I just, I meant more like, that it's been love…ly to, um. Be together."

"We get it." Hayden shrugs himself off the bed. "You're just *so* in love with us you *had* to say it."

"Shush!" My face is burning hot.

Buffy slides up too and plants a kiss against my cheek. "We love you too, Charlie."

What surprises me even more than hearing her say it is knowing she means it. I never knew love could feel this easy. After everything with my dad and sister, with Hillside and Mako, I swore I'd never make my home in another person again. And I haven't, really. Because instead, we've made a home *together*, one that travels with us wherever we go. My heart's never been so full.

"Guess we really don't have any more secrets now." Hayden

kisses my other cheek and tousles my hair. "Yep, we love ya. Now go on already. See you soon."

Hassan arrives fifteen minutes early with a rhythmic knock at the door. As if there was any doubt he'd be late. Though he was still at the office when I left just half an hour ago, he's managed to change from his standard suit and tie into a sharp green vest that brings out the rich brown of his eyes. He's also somehow procured a casserole dish, which he passes over with a warm smile. "I know you said no need for snacks, but I thought I'd bring just a little something to nibble on."

"Hey, we're not complaining!" Mako sweeps out from under me and snags Hassan's platter of basbousa from my hands. "Good to see you, bud!"

"Mako!" Hassan's whole face lights up as he sees them. Sharing a hug, the pair step together into the living room. "It's been way too long, how *are* you?"

"Oh, you know, just changing the face of the beauty industry." Mako pries one of the golden squares from the casserole dish and nibbles happily on their pilfered treat. "What about you, when's the wedding? Those engagement photos you posted are *so* cute."

"Do you not have a set of salad tongs?" Hayden calls out while digging through my kitchen cupboards.

"I usually just eat it right from the bag," I admit with a shrug.

"All good." Buffy dumps a bag of chips into a large bowl. "We'll make it work."

There's another knock at the door. Cashew weaves around my feet, ready to greet our next guest. Augustine arrives in a bright yellow raincoat, droplets falling from her curly hair. "I walked," she states, and hands me a tightly sealed Tupperware. "Deviled eggs."

"Thanks." I take her coat. Cashew dashes off to avoid the splash zone.

Aditya arrives shortly after, with Sophia. Turns out both of them live in the apartment complex just across my street. They settle in with the rest of the group and soon chatter starts to blossom. It starts with workplace gossip but shifts to what we did this weekend, to what summer plans await us. Laughter sprinkles among pockets of conversation. Mako sets the trend and soon everyone has loaded their plates. Good food makes everything flow easier and someone gets the idea to put some music on. Hassan gets the dance party started while Cashew hops onto Augustine's lap for pets. The windows of my high-rise apartment are streaked with rain, the lights of Toronto are cast in misty grey fog. Inside, my bachelor pad has never been so warm and cozy.

I sit shoved into the corner of the couch, snuggled next to Buffy. Our hands linger intertwined, just out of sight from the rest of the group. Since I first clocked her feelings about crowds, back at Saint Brigid's, I've learned to watch her signals. I know she's got this, but I squeeze her palm in mine anyway and whisper, "You holding up okay?"

She quietly smiles back me. "Thanks." Glancing around the room, she nods. "It's a small group and so far I'm pretty okay."

"We're here if you need us, babe." Hayden scootches in beside her and offers a cookie. He's brought a whole tray of goodies for us to snack on.

"Thanks, hon," she says with a quick peck on his cheek. "Love you."

It doesn't take long for the questions to arise. Why have I asked everyone to come over, on a Sunday no less? After circling the point for a while, I just come out and say it. I spill the news about Angie's retirement, my potential promotion, the risk of more layoffs—all of it.

Mako sits on the floor, an open jar of Nutella in one hand and a spoon in the other. "So have you decided or what?" they ask. "Are you gonna take the job?"

The whole room turns their eyes on me. I look to Hayden, who tilts his head. Buffy juts out her lip. I nod. "I am still thinking it over," I tell them. "There's a lot to consider."

"What's there to think about?" Mako pops a scoop of Nutella in their mouth. "That job sounds like way too much work. Why not just do like I did and quit? It feels way good."

"Technically, you were laid off," says Augustine. Cashew mews for more attention, still curled up in her lap.

"Hell yeah I was." Mako goes in for a bite of basbousa. "Get yourself that severance money!"

"But who would benefit from that scenario?" Hassan circles us back to the point. Hands behind his back, he paces by the window. "Angie would still step down and who knows who might come in her place? If you were to come up next, then at least you'd have some influence."

"What if we were to approach the board?" Augustine suggests. "Speak to them directly about our concerns. I have some friends on there, they may listen."

"But for how long?" says Hayden. "In my experience, even if you've got some higher-ups on your team, there's no guarantee they'll be able to swing a vote in your favour."

"Not to mention," says Sophia, "it sounds like Angie herself has not wanted some of the latest changes. Who's to say Charlie would hold any more sway?"

"We could try a fundraiser?" offers Aditya.

"Too short-term," says Augustine.

"Maybe a new grant?" Hassan suggests.

Mako shakes their head. "I still think you all should just bail. Let the place crash and burn."

Buffy waits until the room quiets, before she speaks. "Money is a short-term solution," she tells us. "As are allies in positions of leadership. What you need is something more tangible, a position from which you can influence things as a collective."

"That's why I asked you all here tonight." I nod. "So we can—"

Knock-knock-knock. The whole room exchanges a series of puzzled looks. Augustine counts heads. "Who are we missing?" she wonders aloud.

"One second," I mutter, and push myself up.

"Hey, Hassan," Mako whispers as I step out of our circle. "I never got to ask, how's it been reporting to the HBIC ever since she fired all the cool people?"

"Literally, the worst," Hassan grumbles. "I've been dying to text you about all the stuff that's gone down—like, you should have seen the week she got a new glasses chain!" He snorts. "Finding every little excuse to take them on and off, like we were all in the opening bit of a bad *CSI* reboot."

Mako mimes adjusting glasses on their face. "It looks like this sheet... Will have to spread a little more." They snatch the faux glasses off and scream, "Yeah!"

Hassan bursts out into laughter and claps. "Yes, exactly like that!"

"Hello, Angie." Augustine gives a small wave. The whole room turns as one to where I stand, my hand on the door.

Clutching her umbrella under one arm, Angie wipes the fog from her glasses and peers around the room. "Apologies for my tardiness."

The hangers in my hall closet are packed tighter than they've ever been. They clatter amongst one another as Angie struggles to offload her coat. Somewhat awkwardly, she hunches over and peels off her short black heels and places them carefully among the pile of discarded boots, shoes and sneakers at my front door. Everyone remains silent as she stands at the edge of the living room circle, clutching her purse.

"Well," she tuts, "it seems you're in the need for more seating."

"You can have my spot!" Mako pats the pillow they're sitting on, which is now stained with fingerprints of Nutella.

Before Angie gets a chance to answer, Hayden hops up to

help. "How about you take the stool?" he offers, gently guiding the chair towards her. She gives a nod in thanks.

Angie's silhouette is a lot less intimidating when outside the glass walls of her office and broad desk chair. Perched on the stool, legs not quite long enough to reach the floor, she reminds me a bit of a large bird who's found its way to an unsteady perch. "Now," she addresses the room, "I'm sure you're all wondering why I'm here."

"Just a tad," Hassan mutters under his breath.

"To be honest, I've been asking that myself." Angie holds tight to the purse on her lap and fiddles with its clasp. "As Charlie put it this morning, I *am* the most senior member of CMM, in more ways than one. With that, I can lend a certain perspective."

I nod. "Plus, I was thinking with Angie gearing up for retirement, this is the perfect time for her to really go out with a bang, right?"

"That is a fair point." Augustine thoughtfully thumbs Cashew's furry chin, much to his appreciation.

"Still, having upper management join an organizing meeting is pretty unorthodox," says Buffy. "But Angie, if you're truly here to help us make change, I, for one, welcome you."

Angie tilts her head. "Sorry, who are you?"

"My name is Buffy Hawthorne. And I was just getting to the good part."

Leaning forward in her seat, Buffy takes a moment to look around the room and make eye contact with every guest. She stops on me and winks. "Now, whether it's Angie or Charlie, or someone else altogether in that Executive spot, what you're all really in need of is some solidarity." She begins to list off points on her fingers, "Protection against future layoffs. The right to have a say in the workplace and where you're heading. Fair hours, better benefits, a seat at the board. You're hardly the first group facing up against these issues, so let's talk strategy."

She puts a hand on Hayden's shoulder and asks, "Babe, would you like to do the honours?"

A smile spills across Hayden's cheeks. "Have you all ever considered forming a union?"

Epilogue

The warmth of the oven fills the kitchen with ease. I lean over to check on the progress of our casserole. The cheese is bubbling just right, golden brown.

"And what's that part?" Buffy points at a small turret at the edge of her daughter's latest sculpture. We watched a video online last night on how to make homemade playdough and she's been unstoppable ever since.

"It's where the Pegasuses can touch down," she replies, carefully focused on tiny shingles that decorate a slanting rooftop.

Hayden glances up from the cutting board. "Are you sure they're not Pegasi?" he asks.

I stir our fresh veg into the pan and add a dash of extra spices. "Looks like it's coming along nicely, Rebel."

She glances up, massaging a mash of multicoloured dough. "Actually, I'd like to go by Rainbow again. That was my favourite of all my names."

"I think that's the first time Reb—*Rainbow* has ever gone back to a name." Buffy grins. "Must be a good one!"

"Or maybe I'll just go by Rain." She shrugs and returns to her crafting. "I'll decide after dinner."

Just as quickly, the doorbell rings and soon enough our company has arrived. First, Hassan, of course. With him is his now-husband, Jay. They tote a large bowl of fresh greens, a lemon-based vinaigrette and a pair of salad tongs. We laugh and greet each other with warm hugs. Augustine sidesteps the rest of us to go visit with Miss Kiki at the cat tower. Mako brings with them two bottles of sparkling wine and Frances parades in shortly after, half his makeup still on. He just finished drag storytime at the Sunday school. Mango sings along, announcing each new guest. He's joined by a new friend, who Rainbow has named Papaya.

We pull chairs from every corner of the house and squeeze ourselves around the table. Elbows and knees clack and bang into one another as we squish and reach and pardon ourselves. Rainbow refuses to put away her playdough but accepts her castle getting its own seat on top of the fridge. Plates of various sizes are all passed around the table along with mismatching cutlery. Ladles and spoons and tongs and forks all dish out the many potluck dishes that grace our summer table. Firsts become seconds become thirds, streaks of sauce dribbled and dipped and licked clean. I lean back in my seat, my stomach full and heart warm.

"So, how's the new place?" Mako ventures the question.

"Nice." I pat my stomach. "Really nice, actually. Not fancy or anything but a lot bigger than what I could afford back in Toronto." From the kitchen window, I can see a hint of my new-to-me apartment complex. "I think Cashew likes it too. He's got a little spot at the back where he can watch the squirrels running on the power lines."

"I love that for him." Mako smiles as they pour themself another glass of wine.

"I have to say, it's nice to have you in walking distance."

Buffy leans her head on my shoulder. "All that driving back and forth was doing a number on our gas budget."

"Though, if you ever *want* to move back, we'd support that too." Hayden squeezes my arm.

"I know." I chuckle and pat his knee. "But, honest, I'm doing good out here. It's quiet, most folks are friendly—"

"And if you ever get bored, you can always swing by Saint B!" Frances reaches across the table to finish up the salad mix. "I've been meaning to ask, how's the dog walking going? There's a few congregants who have been asking."

"I'll have to check my schedule." I smile politely. When I first got back into the dog-walking thing, it felt like a step backwards. Especially to my dad, though he tried to be nice about it. But honestly, I've never felt better about where I'm at careerwise. And Mako loves the fact that they were right, starting my own business turned out to be the right call.

"Charlie's been swamped since they moved out here!" Hayden pokes my shoulder. "There's a real demand in Elmridge for someone who's so good with animals."

"I could help walk the dogs!" Rainbow wiggles in her seat. "I could, I could!"

"Maybe when you're a little bigger," says Buffy. Rainbow pouts. "We could start by letting you take Wellesley on his own a couple times?"

"You make it sound like paradise." Jay swirls the sparkling water in his mason-jar cup. "We've been thinking of moving to a smaller spot but." He shrugs. "I don't know. It's not an easy call."

"It helps if you already know some people." I nod. "Anyway, how's life back in the city—what's the office like these days?"

"Angie still hasn't stepped down." Hassan shakes his head. "She keeps promising to do it next quarter, and then *next* quarter."

"She's backing the union efforts, though," says Augustine. Wellesley snores at her feet. "Which makes organizing much easier. The vote is coming up again; hopefully we can make it happen this time."

"Speaking of!" Buffy sits up and digs out her phone. "I heard back from the Steelworkers—I'll forward you the email."

A second later though, my own phone starts to buzz. "Sorry!" I sneak it from my pocket to silence the ringer. "It's Emma— she's been living at Dad's for a couple weeks now and he's driving her up the wall!"

"*Your* father?" Hayden gives an over-exaggerated gasp. "Getting under someone's skin—I can't imagine!"

"Well, hopefully she finds her own place soon." I laugh along with them. "Turns out it's not so easy to just *hop into* the Toronto market."

"Well, make sure you tell her your old spot is *not* up for grabs!" Mako prods their fork at their plate. "I've already moved over all my plants and they are *loving* the natural light. You wouldn't take that away from them, would you?"

"Don't worry," I promise. "The place is all yours!"

"Good." Mako sips the last of their drink. "Oh, and I almost forgot! I think I left something in my car." They shuffle up from their seat. "Franny, would you be a dear?"

"Already on it!" Frances hops up after them. They hurry out the door together, giggling like mad.

"Franny?" I whisper to Buffy.

Hayden leans over to ask, "You don't think they're—?"

Suddenly, the room goes dark. Hassan stands at the light switch and moments later, Frances reappears with stack of cupcakes covered in candles.

"Happy birthday to you!" Mako starts to sing after him, "Happy birthday to you!" The room starts to join in chorus. Buffy and Hayden harmonize while Hassan rises to a falsetto. "Happy birthday to you, dear Charlie!" Rainbow bounces in her seat, her attention fixed on the flaming treats. "Happy birthday to you!"

The medley erupts into cheers as the cupcake tower is placed at my seat. "What—cupcakes?"

"Since you stole your own cake last time," Hassan reminds me with a smirk, "we went for something different."

"Surprise." Hayden kisses my cheek.

Buffy nuzzles me and whispers, "We love you."

"Go ahead and blow already!" Mako shoves the cupcakes towards me. The collective flame flickers, daring to almost go out.

"I've heard that one before." Hayden laughs with a hiss.

Buffy rolls her eyes. "Just go ahead when ready," she tells me. "You're allowed to have nice things, Charlie."

"Don't forget to make a wish!" Frances claps.

Bathed in the orange glow of candlelight, I take a deep breath and close my eyes. Hayden's hand sits on my shoulder. Buffy's palm gives mine a squeeze, our fingers intertwined. What else could I possibly wish for?

★ ★ ★ ★ ★

Author's Note

Chosen family is often considered a novel concept. Some might even say it is a "radical" act to form meaningful bonds that go beyond those of biological kinship and/or monogamous coupledom. However, I believe this is a misconception. Humans are social creatures, born with a deep need to be known and loved for all that we are. Over millennia, we have found, chosen, and made our own families. If anything is "radical," it is the age in which we live wherein so many people are isolated from genuine connection and community. While I don't expect a romance novel to change the world (though stranger things have happened), I hope this story offers a glimpse of possibility, a window into another way of doing things. In the love between Charlie, Buffy, Hayden and their interwoven families, may you encounter something different yet familiar; something deeply human.

I would like to state clearly that no character or community featured in the story is intended to be based on the exact likeness of any real person or group. Any similarities present are likely due to the fact that my own life experiences often inform my creative imaginings. I would also like to express special thanks to those individuals who lent their own names (or the names of their pets) to my characters.

Really Cute People has been a queer project from the start. My intention was to play with familiar tropes in romance fiction, especially forced proximity and the love triangle. I had a lot of fun getting to know these characters, trapping them inside a snowstorm and seeing what might happen. This story was intended to challenge some of these classic dynamics—after all, why *can't* a triangle turn into a triad? Additionally, there was something deeply healing in crafting a non-binary protagonist (whose assigned sex is never revealed, not even during the steamiest of steamy scenes), pairing them with a proud trans man and a burnt-out bi woman. For anyone who feels this story is "unrealistic" because of its many LGBTQ+ cast members, I would encourage you to crawl out from under your rock and look around—we are everywhere!

Even as I tried to focus on the romance angle, side-narratives kept sneaking into the main plot. Charlie's dad, their sister, Mako, Frances, all the folks at CMM, Saint Brigid's, and Hillside—none of these were supposed to become such big players. Now, I can't imagine the book without them. I think that's because we are all always carrying pieces of the people we've encountered. They make us who we are and help us know where we need to go. Even the concept of "chosen" family is itself a misnomer; relationships are rarely something we truly choose for ourselves but instead are formed through a medley of chance, fate, and circumstance. With all that said, I am truly grateful for my own good fortune in getting to share this unique story with all of you. Maybe you will even see a part of yourself in there, too.

Acknowledgements

I want to take a moment to thank my husband, Andrew McAllister, for all his steadfast support through this and so many other creative projects. Thanks also to Hannah Dees, who took on many long days of solo-parenting so that I could focus on my writing. And River, thank you for all your smiles and silliness—you continue to be the best part of every day.

Much appreciation goes to my grandparents, Bill and Cheryl Telford, Heather Dixon and Tony Harwood-Jones. Thank you for always believing in me. I pray you skipped over the steamier chapters in this book. If you didn't, please at least pretend that you did.

Thank you to my editors Kerri Buckley and Stephanie Doig. You saw all this story could be, even when I could not. Thanks also goes to Mackenzie Walton, for your detailed insights. I am grateful to my dear friend Ronan Sadler who originally encouraged me to draft this manuscript, and to Carina Adores for taking on my submission. To Myriad Augustine, thank you for all your thoughtful guidance, feedback, and sending of top-notch memes.

Michiko Bown-Kai, thanks for hosting me in your beautiful home and staying up late to swap stories about the good old days (some of which found their way into this book). Thank you to Tamiko, Chris, and Evelyn Lupa, for being the family of the real-life Wellesley and allowing me to borrow his name. Many thanks go to Caitlin and John Chee for running the real-life Fisticuffs (and making such good food, I had to put it in my novel). To Shane Forrest, thank you for being my best friend and dedicated superfan. Thanks to Mac Stewart, for all the last-minute breakfasts and dinner hangs. Lauren Munro, for commiserating with me through all kinds of big feelings. And to McKenzie Grey, thanks for being the best metamour a gay could ask for (and a super auntie, too).

Finally, I truly thank everyone who has ever been a part of Phoenix Nest. I will never forget our time together. Thank you to all the folks at LGBT Youth Line, for all the truly impactful work that you have and continue to do. Thank you to all my Dirty Chat pals and fellow Rugrats for always texting back. These community spaces, past and present, have made me who I am today and for that I am so grateful.

A former firefighter at loose ends and an academic with a confidence problem join a friendship study—and quickly become more than just friends...

Read on for an excerpt from
The Friendship Study
by Ruby Barrett.

Chapter One

Jesse

Between the music and my pulse thrumming in my ears, I think the pounding on my front door is thunder. The sky outside my window is slate gray, the clouds full to bursting.

But the pounding comes again, along with the ring of my doorbell, the two-tone sound distinctly un-storm-like. I turn my music down as I drag a balled-up T-shirt over my sweaty chest. My heartbeat is still coming down from the last set of back squats and my thigh aches from when the leg was in traction. A phantom pain that the doctors have hummed about skeptically in the two years since.

The doorbell rings again, three times in quick succession. "I'm coming," I yell.

A broad-shouldered, stocky person stands on the other side of the glazed glass door. "George?" I ask as I yank it open, already knowing the answer. I'd recognize the shape of him anywhere.

He narrows his eyes and gives me a once-over, his lip curled in disgust. For a panicked moment, I wrack my brain for some event I've missed. One that I agreed to attend with him and forgot to cancel.

"You need a shower."

I look down at myself. He has a point. My sweat has acted like glue, sticking dirt and dust to my skin. I need a shower and clearly my home gym needs one, too.

"I was working out," I say stupidly.

He walks past me, careful to avoid skin-to-skin contact. George never liked to join me at the gym when we were together. We'd hit the yoga studio or spin class but he "declined to participate" in the toxic bro culture of most weight rooms. The result is that George has stacked, lean muscle and some of the best cardiovascular stamina of anyone I know. Since my accident he's tried to get me to come with him to yoga again, and I've even acquiesced a few times, but I'm positive I didn't agree to that today.

George stands in my entryway, his head swiveling between the living room and the kitchen.

"Not that it's not nice to see you but...what are you doing here?" I ask.

He nods once and, seeming to make a decision, moves into the kitchen, placing a tote bag I hadn't noticed on the counter and opening the fridge. Bottles and jars clink as he moves stuff around, placing a six-pack of beer inside.

This is officially weird.

The last time George drank beer, we'd stolen it from my grandfather's beer fridge in the garage.

A fly buzzes past me and my still-hot skin puckers against the cool air. I've left the door open. I pull it closed and follow him into the kitchen. "Did we have plans?" I finally ask.

The answer is no. I know that it's no. Not for his lack of trying. I've just been a terrible friend—ex—whatever, this past year...maybe even longer.

"Why don't you go shower, Logan. You stink." He places a bag of tortilla chips, a brick of cheese, sour cream, salsa, and avocadoes on my counter. He opens the cupboard at his feet. Shuts it.

"Where'd you put your casserole dish?" He sounds livid. Like rearranging my kitchen was a personal attack. But I'm still stuck on his use of my last name. He hasn't called me Logan since we were in high school. Since we were both dragging ourselves through comphet in public, while giving each other hand jobs in his parents' basement in private.

He came out first. By baking a cake and piping *I'm gay* in rainbow icing on top, serving it to his parents after dinner. They were happy for him. His mom cried—out of happiness that he'd shared such an important part of himself with them, not out of any sense of disappointment. George came out and came into himself.

I came out more slowly. First, just to him.

I * don't * just like girls, I'd typed into our private chat. Words I had written and deleted what felt like hundreds of times. The backspace button was practically smoking.

I know ☺, he'd responded. He'd promptly asked me on a date.

Then I came out to our friends, but since most of my friends were George's friends, other outcast kids he'd collected over the years, mostly queer theater kids, telling them felt less like coming out and more like landing in a loud, fluffy pillow of love and acceptance.

I came out to the fire station, too, but only after a few years on the job. After I made sure they saw my contributions as invaluable, and after a few of the old-guard vets, who used "gay" as an insult, had retired. For the most part, they were chill. A few blank faces that I'm sure were working hard not to show disgust, some confusion since bisexuality continues to be one of the most perplexing of all the sexualities known to straights. After I dropped a few "hose" jokes at my own expense, everyone calmed down. Since having sex in the firehouse, regardless of the gender of your partner, is expressly and certifiably prohibited, I didn't have to hide much. But I was always worried that someone—one of my older coworkers who kept in touch or a rookie who'd idolized him—would out me to Pop.

Even when we were dating, to Pop, George was always just a friend. My best friend, but *just* a friend. Back then, we'd used all of the same tools that straight boys used to emotionally distance themselves, including calling each other by our last names.

I probably don't have the right to the feeling, but *Logan* makes me angry. Pop isn't here and to George, I'm Jesse. Jess. I'd even accept *Juicy*, the name he called me only when he wanted to make me blush. A name I'd asked him to stop using once we stopped being boyfriends.

I let that anger dictate the next words out of my mouth. "Listen, you can't just barge in on a Saturday afternoon, *uninvited*, and start making lunch. What the hell are you doing here?"

"No, *you* listen." He points a finger at me. George has always been able to give as good as he gets. "I tried giving you space. We all did. You've got yourself some new job you didn't even tell me about, which is…whatever. You haven't been dating and I get why you might not want to share that with me, anyway. Hell, you're a private guy, Jesse. OK? I get it. But you are also my best friend." His words end on a sigh, losing all of their bluster.

He slides his hand across the countertop, the tips of our fingers touching. My heart squeezes and I hope it doesn't show up like it feels, a crack down the center of my face.

"You're my best friend, too." My voice is shaky, and I swallow the other words down, that he's the person I'm closest to in this world, other than Pop.

George doesn't let me off the hook, though. "You haven't

been texting anyone back for months. You don't pick up the phone. You didn't join the softball team this year. I'm trying to be understanding, but I miss you."

After over a decade of knowing each other, George is used to my silences. Still, I can't help but feel self-conscious about them. I stare down at the old Formica countertop, trace my finger over the faint brown crescent moon burned into it, marking the spot where Grandma had once put a hot pot down without a trivet.

"So, you're going to shower," George says, softer. "And I'm going to make this new nacho dip I found, and you're going to drink beer, and we will watch some rugby match on whatever channel you pay too much money for. And we're going to start again."

"Start again?"

"Our friendship," he says, quieter still. "We're going to restart it without the baggage of being exes and the decade that we've already accumulated between us. We're just going to be two queer dudes, hanging out. Being friends." He clears his throat and clenches his jaw, a little embarrassed.

"The casserole dish is above the stove," I say after a moment.

The shower is too hot, then too cold. Never an in-between. I dress still a little wet, my shirt sticking to my back. I putter around my weight room, what used to be my bedroom until I moved everything into the master bedroom last year, after Pop moved into the assisted-care home. I wipe down the floor mats I installed, and the bench, the bar and the plates, the mirror on the wall, with an all-purpose cleaner.

Pre-match commentary blares as I enter the living room and I join George on the couch, a bowl of chips and the casserole dish—now filled with some sour-cream-salsa-cheese concoction—between us. "I also ordered a pizza," George says, his eyes on the TV screen as if he's actually interested in what two old white Welsh men have to say about these random teams' prospects this season.

I shrug and dip a chip. "It's good," I say with a full mouth.

He preens. George has a separate Instagram account dedicated to his cooking and baking projects. I assume he's already uploaded photos of this dish to the account. Meanwhile, I have an Instagram account I have forgotten the password to.

I sip my beer; it's still warm after too few minutes in the fridge. A rugby player drop-kicks the ball from the middle of the field. George scrolls his phone. Despite his claims that we are starting fresh, he's as comfortable here as I am. He's as familiar as the furniture that's been here for twenty years at least, the school pictures and my grandparents' wedding photos hanging over the fireplace; nothing's been changed since my grandmother was alive. The only new things in this house are the television and the close-cropped haircut I got last week.

Eventually, the boredom gets the best of him, and George regales me with the drama at his job. He's the administrator for the psychology department at the University of Wilvale, the school that's the only reason this town is on a map at all. George is also, slowly, getting his PhD part-time. He doesn't want to be a psychologist, he says. He just wants to be able to psychoanalyze our friends. Since this is the exact level of meddling I expect from him, I've never said anything about how he's spending a shit-ton of money to be able to dole out the best advice in our friend group.

"OK," George says, breaking the comfortable silence that has settled between us. "There's more to this intervention than just starting fresh." His voice is pitched high. He catches his lip between his teeth.

I freeze with the beer bottle halfway to my mouth. This is what his nerves are about.

"Don't be mad," he pleads.

I place my bottle on the coaster and resist the urge to say I'm not mad, I'm just disappointed. Because George does this. He's the king of not-always-welcome surprises. Most of the time I'm quiet because I don't know what to say but this time, I let the silence hang thick between us.

The doorbell rings. George winces at the door and back at me. "That's the food."

George's eyes are bigger than my stomach. I'm already full.

He says quickly, "You're going on a date tonight." Then gets up to answer the door.

"A what?" I ask when he comes back carrying a pizza box. Normally, I'd reach for my wallet, but he can cover this one. "A *date*?"

I'm not disappointed. I'm definitely mad. But underneath that anger is the gripping fear that makes it hard to speak, to breathe.

"Why?" I ask, then before he can answer, "With who? When? George, *why*?"

He slides the box onto the coffee table. "Just listen."

"No." I stand up. Sit down. It's been two years since my accident but in this weather—unseasonably cold, damp, the air heavy with rain that hasn't fallen yet—my leg stiffens, aches. I press my fist against it, as if the pressure on the muscle will distract my nerves from the metal in my bones, the muscles that were torn and shredded.

"No. I'm not going on a date with anybody. You can't do this to me, George."

"There's this woman who works at the university." He plows ahead as if I haven't already said an adamant and resounding absolutely the fuck not. "And we've become lunch buddies and we've been talking and she's really lonely—but gorgeous—and she hasn't been on a successful date in forever—I don't know why, she's lovely—and she reminded me of you."

He walks into the kitchen, the floorboards creaking under his feet. The sound of cupboards opening and closing drifts in over the quiet hum of thickly accented rugby match commentary. As if this is just a casual conversation and not George meddling in my personal life. Again.

"She reminds you of me because…we're both lonely and can't get dates?" I ask. "Do you know how rude that sounds?" I don't get angry often. Even now the feeling is burning up, leaving something empty and airless in its place. But my voice still trembles.

He comes back with two plates and starts doling out slices. "And I told her about you, and she said you sounded great and how about this Saturday, and I said I'd set it up and now…" he says, breathless. "It's Saturday."

"What if I had plans already?" I ask, as he shoves a plate into my hands.

He snorts.

"I didn't say I *did* have plans, just *what if*," I grumble.

"Maybe if you'd answer your phone or text me back once in a while," he hisses, his hand still gripping my plate. "We wouldn't be finding ourselves in this predicament."

George leans back, holding his plate up at his chest to avoid crumbs falling everywhere. He takes a huge bite of his pizza, grumbling around greasy pepperoni. I dump my plate onto the coffee table. My stomach has soured to the thought of food, and instead I worry; about how terribly my last date went, with a man I'd met through an app, who turned out to only want sex but definitely not sex with me; at how I used to be strong, capable, a firefighter, a man who trusted his body, and how now I'm not strong or capable of much at all, how I'm not a firefighter, how I've lost that trust.

I know, somewhere deep down, that this is probably anxiety. I know that I should probably do something about that but losing my job didn't just affect my identity. It affected my access to things like therapy at anything close to an affordable rate.

Mostly, I worry about George's supreme ability to meddle.

And my inability to say no to him. Because he does meddle, but George also loves me, and he worries, too. And if he's done this, knowing how I'd react, I've made him worry. A lot.

"I need to visit Pop," I say, a little helplessly. A last-ditch effort at no.

"Lulu said you should meet her at The Pump at seven. You have lots of time."

"Lulu?"

He shoots me a look. "Yes. Lulu."

"Sounds like a cartoon character," I mumble.

He shoves me, his shoulder to mine. With the difference in our size, I don't move. "It's short for Eloise. Don't be rude."

"I'm not," I say. "I'm sorry." I feel sheepish. "This is just…a lot."

The match plays on, the Welsh accents on the announcers so thick I can only pick out every third word or so. But I don't want to hear them talk. I watch since it's better than not watching. If I can't play anymore, at least I have this.

"Jess," he says, softly. "I really am sorry for meddling." George nibbles his pizza.

"I know you are." The invisible fist wrapped around my chest loosens. Everything feels a little bit better now that I'm Jess again.

"It's just cuz I want—"

"What's best for me. I know." I sigh. And I do know. I love him enough not to care…too much. "Next time could you just set up a dating profile without my permission instead, though?"

George throws his head back as he laughs, his dark curls flopping on his forehead, and it's not until hearing it that I realize how much I've missed it. Laughter: his, Pop's, my own.

"So, you'll go?" he asks.

I sigh. "What's she like?"

George lights up. He knows he's winning and I hate it. "She's smart and funny and a little quirky. Here." He pulls out his phone and navigates to an Instagram account for someone named @luluvsyou.

And she may not be a cartoon character of the Saturday morning TV variety. More like my thirteen-year-old Sailor Moon obsession. Her eyes are big and blue, framed by winged eyeliner, her lips a shiny bubble gum pink. Her hair is a purple cloud around her head.

"She doesn't have that hair anymore," he says. "She just doesn't update her social media a lot."

So, we're both lonely, bad at getting dates, and terrible at content creation. At least we'll have something to talk about. "George, she's..."

He won't let me get away with saying she's too pretty for me. But he can't stop me from *thinking* it. And not even in an "I'm ugly" way. I know what I look like. But there's more to a relationship than attraction and I'm not sure I can bring the rest.

"If you really, really don't want to, I'll text her right now and cancel but... I really do think you'll like her. And at the very least, you could be friends." His gray eyes are big and pleading. He's got his palms pressed together like he might beg.

"It's weird," I say. "That my ex is setting me up on dates."

"The straights could never," he says and this time I laugh.

"Yeah. I'll go," I say, even though it makes my chest feel tight, a date that might end like the last one. Or a person who might expect me to fit within their life when I can barely fit into my own. "On one condition," I say.

"Anything."

I can tell he means it.

"You stop meddling."

George is quiet, staring blankly at the TV screen. Like he has to think about it and he's weighing his options, as if it might be worth canceling on this "Lulu" for the right to keep sticking his nose in my business.

"*George.*"

He sighs. "Fine."

I sit back against the couch and focus on the match. This feels like a win, even if it isn't really.

Chapter Two

Lulu

Wilvale University boasts fewer than ten thousand students on one hundred and fifty acres of land and yet I always seem to run into the same people. I expected the history department to be quiet today since the Phillies have a better chance of winning the World Series than an academic has of dragging themselves to campus on a Saturday, but the bathroom door swings open just as I'm ready to flush and I freeze in my stall.

I try to catch a glimpse of the shoes that enter the stall next to mine but they're not the heels that Miranda wears or the orthopedic sneakers that the semiretired Dr. Hoff wears. They're flats, but fancy, the kind with a pointed toe. They tell me all I need to know about who this is. My bathroom companion finishes their business as I stand stock-still and it doesn't occur to me that they a) probably know I'm in here, too and b) think it's weird that I'm just standing here listening to them pee?

Get it together, Lu.

And yet. I wait until the door opens and closes on their re-treating footsteps before I unlock the door. I lean against the sink after I wash my hands. The summer semester started last week and I find myself teaching the same first-level course that I've taught since I started here in the fall: Introduction to West-ern History, which is really just a sterile way of saying, we're going to teach you about a bunch of old dead, white guys from the fall of Rome until the First World War. And let's face it, that's already a pretty sterile topic.

"Imagine," I say to my reflection. "The horrific finality of being remembered only for the worst thing you've never done."

I make a face like *blech*. It's a bit dramatic and over the top, but it's gripping. It's exactly the way I'd want to start my gen-der and witchcraft course, if I could ever get out from under-neath this first-year survey course the department has saddled me with.

As I finish washing my hands, I recite more of the lecture that I've lain in bed crafting, that I've spent hours working on when I should have been reading a new article about gender theory or grading exams or working on a proposal for a book.

"Between the fifteenth and eighteenth centuries, thousands of people—mostly women—were murdered because they were believed to be witches…" I swing the door open with too much force, the handle hitting the wall with a loud bang. I cringe and poke my head out into the history department hallway but whoever was in the bathroom with me doesn't seem to be around now.

A lot of academics see teaching as a speed bump, something that gets in the way of research and writing, but I grew up watching my dad take hours to prepare his lectures. He'd prac-tice in the mirror and rehearse for mom at the dinner table. He cares so much about his students, about giving them the chance to love history as much as he does. I didn't have any other choice but to feel the same way.

"Other than their alleged crimes, historians don't know much about them. Sometimes names were recorded, sometimes ages. But their lives before they were 'witches' are lost." I pause, patting my pockets down for my phone. I open the notes app, ignoring the red notification from my lunch buddy, George, and type: "Anonymous. Erased. Their history was burned up along with them, on flaming pyres."

Damn. I'm good. That's good, right?

Behind me, someone giggles, sharp and high. In this hallway, with the tiled floor and cement brick walls painted white, the sound echoes, matching the stark and impersonal feeling of the history department. I hunch my shoulders up to my ears, a defensive position before I've even turned around. Dr. Audrey Robbs and Dr. Frank Hill peer out from the now open doorway of Dr. Miranda Jackson's office.

"Who are you talking to?" Audrey asks. Her tone makes it clear she knows I was talking to myself and she thinks that's a little bit weird.

"No one," I say quickly. "I was…" I clear my throat, trying to buy myself time to come up with an excuse, but I've always been a terrible liar. "Practicing."

"Practicing for what, Dr. Banks?" Miranda smiles, welcoming and warm where Audrey and Frank are skeptical, sharing a look.

"Um." I clear my throat again. They're going to think I'm getting sick if I keep this up. "A lecture."

"For Intro to Western History?" Audrey asks. Audrey's style resembles Miranda's more than the grad student chic that I still sport, despite receiving my doctorate two years ago, which consists of any available clean clothes that match my Keds. Which means really any type of clothing at all. Everything matches Keds.

Audrey wears a pair of pointy-toed flats, made to resemble animal hide, a skirt in the graphite-est of grays, and a blouse that buttons to the collar. She'd never be caught dead in sneakers, or talking to herself. Frank already looks bored and disdainful, offended by my presence, though he doesn't reserve that for just me. He thinks he's God's gift to the study of eleventh-to-thirteenth-century monastic orders and manuscript illumination.

"For a…" I wasn't planning to pitch this idea until the planning meeting later this summer, but Miranda's here now, I guess. It would be good to get her input. I look from Audrey to Frank, gauging the level of judgment on their faces.

Ever since my own survey course in European history in high school, I've wanted to understand the women I study, to speak their names into the history books. Those too old, or poor, or angry, or independent, deemed not good enough by men who were too scared and powerful to see them for what they were: mothers and sisters and daughters, neighbors and friends. Healers. Humans. I want to give my students the chance to love history as much as I do.

But right now, staring down Audrey and Frank, I wouldn't mind a little bit of my witches' anonymity.

An anemic oscillating fan whirrs in the corner of Miranda's office, gently lifting papers and blowing Audrey's hair against the back of her neck. Sunlight hits the window behind the desk at just the right spot this time of day, reflecting off the picture frames on Miranda's bookshelf and the shiny lacquer of her desk, blinding me if I glance in her direction. At least, I tell myself it's the sun and not the hero worship I feel at the sight of *the* Dr. Miranda Jackson, the only Black woman in the department, a tenured historian of Africa and the Caribbean, race, gender, and power, and African diasporic religions, waiting for me to explain what the hell I'm muttering about in the hallway on a weekend.

"Actually, it's for a class I'd like the opportunity to pitch at our next planning meeting," I say.

There's a half-empty tub of hummus on Miranda's desk, and

laptops in Audrey's and Frank's laps. I've interrupted a meeting, something friendly and personal. Something I wasn't invited to.

"Let's hear it." Audrey's smile is as sharp as her tone.

"You don't have to, Dr. Banks," Miranda says quickly. I want to think that she's uncomfortable but truth be told, I don't know Miranda all that well. Dad always speaks so highly of her. I'll swallow my tongue before I back down in front of her.

I wave my hand like it's nothing despite the ice in my veins. "It's a history of gender and witchcraft course. Something we could offer to second- or third-year students after they've taken the survey course." The one that I'm teaching. "As a popular grassroots movement that was informed by the geopolitical issues on the European continent, I think there are connections between this cultural hysteria and—"

Audrey makes a humming noise, her face scrunched up in an apology that she doesn't mean. "Sounds a bit…derivative."

"Well, you haven't heard anything about it yet—"

"And I'm not sure we have the budget for a new course," Audrey continues, turning back to Miranda, as if she knows anything about the department's budgets. As if she's not a contract instructor holding on to employment by her fingernails, just like me. "Right, Miranda?"

I shouldn't be embarrassed, I know. It's just a pitch, just an idea. That's what I tell myself, over and over again even as my face flushes, the heat of embarrassment scalding like a wash of hot water.

"Well." Miranda winces. "We do have to review the budget, yes…"

"See." Audrey shrugs like that settles it, her face contorted in what I think is supposed to be sympathy.

I don't know what I'm more embarrassed by: the fact that I was fool enough to pitch it at all, to share something that feels so precious; or how, despite her obvious dislike for me, I'm desperate to be Audrey Robbs's friend. Frank I could take or leave.

"Plus, we're offering my new course next, History of Magic."
Audrey sets her jaw, squares her shoulders like she's challenging me to respond. But I won't. I never will.

Sometimes I wonder if I wouldn't be better off back in the UK, trying to make it work. Sure, my history prof boyfriend, Dr. Brian Mason, cheated on me with my best friend and colleague, Dr. Nora Carpenter, effectively blowing up my entire professional and personal life and making every migration to the department's shared kitchen a walk of shame, but at least when I taught at the University of Lancaster, my dad hadn't had to get me the job after all my other academic leads had dried up. News of Brian and Nora's twin betrayal reached my coworkers here at Wilvale University before I did since academia is basically a gossip magazine with tweed elbow patches. So, now not only am I that fishy nepotism hire, I can feel their stares when they wonder what kind of social deficit I had, like a witch's mark, that pushed my bestie into my boyfriend's bed.

I've only been teaching here since last September but I've spent every minute trying to prove that I didn't just get this job because of my dad—that I am actually good at this. It's why I volunteered for the intro course this semester.

Frank huffs, turning his back to me. His body shakes. He's *laughing* at me.

Maybe it's to check if she's noticed—as if she could somehow not notice—or maybe I'm just a glutton for punishment, but I can't read the expression on Miranda's face other than to know I don't want to see more of it.

"Right. Well. I'd better..." I jerk my thumb behind me, turning on my heel fast enough my sneakers squeak. A sound, like a snort that's been contained, then Audrey's quiet shushing, follows me out of Miranda's office.

I love my work, when it's just me and books and words. Me, standing at a lectern teaching; sometimes people want to be

there, they've chosen that course because they're interested, but
sometimes they have to be there to fulfill a history credit before
they graduate. Those ones are my favorite. I love persuading
them that history is more than just a requirement.

History is fun, but *this* isn't fun. Sometimes it feels like every
academic got a rulebook, one that counsels competition over
partnership, to step on the throats of anyone who might be in
front of you on the tenure track. One that champions working to burnout, past burnout, as the best indicator of success.
It expects you to work for free and give feedback even if you
won't get any. It teaches you how to posture, to demean. And
everyone got a copy of this rulebook except me. I'm sure of it.

I manage to close my office door behind me with a soft snick
instead of a slam. But just barely. I'm sweaty, my heart thumping like a punk band's drum. I left Lancaster to get out from
under the shadow of a man only to find myself so desperately
in need of a job that now I'm stuck under the shadow of my father. And while I now have a job, I've alienated the very people
I was once so excited to work with.

My phone buzzes in my pocket, another reminder of the text
message I still haven't opened from George.

**Jesse said he's SO excited to see you tonight. He wants to meet
at the Pump @ 7. I told him that would work for you, right? G**

Crumbs. I slump down into my chair, the wheels rolling me
back into my desk.

Can't wait!!!

I type back with the kind of false bravado that is only capable through text message. I won't ever admit this to George
because I'm pretty sure he'd freak out but I definitely forgot I
agreed to go on a date with this Jesse.

★ ★ ★

Gravel pings on the undercarriage of my new—to me—car as I pull into The Pump's parking lot. Little Texas, the restaurant next door to The Pump, has leaned so far into their rustic theme that despite being located in a college town in Pennsylvania they cover their floors with sawdust and kept the parking lot unpaved. The lights in Little Texas are still dark; it's too early in the evening for them to bother opening yet. But a warm glow comes from The Pump, with its decidedly more steakhouse vibe.

I don't know why I even agreed to The Pump. I'd be more comfortable at Little Texas, with its neon signage and combination of pop and country music. Although, now that I think about it, a loud combo of pop and country probably doesn't make Little T's a good "date" location, and if I've somehow gotten myself talked into a date with George's friend—maybe ex? The way he talked about him, I thought he could be—I should at least be able to hear him.

"You could cancel," I whisper to myself, the desire like the small, sputtering flame of a Bic lighter. After the afternoon I've just had, all I want to do is go home, sit in bed in my underwear, and scroll social media for satisfying cleaning videos.

"No, you absolutely cannot cancel," I hiss back. "You're supposed to meet him, like, *now.*"

The door to The Pump swings open and two women walk out, laughing. "Must be nice," I grumble at them, then immediately feel bad about it. It's not their fault they're normal, adult humans who can make friends.

I shouldn't have agreed to this. Not when the burn of Nora's betrayal aches like a phantom limb. Not when the thought of meeting someone new, of trying to convince them that I'm worth the time, makes me feel sick and exhausted. I was just so excited to be making a friend in George. The first time he spoke to me

I assumed he was talking to someone behind me and kept walking until he waved his hands in the air.

And now we're…friends…almost. We're at the very least semi-consistent lunch dates. Our conversations don't get into very personal territory, mostly sticking to work, my teaching position at the university and his work running the psych department. And at a time when my desperation for human connection outside of my parents borders on rank, it's so stinky, I didn't want to say no to him about his friend Jesse.

I bare my teeth into the rearview mirror and pat down my hair. I hike up my jeans and adjust the crop top that seemed like a good idea when I tried it on but now seems too cutesy and far too underdressed in the fading evening light. I review my list of acceptable conversation topics: my work/his work; the Phillies/whatever sports team he likes (though if he doesn't at least tolerate the Phillies, I'm not sure what more we could say to each other); recent travel; summer holiday plans.

Safe, normal topics of conversation.

Pausing at the front door, I pull my spring jacket on, despite knowing I'll have to take it off in a few moments anyway. The air is cool enough that my nipples are pressing through the fabric of my shirt. I'll never apologize for having nipples that react to the temperature, but I just know I won't be able to keep my mouth shut about them, if I walk in there like this. I'll make some joke about my breasts and then his gaze will fall to them because where else would they go and he'll either be horrified or think it's a desperate come-on.

Unacceptable conversation topics: the aforementioned nipples; if he has a favorite tree; the top ten stupidest ways early modern men attempted to identify witches; why the 1983 Phillies' uniforms are the best uniforms, which is really less of a topic of conversation and more of a slide deck.

"Just a drink with a nice guy," I mumble. "George wouldn't set you up with a serial killer."

Although, how well do I know George, really? What if George is a serial killer? What if they're a serial-killing duo?

"Go inside, Lulu," I growl.

The hostess who stands at the front is a young Black woman with a bubbly smile. "Do you have a reservation?"

I search the restaurant, but the few men all have a dining partner already. At the back of the room, where a dark bar fills the space between the "in and out" doors to the kitchen, one broad-shouldered, white man in a navy blue pullover sweater sits perfectly centered. Part of me is tickled by the symmetry of it all. The girl who takes pleasure in this kind of movie-scene kismet wants to frame him between my thumbs and forefingers and take a mental snapshot. But I can't get hot for kismet anymore.

I try to channel a little bit of the kismet-loving, happy-go-lucky girl I used to be as I let the hostess know I'm all good, stride between the tables, and hop onto the stool next to him. Letting my hair fall over one shoulder, I smile, following a template for flirtation. Fake it till you make it or whatever.

"Hi, Jesse Logan? I'm Lulu." I stick out my hand to shake.

Jesse turns toward me, his mouth flat. Not the reaction I expected. Maybe since this is technically a date we shouldn't shake? Maybe we should hug? Should we kiss? A double-cheek peck? Surely, we shouldn't. Now that I've thought the word "kiss," my brain must immediately collect data about the kiss-ability of this man, and my eyes drop to his mouth.

Double crumbs, he definitely saw that, and what if now he thinks I want to kiss him?

"Can I get you anything?" the bartender asks, saving me from this spiral. He has that classic style, a white cloth folded over his shoulder, a perfectly crooked smile aimed at me, suspenders and a slick haircut. He looks like he can call a woman "doll" and it doesn't even come off that patronizing. I feel Jesse's eyes on my face while I order a beer and the bartender asks for my ID, confirming that the crop top was definitely the wrong choice. His stare feels heavier as I flush, rummaging through my bag, which is one-third purse, one-third work tote, one-third gym bag, for my wallet.

Jesse Logan shifts in his chair, sighing, and if I dropped dead right now the coroner would have to put humiliation as the cause of death because heck am I rattled. My eyes are so wide from trying not to suddenly cry, they feel like they could fall out of my head as the bartender studies my license, my face, my license again, and finally nods. As I tuck my ID back into my wallet and ask once more for the closest beer on tap.

He looks at me out of the corner of his eye as I settle beside him. The bartender returns with my beer, refilling Jesse's drink, which is...soda water? Silence descends as the bartender walks away, wiping down the dark wood of the bar. The dining room behind us tinkles quietly with the sounds of utensils on plates and clinking glasses. I have to have arrived at least two minutes ago. That span of time doesn't seem so long in general but in the context of a first date with a man I've never met before, it's an eternity.

My heart doesn't beat any faster, just harder, like each pump is more difficult than the last. My palms sweat. I don't know when this happened, or how. All I know is that I left the UK, where I'd built a healthy, thriving social life, a best friend I trusted, a boyfriend I loved, all to have it blow up in my face. I came back to beg for a job at my hometown university, with the early modern historical equivalent of a rock star in Dr. Miranda Jackson, and found that most of my high school friends had moved away, moved on. I was left with a vacuum, of time, of space. Wake up, teach classes no one seems very interested in despite my efforts, grade mediocre scores, go home, repeat. And now this: sitting here in the kind of silence that grows louder and louder. This must be what it feels like to burn alive, every second longer than the last.

His jaw works, his five-o'clock shadow thick by seven. "Hello, Eloise." His voice is deep, flat.

Eloise?

"How do you know my name?" I ask, my voice prickled with irritation. I *hate* Eloise.

He studies me. "George. He said your name is Eloise." He sounds accusatory, like either I or George has lied. After a beat, he smiles, mouth closed, lips tight.

I turn my chin toward the bar to hide the flush that I can feel creeping up my cheeks. "Right." I make myself laugh, like *ha!* "You're not going to call me Eloise all night, are you?"

I was named after my father's mother's aunt; an oops baby according to me, a delightful surprise according to my mother, when my parents were already well into their careers. I was nameless for the first week of my life before they finally pulled Eloise out of a literal hat. My father still owns the head covering in question and wears it on particularly sunny days in the garden. I met my great-great-aunt Eloise once when I was seven and Dad took us back to his home, a small village in Kent. Eloise loved my father dearly, but she did not even tolerate seven-year-old me. Which didn't offend me too much once I found out that she coughed up phlegm almost constantly. The incident that sealed our resentment was when I watched her eat a piece of her own long hair like a slowly slurped noodle. Even my young seven-year-old self knew that was a bridge my over-active gag reflex could not cross.

I say *none* of this out loud.

Add that to the list of inappropriate conversation topics.

Jesse frowns and it takes putting my hand to my forehead to understand why. I was frowning at him first. I smile instead, a duplicate of his closed-lip version.

He says, "I'll call you whatever you want me to call you."

With his deep voice and the frown still marking up his face like my red pen on an undergraduate's essay, he doesn't sound the least bit accommodating. More sinister. I lean back in my chair.

Who are you, George's friend?

He shifts in his chair, looking immediately uncomfortable. The bartender, who'd stopped in front of us, must feel the awkwardness settling because he turns on his heel and walks away. Jesse drops his gaze to the bar, flushing, and *oh*. I was so busy feeling nervous, not wanting to come, I never considered that he might also be nervous. But as he turns away from me, grabbing a few cocktail napkins and dabbing at the water ring around his glass like he's defusing a bomb, huffing another sigh that upon reflection could be a deep, steadying breath, I'd say yeah. Jesse is just as nervous as I am.

He clears his throat. "What do you prefer?" he asks. "Lulu or Eloise?"

My mother has called me Lu or Lulu since before I can remember. Eloise has never felt like my name. More a label, the wrong one, slapped on a bag to say "these are caramels," when they're Fun Dip or Fizzy Pops or…gosh, anything but caramels.

Brian was the only person who ever called me Eloise. Even before we were anything but colleagues, he'd insisted. Lulu was a child's name, according to Brian. Eloise was distinguished. I let him, desperate for someone like Dr. Brian Mason of Lancaster University to think I was distinguished. Now, every time he called me Eloise feels like a betrayal. Brian trying to fit a square peg into a round hole and the square peg desperately wishing she could wear down her hard edges to fit.

"I like Lulu." Even now, saying it sounds like asking for permission.

"Sure, Lulu."

A bloom, something affectionate and warm, floats in my chest. He flattens his sweater down his torso, navy blue merino wool giving way under his hand, hinting at the muscle definition underneath. In this light, his brown eyes are a perfect contrast. I can't tell if Jesse is the type of man who would pick a sweater that purposely complements his eyes, but I'm tickled by it either way. His forearms fill out the sleeves, his biceps stretch the fabric. As I follow the wool over the wide line of his shoulders, I notice a square of white cardboard sticking out of the back of his collar.

He's left the tag on.

"Were you planning on returning that sweater?" I ask, my hand halfway to his collar.

He eyes that hand like I'm holding a knife. "Uh…no. What?"

I give the tag a tug, snapping it off. *The Gap. $59.99.*

"Tag." I crumple it in my fist.

Jesse makes a mumbled sound like *oh no*, patting at the back of his shirt, his face turning a deeper and deeper shade of purple. This date is a bit of a disaster. I reach for whatever I can to save it.

"George said you were a firefighter?"

He blinks through a moment of pointed silence. "Yes." His tone is flat, flatter than normal. Final. "He said you have a PhD in witchcraft? At the university?" Jesse frowns like that's not right.

I take a big gulp of my beer, now warmer than it should be after sitting.

"I have a PhD in the history of witchcraft. I'm not a witch."

He nods very seriously.

"That would be cool, though."

He keeps nodding.

I can feel the silence threatening to descend again like a funeral shroud ready to declare this evening dead.

"I read that candles are one of the top five causes of house fires," I offer.

Jesse blinks, his brow furrowing. To be fair, I'm not sure what I expected him to do with that information. "I really love scented candles." I laugh like, *what can you do?* "But like what if they…start a fire in my house…" I trail off. It's either that or I physically restrain myself from speaking.

"As long as you leave twelve inches of space around the candle and don't leave it unattended, you should be safe," he says.

"Oh. Great. Thanks." I take another deep pull of my beer. At the very least I can walk away with this important safety tip.

"What do you enjoy about firefighting?" I ask. "Fighting fires? Fire…extinguishing?"

Jesse takes a sip of his water, shaking his head with a quiet "no thank you," like he doesn't want to answer the question. I was not aware that we could just decline to answer questions, but he does it so seamlessly I catalog the interaction away for myself. The next time a colleague tries to ask a leading question about my productivity I will simply do as Jesse does and decline.

"Tell me about your research," he says and either he knows other academics and thus knows we can't shut up about our research, or he's secretly my evil nemesis who somehow knows my one and only kryptonite. So, I spend far too long talking about the history of witches and the Witch Craze, gender and perceptions of witchcraft, especially within the context of early modern Europe, especially, *especially* in England and how, now that I've moved home I'm focusing on witchcraft in the colonial period; witch hunts, the bubonic plague, war, fear-mongering misogyny, and law in the sixteenth to nineteenth centuries. Once I start devolving into torture devices used to coerce confessions and Royal Witch-Hunter King James VI or I and explaining how he was both a sixth and a first at once, I stop myself. I've definitely wandered into unacceptable conversation topic territory. I don't know how long we've been sitting here but my butt is sore from this hard barstool, and I've finished one beer and started halfway into another. *Whoops.*

It's time to pull this back into safe conversation territory, although Jesse doesn't seem too concerned about anything I just said. He sat and listened quietly, maintaining eye contact the whole time, nodding, *hmm*-ing and throwing in a couple well-timed *I see*'s.

"What about you?" I hiccup into my hand before taking another gulp of IPA. "Why'd you get into fighting fires?" I try again.

He fiddles with the hem of his sweater but at least doesn't deflect me this time. "Family business." He says nothing else, and I resist the urge to duck to his level and catch his gaze. It's probably just the beer but something about Jesse's attention feels warm and familiar.

"George mentioned you're not doing that anymore, though?"

Jesse is the All-American type. Like he'd have smiled into the camera of the local TV station on his football field in high school after making the game-winning play, with an *aw shucks*. He fills his chest with air, like he wants to say something, then never does. He catches me staring, admiring the line of his sweater, his straight back, his freshly buzzed hair. I smile—because that's what I always do—and something about him loosens.

"Can I get you anything else?" the bartender asks.

Jesse and I lock eyes for that awkward moment where both of us try to decide who's going to answer. The silence ticks away again, filled only by the few diners left in the restaurant, the sound of the kitchen behind the swinging doors.

"Do you…?" I ask.

"Maybe we should…" he says at the same time.

I smile. His mouth flattens. He looks over his shoulder then back at me. "Just the check, please."

"I can pay for my drink."

His throat bobs. "I'd like to pay for it, if you don't mind," he says quietly.

The bartender slides the slip of paper between us, his eyes bouncing back and forth, like he's placed bets on this standoff. After a moment I reach for it, pulling some bills from my wal-

let. Jesse nods and I feel like I've disappointed him and care that
I've disappointed him, even though I shouldn't care. I barely
know him, other than the weight of his gaze on the side of my
face and the sound of his companionable silence.

I stumble as I hop off the barstool, staggering a step, the stool
next to mine making a loud, scraping noise along the floor
when I bump into it. *Perfect.* Now he'll think I'm drunk, when
I'm not drunk. I haven't been drunk since England.

Brian's hobby was wine. He'd bring rare and expensive bottles to my flat, with never enough cheese, and make us listen
to French singers he knew I couldn't understand.

The urge to tell Jesse about the distaste on Brian's face when
I played "Bitch Better Have My Money," dancing in my underwear after too much wine, bubbles like Brian's favorite cava
on my tongue. He'd frowned, said *Eloise*, like the word left a
bitter taste in his mouth, and left. At the time I was hurt, but
looking back, I think he was withholding sex and punishing
me for behaving in a way he didn't approve of. Also, he left to
have sex with Nora, so.

I rummage through my purse, weaving between the empty
tables and out the front door, Jesse trailing quietly behind me.
"I'm not trying to find my keys," I say over my shoulder. The
sky is blank, the stars covered by storm clouds I can't really see
but feel low and ominous nonetheless, like they'll sink lower
and lower until Wilvale, Pennsylvania, is nothing but fog. The
wind blows my hair into my face, catching on my lips. "I'm
trying to find my phone so I can call a ride. I'll get my car tomorrow. My dad can drive me into town."

"Your phone is in your hand, Lulu."

And he's right. I shake it at him, showing him the case with
a flower that says "Votes for Women" in the center to distract
him from the complete mess I am right now.

He scratches the back of his head, undistracted. "And I can
give you a ride."

"It's fine." I wave his words away. "I can get a cab." The lights are on in Little Texas now and music isn't exactly audible but the bass of it reaches my feet on the pavement. Soon there will be a lineup of people outside and a procession of cabs coming in and out of the parking lot as students from the university and nearby technical college arrive to kick off their summer vacation.

He points to a rusty blue truck a few spaces down. "I'd feel better if I dropped you off at your door, but I understand if you're not comfortable."

We stand off in the middle of the parking lot, the wind growing stronger. I hiccup and close my eyes; if I can't see him then he can't see how red I'm getting. And it's not that I wouldn't like a ride from him, it's just that I'm still not sure what he even thinks of me. "OK," I hear myself say. "That would be really nice of you."

He opens the door to the old Ford Bronco, the rust most prevalent around the tire wells. It smells like leather and car air freshener and, I imagine if I knew him better, Jesse: peppermint and pine. There's a bench seat and as I climb up my eyes slide over it, the leather soft and cool—and OK, this is definitely the beer talking but—sensual.

I wonder how many people Jesse has had sex with on this bench seat. If I were Jesse, I'd have sex with everyone on this bench seat. He's pulled on a plaid jacket over his sweater, and he fills it out so well, I think I answer my own question: he probably has sex with *a lot* of people on this bench seat.

"Just be cool," I whisper as he walks around the front of the truck. "Be cool, Dr. Banks."

Jesse cranks the engine as he settles in. His hands are big and veiny and a quick, sudden image of how those hands would look on my bare thighs imprints itself on the back of my eyelids, real enough that I can feel his palms, how rough they'd be on my skin. I'm so caught up in wildly inappropriate thoughts it takes me too long to notice that the truck is rumbling, the engine warm, and Jesse is staring at me.

"Turn right on Main," I say too loudly.

We drive through town in silence, except for my quiet directives. In no time, we're in front of my parents' house, which I moved back to last September, heading down their long and bumpy driveway in silence. He cuts the engine and the headlights shut off. A raindrop falls here or there on the windshield then stops.

"Do you, uh, want to see my room?" I ask to break the silence, then immediately wish I could just shut up.

Jesse's mouth is a flat line. A very grumpy face. He says nothing. *Shocking.*

"I just mean that, my parents let me live in the studio apartment that's attached to the house. It has a separate entrance but it's around the back. I don't still sleep in my childhood bedroom. My mom keeps her art supplies in there now." I wonder when—or if—I'll ever stop talking.

He peers out the windshield at the dark pathway that leads to my apartment and opens his door. I shiver at another gust of unseasonably cool air. "I'll walk you," he says.

I rummage through my bag on the short walk around the side of my parents' farmhouse, almost plowing into his back when he stops at my front door. It takes me a second to line the key up with the lock before I can shove it in and open the door to my dark, tiny home. The crisp air has cooled my beer buzz enough that I know what I'm about to say is a bad idea. But the thought of walking into this dark, cold little apartment, alone, makes it so I can't stop myself.

"Do you want to come in?"

I'm not even sure what I want him to do if he came inside. We could sit and watch a reality TV show or a baseball game on my laptop while I scrolled my phone or read student papers, sex the furthest thing from either of our minds. It just seems better than the alternative of being alone with my thoughts. Jesse pokes his head through the door, surveying. His mouth twists into a little pucker. Not grumpy face.

"What's this?" I point to his mouth. "You're not making your Grumpy Face anymore."

He seems skeptical. "What's Grumpy Face?"

"It's like this." I flatten my mouth and do my best to shape my forehead in a way that will create a V between my brows. I jut my jaw. "Hello, Eloise," I say in a barely passable impression. Jesse Logan laughs. He actually laughs. It's quiet, *duh*. But it's a laugh and it transforms his face, lifts a load from his shoulders. It turns a little personal sun on above him, to follow him around until he frowns again. He has one dimple in his flushed cheeks. His jacket stretches across his shoulders. And curses to the beer and the cold and the loneliness, but all of these seem like Very Good Reasons to kiss him.

So, I do.

Jesse Logan, who drinks soda water quietly, and drives for fifteen frickin' minutes quietly, and laughs quietly, does not kiss quietly. A moan rumbles up his chest, against where my nipples are firmly pressed to him. He lets me kiss him for a few more seconds before gently pulling away, his hands wrapped around my biceps.

"I'm sorry," I say, the pads of three fingers pressed to my lips. "Was that OK?" I ask.

"Yeah." He seems surprised by his answer.

"Do you want to do it again?"

He thinks for a moment. "Yes."

Jesse pulls me into him, gently pressing his hands to my lower back. I should feel cold, standing in the open doorway to my house, the wind picking up, the rain about to fall, but heat radiates off him. My body jolts every time my nipples brush against him through my thin jacket, tiny lightning bolts right through my skin.

His lips move softly, almost shyly, and who is this man? So quiet and kissing me, holding me, like I'm something that might break. Honestly, I might, and I hate that. I want to kiss this gorgeous man on my front doorstep without thinking about the ways I am jagged pieces held together by masking tape and sheer force of will.

I slip my tongue past his lips to quiet the tiny implosions in my head. And it works. Jesse squeezes me. A rumble moving through his chest, the sound like melted butter or falling asleep in a sunbeam or the smell of turkey on Christmas morning: good and warm and safe. I sink deeper into him. His hands travel up my body. He cups my face, pulls away just enough to press his thumb to my lower lip.

A joke, maybe another invitation inside, the urge to speak bubbles up—but whatever words I want to fill this silence with, he presses them back into my mouth with gentle pressure. Jesse's brown-eyed gaze travels over my face and I think this might be the first time he's really seen me. That little V returns to his brow, and I smooth it with my fingertips. He inhales, a sound like resolve, and settles lower against the doorframe, pulling me against him, his thigh between my legs. He presses his lips to mine, slipping his tongue into my mouth, and I moan; his leg holding me up, his hands cupping my face, fisting my hair, our mouths, pressing and pulling at each other. I laugh, surprised, into his mouth and it doesn't stop him. He kisses the smile on my face. Tips my head back and works his mouth over my chin, my jaw, my neck.

Cold water hits my shoulder, another drop on my cheek, startling me from where the rest of my body is warm and liquid. I lift my face to the sky and another raindrop lands in my hair. Since this night has been full of me having bad ideas and now the weather has provided the perfect excuse, I ask again, "Do you want to come inside?"

It sounds illicit, combined with how close we're pressed together and my open door. It sounds like I'm asking him something else, and even I can hear the desperation in my voice when I toss each word over the cliff into this cold, quiet evening.

Jesse cools against me. His lips against my jaw slow. He doesn't so much push me away from him as plaster himself against the doorframe. He blinks, frowns, says, "Eloise."

The nebula of lust dissolves and leaves me numb. "Lulu," I say.

"Sorry." And he does sound sorry. "Lulu."

"It's fine," I say quickly, even though it isn't. "I almost bailed on this date," I say loudly and stupidly. Maybe he thinks I'm trying to save face but really I'm just trying to show him that this, stopping, is the right choice. I'm a fucking mess.

He makes a fist, tucking his hand under his arm, mirroring my own stance.

"I've been having a hard time meeting new people."

I want to punch my own mouth.

"Did George tell you?" he asks. "About us?"

"That you two were together?" I ask.

He nods.

"Not in so many words but I assumed…from the way he spoke about you."

He laughs in that way that makes it clear he finds none of this funny. "What way was that."

I shrug. "Like he cared about you. Like he loves you."

"He didn't tell me about this date until earlier today," Jesse says. He winces. "I just mean that he cares maybe too much sometimes."

A familiar sadness blankets me, warm and comforting in a sick sort of way. At least I'm used to the feeling of my colleagues' rejection, compared to this new rejection from an almost stranger. "You're not going to come inside," I say.

When I blink up at him, there's something about the shadow

from the motion-sensor outdoor light, the slope of his shoulders, that makes me think he's wearing a sad blanket, too.

"No. I'm not."

"It was nice to meet you, Jesse." I hold out my hand. He looks at it and, like last time, he doesn't take it. He steps out of the doorway, shoves his hands in his pockets.

"Thank you for the date, Lulu. It was..." He pauses for so long I think he'll let it hang. "Interesting."

I don't know what I wanted Jesse to say. I don't know if he could have said anything that would make me feel not so lonely right now. But whatever I needed him to say, it wasn't that. Silence would have been better. So, I say nothing back, and close the door, and wait in the dark until I hear the crunch of his boots on my gravel walkway. Leaving the lights off in the main room, I wash my face, brush my teeth, and crawl into bed in my underwear, just like I'd planned a few hours earlier. I open my laptop and there, in my inbox, is an email. The subject line reads "I'm Sorry." I delete it without opening it. There's nothing new to be said.

It's still disorienting sleeping here where everything is so quiet. My bed in my UK flat rested beneath a transom window; every night I heard cars from the high street below, and every morning I woke up with the sun on my face. This place doesn't feel like home, even though it's attached to the house I grew up in. Even though I've been home since last September, my entire life jammed into three bags, and the bright-eyed, bushy-tailed hope that academia wouldn't chew me up and spit me out.

The bed is cold and empty. Outside, the rain is falling in earnest, thunder rolls like the sky's steady heartbeat, and the wind isn't loud but the house creaks around me.

Things with Brian were passionate, red hot. Something about his elbow patches and tortoiseshell glasses, juxtaposed against the soft curl of his hair and his crooked front tooth, really did it for me. We couldn't keep our hands off each other. He also couldn't keep his hands off Nora. I'd tell myself that there was no passion with Jesse, not like with Brian, that the familiarity with which I spoke to him, the ease I felt even in my awkwardness was a sign of a dimmed lantern rather than a blazing bonfire. I'd tell myself that, if it wasn't for that kiss. I'd tell myself we're Just Friends but he wasn't interested in even that. Of course, I'd thought he was nervous, too. I was projecting. He wasn't nervous. He wanted nothing to do with me at all. It was all a favor for George, a last-minute hand for his old friend.

"It wasn't going to be anything," I say into the quiet. Since I moved back to Wilvale, I've lived and relived my entire relationship with Nora, from flatmates to coworkers to best friends, trying to identify the moment it went wrong. Searching for what made me disposable. I've googled "how to make friends as an adult." I've bought books, opening the packages once I get them into my apartment, so my mother won't see the titles on her kitchen table. I've listened to podcasts and watched old talk shows. All the advice comes down to this: be yourself and your people will find you.

When am I going to learn that myself will always be a little too much—and somehow not enough?

Chapter Three

Jesse

I make it home just as the sky opens up. In the time it takes for me to run from my driveway to my front door, I'm soaked. I hang my jacket on the hook by the door, throw my keys in the same dish Pop always did, and leave my clothes in a trail behind me as I strip all the way to the bathroom. The shower is lukewarm. I really should get the water tank fixed. Another problem on an unending list of things I need to save up for now that I'm bringing home a security guard's wage rather than a firefighter's salary plus benefits.

The discomfort of my shower's lackluster performance does nothing to calm the erection that started when Lulu pressed herself against me. Despite a double body wash, I can't get the smell of her, lavender and light, out of my nose. The water splashing over the tiles can't drown out the sound of her voice, excited and confident when she talked about witches—*fucking witches*—and gay kings and early modern whatever the fuck;

then breathy and hopeful when she asked me to *come inside* like she was auditioning for my next wet dream.

"Fuck," I growl. "*Fuck*."

I stare at the slate gray shower tiles as I wrap my hand around my dick. But all I see are her cheeks, flushed from the beer and the sudden, unseasonable cold. Her lips swollen from *me*. This time when she invites me to come inside, I say yes. We'd shut the door, keep the lights off. She'd push my jacket from my shoulders, and I'd do the same to her. She'd kiss me with my back against the door for what felt like hours. I'd suck her nipples through her shirt, and I hear her cry out, the sound so real it echoes off the tiles. We'd fall on the bed, our clothes gone. I'd touch her everywhere. I'd taste her while her thighs and hands pinned my mouth to her body.

In the fantasy, I'd fuck her for hours.

In reality, I don't get past the part where I thrust into her, her body hot and soft, her fingers in my mouth. I come and the water washes it away. My skin prickles, suddenly too hot in the cooling water.

I dry myself off before the sputtering bathroom fan can even consider defogging the mirror. Lie in bed with the lights off and my phone silenced, George's text—Let me know how it goes!—unanswered. The rain has picked up outside, the wind throwing it like a sheet against the windows. I stare at the random patterns in the stucco ceiling, as the vision of Lulu slowly disappears. Until all that's left is disappointment, mostly in myself.

If she ever saw me again, she'd be able to see it all over me. Not only what I just did to myself in the shower, my lips still hot from her warm exhales. She'd be able to see it all. That I *wanted* to come inside. And not just for sex. That I wanted to sit beside her and listen to her talk about just about anything. George knows one thing, at least: I have a type. They're talkative, where I am not. But what he doesn't know is that getting me out of whatever rut this is can't be cured by one date.

No matter how horny my bi ass might be.

How long will it take her to realize that my silence isn't the kind that wears off with time, that my résumé has two lines: firefighter and security guard—and that I'm only considered good at the latter because I have experience not falling asleep on overnight shifts and my size makes me "intimidating" even if I feel anything but. How long until she finds out I can't even come out to my grandfather, that I waited so long to tell the man who raised me the truth that now it's too late. How long would it take her to see that I don't fit into her life the way I didn't fit into George's or my grandfather's or my own.

"Stop whining," I tell myself. Because that's a great way to cure myself of self-pity. George will be happy, though. He was right, about Lulu being my type, and that I need to make a change.

I just wish I knew how.

Pop was huge once. He fit into his size, filled rooms with his smile and his laughter, carried others' worries on his shoulders. Mostly mine. I dwarf the man standing in front of the window now, his soft gray T-shirt swallowing him whole.

"Pop." My voice sounds too loud in the quiet hush of his long-term care home. A lot of people complain about the smell. It's not that the nursing home is unclean; there's an astringent bleach smell that permeates every cell. The smell I can get past. Maybe because I've worked with a bunch of smelly firefighters or I've learned, in the many traumas I've been called to, that the human body produces a surprising number of odors.

It's the quiet that's the worst, especially at this time of day. I should have just visited tomorrow, but I wanted to be awake, present, and I knew I wouldn't be after dinner with George, then an overnight shift guarding a construction site. So, I'm here now, my grandfather sundowning or not.

My voice breaks through whatever fog he's lost in, but his anxiety looks high tonight, creasing his quivering lower lip.

"Have you seen your mother?" he asks, his voice raspy.

I've never met my mother, and I can remember only glimpses of my dad. They're vague enough that I am never quite sure if they're memories or if the many photos my grandparents showed me as a child imprinted on my mind. "I...no, Pop."

His hands shake as he presses his fingers to the glass, the skin on the back of his hand pale and thin, his fingernails bitten short. "It's been over an hour. I'm worried about this blizzard, Joey."

I follow his gaze out the window. The sky is shot through with purple and pink and orange, still dramatic after last night's storm. It brought down trees and blew over my neighbor's trampoline, and it's probably what's got him worrying about the weather. Hearing my grandfather call me by my father's name will never not rip me apart inside. It's the combination of the reminder that Joseph Logan is dead and the hurt—even if it's unintentional—of being invisible to my grandfather. I haven't been Jesse since before my accident.

"She'll be home soon, Pop."

The doctors say that sometimes it's best to go along with him rather than confuse him with a gentle course correction. He thinks I'm my father and he's remembering a time my grandmother was out in a blizzard, but it feels like lying, and I've already spent so much of my life lying to him. Each new lie gets heavier than the last.

He mutters to himself, pacing slowly up and down the length of his room, his brows twitching in silent argument. I drop into the armchair by his window. My quad is sore, the bone aching, as if the plates the doctors screwed into me are rattling to get out. A common occurrence after rain.

"Have to put chains on the tires," he whispers.

After the car accident that effectively ended my firefighting career, George visited Pop while I was recovering in the hospital. He warned me that Pop's lucidity was coming in moments, in glimpses. He'd encouraged me to tell Pop before it was too late. "Now's the time, Jess," he'd said. "I know how badly you've wanted to do this. He'll hear you and understand."

I'd swung into this room a week after my surgery, still trying to navigate the world on crutches, but ready to speak the truth to the man who raised me.

"I'm bi, Pop," I'd wanted to say. But Pop wasn't there. My grandfather hasn't had a lucid conversation since; a switch has flipped in his mind, and the man I knew is gone. At least the version of him I wanted, needed, was gone, ripped out of him by this invisible disease that could, at this very moment, be taking root in my own brain. I felt like, once again, I'd missed my chance at something important, life changing.

I could tell him like this. There's nothing stopping me from saying the words now into this quiet room. His ears still register sound. He just doesn't know who it's coming from.

"There's something I wanted to tell you," I say, testing it out.

"The chains," he whispers. I step in front of him, hoping to catch his attention, but he stares over my shoulder, his mouth working silently.

"Pop, I..." It feels like cheating. Like when he used to ask me where I was going on a Friday night and I'd tell him "the movies," but not who with or why.

He grabs my arm, his grip surprisingly strong despite the near constant shake in his muscles. He looks up at me and his eyes seem so clear, focused in a way I haven't seen in a while. My heartbeat kicks up. This might be it. He might be *here*. Finally.

"Get your coat. We're going out to find her, Joey."

It's silly to be this disappointed. I should have expected it, and it's not his fault anyway. But I've been hiding myself from him for so long, it's starting to suffocate me.

"It's Jesse." I take his hand and press it to my chest. "I'm not

Joey, I'm his son, Jesse. And I'm trying to tell you something important."

His cracked lips part in a gasp. The sound of water trickling onto the floor interrupts the silence between us. I look down at the urine soaking into Pop's pants and socks, pooling around his feet.

"Joey?" he asks. "What's happening? I'm so tired."

I close my eyes. Close up the rip in my heart with the reminder that none of this is his fault and the hope that one day he'll see me again. Today's just not his day.

"Let's get you cleaned up," I say, keeping the truth buried firmly inside my chest.

There are many voices coming from behind George's apartment door. When he texted me this morning, demanding that if I'm not going to answer him about the date the least I can do is come over for dinner tonight before work, I stupidly assumed it would be just us.

Already, I can recognize the voices singing along to "Winner Takes It All," with George playing the piano, the same one he learned on at his grandmother's house growing up. I take a deep breath on this side of the door. It's not that I don't want to see them, or that I'm mad at George for not telling me. It's the energy; I'm drained from seeing Pop, I'll drain more once I open this door, hug RJ and Annie and Lacey, if my ears are correct; once George corners me in his galley kitchen and gets the truth out of me. Then there's work tonight, the overnight shift that doesn't require me to talk to a lot of people but does require me to stay awake and alert for none of the reasons that I used to.

So I breathe here, on George's quiet apartment landing, squeeze the loaf of fresh French roll maybe a bit too hard. But it feels good, at least. I open the door just as they hit the second verse and the ABBA is quickly abandoned for squealing and RJ taking my coat and Lacey petting my hand and George slipping the loaf from me and whisking it into the kitchen, where a pot of his mother's spaghetti sauce bubbles. We eat on the couch and living room floor. George insists I am the one to take his new "adult" beanbag chair since it's comfortable and allows me to stretch out my leg, even though it's not bothering me right now. They have pink sparkling wine, celebrating RJ's new part in a Tennessee Williams play at the Walnut Street Theatre. George slices a lemon for my water.

It's nice even if it is tiring. My friends don't expect me to talk much but then they usually don't, and I get by answering only direct questions. Eventually, Lacey curls up on the floor next to me, resting her head on my lap, and the weight of her friendship is familiar and comfortable.

"We're going to go out tonight," she says. There's a sparkling wine and oysters special on Sunday nights at the local queer bar.

"I've got to work. I should leave soon," I say, checking the time on the clock above the empty dinner table.

"Help me clean up first," George says, stacking plates.

Here we go.

I dutifully follow behind him, collecting champagne flutes, and when I enter the kitchen, he turns on me. "You didn't stand her up, did you?" he asks.

I blink, confused for a moment. "No." I thought Lulu would have told him by now what a terrible date I was. "I wouldn't do that."

He starts loading the dishes in the dishwasher and I flip the faucet, letting the sink fill with water. "She didn't…" I start. "You haven't heard from her?"

He leans against the counter beside me, his forehead scrunched in concern. "Did you two make a pact to keep me out? An anti-meddling task force?"

"A…what? No. George. I haven't told you anything because

there's nothing to tell." I pull a pot off the stove and dunk it in the sudsy water.

"You didn't like her?" He sounds affronted. He gasps. "She didn't like you?" Now he sounds aghast.

I shrug. The tips of my ears feel too warm under his gaze and I itch to get away from this conversation, but after yesterday's attempt at an intervention, I know I won't get away with that. Whether or not Lulu liked me isn't really the point. "Maybe dating wasn't the right strategy," I say. "For getting me back out there."

"Don't give up yet," he says. "I know a guy I could set you up with. He works in special collections at the library." He pops his brows like "sexy librarian."

"It's not a gender thing. It's a me thing. I just…" I sigh as I scrub at the pot. There's no sauce left on it; at this point I might rub a hole through the metal. "I need you not to rush me, OK?"

"I'm sorry," he says quietly, squeezing my forearm until I stop scrubbing. I turn to him, drying my hands on the dish towel he passes over. "How would you feel…" George asks slowly. "About being a part of a study?"

I check the time on his microwave, cookbooks and little orange bottles filled with his ADHD prescriptions sitting on top. "Do you have another survey for me to fill out?" As part of his research for his PhD, George is always sending us surveys to fill out, usually about the correlation between mental health and queer communities. "I don't know if I'm going to have time. I have to leave for work in half an hour."

George shakes his head and pulls a stack of papers off the kitchen table by the big bay window. George's parents set him up here in his sophomore year and as he's gotten more financially stable he's taken over paying the mortgage. I've had many a breakfast in that little nook, squeezed in next to George and the heater underneath the window, tasting the recipes he's tested over the years.

"I'm running a new study. It's cross-disciplinary, the medical school is involved, sociologists, too." He makes a face like *ugh*; George hates working with sociologists for methodology reasons I've never quite grasped. "Basically, it's a study to find out why adults, specifically millennials, have such a hard time making friends." He holds up the flyer on top of the stack for my perusal.

I laugh, a quiet *ha*. "If I knew the answer to that life would be a lot easier." I know what he's going to say before the words leave his mouth.

"You should apply," he says, like it's that easy. Like the terror invoked by the thought of walking into a room full of strangers isn't one of the reasons I'm like this to begin with.

"Yeah," I say. "Maybe." Sometimes it's easier to just go along.

"I'm serious, Jess. I think it might be good for you to meet new people."

"I thought y'all were pissed I wasn't hanging out with *you* anymore. Now you want me to find new friends?" I'm being petulant, I know, arguing for the sake of it. To get out of whatever new self-improvement project George is trying to assign me.

"First of all, I'm not pissed at you." He pauses. "Anymore. You're a different person than you were before the accident. Maybe you need to meet different people; maybe they're necessary for this different you to flourish."

The living room is silent, our friends clearly eavesdropping on us. I sigh. "Should I join the study?" I ask, projecting my voice to them on the other side of the wall. There's silence, then shuffling, a giggle. A sock puppet with a disturbingly human-shaped mouth peers around the corner and George cackles with laughter.

"We just want you to be happy, Jess," the sock puppet says in RJ's squeakiest voice.

Annie snorts and Lacey bursts into another song, playing the piano badly, and I think, even if I am a different person now, who could ever want for better friends than this?

★ ★ ★

Eight hours later, the words on the page of my hardcover swim together. Call it confirmation bias or coincidence, but after listening to Lulu's explanation of the history of witchcraft, I'd found a book about the witch craze in a pile of my grandmother's things in the crawl space. Both of my grandparents were big readers and they passed along their love of reading to me, even if I don't have as much time for it anymore. I'd spent a few minutes flipping through it, after giving up my search for the electric hedge clippers I knew Pop had stored somewhere before he moved out. The cover was clearly meant to shock the reader, with the painted image of two women hanging by their necks over a burning pyre, but the information inside is too dry for a night shift on security duty. I readjust the book light clipped to the cover, but it doesn't help. Close my eyes and let the printed words dissolve behind my eyelids. Lulu's explanation was far more compelling than this. I think I might leave the history to her. I scan the parking lot outside the security car's windshield.

A puddle the size of a small house halfway across the empty lot ripples under a faint wind, the last gasps of the storm that blew through last night. I glance at the clock on the dash. Fifteen minutes until I can go home.

I click the light, snap the book shut, stamp my feet on the floor mats to keep the blood in my legs moving. The company that contracts out our security detail to different construction sites around the county said security guards can leave the car on for the A/C to keep cool in the summer but leaving the engine running for eight hours a shift seems like something Cruella de Vil would do. In a way, this is just like firefighting. Hours and hours of nothing, then *boom*. Except I'm positive there will be no boom this time. Unless the sudden urge to pick up this book again counts.

Headlights from another security vehicle move across my windshield. My colleague, early for his shift replacing me, flashes his high beams twice. I flash them back and start the car, pulling out of the lot, the tires squealing unnecessarily on the asphalt. I drive toward the four-story glass building in the middle of an industrial park, five minutes away, where our offices are. As I step inside, the fluorescent lights blind me. Everything looks sleepy at two in the morning. The couch in the breakroom sags. The floors and furniture are washed out in the artificial light. Amir, my boss, isn't at his desk in the expansive and empty office off to the side of the breakroom, but his keys lie on the desk, and a half-eaten tuna sandwich sits on a square of waxed paper.

The A/C kicks on as I clock out on the computer, a process that takes too long since the machine is about fifteen years past its prime. Flyers on the corkboard above the computer flap in the breeze created by the artificial air. The computer fan whirs, the high-pitched whine like the dinky, secondhand dirt bike I got when I was fourteen and promptly wrecked. I input my hours, hitting Enter and waiting again for the processor to catch up, the cursor spinning in a blue circle of death. Finally, the screen shows the landing page, confirming that my hours have been inputted, and I stand to gather my things from my locker. Another gust of air blows from the vent above me and flyers flutter again, this time one falling off the corkboard and landing on the keyboard.

It's a notice for a rec touch rugby league and the grainy, unfocused photocopy of a rugby player in motion is a punch to the gut. That used to be me. Touch leagues, tackle, whatever. I've played since I knew how to toss a ball; instead of playing catch or teaching me how to throw a perfect spiral like all the other parents, Pop had taught me rugby rules in the backyard, while Grandma gardened. He drove me an hour each way to rugby practice two towns over when I was thirteen and showed up to my local league games after graduation. I was never good enough to play in anything more than an amateur league, but I loved it. Loved the sweat and the sometimes blood and the way we could lay all of our aggression out on the field and then crack open a can of soda together after. I loved pushing myself, feeling my lungs burn and my muscles scream. I loved winning.

And maybe George is right, because I don't know who that man is anymore. Even if my doctors hadn't told me I probably shouldn't play again, I don't think I'd play anymore. I want to, though. I miss the guy I was before the accident. I miss me. But the flyer is at least enough to remind me that George shoved a stack of flyers into my hands before I left tonight, asking me to share them at work. I wrench open my locker, flatten one out on the desk, and find a spot for it on the corkboard.

How to Make Friends as Millennial Adults: Psychological and Sociological Challenges in Forming and Retaining Adult Friendships, A Multidisciplinary Study, it says. Other than Amir and me, I don't think there are many millennials here. Mostly Gen Xers and a kid who barely seems legal to work past eight in the evening.

Are you a millennial adult (between the ages of 27-37) who:

- *Has difficulty creating new, lasting friendships?*
- *Experiences feelings of depression, anxiety, and/or loneliness?*
- *Feels that factors such as shyness, busyness interfere with forming or retaining platonic relationships?*
- *Believes friendships require too much work?*

Consider applying for the Millennial Effect: Challenges in Making Adult Friendships. This cross-disciplinary exploration of friendship and its effect on our physical, mental, and emotional well-being will take place over six weeks and could pay $1,000 upon completion (per the results of a participant lottery).

It's the $1,000 that gets me. And yeah, OK, I'd answer yes to all of those questions, but with $1,000 I'd have enough for a new water heater. Between Pop's savings and pension, I'll be able to keep him comfortably in the nursing home until his death. Pop and Grandma had put money away for my education but then I never got one. It feels unfair to use that money for home repairs.

I pull the paper back down off the corkboard, stuff it back into my backpack. I won't fill out the application form on this computer. Amir will be back before I can even get the internet browser open. I'll do it at home. Where no one can see me. I'll apply and might get chosen and hopefully I'll make $1,000. And if, in the process, I learn how to get back to the man I was before my accident? Well, that's just gravy, as Pop would say.

Don't miss The Friendship Study *by Ruby Barrett,*
available wherever books are sold.
www.CarinaPress.com